University of Western Australia Press

The Sinkings

AMANDA CURTIN

First published in 2008 by UWA PRESS
Reprinted in 2014 by UWA PUBLISHING
Crawley, Western Australia 6009
www.uwapress.uwa.edu.au

National Library of Australia
Cataloguing-in-Publication entry:

Curtin, Amanda.
The sinkings / Amanda Curtin.
1st ed.
ISBN 978 1 921401 11 4 (PBK.).
A823.4

Cover painting by Jill Kempson;
Jill Kempson represented by Galerie Düsseldorf, Perth

Edited by Susan Midalia
Design by Anna Maley-Fadgyas
Typeset in 10pt Janson by Lasertype
Printed by Lightning Source

FT PBK

For
Ric, Robyn, Richard

Life can only be understood backwards,
but it must be lived forwards.

— SÖREN KIERKEGAARD

2 October 1882

The Sinkings, near Albany, Western Australia

Wild-eyed, the little man pants by the well, writhing on his back like a stranded beetle.

The first blow was clumsy, a rehearsal with no weight behind it. The man with the axe has better in him. Raising it above his shoulders, he brings it down hard.

Thunk.

The skull fractures with a force that sends the brain ricocheting between the frontal and occipital bones. The little man is gone, his eyes vacant but for the reflection of the Great September Comet, a celestial aberration that has branded the night sky these two weeks past.

The man with the axe is not yet done. He slashes at the plaid shirt, laying open the chest. Mutters as blood soaks through his trouser knees. And again he strikes, frenzied still, stripping warm flesh from bone.

Finally, he thumps a fist against his own florid skull. *Think, man, think.*

Up on the wagon, among a clutter of cooking pans and tools and bundles of clothes, he rummages for a flour sack and spade, and then snatches a bucket from the fire on his way back to the corpse. It takes him more than an hour to hack through the third and fourth vertebrae, to smash and splinter the sockets of the thighs, but by the time he is done he is as calm as a priest.

The earth around the well is damp and smells like a butcher's scrapery. He pours fresh sand over it. Washes his hands. Yawns. Throws at his tent a longing glance. Just one more thing to do, and the rest can wait till daylight.

By the dying coals of the fire, he sits, humming, sewing up the neck of the bloody sack with coarse blue thread.

The look of a shadow

She had the look of a shadow about her. A greyscale version of the colour photograph on the driver's licence that she passed across the desk. Willa hoped they wouldn't look too closely, that it hadn't expired. On the APPLICATION FOR RESEARCHER'S TICKET, she used, as a reference, a colleague she hadn't spoken to for a year, but when it came to the space for 'Subject of your research', she paused. A little coil of anxiety. A loop became a knot. This name had lain dormant in her memory for the longest time. 'John (Jock) King,' she wrote. A name nobody would know. And what would they make of that? Did the custodians of archives scan these requests, favouring worthy subjects, filtering out the rest? She watched as the woman glanced over the form, but there were no questions asked.

It was twelve years since she had come across the story of the murder. The manuscript – *A quick copyedit, please, nothing fancy* – was a collection of articles written by members of a local historical society for the group's yearly journal, *Past Lives*. She had wanted to contact the author of the article called 'A strange case of murder and mutilation' right away but her client, the compiling editor, had warned her off. *George Sullivan is an elderly gent, in poor health now. I'll be handling the author queries for him.* But Willa didn't want to check on inconsistent dates or the spelling of names or incomplete citations – the usual things a copyeditor needed to follow up. It was the human inconsistencies that had caught her eye. She wanted to know more, all that George Sullivan could tell her. And she wanted to sound him out on a theory about this 'strange case' that might not have occurred to an elderly gent.

Back then, every minute, every space in her life, had been taken up with Imogen and the work she'd managed to fit in while her daughter was at school or asleep. She'd had to lay aside her gratis copy of *Past Lives*, journal of the South West Historical Society, no. XIV, 1992. To forget about Jock King. But now things were different. Now she was free of commitments, her days awash with time, and time had brought her here. George Sullivan had died years ago, but she hoped his sources would lead her to the heart of this story that had haunted her, that she couldn't forget. For she had read about a horrific nineteenth-century murder and she had seen the connection clearly. She had seen Imogen.

As Willa gave her request slip to the archivist at the State Records Office, she was acutely aware of other people: waiting at the desk for help, talking on phones in unseen cubicles.

A man tapped her on the arm. *Do you have a spare pencil I could borrow?*

She didn't, but had to remind herself that the words must be spoken out loud.

They came from her throat so softly that the man asked her to repeat them, cupping his hand over one ear.

No, she said, *I'm sorry*, and shook her head this time.

Sorry.

Shrinking.

If only she could access what she needed on-line. Over the last six months, her world had contracted to the frame of her computer screen, the daily transactions of life conducted at a distance, via the net. Occasionally a courier would deliver a package and require a signature, but he was an incurious sort. If he thought anything at all of Willa, it was probably a passing expression of mild contempt for women who *let themselves go*. Even when she had still been working, the need to meet with other people face to face was rare. And now if anyone ventured near there was the standard excuse for her self-exile, the everything and nothing of it: *I have lost my daughter...*

The next retrieval is not until 1.00 pm, the woman at the desk told her.

Oh. She was surprised at her disappointment, at how soon the desire to begin had taken hold.

People with books, laptops, folders full of papers, filed past the expanse of glass that separated the library foyer from the coffee shop. From her table in the corner, she saw a closely cropped skull that curved in familiar contours. The cup jolted in her hands, splashing hot tea onto the veins of her wrist. But no, it was not Imogen, of course it was not Imogen, not that beautiful face she missed and longed to see. The young man passed, and Willa slumped back again to watch the flow of bodies. What needs and obsessions brought people to places like these? Could she really explain her own motives if someone were to ask her?

Taking the well-worn copy of *Past Lives* from her satchel, she began to read again, as though the words might offer up something new simply because she had broken her exile to pursue them.

John King, known as 'Little Jock', was last seen alive just before midnight on Sunday 1 October 1882. He and his team of five horses, with a wagonload of sandalwood bound for the export yard of merchant John Hassell in Albany, were camped at a clearing called the Sinkings, so named because a shaft had once been sunk nearby in a vain search for coal. Five miles north of Albany on the King River Road (now Chester Pass Road), the Sinkings was a popular place for teamsters to rest overnight and water their animals at the well. Three people stopped there on the night in question, and the last of these, mill owner Horace Egerton-Warburton, saw only one other teamster sharing Little Jock's campfire. That person was John Collins.

A month later (31 October), while at the Sinkings to water his team of bullocks, John Garretty came across two bones protruding from the earth, disturbed, it seemed, by the scratching of a native dog or a kangaroo rat. His brother James, who had ridden out to meet him, found him squatting on the ground, wondering what to do. John Garretty was apprehensive and fearful, as there were vestiges of cloth adhering to the bones. James had no such qualms: he grasped one greasy bone and pulled. It gave, with a stomach-churning squelch, and the brothers could see what looked like trouser fabric where the bone had been...

It was a gruesome story. What the Garretty brothers found in the vicinity of the protruding bones was a sack, crudely stitched, containing the remains of a human torso. The head, legs and part of the left hand and arm were missing. At the subsequent inquest, Albany's colonial surgeon testified unequivocally that the body was that of a woman, but changed his mind later when the head was found nearby and identified as that of Jock King, a sandalwood-carter and former convict.

Willa fingered the crisscross of thin white lines on her shoulder. She could still remember it: that shock of recognition she felt twelve years ago when she had first read the article. She had dropped the manuscript, spun around suddenly in her chair, startling the kitten that had a fondness for nestling between her ear and shoulder. That day was marked by the certainty that there were things she could see in Sullivan's article that others could not, and by the slash of Lucifer's sharp little claws deep into her skin.

Who were you? she had wondered then, and wondered now as she sat restlessly stacking sachets of sugar. What was your story, Little Jock?

1838

Near Ballynahatty, County Tyrone, Northern Ireland

Perhaps it begins with a lone carrion crow flying over a cabin. An ill omen.

The Handywoman shivers, pauses. It is only the familiar rhythm of the keening coming from inside that keeps her from turning back to the village. She had promised the widow she would do for her girl, and who would break faith with a widow?

In the gloom of the windowless cabin, lit only by a scanty fire of turf and hazel boughs, she rummages through piles of rags, gently lifts the corners of the mattress of straw and rough brown linen, searching in vain for knots to untie, twists to unravel, to ease the next onslaught of pain. Vexed, she pats down her own body, feeling along seams of calico, the shawl's woollen fringe. But it seems there is to be no relief for this girl.

The Handywoman turns her attention to less earthly concerns. *Have you iron?* she rasps, urgently. The girl convulses, conscious only of the spasms racking her body. *Iron, child! Iron to keep Them away.* When there is no answer, the Handywoman glances around the room, taking in its meagre offerings, and crosses quickly to the fireplace. There is naught but a blunt knife. She runs her thumb along the blade and mutters in disgust: scarce to slice through a boiled potato, this. But still she slips it into the folds of the girl's long, shapeless garment. A poor charm is better than none.

The pot? she demands. She shakes the dazed, exhausted girl. *The pot, child!* But a fresh wave of pain begins and the girl cannot speak. The woman finds the vessel outside the door, upturned and empty. Grunting, she sweeps up her skirt and squats.

The world into which the infant is half pushed, half pulled, reeks of fresh urine sprinkled liberally about the cabin, for protection, and the ferric tang of blood that the Handywoman hopes will be a stronger talisman than the knife fallen on the dirt floor.

Near nightfall a widow returns from her plot to find her high-spirited daughter too late for the priest's goodbye, and a rag-swaddled infant sucking a gauze of flax soaked in weak buttermilk, held at arm's length by the Handywoman.

She twines a tendril of her daughter's hair around her finger, traces a cross on her heart.

The Handywoman watches, cheated and more than a little afraid. Her skills as a midwife could not save the girl, but that was sometimes the way of it. She has older skills, though, passed down, and has always had more faith in these. Her blessings are meant to come in twos – mother and baby, body and soul – but the balance has been skewed. She has failed to produce even one pair.

The widow turns to her. *A boy?*

What could she tell this woman, to whom a grandson, if strong and sound, would be as gainful as a crop for tending now and harvesting later? A boy? Ah, if she had been here to ask that three hours ago. But this room, this room she had charmed and protected, had been fleeced and a deception played. There is nothing They desire so much as a healthy boy-child. She had turned her back so briefly, no longer than it took to retrieve a coin from her cloak to handsel the newborn, and that was all it had taken for Them to steal the boy and leave a copy, imperfect, in his place.

She hesitates. She has no desire to confess or explain. And what need? There is no taint to the changeling's face, no wizening or canker, no grotesquery of limb. No sign to implicate the Otherworld and, with it, the one whose job it was to turn it away.

She looks again at the widow. One could say *a boy* or *a girl* and it would be so. For years it would be so. The child could pass, causing no more than a puzzlement of the brow to the few who would see. A *man* it would never be. Nor a mother, surely. But need that be said now, and need she be the one to say?

She hands the bundle to the widow, barely concealing a shudder. Let God take the blame, and let this woman choose.

A new language

Willa clicked on 'save' and looked up at the clock on the reading-room wall. Nearly closing time. She stretched like Lucifer but with none of that visible flow of tension that ripples out so cleanly from the feline body. As she gathered up the pages, a flake shed from the deckled edge of the brittle, browning pile, landing on her arm. It unsettled her to think that her research was contributing to the eventual disintegration of this archive. The more these pages were valued, the more they would be worn away. Still, she suspected that the last person to read them might well have been the late George Sullivan, and they would probably remain untouched now for years to come.

She scratched her arm, the back of her head, imagining what else might be shedding from these pages, what invisible dander of history she was breathing in.

It had taken her two weeks to transcribe the Supreme Court file of criminal sitting number 1031, the trial of John Collins. Each day she had withdrawn the thick folded sheaf from the acid-free envelope reserved in her name, and balanced it on calico cushions. It was slow work, painstaking, for the handwritten pages were often difficult to decipher, and of course had to be handled with extreme care – far more care than was shown by the clerk who had bundled them together and tied them with cord in 1883.

The sheaf contained official forms relating to the trial, pages and pages of depositions, a list of witnesses – and, shoved in with all of these, a bill of sale and several notes handwritten by Little Jock and the man found guilty of his murder. Collins had appeared in Albany with Jock's loaded wagon and team, claiming Jock had sold them to him before heading off towards York (or Bunbury or Perth or Kojonup or Eticup – Collins was inconsistent on this point). When timber merchant John Hassell demanded proof of this transaction, Collins had eventually produced a dirty sheet from a pocket book, written by him in pencil and supposedly signed by Little Jock. At the trial, the prosecutor claimed that the bill of sale was a forgery.

Willa handled with awe the fragile, much-folded letters that had been submitted in evidence, bearing the signatures of each man – signatures whose peculiarities had been analysed at trial by witnesses, hardly expert, such as the timber merchant's clerk. The paper was streaked and faded into sepia tones, but the ink remained bold and black, confidently setting forth working men's wishes:

> Please send 1 pound of butter 1 pound cheese a loaf of bread a tine of Jam...
> Please to pay W. Munday and Place the same £1.13 to my account...

She was struck by the disjunction between the triviality of such small, domestic transactions and the significance they had acquired at the trial in 1883 when viewed with the hindsight of their writers' fates. And now, with the passage of time, they were precious to her for another reason, as physical artefacts that turned disembodied names in newspapers and archives into real people. Handwritten words, caught and preserved. Proof of life.

With the contents of the file deciphered and recorded and her laptop packed away, she retied the bundle, with a sense of loss, and returned the envelope to the desk, the accession slip marked 'Finished'. On the way out, she was seized by the thought – reckless, fleeting, but hardly original – that she should have spirited those handwritten letters away, for who else would ever value them as much as she did?

At this time of the year, the cottage she had grown up in was festooned with wisteria, scalloping the bullnose verandah in lacy clusters like icing on a wedding cake. Bees droned among the purple blooms, seduced by a scent so sweet and strong that Willa could never tolerate it for long. It seemed to linger for hours after she had shut the front windows.

Chas and Orla had bequeathed her the house, imagining she and Imogen would live in it forever, together. In one of her mother's favourite photographs, Imogen was posed in front of the wisteria in a pink satin dress with a stiff white ribbon in her curly hair – one of the few times she had consented to be prettied up in froufrou. You could just see the tip of Babar's ear clutched in her right hand (had Orla deliberately cut off this favourite toy?), and Willa remembered how Imogen had shunned the princess doll her grandmother had tried to arrange on her lap in favour of the enigmatic little elephant, so dapper in his human clothes. Orla set the portrait of her granddaughter in a heart-shaped frame of polished brass. It always surprised Willa that her mother seemed oblivious to the joyless cast of Imogen's face caught within the heart, as though Orla could choose the details she wanted to see and screen out those she didn't.

It was still cold inside, the house not yet responding to spring, and Willa donned thick socks and a sloppy jumper while the kettle boiled. Setting the laptop to print her day's transcriptions, she took out the folder containing the rest of her research and was about to start working through it when there was a muffled sound from the direction of her bedroom, a sound she recognised as the scrabbling of claws on wood.

The door of the wardrobe, loose on its runners, had slid open. And there, in the corner of the recess, was Lucifer, spread-eagled on the side of a tea chest and desperately trying to gain purchase. He began to purr as she gently unhooked his claws and lifted him out. *You're getting too old for this, boy.*

The chest, made of light wood, the kind that splits when a nail is driven into it, held the detritus of a time long past: books and medical journals; photocopied articles, correspondence, thick envelopes of X-rays, ultrasound films – items she wished never again to see but would nonetheless doggedly keep. Six months ago, when she lost Imogen, she had hammered tacks into the top of the chest, thinking to form a permanent seal on that other time, on all the mistakes she'd made, all the things that could not be undone, or forgiven. But now she looked at it speculatively, wondering.

The tacks came out easily with the claw end of a hammer, the top springing free, but she was unwilling to confront all that the chest contained. She felt around gingerly, selecting by touch. All she wanted was the books.

A small paperback slipped from the pages of one of the medical volumes: *Best Baby Names 1986*. Matthew's mother had given it to her when Willa first discovered she was pregnant. She picked up the book and a still frame flashed into her head:

Matthew is lying on the sofa, endearing in those threadbare jeans she could never get him to throw away.

If she lifted her finger off the pause button, the frame would jerk into action:

He is smiling, scratching the stubble on his chin, and calls out to her: *How about Aloysius? Do you like Zerelda?*

And Willa laughs and tells him, *No, no, names can't be chosen from a book.*

The frames shuttled forward to another painful happy scene:

It's like buying clothes from a catalogue, she is telling Matthew, snatching the book away from him in bed. *You can't be sure they're right until you feel them in your hands, try them on.*

Fast forward again:

They are driving to the hospital, bickering to ease the tension, still unable to agree on two perfect names: one for a boy, one for a girl. They look so young, sound so young. Children playing grown-up games.

Stop.

Forward to the aftermath, the space between birth and naming, and the trivial incidents that punctuated her panic. Hospitals are no keepers of secrets. An elderly sister, a gold cross pinned to her breast, hovered daily over the bassinette, quavering what Willa supposed was a hymn but felt like a rebuke: *Trust and obey, for there's no other way.* The morning cleaner, whipping at stainless-steel surfaces with an antistatic cloth, avoided her eyes but deposited on the end of her bed a smiling white pig with a corkscrew tail made of pipecleaner. Soft, embarrassed glances came from women in pink and blue nighties, newborns sucking robustly at their breasts. Always, always, there was the acid drip of pity corroding kindness.

It was in those days between birth and naming that she and Matthew learned a new language. *Karyotype. DNA polymorphism. Radiographic genitography.* At first the idea that such turgid, forbidding words could have anything to do with the small, cherished life she had brought into the world was simply beyond comprehension. But soon, alarmingly soon, these same words became absorbed into the familiar as she and Matthew tried to grasp what they were being told: that this ambiguity was not some matter of diagnostic uncertainty that time and science would solve. Their baby's chromosomal profile was 46XX/46XY, confirming the presence of male and female cells. Those *gonadal structures* on the radiographic film were not a matching pair. Far from clarifying ambiguity, science was in fact confirming it. *Very rare*, they were told. *But always a theoretical possibility, given the circumstances. Not without precedent in the literature.*

She closed her eyes but the memory spooled out anyway like one of Chas's old family films.

The specialist is a large man, his body as weighty as the intimidating title on the door: *Paediatric Endocrinologist.* When he leans over the examination table, the shadow cast on the pale green wall rears up like a giant, and Willa expects a thundering *Fee fi fo fum!* The burden of what he says crushes her.

What we must focus on is socialisation. A flick of his hand dismisses chromosomes and genetics. *Can this infant ever hope to function in the world as a little boy, as a man? Does it have an adequate phallic structure to make this possible?*

She flinches as his thick fingers grasp the baby, stretching, stretching.

And clearly, he continues, *it does not. Anything less than 2.5 centimetres in fully expanded length is not an acceptable penis.*

Willa looks at Matthew, and although the loss of a maybe-son is apparent on his face, she can see he feels more comfortable in the territory of measurements and parameters. She turns back to face the doctor.

I don't understand. A decision like this. Surely it can't come down to a few millimetres?

The baby has a testicle and an ovary, Willa, Matthew snaps. *It has to come down to something.*

She persists, does not look at Matthew. *Are you saying the baby is a girl?*

I'm saying you can feel confident in raising her as a little girl.

Willa feels stupid, still does not understand.

Will she be able to have children?

No, not of her own; she has no uterus, he concedes, and then immediately brightens. *But there is a short, blind introitus that our team can fashion into a functional vagina – so she will be a true woman in other ways.* He looks at Willa sharply. *I would be surprised to hear, Mrs Gates, that a young, intelligent woman in the 1980s would be advocating we rest the issue of gender on biological fertility.*

No, no, but…

You're worried, and understandably so, about the unsightliness of the genital structures. Well, let me put your mind at rest. We have an impressive record in reconstructive surgery. And the offending gonad can, of course, be excised.

When they leave the examination room, the giant becomes almost jolly, shaking Matthew's hand in one huge paw, clasping Willa's shoulder with the other, uniting the three of them, with the baby, in some pantomime embrace. *Congratulations!* he says, smiling. *You have a daughter!*

Her mind is dizzy with a new battery of ugly words – *introitus*, *orchidectomy*, *genitoplasty* – and those blithe assurances of all that can be done to *normalise* and *correct*, as though the whole thing has been some horrible mistake. But when she looks down at the sleeping infant in her arms, the rare and special child who had been born not-quite, more-than, all she can think of is the pressing urgency to give her a name.

By the time they reach the car, she has chosen, without even consulting Matthew. *Imogen*, she whispers, breathing the name into a halo of babydown.

∞

It took will to halt the memory there. She was about to toss *Best Baby Names 1986* back into the chest when she changed her mind and flicked through to the *I*s, running a finger down the list.

> Imogen: *Latin* image, blameless, innocent; *Celtic* from 'Innogen', meaning 'daughter'.

She frowned. Had she known this before? Surely not, for she could recall that moment of naming with wounding clarity. Her daughter's name had *not* come from a book. But suddenly her face burned. Imogen would have had a good hard laugh at this one. *Could you have picked anything more obvious, Mother? More sentimentally symbolic?*

She threw down the book, frustrated that a name she had loved for a lifetime now felt lost to her, all over again.

∞

The front room, her study, had curlicued cornices and a ceiling rose fluted with eucalyptus leaves and was beautiful in spite of the clutter of Willa's former working life: shelves of page proofs wrapped in plastic, archive boxes of files and manuscripts stacked three-high in each corner. A wide sash window faced the street, but the computer desk looked on to a blank wall, where there were no distractions.

She stacked the medical books on the shelf above the desk, and moved Lucifer, who was neatly perched on the folder containing the transcript of the Supreme Court file and staring at a screensaver shimmering with tropical fish.

She read the printout from beginning to end, and then started again, this time making notes in a kidskin journal, never used, that Orla had once given her. In the depositions there were continual references to Little Jock's diminutive features. A shoemaker said: 'He had a very small foot – much smaller than ordinary men – four would fit him – I know this because the previous pair I made for him I took his measure for, and he took four...woman's size.' The surgeon 'noticed the hand as being remarkably small, as also the bones of the arm – the hand measured in length six inches and in breadth two and three-quarters across palm on examination.' Another witness described the deceased as 'a small-built man, his hands and feet...more like a woman's than a man's,' and the murderer even nicknamed him 'Napoleon Bonaparte' after that famous 'little man' of history.

There was a grain of sand in Willa's memory, something she could not quite isolate. She pulled down one of the medical books and quickly navigated her way through the once-familiar pages.

Here it is, she told Lucifer, who watched, golden eyes glazed. The condition was known as *congenital adrenal hyperplasia*, and she scanned the causes and symptoms:

inborn error of metabolism
high level of foetal blood androgens
masculinisation of genitals in the genetic female
    (pseudohermaphroditism)
penile and fused labioscrotal structures
development of breasts often fails to occur
irregular/absent menses
early development of some secondary sex
    characteristics
child may exhibit facial hair in the form of a light
    down
untreated individual does not attain sexual maturity
progressive early virilisation advances bone age, often
    resulting in the paradox of a tall child becoming an
    adult of extremely short stature

So, Little Jock, she thought, underlining the phrase *adult of extremely short stature*, does this explain the name they gave you?

The medical evidence was what interested her most – what the Albany doctor, Rogers, had to say about the sex of the remains. George Sullivan had suggested in his article that there was an agenda of self-preservation behind Dr Cecil Rogers's trial testimony as he struggled to extricate himself from his earlier findings.

> I stated at the Coroner's Inquest that from the measure-ments I had made and from the slight obliquity of the thigh bone the smallness of the hand and fineness of the hair I formed an opinion that the trunk there before me may have been the body of a woman...with reference to the pelvis I have since ascertained that

my original measurements were not correct – I have subsequently measured it with new measures – I would also remark that you cannot invariably depend on measurements of the pelvis as characteristic of either male or female adults.

Willa compared the wording of Rogers's original findings with the trial testimony, and had to agree with Sullivan's conjecture on this point. The equivocation of 'may have been the body of a woman' was not there in the inquest deposition. It stated: 'I believe from the structure of the pelvis & other indications – the smallness of the bones & hand, that it is the remains of a woman.' *Structure*, he said – no reference to *measurements*. Shape, configuration, as well as size. This back-pedalling focus on new measures was nonsense.

She opened her web browser and found the on-line edition of *Gray's Anatomy*, searching *pelvis – male – female*. The comparative illustrations showed distinct differences. Yes, she thought, size *and* shape – *and*, according to the text, density of the bones, as well. Even colonial doctors, who were often not the finest the Empire had to offer, would have been aware in the 1880s of *Gray's* and its successors. To Rogers, versed in texts like these, the differences between male and female pelvis must have appeared an almost conclusive determinant of sex, no small thing to be forced to walk away from.

According to George Sullivan's article, Rogers pestered the authorities in Perth about a second opinion long after declaring himself satisfied that the body was male.

He sent another telegram to the Colonial Secretary: 'Am still of opinion that a medical board should examine the remains & would suggest that as Sergt McLarty has been with us through the whole case he could take charge & accompany remains to Perth. I have serious cases of illness & accident under treatment will also write fully on the subject to Dr Waylen.'

Rogers was clearly still uneasy, agitating for confirmation of his findings – and perhaps even seeking to avoid giving evidence at the Supreme Court trial. No attention, however, was paid to his concerns. The Colonial Secretary ordered him to attend the trial, privately moaning to Colonial Surgeon Dr Waylen: 'Re remains I don't understand what Sergt McLarty knows about medical examination of dead bodies. Dr Rogers as usual trying to escape coming to Perth…Other medical men leave their activities often to attend trials.' Waylen agreed, adding waspishly, 'I don't see what difficulty there is for a medical board to solve.'

In a recent talk given at the State Library, researcher Brian Purdue proposed that Jock King was actually a woman, and implied that the authorities coerced Rogers into changing his testimony because 'it would have been some embarrassment to [them] to reveal that a woman had "slipped through the system"' (the terms of the scheme to transport convicts from Britain to Western Australia specified that only male convicts were to be sent). There is no evidence of coercion or cover-up in the extant archives, only a palpable sense of irritation with Rogers generally.

Lucifer landed on the desk with a skid, scattering paper left and right and knocking Willa's empty mug onto the carpet.

She glanced at the display in the top right-hand corner of the computer. Nearly 8.oo pm.

OK, boy, OK, she said, slowly uncurling her stiff limbs.

Lucifer led the way to the kitchen, yowling lest Willa should think of changing her mind.

There was a time when Willa would spend hours in the kitchen of her small, cramped flat, preparing food for Imogen using Chas's homegrown vegetables, seeking out organic poultry and beef and free-range eggs long before these became commonplace. She had been obsessive about nutrition, balance, the benefits of whole foods over processed, the danger of additives. Fast food was something she simply never considered.

Now she didn't care.

After spooning a can of gourmet tuna onto Lucifer's plate, she took from the freezer the first package her hand touched and threw away the box without reading the instructions. It was pasta of some description, plastic food in a plastic bowl, and she put it in the microwave for five minutes on high.

Soon she was back at her desk with a fresh mug of Darjeeling at her elbow and a content Lucifer reclining in the space between keyboard and screen.

Did Little Jock have CAH? She scoured Rogers's testimony again, trying to divine meaning from the forensic inventory of skin and hair, bones, organs. And there, in the long deposition by Rogers for the police investigation in Albany, something caught her attention:

> The appearance presented to me then was the body in a very advanced state of decomposition, the whole of the muscles of the belly and stomach were gone – the

muscles covering the hip bones were also gone, the thigh bones were not there – there were no signs of any organs of generation, the pelvis was a mere skeleton... I found on the right and left side of the pelvis two inorganic substances covered with tissue, the nature of which I cannot state on account of the decomposed state of the tissues – but I feel confident they are the result of disease.

Two inorganic substances. She frowned, considering the word *inorganic*. It was a strange word for something found in the body. She flicked through the pages of her *Macquarie*, the thick green volume still, through habit, always open on her desk, and read each definition. Her finger stopped on number 4. Could Rogers have been using *inorganic* in the sense of *extraneous* – matter not belonging, something whose function he could not fathom? She pulled her book from the shelf again, scanning the section on congenital adrenal hyperplasia:

ovaries usually normal...
may later become cystic with thickened cortices...

By this time, Rogers was – for whatever reason – toeing the party line, desperately trying to convince himself he was looking at a body that had been identified as that of a man. He was committed now, scrabbling to save face. The last thing he would have wanted to voice, even if he possessed the expertise to contemplate it, was that here before him were atrophied ovaries, *cystic with thickened cortices* – the hard, shrivelled, useless ovaries of a man named Jock King.

Willa sat for a long time, mulling over her lay diagnosis, stroking Lucifer's short black fur with the end of her pen. She was sure she was right, had sensed from the first time she read George Sullivan's article that this murdered convict was intersexed – a *hermaphrodite*, they would have called him then, had they known. And if they had known...What kind of life would he have had? What was the fate of an ambiguous body in the nineteenth century, a body surgically intact – *unedited*, as Imogen would say?

Pulling out the article again, she skimmed through to Sullivan's account of Little Jock's death.

> The deceased had been struck on the top of the skull with a blunt instrument, and there were two wounds across his forehead, one crossing the other, thought to have been made by an axe. Before being partially dismembered, the body was mutilated. The chest was gashed and the muscles cut away, and at trial Rogers made the sensational claim that King had been disembowelled.

The breath caught in her throat at the ferocity of such an attack. There could be no defence against savagery like this. Surely it was the work of a madman, not a teamster who saw a random chance to make a few pounds out of a wagonload of sandalwood and a few horses. What could have prompted it if not rage and loathing, the compulsion to obliterate? Little Jock was disfigured, dismembered, utterly destroyed.

Carved up, said the voice in her head. *Carved up just like...*

She crossed to the window and pulled up the blind, feeling a sudden need for the blandness of her suburban street. The streetlight across the road cast a glow over the verandah, revealing the aggressive, woody creeper that twisted and twined around the timber fretwork, supporting the wisteria's ethereal blooms.

She knew nothing of Little Jock's life but she knew the manner of his death, and she could not get it out of her mind. From what Rogers could tell from the one intact hand, Little Jock had died with his fingers clenched.

Midsummer's Eve 1842

Cornabracken, County Tyrone

The mud path, slushy from a mist of summer rain, is alive with distractions: moon-bright gold, knobbly green, sleek black. A clod of peat sprouts webbed feet and slithers out of the way. Glassy stones lying in the mud suddenly blink into eyes. Froglets leap from sword-grass spears into the depressions left by bare feet and cluster wetly. The child claps her hands and laughs to see a scatter of frogs this way and that.

Keep up, keep up, you must, the grandmother calls over her shoulder. *We've longer to walk today.*

It is a familiar path; the child, barely four, has walked it alone many times and knows the markers that lead to and from home. They pass tall beeches, where she hears the cry of rooks but cannot see the dark birds high in their nests among the topmost branches. Her grandmother's strip of land is next, the smallest in a row of subsistence plots in the bog bordering the arable land. They stop to empty another day's waste on the dungheap, and look longingly at the crop, profusely green and budding. Autumn harvesting will bring an end to the hungry late summer, when their year's supply of potatoes, stored in a shallow pit, dwindles away to nothing.

Further on is Mrs Spiller's good land, away from the bog, rented for profit, not subsistence, by more well-to-do tenants. The child, seeing nothing more than row after row of Ga'ma's plot on a larger scale, is unimpressed. What is so *good* about it? But soon they come to fields that rise gently from the path and roll away as far as the sky, as smooth and clean as church glass. No stony furrows – just endless green spotted with snowflakes that Ga'ma says are sheep, though the child has seen dirty, greasy sheep at the markets at Omagh and does not believe this. She would like to clamber over the low granite wall and run up the hill all the way to the sky and stay there with the snow-sheep forever.

They reach the bleaching greens where Ga'ma works, where she says the child will work soon *and never-you-mind about running wild with sheep*. The child wonders whether it will be today she joins them, the small girls and old women ladling water over the bleached webs of flax pegged out on the grass. Or perhaps, having strong arms, she will be given the job of carting water in buckets from the Owenreagh. But no, the greens are bare, and the child becomes excited: it must be market day! When they reach Omagh, however, there is nothing of the usual scene in the square – the pigs and geese, the blocks of pale butter, the squabbling voices rising and falling in the rhythm of trade, linen for cash, cornmeal for sausage. She struggles to keep Ga'ma in sight, jostled along by more people than she has ever seen. Outside the full-to-overflowing White Hart Inn, a man plays a fiddle; another drums strong fingers against the skin of the bodhrán. She watches, mouth agape, as a boy with a tin whistle catches in one hand a coin flicked from the balcony of the inn, without missing a note of his tune.

Ga'ma grasps her by the arm. *Come, we've a mile to cover still.* And the child is hurried along the Gortrush road away from the town and into unfamiliar terrain.

The crones come each year, on the eve of the summer solstice, to watch over the holy well at Cornabracken. Ailing children from miles around are carried, wheeled or led on this day to be healed by the spring's ancient powers, which, purified by the staff of St Patrick, have now been pressed into the service of Christianity. The presence of the crones provides a witness to miracles – pagan or church-blessed, who can say? – and a steadying force on desperate mothers, a reminder to dip, not drown.

The Handywoman, from her place among these guardians, watches the widow and the child as they struggle through the bright gorse. Other women and children have already gathered, waiting for the rays of the sun to strike the well and light its dark waters. The Handywoman knows why the widow has brought her grandchild on this pilgrimage. She knows, too, that no good will come of it, but she will not take hope from a widow.

The child whimpers as another branch whips free of her grandmother's skirt and scratches her bare skin. By the time she reaches the well, her arms and legs are bleeding from welts raised by the treacherous gorse, but she seems not to notice. Her attention is claimed by the looming figure of a whitethorn, its branches tied with hundreds of strips of weathered cloth.

The crones wordlessly begin the ritual of the patterns, leading a circle of women around the well in the direction of the sun and placing around its circumference small egg-shaped stones, plucked from the shallows of Fairy Water. At a signal from the hand of one of the crones, the circle sits.

The children are stripped of their outer clothing and dipped, one after the other – sickly babies, the lame, infants with festering flesh, cheeks ashen or luminous with fever. Some are passive; others, especially the older ones, are afraid and struggling. After each child is dipped, its mother looks into the rippling water, hopeful of a sign, an omen, but the appearance of the sacred fish is rare.

When it comes to the widow's turn, the child protests loudly that she will not remove her thin little blouse, her canvas skirt – no, she will *not*. The Handywoman looks sharply at the child's face, surprised to see will where feebleness was expected. The assembly can only wonder at the nature of the disease as the widow plunges the fully clothed child face first into the holy waters of Cornabracken.

Blood freezes in her temples and she gasps, gulps in a mouthful. But Ga'ma has drilled her: *Open your eyes, mind what you see.* So she forces her lids apart against the water. Filmy threads of green sway, slide over her face. Particles dance. Bubbles of silver rise. Strands of her own dark hair fan out around her, but there is nothing else, nothing but the pressure of silence, thick in her ears, in the brief seconds before she is hauled back into the grip of air. Ga'ma is staring into the water, looking for the sacred fish. The child looks, too, knowing Ga'ma expects her to, and is startled to make out a form in the disturbed waters. She smiles up at Ga'ma but the woman is still searching intently. Can she not see? The child looks down again. The shape forming and re-forming in the ripples of water, between the shadows and the light, is not a salmon, not an eel.

Perhaps the Handywoman will mutter a blessing as the widow tears a thin strip of flax from the hem of the child's blouse and ties it to a branch of the whitethorn with all the other clooties, to be whipped and savaged by the wind.

August 1847

Near Ballynahatty, County Tyrone

The child kneels between the lazy-beds and plunges her hands into a ridge built up with sods of peat. A puff of fine powder rises as her elbow brushes the sparsely leaved plants. The soft lavender flowers have only just begun to blanch and curl. It is too soon to be pulling tubers: if there are any, and if sound, they will be small and bitter, unsuitable for storing. But she is half mad with the craving for starch in her stomach, for bulk of any kind, and willing to gamble starvation tomorrow for one new potato today.

She scrabbles feverishly, a small, ravening animal.

In the suck of the bog, her fingers feel along the fleshy rope tuber for swellings. Elated she pulls them up, a string of pearls, crisp, white and gleaming – but they are none of these things. The pressure of thumb and finger is all it takes to pop the skin, render them pulp in her hands. As it was the year before, throughout the village, all the county, all of Ulster, the crop is blighted.

Weeping, she flings the nauseating mush away, but a cavern inside her howls, admonishing her for the sheer waste of it. She picks up another potato, jabs it with her finger. Could Ga'ma cook the pulp; would it be like mash?

She re-inters the precious, rotten tuber, carefully patting over the sodden ground.

Only a few remote descendants of the ancient landlord remember where the castle of Ballynahatty once stood, for every stone of it, right down to the footings, has long since been carried away and put to use – in the drystone walls and ditches carving up fields, in clochauns built to shelter pigs and fowls, in the superior stone cabins that now form the heart of the village.

The child approaches the first of these dwellings. She has, on the way, passed cottier cabins like Ga'ma's, of mud and limewash, but knows there will be nothing to spare here. No food, no charity. Surely, she thinks, she can appeal to the Stronges, the O'Neils, the Gwynns, with their thatched roofs and real chimneys. She creeps cautiously, on the lookout for an egg, a row of cabbages. Ga'ma has sent her to beg, but she is prepared to steal.

There is no smoke spiralling from this chimney, or the next. This child notices, and might have found strange, were it not for the litany of strangenesses that could be recounted daily, leaving her numb to all but the fact of them. A clochaun close to the cabin is bare of either fowls or scraps. Rooks wail in the distance but the village is otherwise silent.

As she reaches the half-door of the cabin, anticipation buzzes in her ears. Perhaps there will be a pot on the fire, awaiting the family's return from the looms. She will not take it all, she promises God, but she has been days now with nothing more than cabbage water. A little for herself, a little for Ga'ma. She can almost imagine the taste of it. She looks in.

The buzzing becomes incarnate: fat little bodies hovering and settling, jostling for choice space in sockets where eyes should be. A scream rips raw from her throat and echoes through the empty village laid waste by the Famine.

When she leaves Ballynahatty, stinking of death, she is a thief with a turnip in her pocket.

November 1847

Omagh, County Tyrone

The Poorhouse is full, over-full, with inmates sleeping in hallways, under long wooden benches in the dining hall, spilling out into the grounds, in stables, turf-shelters, churning-sheds. And still they come, pouring in from all the townlands in the Drumragh parish, evicted from their niggardly cabins, their half acres of blighted bog. Turned away from the Poorhouse, they must beg in the streets, sleep in ditches, queue, fretful and spoiling for violence, outside the government soup kitchen for a foul-smelling broth so remarkably devoid of a shred of meat, grain or vegetable that the question of its substance is a wonder to all.

They have lived the Great Hunger, a slow marasmus that begins with diarrhoea and disorientation, advances with hair loss, pellagrous eruptions of the skin, and gradually picks off organ after organ until bodily functions simply cease. Dysentery has taken families; typhus, whole villages. Many have sunk their teeth into the flesh of rats and starved dogs, or sickened themselves on the unexpected bounty of a wild pheasant still pumping blood. Every one of them has seen death.

Emaciated shells, mere bags of bones, they are differentiated only by the distance between them and their maker, calculated in days, hours, minutes.

What a waste, thinks the man leaning against the churchyard wall of St Columba's, watching as the same trapdoor coffin expedites the dispatch of another dozen bodies into a communal grave. Such a windfall it would have been twenty years before, when he was getting four shillings a corpse in the dockyards of Belfast, as much as ten if he delivered them to Glasgow himself. And it was harder work then. At a time when the dead, in fewer numbers, were consigned reverently to the earth while all was done to release their spirits skywards, loved ones did not take kindly to the midnight pillaging of the sack-'em-up boys. The bereaved here had never resorted to explosive traps, mort-safes and two-ton resurrection stones, as had happened at home across the Irish Sea, but more than once he had felt the sting of buckshot on his boots while throwing another sack onto the back of his cart. Ah, there would be none of that today; it would be easy takings, with quantities never before seen and none to weep over them.

The Act of 1832 had spoiled his contract with the anatomists. They had been desperate for teaching cadavers, available to them then only from the gallows; now they could legally take the remains of those other criminals, the poor. But still he is in the business of bodies: a Collector, procurer of fairground fancies, trawling Ireland for dwarfs and giants, Siam twins, bearded ladies. And what he cannot package with lurid words to titillate the hard-nosed fair-men back home (*The Amazing Eel Man – One Touch of his Slimy Skin Will Pleasantly Shock the Blood from Your Veins!!!!*) is invariably of interest to his old contacts at the university, always on the lookout for aberrations. It has been a task of little work to entice unfortunates away from villages with the promise of adventure – or, in the case of the young, to exchange a few shillings for cursed progeny – but the Famine has confounded his luck. On the one hand, there is little people will not do, will not sell, for an onion. On the other, these freaks of nature are a weakish bunch, and the privations of the Hunger have culled his supply.

At the approach of the town's orphan beggars, he straightens up, alert.

He'd first heard gossip of the child in Gortaclare and then again in Seskinore, from villagers casting round for scapegoats more tangible than blight. Wherever there is talk of changelings, there is sure to be something for him. He is confident of success. The child's family has perished in the Famine; she is without sustenance or future. He is expected in Glasgow and is, for the first time, without consignment. He *will* make the trip, empty-handed or no – his own supply of food has nearly gone – but better still if he has a curiosity to sell.

A man limps by, stooped but not old. The Collector inclines his head towards the ragged children: *The changeling from Ballynahatty – which?* The other passes without a glance or word. The Collector reaches out to touch him on the shoulder, repeat his question a little louder, but sees the running sores and lets his hand drop.

He studies the children from across the churchyard. They are no different from others he has seen throughout the county (there *must* be some market for them), and amorphous in their featureless grime. There is a pitiful solidarity in the way they huddle as a pack, all cupped hands and dropsied limbs, but it is a fragile alliance. Listless when ignored, they are prone to bursts of savagery at the least sign of kindness, as likely to turn on a benefactor as they are on each other.

There is one who follows a few feet behind the pack. The Collector gives a satisfied grunt. Yes, he has an eye for these things.

He will need a quiet place to make certain verifications, for she is not like his usual specimens, not obvious fairground fodder. She is taller than the other starvelings, even with her head drooping, but otherwise unremarkable. Yes, he will need to assure himself that despite the lie of outward appearance, she is monstrous enough to be saleable to the Professor if not to the fair-men, worth the resources it will take to ship her to Glasgow. He will need to *see*.

It should not be too difficult. She will be wary, of course, she will resist, but what choice has she? And in his haversack he has the ultimate prize for compliance, more persuasive than word or fist: the uncompromising substance of oatcake.

The children spy him across the road, a stranger, fair game. They approach with their hands out, a mass of dark, distended bodies on swollen legs, and he is reminded of the awkward gait of crows. If they suspected what was in his canvas sack, they would descend on him and peck out his eyes. But they are accustomed to rejection, indeed expect it, and when he waves them away the mass simply changes direction and moves on. Only one glances back, expressionless, when he grabs the straggling child by her skinny arm.

The collective wheezing of the children recedes. The undertakers have long gone. No one offers prayers in St Columba's today. As the child looks up at the Collector, limp tails of hair fall back and he can see a pale down on her face.

Distinguishing marks

Willa still thought of it as Orla's garden, as beautiful as her mother had been and every bit as formidable. She gazed around at the old-fashioned roses, the dense plantings of gardenias and orange jessamine, the cottage beds with plants whose names she knew only because they were the names of flower fairies on a frieze that had run around the wainscot of her childhood bedroom: red clover, scabious, heliotrope, yarrow. What strong foundations this garden must have. Four and a half years had passed since it lost the guiding vision of her mother, along with her father's willing labour in turning and composting and mulching and fertilising. Suddenly all it had was the summer reticulation set for the twice a week allowed under water restrictions. And Willa. She had weeded – she could do that – though not as often as the garden deserved, and she knew about dead-heading the roses. That had always been her job as a child; Orla had drilled into her that the hips, if not removed, would *bleed the bush dry, with nothing to spare for new buds*. It should have given up, but somehow this garden had survived the loss of Orla, of Chas, the years of Willa's neglect, and as she squeezed down with blunt secateurs, she could only think that it was her mother's will, as indestructible as morning glory.

The train into Perth swept through suburbs that were already beginning to look hot and dry. Willa turned from the window, from her reflection in the glass.

Six months ago, she had begun to lose the substance of her own body. In part, it was a response to failing appetite, a sudden aversion to the sensation of putting food into her mouth, feeling it there, alien, without taste, without relevance – impossible to imagine it becoming a part of her. But the rest she had orchestrated, feeling compelled to pare back surfaces, attenuate, contract. She had taken a pair of dressmaking shears and cut the dark plait that hung to her waist, hacked into it at the base, the curve of her skull, feeling the blades strain against the thick mass of it, her back to the mirror. She had pulled thin gold hearts from her ears, a circle of moonstones from her ring finger. She had scrubbed the skin from her face, lashes falling from her eyes, lines appearing like stigmata. She had lit a match and looked at the smooth white page of her forearm, but then snuffed out the flame, denying herself the ostentation of scars. She had shrunk into black sweatpants, black T-shirt, feet bare, and every day stared her down.

Useless acts of contrition, she told herself now. Imogen wasn't coming back.

She could hear her father's voice: *Pull yourself together, girl. What you need is work!* It was capable, still, of unsettling her resolve, even though she had not heard it all these years. Her parents would be turning in their graves. Chas and Orla would never have understood.

What you need is work.

But she could not work, could not imagine transposing onto the present the rhythms of her life when her daughter had been in it. And yet she could not sever the past, either, could not contemplate anything that was unconnected to Imogen.

She leaned against the cool glass. It would have been clear to her parents what she had to do, criminal that she would not do it. To them, things were always black and white. God and the devil.

How she had always longed for such certainty, for the smallest sign of what was unequivocally right. Perhaps, she thought, as the train slowed to a stop at the central station, that was what drew her to history, for surely certain things were simpler when there were fewer choices to make. A cheerless smile at her own naivety crossed her face as she stepped down onto the platform and headed towards the library.

Choices. They preyed on her mind, commingling with other preoccupations, as she threaded her way through the shelves and tables to the State Records Office. *What were your choices, Little Jock?*

She knew that expiree convict number 7756 had no choice at all about his emigration to Australia – as unlucky for him as it was serendipitous for a researcher. It gave him a visibility in the records, for at least a part of his life, that simply would not exist had he been a law-abiding arrival at Swan River Colony. Nearly ten thousand male convicts from Britain had been transported to the struggling settlement between 1850 and 1868. They had been petitioned for, and welcomed, by many colonists as a source of cheap labour for public works and private development, not to mention the much-needed capital they brought from the British Government in support of its newest penal outpost. However, those who considered themselves keepers of public morality had damned them for the stain they cast on the colony's pure pedigree, fearing for the future of a populace irrevocably besmirched by convict blood.

A gem of a dictionary called *Convicts in Western Australia* had given Willa a brief sketch of Little Jock's convict profile. She knew he had arrived in Swan River in April 1864 on the *Clara* at the age of twenty-six, a semi-literate Roman Catholic shoemaker convicted two years earlier of housebreaking in Glasgow. He was given a ticket of leave in 1865, releasing him to work on probation in Albany, Perth and Plantagenet, and his conditional release, a form of probation with fewer restrictions, two years after that. His certificate of freedom was not granted until 1871 – could that be right? It was nine years after his original seven-year sentence began.

In the microfilm area of the State Records Office, there were people lacing up microfilm readers, typing on laptops, pulling out clattering drawers of films in boxes; people coughing, tapping pencils on files, muttering to themselves, exclaiming; people asking for assistance with births, deaths and marriages, with maps, enquiring quietly about lunacy records. Willa felt vaguely fraudulent, as though she was intruding on a place for people with better reasons to be here than hers. But she stumbled out her request and the woman at the desk beamed at her.

Oh, yes, she said. *Best to start with the Convict Registers and the Distribution Books. And you've got the number of your convict, and the name of the ship, so that will make it easier.* She showed Willa the thick black file containing an inventory of the state's convict archives. *You'll find accession numbers in here, and the films are over there in the drawers.*

Is he a relative, your convict? she added.

Willa shook her head, and wondered whether an explanation was required, whether she should make some claim to adopting *her convict*, but the woman was already speaking again.

It's very fashionable now to have a convict in the family. Wish I had one myself!

The Convict Register for the *Clara*'s cargo of 301 transportees, scripted in slanting letters of black ink, was a gift from another time, and Willa sat, transfixed, in front of the screen.

Little Jock was five feet one and a quarter inches tall, with a stocky build, fair complexion and a round face. His hair was dark brown, his eyes light blue, and he had a scar on his forehead and several tattoos: a star, a crescent and a flower on his left arm, and on his left hand a symbol, unfamiliar to Willa, drawn as a cross dividing four dots. Before transportation he had been incarcerated in Portsmouth Prison, where his character was described, cryptically, as 'indifferent'. Willa was strangely moved to find, in a space on the register headed 'Name and Age of Wife or Next of Kin', the notation 'Mother, 23 High Street, Glasgow.' She turned the wheel of the microfilm reader back and forth, scanning random register entries, and found that, for whatever reason, perhaps a deliberate avowal to sever family ties, it was no common thing for a convict to identify his next of kin. Locating the entry for Little Jock again, she wondered about *Mother, 23 High Street, Glasgow*, drawn to this woman by what they might share despite the years and distance between them. The people seated at the microfilm readers beside her, the friendly archives assistant, the queue of researchers with their notepads and their questions – none of them understood. But this nameless *Mother* might. Willa wanted to know who she was. Would it be possible to find her somewhere in the records, too?

According to the register, the boundaries of Jock's life in Western Australia were narrow. Apart from two early ticket-of-leave engagements in Perth, he seemed to have roamed between Kojonup and Albany, and the trial records suggested that he had not strayed from this pattern once a free man. Fascinated, she read of minor convictions – 'under the influence of liquor at the depot,' 'loitering about Public Houses while on Pass' – and she could see now why he had served more than his seven years: there was another sentence of three years' hard labour for selling gin. An 'Act of Leniency' remitted a year from his lengthened sentence, but Willa was disconcerted to find, when she asked at the counter, that the document explaining *why* no longer existed. It was one of those gaps that could never be filled.

She laced up the microfilm reel of the Distribution Book containing Little Jock's record. A complicated accounting of marks was tallied, itemising the convict's progress, based on his behaviour, towards ticket-of-leave status. Much of the information from the Convict Register was duplicated here, but Willa was discovering that each new archival record added something to the picture. This time, under 'Next of Kin', there was a name alongside 'Mother, 23 High Street.' Little Jock's mother was Mary Lennie.

Deciphering Jock's allocation of marks was beyond Willa, and she realised she would need to find out more about the system before she could work out whether he was a very good convict or a very bad one – whatever that might mean. The ship's superintendent had added thirteen days to his sentence based on conduct – unspecified – aboard the *Clara*, but it seemed a common thing for convicts to incur such penalties on the journey. She sank back in her chair for a moment, thinking about what she had read in books, seen in movies, about convict ships – mostly those of the First Fleet: horror stories of filth and disease, rats, rape and violence. What feat of endurance might such a voyage have been for someone with something to hide?

Returning to the microfilm, Willa saw that during Little Jock's first fourteen months in the colony, when he would have been working on public works gangs, there were five sixpenny deductions for postage. Who would he have written to, this semi-literate convict transported to the other end of the world? Mary Lennie? What would he have told her? Would she have written in reply? There were no records of correspondence in or out, and again she was frustrated to realise there were things, important things, she could never know.

Do you have records for Portsmouth Prison? she asked at the desk, and was directed upstairs to an index compiled by local genealogists.

Some of the documents in the National Archives in London have been microfilmed, the woman explained, *and if your convict is included in these, you'll find him in the index.*

The doors of the glass elevator closed with a huff of air and Willa braced herself against the handrail as the lift began to move from the ground floor, up through the mezzanine. Thousands and thousands of volumes passed by. Deceptive, she thought. It was hard to imagine that, surrounded by so much knowledge, *anything* could remain unknowable.

On the first floor, a volunteer at the genealogy desk helped her find number 8092 of Portsmouth in the Prison Commission index and showed her where the microfilms were stored. How grateful she felt for the generosity of these local genealogists who compiled indexes and shepherded novices. Her helper, a sprightly older man with a brace of ballpoint pens in his breast pocket, chuckled as he read the index entry. *Well, well. Looks like your fellow had his own name and someone else's!*

The microfilm record added to the story of John King *alias Peter Lennie*. His 'character and conduct' in Glasgow and Millbank prisons were 'good', he could read and write, though 'imperfectly', and he had been a boatman, not a shoemaker as stated on the later documents. But here she thought of Scottish accents she had heard, and wondered whether there might have been some confusion across the records: did *boatman* become *bootman*? Did *bootman* become *shoemaker*?

There were four summary convictions before his first major one, in 1857, when he was sentenced to four years' penal servitude. And when Willa did another search, looking for the register number for this earlier sojourn in Portsmouth, it was under the name 'Peter Lennie, collier'. All of Jock's early convictions were detailed here, the first in 1851, when he would have been just thirteen years old. Once again, he named his next of kin: 'Mother, Mary Lennie, 23 High Street.'

She collected her copies from the printer and returned to the index to search for *Lennie*, hoping to find records for Millbank or Glasgow, but there was nothing. Her head was spinning and she had no idea where next to look.

Almost as soon as the train gathered what speed it could manage, it began to slow again, in a rocking, rattling lurch from station to station. Willa watched the late-afternoon bustle, the ebb and flow of shoppers and shop assistants, office workers from the city and inner suburbs, schoolchildren heading home from extra-curricular activities with sports bags and heavy, black cases in the shape of musical instruments. There was a rhythm to it all, more alien to her than history.

She took out the pages folded in her bag and pored over the physical description of Little Jock. He was twenty-six years old when he arrived in the colony. A quick calculation and she realised for the first time that he must have been forty-four when he died. Forty-four: her age. Not young, but not old – not old enough. She tried to imagine a face made up of the features the convict authorities thought necessary to note: dark hair, pale blue eyes, the fair skin scarred across the forehead. How much more there was to a face. Her eye was drawn to the little diagram under 'Distinguishing Marks' – the tattoo that could not be assigned a word like the others, *star*, *crescent*, *flower*.

The symbolism was obviously as cryptic to the person recording it then as it was to her now. And yet it must have meant something to Little Jock, for the inscription of a body with needle and ink is an act of will – a claim, perhaps, to belonging.

She closed her eyes, imagining the tattooist at work, puncturing the skin, point by point, forming first the cross and then the points within each of its right-angles; Jock watching intently as the symbol he had chosen materialised and became part of him. And her mind drifted to a time when *she* had watched symbols appear on a page, watched and tried to understand what miracles skin could be made to perform.

The paediatric surgeon is doing all the talking, and on a slab of notepaper bearing the logo of some new laxative he draws simple representations of organs, blood vessels, nerves – all circles and arrows and crosses – and makes sweeping flourishes with his fountain pen to show what his team will do.

Matthew sits there fully engaged, keen-eyed and making the occasional sharp inclination of his head to acknowledge perfect understanding and agreement. A nod to *labial separation*, to *resecting excess tissue*, to *trimming and wedging*, to *burying the erectile shaft*, as though the engineering is the thing, the neatness and aesthetic soundness and fitness for purpose that one expects from any finely crafted product of science.

The neovagina is lined with the baby's own skin, the surgeon says. *We take it from her thigh.* And he glances up at them, from one to the other, as though expecting some gasp of appreciation at the sheer ingenuity of this surgical performance.

She looks at the stick drawing of her baby's remaking, and then at this man with his sharp-nibbed pen and his smug, problem-solving, making-the-best-of-a-botch face.

What about side effects?

There are always risks with any surgery, Mrs Gates.

Yes, but specific side effects, I mean. Consequences for her future.

A tremor of self-pity runs through her. It should be her right, her privilege, as a new mother to dwell in the baby self of her daughter, with no thought yet to anything but the blank slate that is a newborn child: innocent, unknowing, desiring nothing more than sustenance and comfort and love. But here she is, being forced to project on her four-month-old daughter a future self, imagine her as a woman, make some attempt to protect rights to different desires that she would some day claim. Surely no new mother should have to make that leap of imagination from newborn to sexual being with nothing in between.

She gestures at the drawing. *The endocrinologist said it was too small, but now you're talking of cutting…Doesn't that…*

Too small as a penis, yes, unquestionably, but as a clitoris it is oversized – monstrously so, I'm sure you would agree.

He appeals to Matthew for confirmation – and there it is, that nod.

Anything over 0.9 of a centimetre is unacceptable and will cause her embarrassment in the future.

But what you're doing, surely…Will she have any…will there be any feeling?

She can sense Matthew staring at her, incredulous.

You're concerned about loss of sensation? the surgeon says, raising one neat brow. *Well, perhaps. But we've had a very good success rate with reconstructive surgery, and we must focus on what is best for the baby. There will come a time when all she is going to want is to look like every other little girl, and we can make that happen. We can do that now.*

There had been a moment, a split second, when she wished she had died giving birth, wished that all the mother-decisions to be made about her precious child had fallen to Orla, for whom *what was best* was always as clear as air. What a monster that made her sound, but no less monstrous was what she had consented to in the name of love. Would Little Jock's mother, transplanted into the twentieth century, have made the same choices for her child? *If they offered you the grail of normalcy, Mary, would you have taken it?*

The train stopped at the station before hers, expelling another group of commuters into the cooling air. She gathered up the pages in her lap, copies of documents that had survived more than 140 years, and as the train moved off again she was thinking of what she had to do: organise the information she had gathered so far, make a list of leads, a plan. Some things already seemed obvious, the *where* if not the *how*. Albany and Kojonup. Glasgow. Portsmouth and Millbank. And the convict ship the *Clara*. People leave residues in the places they inhabit. Could the imprint of a single life be discernible among the communal parings, peelings, scrapings wrought by history?

Walking away from the station, she wondered where, 140 years from now, someone would begin if faced with the task of unravelling Imogen's story; how confounding the records might seem, how impenetrable the decisions. And by the time she was fumbling with her bunch of keys, the familiar dialogue of recrimination was playing its endless loop in her head, broken only by Lucifer's wails of grievance on the other side of the door.

Would a day ever come that did not begin and end with Imogen?

December 1847

Belfast

The SS *Aurora* pulls out into Belfast Lough at sundown, thronged to the gunnels, leaving behind a hundred more would-be passengers fretful and shivering – and with a sudden pressing need for shelter. Icy winds howl through the dock and there is no question of remaining here until morning, when the next ship, the *Tartar*, will leave. Not even the robust would survive, and in truth there is not a robust one among them.

The Collector, unlike most of the others, is no stranger to Belfast and hurries towards the Night Asylum, knowing its doors shut soon and there will not be room for all, besides. He casts a speculative eye over the child. Even out of her rags, clad in a skirt and tunic of thick worsted and charity boots, she is a sorry spectacle: dirty, scabby, skeletal. They are sure to take her in.

He has no intention of applying for night relief, not when the shebeens of the dockyard beckon, but he wishes not to be saddled with a wretched child with wide eyes. *Say nothing*, he admonishes, shaking her bony shoulders. *Keep yer mouth shut and say nothing o' me*. It is just a precaution: he has no real fear of investigation of any kind. She is just one in a city inundated with waifs. Nor does he fear her absconding when she is so clearly stricken at the frenetic throb and pulse of people hurrying along cobbled streets, spilling from the open decks of horse-drawn bians, singing in the doorways of noisy inns, lurching, fighting, begging, drunk.

He gives her a push at the foot of the steps. *Go now*, he hisses, gratified to see her cower. *I'll be back for you at sun-up. And mind yer boots.* At the street corner he turns and watches as she climbs the stairs, is questioned at the door, is taken, mute, into the asylum.

The bath-house is an innovation, an ambitious attempt at institutional hygiene that, based as it is on two tubs for 300 – children first, then the adults – is doomed to fail. Long lines of crusty children, boys to the left, girls to the right, wait their turn to be doused in the same rancid soup of water and lysol and drowning lice.

The child is shepherded to the end of the queue of girls and ordered to strip. She twists in an agony of distress. There is the question of her clothes, warm and barely a patch on them. She dares not discard them with the others left in heaps against the walls. And her boots, especially, she has been exhorted to safeguard, and what would he not do if she were to lose them? She cannot take them off.

Blood flushes hot through her face as she glances around furtively. She has never before seen naked bodies, nor, until the man and his prying hands, exposed any part of her own. The others do not seem concerned. Some wait, solemn and quiet, in anticipation of broth and warm sleep. Some are laughing and jostling, and a few lively boys make a game of ducking the cuffing hand of a passing attendant. Children squeal as they are dunked, but no one seems to share her rising dread.

For a long time, until the man came, she had survived by keeping her eyes open, watching for luck and chance, but lately it has been better not to see. And now the shock of so much skin is blinding. Awareness of details is slow to break over her, but gradually her focus narrows. Here are the girls. There are the boys. The girls. The boys.

The child opens her mouth and an animal cry breaks loose, tearing through corridors, clawing at walls, scarifying every surface with the story of its wounds. The sour retch of hunger, the buzz of blowflies, the frenzy of dogs and the calm picking-over of crows. The loss of home, of Ga'ma, of love. The anguish of surviving. The shameful, nameless ordeal of the man and the things he has done. And now, this sudden, terrible revelation, the slap of awareness that she is *different*.

A plump woman carrying a bundle of rags for drying makes a clucking noise with her tongue as the child flees past her. *Ach, such a noise to be making and 'tis only a bath!*

She cannot sleep.

The bright face of the moon lights up the grandly named 'sleeping gallery', one of several vast dormitories where mattresses of chaff lie side-by-side, end-to-end, filling every square inch of the rough oak floors. The child sits with her back against the wall, arms hugging her thighs, chin on her knees. She misses the stillness of Ga'ma's cabin. Even the ditches on the outskirts of Omagh where she slept after leaving Ballynahatty were peaceful. The rustle of voles in the grass, owls hooting in the distance – these things never frightened her. They belonged, as she did. Where, now, does she belong?

Here the gallery snores, snorts, sighs, wheezes, whispers, farts, groans. It never stops coughing, and the coughs are of every kind: ratcheting, catarrh-gobbing, lung-gurgling, bone-racking. Feral grunts and gasps, strangely punctuated with giggles, can be heard from beneath moving sacking.

Her hand slips tentatively under the thick folds of her skirt to that place that is not like the smooth absence, the pale, cloven mound, she saw on all those skinny girls. The man had looked there, was always looking, always poking and pawing, holding his lantern so close that she feared the hot glass would burn her skin.

She touches herself, but jerks her hand away when a sibilant whisper comes from the mattress next to her.

So, what's wrong with ya?

A face materialises in the moonlight.

I say, what's wrong with ya? Y've a face as long as a Lurgan spade.

She shrinks further into the wall but the face just gets closer.

So, where's yer mammy?

I've none.

No mammy? Ah. It seems to give him food for thought and he is quiet for a moment. *So, I saw ya. Running from the tub.*

She flushes, remembering the line of boys, their pink, jiggling bodies.

Wish we dunnit, too, me and Felix, so we did, when we saw ya up and run like…

Patrick Lunney! The sharp whisper cuts through from the mattress on the other side of him.

The child watches as the boy is grabbed by the arm and jerked back.

Now, you be silent, boy. You close your eyes at once. We've an early morning and a long, long way to be going.

In spite of her gruff voice, the woman's expression, caught in the blaze of the moon, is mild. She smiles when she sees the child watching.

It is a fleeting kindness, this smile, but to the child it is as warm as a sack of down.

It is still dark when the gallery begins to stir, roused by a thick, yeasty cooking smell, unfamiliar but no less welcome for that. The child is torn between her habitual hunger, never sated, and the imperative to be where she was told to be. The only thing greater than her fear of the man is fear of the consequences of keeping him waiting even for a minute. Sun-up, he said. She keeps one eye on the window.

The boy in the mattress beside her is yanked to his feet, still dreaming, by a coughing man – one of the ratcheters – and at once is absorbed into that most intimate of things: family. He stumbles into two bigger boys, who pummel his chest, growling like dogs, until their mother intervenes with a few amiable slaps. *Bridget, ah, Brid-get, getoffwillya!* he whines as a young girl, blinking and yawning, falls over his feet.

The child stares, fascinated, at the benevolent touch of skin against skin. Something uncurls inside her, want instead of need. The cluster of bodies, the coughing man, the tired woman who glanced kindly. Could she…?

As the woman ushers her family out of the gallery, the child is drawn forward with them, hooked.

The Night Asylum discharges another burden of inmates into a cold, white dawn. The child floats down the steps, a pale wraith hovering on the edge, as invisible as any lone child in Belfast in the hungry years. She looks this way and that down the empty street, pulls her cold hands into the sleeves of her tunic, stamps her feet on the cobbles, glad she minded her boots. If only she can just keep shuffling forward, moving with the others, somewhere else.

A strong hand grabs her shoulder from behind and the glow inside her is snuffed out by a blast of moist, sour breath.

December 1847

Belfast to Glasgow crossing

Tuppence per skull, if yer fit for the deck. The shipping clerk has to shout to be heard. *But mind ya* ARE *fit, Missus.*

Her fingers, waxy as cold muttonfat, untie a twist of calico and count out fourteen pennies. She reties the knot and stuffs the makeshift purse down the front of her dress.

They are elbowed and jostled and frisked as they make their way through the crowded wharf. Mary Lunney keeps her hand on her heart, but the secure warmth she had felt with the weight of nineteen pennies pressing against her has vanished, and the remaining five scoop out a hollow in her chest. It yawns wider, that hollow, when she sees the SS *Tartar*, barely large enough to cast a shadow on the dock and already seething with men, women and children. She is a woman of the land, the wife of a weaver, the mother of children with good bog-peat between their toes; what madness to entrust their salvation to a skittish sea and this stinking bucket. But the land has given them up for dead. They need work. They need food in their bellies. They need more than fivepence will buy them.

Mary looks sideways at her husband, Felix, stooped and defeated, perpetually coughing, leaning on John for support.

What choice but to move on? Sixty miles to Belfast they had walked, sixty miles sleeping on damp ground, subsisting on wild parsley and blackberries and scarce Quaker gruel, but rumours of work in the city were untrue. Hugh, now proclaiming himself a Scotsman, settled and well-fed in a foreign army, has sent word for them to come, sent money (and a sore test it has been, not to turn it at once into meal). It is hope, of sorts, the only one they have, but Mary wonders now, looking at the wasted frame of her man, what good can come of this forced defection. Neither of them is still young. They are destitute now and will be so when they disembark in Glasgow. Will the sum of all this amount to no more than starvation elsewhere? She is too weary to work out what is right any more, and to weigh up the soundness of Hugh's say-so. If they fall, she and Felix both, then Hugh will have to take the consequences, the survival of the others resting with him and John.

They are jerked forward into the straggle of bodies trailing up the gangplank. Few carry anything more than net bags slung across shoulders, containing rags and trinkets too worthless to sell; anything useful has long ago been traded for food. Bridget whimpers against her mother, and Mary gives her a clout, despairing again of ever toughening up her youngest child for the world. Young Felix, Patrick and Michael are surprisingly – mercifully – subdued. Perhaps it is the blow of reality – the mean little vessel, the rocking sea beneath it; perhaps it is simply the unfamiliar stodge of institutional maize lying like lead in their stomachs.

The *Tartar* was never built for bulk cargo, still less the human ballast it now carries. By the time eight hundred people have shuffled up the gangplank, it wallows in a dark swill of sewage and bilgewater, weighed down by thin bodies crammed together in an uncomfortable intimacy, breast to back, shoulder to shoulder, in the hold, on deck, occupying gangways, perched on the roof of the galley and the crew's cabin. Individual movement is impossible; for nine hours, they will stand or drop as one. The smell of despair is rank, ripe with potential for panic.

Mary Lunney, on the afterdeck, spots her husband's brown cap, John wearing Bridget like a haversack – the girl will break his back. She tries to locate the younger boys, who were meant to stay by her, but the steamy press of flesh all around makes any movement of her hands feel obscene. *Michael!* she shouts. *Felix! Patrick!* But the names fly up into the wind, caught in communal babble and the rhythmic sough of the paddles as the boat steams away. Grey hills rise on either side, peeling back into blurred horizon. Great wheels of cloud roll across the sky. When the lough widens out into the North Channel of the Irish Sea, Mary tries in vain to turn her head, to see Ireland receding in the churning wake of the *Tartar*. The wind turns shrill, sharpens its needles on her face.

The child slips free of the Collector's grasp as they are herded on to the boat. He is unconcerned – where can she go? – and heads for the crew's cabin and the possibility of rum. The mate is a colleague from the days when both were in the business of shipping cadavers dressed as sacks of wheat.

When they reach Broomielaw, the crew will disembark first, and he with them. He will claim his goods readily enough then.

Freedom is brief. The child is soon trapped against a solid wall of people behind and the surge of those in front. By the time the boat lurches into motion, she is as tightly packed as a fowl in a basket on market day. She squirms this way and that, bodies towering over her, her forehead grazing against ribcages, belts, coarse winter capes. Suddenly a small hand shoots out, grabs hers. She manages to twist around, fight through winding sheets of wool and worsted, and there, the length of an arm away, is the boy from the Night Asylum. Patrick.

From a distance it sounds like singing, an unruly church choir warming up for a performance. But there is no joy in these voices, and no praise for a God who has abandoned them. Groaning bodies, held upright against their will, spew and void until the deck is awash with seawater and bile and excrement. A wail rises with each wild wave that lifts the *Tartar* to the brink of oblivion, before plunging it once more into a roiling swell.

Those on the low-pitched afterdeck, most exposed to the waves, cannot help swallowing the salty spray, and then retch mucus, bitter and burning. Head and shoulders below them, buried within the mass of humanity pitching left and right, two children bruise against knees and hips, vomiting helplessly, suffocating in the fug of sweat and breath. For them, no glimpse of Ailsa Craig rising from the sea like a ghostly giant haystack, of white foam breaking against the cliffs of Culzean to warn the *Tartar* away from the coast, of the looming bulk of Arran in the distance. All they see, when they are capable of opening their eyes at all, is the knot of their two hands, clasped, frozen.

A hush descends on the wharf at Broomielaw. Word has come through from Greenock, where the little steamer turned into the Firth of Clyde on the last leg of its journey, emerging from a curdle of fog. *Another one doon the watter!*

The *Tartar*'s crewmen, themselves shaken by the ferocity of the crossing, are unnerved by the silence of their human cargo. The beauty of such cargo is that it unloads itself, but those on board the *Tartar*, tuppence per skull, seem rooted where they are. The mate runs nimbly round the edge of the gunnels and takes the waiting gangplank, letting it drop to the deck with a clang. A murmur begins, spreads quickly, and those closest to the wharf begin to peel away from the others. Slowly the deck disgorges its load, among them several who have been dead for hours, beginning to stiffen into the mould of the mass around them. The survivors stagger down the gangplank, dazed and reeking, sick and exhausted. Dockmen shrink back, avert their gaze. *The filthy Irish.*

Mary, desperate to find her own, pushes against the flow of the crowd. Relief as she catches a glimpse of a tall man with a little girl on his back—but it vanishes as the people clustered around them move and the body of her husband slumps to the deck. *Felix!* She weeps over him, clutches speechlessly at John, at the two small boys who wriggle free of the cargo and fling themselves at her. And then she stumbles forward into the thinning crowd, searching still.

What she finds is a child crouching beside the body of her youngest son. The boy is cold and livid, gone from her. Unable to weep any more, she gently prises away his hand, gripped tightly by the other child's, and for a moment holds them together as though offering a prayer for all children.

December 1847

Glasgow, Scotland

The poor end of Glasgow wheezes like an old dosser, gasping in gritty smoke from chimneys and proud new industrial furnaces, exhaling a potent steam from consumptive lungs. It unlooses a dandruff shower of snow to settle on grimy back-courts, freeze on stone stairs. It bludgeons and bleeds in closes notorious for resurrectionists, garrotters, vitriol-throwers. Middens, soaks and streets of dung: the telltale reek of incontinence is everywhere.

Ah, home, thinks the Collector.

He strides out from the wharf, feeling his gut begin to calm, breathing in air that, if not sweet, is at least cold enough to numb the stench still in his nostrils, the legacy of that tub the *Tartar*. But relief at being on land is short-lived. Now that he is here, glum disappointment sets in. His miserable merchandise, sum and all to show for a sojourn of weeks, scuttles along behind, tethered by rope and fear. He won't even venture the humiliation of offering it to the fair-men, whose tastes run to more garish display. His only hope of some meagre profit lies with the Professor, a long walk by gaslight along the river, past the slaughterhouse, up Saltmarket, into High Street, and through the narrow side entrance to the college grounds. The bells of the Tron chime him on his way, drowning out cries that toss around like smuts of snow:

Herrin' three-a-penny!
Buy a bawbee candle, sir!
Will ye no' look at the wee doggie on a lead!

Ga'ma used to tell her about a place called Hell. It was worse than the Otherworld, she said, far worse, because at least you knew where you were with fairies; they could be blarneyed and they could be bought. But there was no bargaining in Hell. Hell was where the church priests sent all bad children and it sucked the soul from them so that all they could feel was the pain of the world. God was one thing, she said, but it was best to stay away from priests and their Hell.

The child follows the two men through a maze of corridors, staircases, heavy doors, rooms, the likes of which she has never before seen. She is dazzled by opulence – gleaming wood, polished brass, stained glass, velvet – but she is not fooled by beauty. Lining the graceful shelves, on the sheen of desktops, are tiny children suspended in glass jars of pale fluid. They float, blind and gaping, crying for the pain of the world, screwed down and trapped under seals of black wax.

This, she knows, is Hell.

The Collector feels the queasy rise of bile again. The dissecting room is no place for a stomach that has been churning for nine hours on the open sea. The skeletons of three murderers swing from the skylights, throwing candlelight shadows of ribs and limbs across slab-topped benches. There are no open cadavers tonight, but the smell lingers, ripe and bloody like any butchery. He lets the rope drop and motions to the child to wait outside while he tries to strike a deal with this new man, Jeffray's proxy. Old Professor Jeffray, frail for years and now nearing death, would have been intrigued, considered the possibilities, but this man, *this eedjit*, can see no value in the living, monster or no, to the college's Anatomy Department. *Should have waited till the Famine did her in.*

The child is already fleeing through Hell. Down two flights of stairs. Into rooms with eyes, rooms with monstrous scarlet feet, rooms with bones in glass cases. There is a noise at the end of a corridor and she follows it into a room where straw is strewn on the floor. Just a few yards away is the promise of escape, a door leading out to a cobbled courtyard. But she cannot get to it: a man is pushing in a large wooden barrow, covered in sacking, and when he leaves he turns the key. Hearing shouts and the heavy fall of feet on the stairs above her, the child hunkers down behind the barrow, exhausted.

Weak light filters in from a gap under the door and the child is woken by voices coming from the courtyard. One of them sounds familiar:

...you can't take...Mother of God, have mercy...

She creeps away from the barrow and peers through a small window. Outside a woman clutches at the sleeve of a uniformed soldier, and both of them plead with another man, the one who left the barrow the night before.

Hugh, please, make him see...

The barrow-man shakes his head, looking only at the soldier. *It's pauper law,* he says, *and it's thankful you should be, man, and no bletherin', when you cannae afford the buryin' yoursel'.*

As the woman weeps, the soldier looks down, shuffles his feet and mutters a question.

The barrow-man pauses a moment, spits to the left in resignation. *Ah, wait*, he says.

Shivering behind a water barrel, the child watches as he locks the door behind him, strides over to the barrow and flings off the sacking. He grapples, cursing, with arms and legs, and the child sees a boy's grey face, a hand still curved into the shape of her own.

He pulls at trousers, at sleeves, yanks the buttons off waistcoats, struggles with boots, flings two caps onto the pile and ties the lot together. Unlocking the door again, he looks out, tosses the loose bundle at the soldier with a curt *Gang away wi' you afore Ah change ma mind*. And not until he is certain they are walking away does he return to the barrow of bodies, pushing it through the inner door, into Hell.

The child sees her chance. Opening the outer door a crack, she slips into the courtyard.

A rook lands on the steeple of the university gate and raucously reproaches all of High Street for heinous wrongs. Behind the imposing entrance of grey brick and slate lie the university quadrangles, with their halls and houses, classrooms and lecture theatres. Further along the cobbled grounds are the library, the Hunterian Museum and the departments of Anatomy and Zoology, with College Green beyond, bordered by the high wall separating this lofty seat of learning from the worst dens of disease and vice in the whole of Glasgow.

The Collector stumbles out of the door of the Old College Bar and into a bitter morning that flecks his coat with a spittle of ice. He has been keeping a half-hearted watch on the university gate across the road from the grimy window of the pub, but it is, he thinks, a lost cause. She must be long gone, and good riddance to her, the useless article of Irish shite. He stamps blood into his frozen feet, the impact impressing on his bladder an urgent need. He is about to turn into the well-urinated alley of Buns Wynd when he notices movement by the gate. A woman, shawled and stooping, a bundle of rags under her arm, and a man in uniform and – ah, yes, will you look at that – a small figure resembling a useless article of Irish shite skulking a few paces behind them.

The child screams as a growling drunkard in a big black coat lurches across High Street. The soldier reacts, cleanly felling the madman threatening his mother and this poor child who has sprung from nowhere. *Run!* he shouts, one boot on the man's chest, just to be sure. *Go!*

Grabbing the child with her free hand, the woman flees up High Street, weaving around lodgers thrown sleepy-eyed from their doss-houses into the cold morning, around scuffling dogs, around barrows of apples, dodging horse dung and stumbling on uneven stones. Suddenly unsure of her bearings, she swings around and finds her son thudding heavily towards them.

Home, child, and quick! he cries, and takes his mother's elbow, steering her into a narrow lane. But the breathless child grasps the woman's skirt. The woman turns and a flicker of recognition, of some inchoate bond, passes between them. But it is broken by a cursing bluster of arms and legs flailing its way up High Street behind them.

The woman grabs the child again and they run into New Vennel, following Hugh, away from the drunken man. With relief she recognises the dank close-mouth to number 97, the front stairs to Hugh's house – so he calls it – with its one room, one broken window, one noxious pail steaming in the corner. She had left the children sleeping on the floor on hessian, bodies two and three a bed, in the squalid room lit by a candle in a bottle. They are lucky, Hugh says, not to be sharing with another family, only Hugh and his lodgers. It is their own room, for now. Their own.

She slumps on the second-floor landing, where there are low doors to six houses. *A minute*, she pants as Hugh makes to push theirs open. *Go, son – and will you not see to Bridget.*

She holds the precious bundle of clothes against her scudding heart, weeps silently, hurriedly, for her dead. When she wills it to be enough, when she opens her eyes, the child is beside her.

For a long time they are both still but for the work of breathing – the woman remembering a lone waif in the Night Asylum, the last touch felt by her youngest son; the child, a smile from a stranger, the enfolding of bodies into family.

The child will tell her and the woman will listen. And then Mary Lunney will unroll her bundle and pick out a pair of worn moleskins, a woollen shirt, a threadbare, buttonless waistcoat, the smallest of two caps, and lay them on the stone landing like the shell of a boy.

Those born somewhere else

Over the top of her book, she could see Lucifer stalking through the rosemary, squinting into the last of the afternoon sun. He sprang onto the bench beside her, his fur fragrant with that sharp scent she would forever associate with a blue plastic bath and a disconsolate child. The antiseptic decoction she used to brew from the oil-laden rosemary leaves was gentler, more soothing, than anything that could be bought from a pharmacy. *You should market that*, Orla always told her, seeing for herself how Imogen's fretful weeping would subside as she sank into the bath half filled with water and Willa's *potion*. But Willa hoped there was no other child in the world who needed a balm like hers.

Lucifer sidled up to her elbow, bumping the book in her hands, and she felt the warm rumble of his contentment as she drew an arm around him.

The sun did its best to light up the pages of her book but they were lost in hues of Dickensian gloom. Judging by these photographs, Glasgow in the middle decades of the nineteenth century was no pretty place. Grim tenement buildings rising either side of impossibly narrow alleys; small, mean windows;

indeterminate garments strung from poles overhead like flags proclaiming poverty; a patina of grime and age on every surface. They were only images in a book, but a shudder ran through her. *Wynds*, the captions called these dark, shrouded alleyways; *closes*, the small spaces between hovels. Airless words. Suffocating.

Here was a group of ragged boys in varying stances of aggression: pointing, swaggering with hands on hips or thumbs hooked under the armholes of a waistcoat, mouths open midway through some crude curse. They were wary and suspicious, likely to pitch a broken cobble at the camera that dared to accost them in their own territory. They did not look like children at all, these miniature adults with their wizened faces, their ill-fitting clothes sewn for larger bodies. A girl in a long skirt and shawl clasped her hands over an apron, ready, it seemed, to serve, and something about her demeanour, the dull presumption of toil caught in the lens, reminded Willa that childhood as she knew it was alien to this little girl, that she and these hostile boys were working units in working families who had lived out the implacable equation between struggle and subsistence. Children of the children of the Industrial Revolution – factory workers, miners, artisans all – had nothing much to smile about.

What am I doing? What am I looking for?

She felt uneasy. Like the photographer who was paid to document the shame of Glasgow's slums before they were torn down, was she trespassing, venturing somewhere she did not belong?

She remembered what it had felt like when the first medical journal arrived in the mail, sent to her and Matthew by the specialist who had overseen Imogen's surgical procedures – conspiratorially, she thought, as though he was keen to include them in *the team*. It was to be a long time before she could bring herself to read the text of the article, flagged by the specialist with a sticky note, but the sight of the journal spread open on the white laminex table caught her squarely on the chin.

I didn't know there'd be photos, she had murmured to the air over Matthew's shoulder. There were two pages of them, harsh images in shades of skin and blood, with comprehensive captions.

> Ambiguous genitalia of newborn true hermaphrodite (chimera), 46XX/46XY, at two weeks. Note phallo-clitoral structure with hypospadiac/female urethral position, vaginal introitus (blind), testis in inguinal position (left).
>
> Postoperative configuration at four months: neovagina and resected clitoris (cicatrised).
>
> At six months (note partial stenosis of neovagina).
>
> At twelve months (additional scarring from vaginal–anal fistulae).

Anonymity was preserved by the absence of names and identifying places, by the close focus of the images that reduced everything that was Imogen to morbid genitalia predominating in an otherwise featureless blur of body.

Looking at the aggressive stance of the boys of nineteenth-century Glasgow, she was reminded again of the capacity of photographs to violate. *Good for you*, she whispered.

∞

It seemed unlikely that traces of Little Jock's life in Scotland might remain, let alone be accessible from Australia, so Willa was surprised and grateful when the National Archives of

Scotland, in Edinburgh, responded to her request for the court records of John King/Peter Lennie. For a fee, it would supply photocopies of precognitions – written reports of evidence taken from witnesses – for nineteenth-century criminal cases. When the package arrived, Willa sat for hours with these papers, slowly deciphering the handwriting of witnesses and court scribes, making notes of anything they could tell her about Little Jock.

The crime that resulted in seven years' penal servitude – a sentence that automatically meant transportation – was housebreaking and theft, compounded past redemption by a list of previous convictions. Jock, in the company of another, had broken a padlock and entered the premises of a grocer and victualler in Havannah Street, Glasgow, carrying away a wooden till, thirty-five shillings and a quantity of tobacco. Willa skipped over the petty details of the crime, but copied into her journal little details that intrigued her:

> 'the accused John King (or Pat Looney as I know him by)'
> seen smoking a pipe
> 'no appearance of drink'
> identified variously as Peter Lennie, Patrick Lonney, Patrick Looney, Patrick Loany

She wondered about those names, whether they were flimsy attempts at obfuscation before the bold graduation from *Peter Lennie* to *John King*, or mere transcription errors by police and court recorders. Were any of them real? In one of the precognitions was another possible variation: Lonie. 'A girl named Bridget Lonie was with me,' a witness said. Was this Bridget Lonie connected to Jock?

When Willa reached Jock's own statement, she was taken aback to read that her Scottish felon was actually Irish: 'a native of Belfast.' At first she thought it was probably another of his lies, but paused when she found the same claim in the precognition for an earlier conviction in the name of Peter Lennie. In other records, even earlier, he declared himself 'a native of County Tyrone'; looking at a map, she saw that Tyrone was a county in the centre of Northern Ireland, lying to the west of Belfast.

He protested his innocence, of course, and Willa smiled to see a familiar name and address – appearing this time as John King's alibi: 'widow Mary Rafferty or King, 23 High Street, Glasgow.' The Sheriff Officer refuted this: 'I have enquired at 23 High Street for a widow Mary Rafferty or King; I found no such person.' But perhaps it was not surprising, she mused, that among the tenements of Glasgow the enquiries of the police would be met with denial or silence.

Mary Lennie. Mary Rafferty. Mary King.

Who were you, Mary? Willa wondered. *Did you even exist?*

∞

There are none so Irish, so the saying goes, as those born somewhere else. Orla proved the truth of that. She had always embraced a divided heritage, thought of herself as Irish-Australian even though she had been born in Australia, as had her parents and three of her grandparents. But that one Irish-immigrant grandmother had bequeathed to Orla a sense of ancestral identity that she was quick to claim, proud to acknowledge.

Willa recoiled at the thought of Orla's St Patrick's Day parties: the garden gnomes brought in from beneath the gardenias to do their yearly stint as leprechauns; all that ghastly diddly-dee music and the women from the bowling club leaping about with stiff arms. She had always thought privately that Orla's much-vaunted Irishness was as substantial as smoke, a selective inheritance, for its greatest manifestation seemed to be in these annual Irish-fests and her mother's readiness to take offence at Irish jokes.

The memory played out so clearly that she was sure she must have seen it just like this before, in one of Chas's Super-8s, everything doused in a dull wash of green.

There he is, her father, pouring champagne into plastic flutes, bestowing on Imogen the grown-up responsibility of injecting into each glass one careful drop of fungus-green food colouring and handing them around to unfortunate guests who cannot refuse her. Imogen is the right age to be costumed, however awkwardly, in Orla's heirloom dress. Willa hated wearing it when she was a child, the kelly-green pinafore with the white puff-sleeved blouse and stiff, lacy petticoats embroidered with tiny shamrocks. But Imogen, normally so definite about what she will and will not wear, seems heroically attuned to her grandmother's fantasies when it comes to the 'Irish dress'. *It's better than that horrible pink thing with the bow*, she confides to Willa.

Orla does not realise that her eight-year-old granddaughter is humouring her. She is delighted, in her element, though from time to time she frowns and pulls at the dress every which way, trying to make it sit right on Imogen's singular frame, and she tells Willa once again *what a shame* she hadn't encouraged Imogen to learn something lively, like the fiddle. *The cello – very clever of her, of course – but not a party favourite. And you can't play the cello in a dress…*

Willa had always disappointed her mother by stubbornly resisting her *Celtic roots*. As soon as she could express herself emphatically enough to be taken seriously, she had cast off the despised name Orla had burdened her with. Declaring her intentions passionately but also strategically, she had taken the unusual step of appealing to her father. She had identified him as a potential ally, hearing him muttering to himself after yet another phone call to the school in which he had been forced to laugh and trot out the same responses perhaps once too often: *c–a–o–i–m–h–e…No, it's pronounced 'Keeva'…Ha ha, yes, Irish…No, my wife…*So she gave her speech, railing against the little Irish cipher of vowels that no one could say and no one could spell, and announcing her preference to be known by her second name, Willa – *Grandma's name*, she added, glancing up at Chas. Orla began to splutter: *Honestly, Caoimhe, that's just…*But Chas had caught her arm gently.

It took a long time, years, for both of them to break the habit, for *Caoimhe* to recede and for *Willa* to become second nature – and even in her later years Orla sometimes slipped if caught in the heat of emotion. But Willa had to give them credit for the gesture of respect and, for Orla, the capitulation.

Orla never gave up believing Willa's Celtic inheritance would claim her yet. *You've Irish colouring*, she would say, affecting an accent to make a Dubliner cringe, *and there's a piece of Ireland somewhere in your heart. There are only two kinds of people in the world: the Irish and those who wish they were.*

Exasperating. But now Willa began to wonder: which was Little Jock?

When she read about the Great Famine of the 1840s, she understood why the Irish were a nation of those born somewhere else. The potato blight, *Phytophthora infestans*, wiped out the country's staple diet and Ireland was unable to feed its eight million souls. More than a million were lost to starvation and disease; one and a half million to somewhere else. And where did they go? It was said that those with money went to America, those with only a little went to Liverpool, and those with nothing at all went to Glasgow.

∞

What are you doing? What are you looking for?

The questions sounded harsher in Imogen's voice, Imogen at eighteen, scathing, and Willa was even more unsure of herself. These imaginary conversations with her daughter always followed the same course, ending in self-recrimination.

Willa laid bare her motivations, cast them down on shaky ground.

I think Little Jock was genetically female.

So?

So? So I want to know whether I am right. And I want to know how he survived, how he made his way in the world, how he dealt with the anomalies of the body he was born with. I want to understand.

She had read about 'hermaphrodites' of the nineteenth century. Until publications by Michel Foucault and Alice Dreger brought them to light, their stories had existed only in the accounts of medical men, some of whom gained modest notoriety as experts in such curiosities, or of scientists studying teratology – a name designed to quench, by immersing it in serious purpose, the threat posed by freaks and monsters of all kinds. Willa felt for the parents of hermaphroditic children, who had hidden the truth, fearful of the wrath of God or village gossip, and it had chilled her to read what happened when these children grew up. Driven by pain or confusion to seek medical or theological guidance, they became unwilling specimens, their private selves the subject of photographs and wax casts traded among the voyeuristic few. Some of the reports by gloating doctors had made her flinch. 'A thorough examination of the patient's body was now made, and the following facts were elicited in spite of much modesty and reticence on his part,' wrote one. 'She begged of us never to reveal her secret,' said another. The most vulnerable were exhibited in travelling fairs throughout Europe, although one turned hermaphroditism to his own advantage, earning a living by exhibiting himself to a stunned medical profession. Willa thought of Jock's loyal claim on *Mary Lennie, 23 High Street*; she hoped this was proof that he'd had at least one enlightened parent to protect him. That he had been loved.

It was true, Willa knew, that unlike those of medieval times, hermaphrodites of the nineteenth century had not been viewed as harbingers of doom, executed as agents of the devil. Small mercies, she thought. But in most accounts she had read it was presumed they led tragic lives. Only one left a personal story. Herculine Barbin, raised as a girl in a French convent, wrestled all through adolescence with an ambiguous body and transgressive sexual desires. When finally doctors decreed she was male and ordered her to live accordingly, she was cast out from the life she had known, renamed Abel, and expected to manage alone. 'This incessant struggle of nature against reason exhausts me more and more each day,' wrote Abel, 'and drags at me with great strides towards the tomb…' Willa had been close to tears on reading the words, despairing at human intolerance, ashamed of her own complicity in the drive to stamp out difference. The piteous existence of the man who was once Herculine Barbin ended in suicide at twenty-nine, ensuring his endurance as an icon of suffering in the history of hermaphrodites.

You don't want to understand, said the voice. *You want to know that Little Jock suffered, how he suffered, how much he suffered. That's what you want: a narrative of suffering.*

No, I...

You want to justify what you did.

July 1848

Glasgow

Bridget wakes before dawn to the sound of clattering on cobbles two floors below. She carefully wriggles free of an arm thrown across her chest, a heel on her shin, and creeps to the window. The thick, grimy glass is chipped and riven with fissures, but Bridget is just tall enough to peer through a clear section near the sill. She gasps to see ghosts drifting in and out of the close-mouth. But as her eyes adjust to the gloom, she tells herself that ghosts don't have spades in their hands, creels on their backs, little lamps smoking on their caps to light their way. It's the scaffies, she thinks, come to shovel out the middens and ashpits from inside the close-mouth, and almost as the thought settles she can smell the proof of it, an evil stench rising like fog and permeating the cracks in the glass.

Bridget turns away from the window and looks around the thinning dark of the room. It is so early that Mammy and John are still asleep; they have usually left by the time she wakes. But no, she remembers suddenly: they will not be going to the colliery today. And Michael and Felix won't be going to the mill. She looks at them one by one, each sleeping figure, only two a bed since Hugh went back to the barracks and the lodgers left. And then her gaze stops at the one who shares her mattress. Patrick. Who isn't Patrick, no mind what Mammy says.

He opens his eyes, as though feeling her watching him, and sits up. *Bridget*, he whispers, *the fair!*

She hugs the thrill to herself, turning back to the window. She will not smile at Patrick-who-isn't.

He always walks behind the boys, watching and learning, trying to match the swing of their arms, the way they scuff their heels and kick at bottles. Felix leaps up, punches an overhanging sign, and the metal flap emblazoned with the profile of a ringleted lady slaps furiously back and forward. Fearless is Felix. He can do anything.

Michael swings round, grins, and Patrick tells himself again for the hundredth time: *What gift is this family, these boys who consent to call me brother. What luck!*

The hair rises about his collar as they pass the college gate. He pulls down his cap, fixes his eyes on Michael's boots, certain that a glance at the college forecourt to the left or the Old College Bar to the right would draw a shout: *There she is!* Mary's gaze is on him as she hurries along the straggling Bridget. He must be tough, she is always telling him; he must be tough and he must be careful.

Look! Look! squeals Bridget, pointing at shadows. *'Tis wee John O'Byrnie a-dancin' in the window!*

Patrick has heard the tale of 'wee' John O'Byrne, the Irish circus giant who was so afraid of the Glasgow anatomists that he pre-paid a captain to take his corpse miles out to sea and consign it to the peaceful deep. But the great Dr John Hunter coveted that prize, was determined to have it, and when the time came he paid the captain a handsome sum to release the body instead to him. And now O'Byrne's skeleton has pride of place in the Hunterian Museum, a testament to science and the persistence of great men.

Patrick shudders. He knows there is more to fear than bones within the university walls.

∽

The Cross is just up ahead – a crush of people pouring in from High Street and Trongate, all headed down Saltmarket towards Jail Square. Mary roughly pulls her brood into the shelter of Tontine Close, and gives them each a piece, a ha'penny and the promise of a skinning for anyone getting in the way of the lawful.

She watches until they reach the Cross, which is crawling with pickpockets and villains and thieves. Curse John for clearing off on his own! From what she has heard of Glasgow at fair time, and what she can see now with her own eyes, they will be lucky to make it to the square without being fleeced of their ha'pennies. She wonders again at the flesh on their bodies where none existed only a few short months before. It is not as though there is food to spare, but they no longer go without, and it seems that potatoes and bread and pease brose build more bulk than potatoes alone can do. At least, so it is for them, she thinks, glancing down at her own scrawny arms.

She counts out pennies and a few shillings under the cover of her shawl, hoping there is enough to buy clothes for stouter frames. When she looks up again, they have been swallowed by the crowd.

She turns off into Trongate, against the flow of people, heading for the old clothes market in Briggait.

∽

The dignity of Jail Square is somewhat dented by the sensory onslaught of its close neighbours: the cacophony of the bird and dog market, the sharp reek of the hide and tallow works and the flapping of shirts, skirts and undergarments on the drying greens. And for two weeks every July, dignity is forsaken altogether when the Glasgow Fair takes root and grows like weeds all over the square's open space.

To a child with a ha'penny, the attractions of the fair are dizzying; the choice from among competing desires an exquisite new agony. Patrick and Bridget, abandoned by Felix and Michael the moment they are safely within the square, wander open-mouthed among circuses with clowns, one with a *real elephant*, waxworks, merry-go-rounds, oyster stalls and pie-shops. There are booths where you can enter and see wrestlers, Norman the Wizard, dancing bears, cockfights, monsters of all kinds. Inside the canvas-lined geggies, your penny might buy a play, a song-and-dance man, a performance with mirrors *and* a lecture – although neither Patrick nor Bridget has a penny, and neither is sure what a lecture is.

A man shouts outside a tent painted all over with crescent moons, stars and flowers in lurid scarlet and gold: *Three Abominations before the Lord! Three Freaks of Nature for a ha'penny! Not one, not two, but three! See the Webbed-fingered Dwarf. The Bearded Lady. The Man with Two Heads. Three for the worth o' one!* An accordion caterwauls from inside.

Bridget will go no further. She stares in undisguised awe. *Two heads*, she whispers. *Two!* And she turns urgently, looking for Patrick, for some confirmation that she really *can* hand over her ha'penny and see the wonder for herself. *Can we? Please?*

Carrn way. Plaze. Carrn-way-pla-aze. Three mocking boys jostle around her, pinching her elbows, pulling at her hair, pushing and laughing. *Wha's tha' in yer pocket, Barney-girl?*

Bridget screams but the noise of the crowd soaks it up.

One of her tormentors howls as a punch lands on the side of his face. Patrick's small balled hand strikes another on the chest before the boys realise what is happening, but then his advantage is lost and he sags beneath the weight of their blows. By the time they flee, warned off by a glimpse of the tip of a policeman's hat, Patrick's face is battered, his forehead streaming from contact with a coin gripped in a fist.

He stays low, arms to his head, and tunnels through the knees of the crowd and round to the back of the tent, grabbing Bridget, still screaming, by the skirt along the way. *Hush, now, hush, it's all right*, he says, wanting her quiet, more frightened of the attention of adults than of any bully-boy.

Bridget stares at the blood, the taut red skin beginning to swell around his eye and on his cheek. *They took my copper*, she wails.

He pats at his trousers. *Also mine.*

As he slumps against the frame of the garishly painted tent that rocks with harsh laughter and teasing taunts, the canvas gives slightly, and Bridget can see inside. She cries out, points. There, in a sliver of air, two heads sprout from a single collar.

Patrick turns a little, squinting with his one good eye into the gap between the two canvas sheets. He will never forget what he sees: a shiny gown, a confection of silver curls piled high, a long cascade of beard. And the eyes of a hunted animal.

The Bearded Lady catches sight of him and her face crumples, as if it is *his* gaze – this fleeting look on top of the thousands she must have endured – that is the one to seal her shame.

Patrick backs away, and the moons and stars and flowers claim the Lady once more. He jumps up, staggering from the sudden pain of his purpling bruises, and pushes weakly through the crowd, fending off elbows and shoulders. On reaching the relative calm of the Green, he collapses, puking in the shadow of the gallows where no grass will grow.

When he finds his feet again, Bridget is beside him, fishing around in the pocket of her skirt. She solemnly holds out her piece, now a mangled gob of lint and bread. *Here*, she says. *Here, Patrick.*

Early March 1851

Glasgow

Mary Lunney shakes snow from her shawl and winds the web of wool around her throat, burying her chin in its scratchy folds. She is bone tired. She is old in the way that the trees lining the Clyde are old, all weary trunks and bony fingers. She is old like the seams of coal that run between Glasgow and Hamilton, the weathered essence of all that has gone before. She is winter old, river old, as old and grey and pinched as poverty. She is, she thinks, though she cannot be sure, forty-five.

The ferry trip back across the Clyde from Govan is short, only a matter of minutes, but six days every week she feels the fear of it, the churn of the river beneath her. It is not so bad on the outward run, when she is half asleep in the pre-dawn gloom, but on this late-afternoon return there is nearly always another little steamer limping up the river to remind her of the losses of that terrible crossing, and it is one more reason to long for an easier way to make a shilling a day.

Even so, she does not know what would have become of them were it not for Dixon's Govan colliery. She glances at John, stooped and coughing beside her. He has stuck it down the pits for three years, breathing dust and marsh gas, juddering his bones with the slam of pick against seam in a crawlspace barely big enough to contain him. It is cruel work for all but especially for those not born to it, not from a lineage adapted to the miner's foetal crouch, raised like moles with sun-blind eyes. He is a young man chafing to marry, and vows his mining days will soon be done. He has made Patrick his drawer, much to Mary's dismay, but the child has muscle as well as fat, he tells her, and boys and girls both had once been used as drawers until the government outlawed the use of women and children in the pits. Perhaps, he says, the lad can take the pick soon if he grows some inches – but here Mary looks at him sharply, wondering whether the pits have addled his brain. Patrick might look tough, but you can't make rope from the sand of the sea.

On the long walk home from the Clyde, Patrick trails behind Mary and John. Since well before six he has been working the tunnels, loading John's coal and fireclay onto the whirley, drawing it to the mouth of the pit, and then racing the empty wagon back to the face where John is working. His head aches from the roar of the engine and the smell of human sweat and human waste thirty fathoms beneath Govan. But he would rather work at Dixon's than with Michael and Bridget at the Saracen Foundry or Felix at the Lucifer Matchworks. At Dixon's he does the work and earns the wage of a half-man – more than Michael, more than Felix, more he can hand over to Mary.

As they turn into Goosedubs, there is a commotion ahead and the cry goes up: *Police! Fetch the police!* Patrick sees a girl no older than he struggling to break free of the grip of a man in a top hat. A note of indignation sounds in the street babble: ...*child stripping, she was...peeled the coat off a poor wee bairn like skin off porridge...*

Mary wheels round to face Patrick, grabbing him by the sleeve. *See? And it's sixty days that lass is sure to be getting. Don't be thinking youth will spare her!*

Patrick says nothing. He had not heard the last of it since the day he came home with a neckerchief the colour of a damson plum. So proud when he handed it to Mary, thinking to gain a smile, but she had given him instead the back of her hand. It had been easy enough to twitch the pretty thing from the throat of a boy who surely would not miss it, judging from his stout trouser cloth and thick coat. And what harm to give it to Mary, whose skirt and jacket are drabness itself, stiff and black with the dust that rises in clouds around her at the pit-head as she picks slate and shale from each new haul of coal. She had looked at him aghast – *Only a fool risks the ease of existing unknown to the law!* – and ordered him to cast the thing into the Clyde. He said he had done just that, but it was not so: the pragmatic Felix had relieved him of it, sold it to a dealer at the matchworks for a penny.

As he looks over his shoulder, he sees a constable tightening snitchers on the girl's wrists and leading her away towards Central.

They have no sooner begun making their way up the front stair, stepping carefully around the day's slops, when a voice like the blade of a saw hacks down from the third floor, quickly followed by the large and formidable person of Hugh's wife. She arrives on the second-floor landing, jigging a fretful baby on one hip and brandishing a parsnip.

That worthless eedjit of a son of yours has slept his way through another week and this is all I've to keep us alive with. Am I to throw myself on the mercy of the parish again, Mary Lunney? Will you see your wee grandson in Barnhill?

Patrick places himself impotently between Mary and the towering bulk of Marnie Malone while John mutters and curses his way through the door, slamming it behind him.

Lord above! Mary exclaims. *The wretch is ailing in his bed, not whiling away the days, and you know I'll not see one of my own hungry while I've breath t' help it.*

At six, when Felix straggles in, the last of the workers home, the room is already thick with fumes from the lantern, and although the porous walls are damp and chill to the touch, none among them could feel cold. If they were not warmed by the struggling coal fire, by the mean little stew of sinew and onions, they could count on the glowering face of Marnie Malone.

There is no need, this day, to rise in the small hours for the long walk to the Clyde, the ferry across to Govan, but Patrick cannot reset the rhythm of his body to take advantage of his one free day a week. Nor, it seems, can Mary or John, for he hears them in the darkness, an argument conducted in whispers that ends with John pulling on his boots and thudding out the door.

The moon breaks through a scudding cloud, lighting up the crazed windowpane, and Patrick watches Mary rise, drawing her shawl about her. She hunches over the ashes, jabbing at them with a poker, defeat in the curve of her spine. He had caught only snatches of her words to John – *what we owe Hugh...our own flesh and blood* – but he understood well enough. John had been saying it for months now, and who could blame him: he would be a pit-man no more. Not for his mam, for any of them. Certainly not for the Malone woman.

Patrick does not think Dixon's will take him in John's place. He is not nearly as tall as Michael and Felix – even Bridget is gaining on him – and he has become stocky. There is nothing in his frame to promise a worker lithe enough and strong enough to swing a pick down the pits.

The moon disappears again, and Patrick shivers.

At 43 Trongate it is a slow morning for Andrew Mackay, and he flicks a rag idly over the brass nameplate of the Old Exchange Loan Company. He rolls up his sleeves, preparing to sort through another boxload brought in by the Sauchiehall linen man with a wee problem, who would not normally be seen dead in this end of the city. When the bell above the door jangles, he looks over his spectacles and frowns to see a coal-stained figure dressed in the rags of the Irish, all kneeless breeches and elbowless hessian shirt, no doubt sent to pawn his father's Sunday coat. Mackay peers closer at the ginger fuzz sprouting on lip and chin, at odds with the squat, childish body, and wonders what ruse this brat is playing at. Nevertheless, he offers up his habitual amen to God for the Irish: the men drink their future and the women pawn their past.

The boy says nothing as he deposits two blankets on the counter, and Mackay is immediately suspicious. The blankets, a matching pair in newly washed blue wool, are not threadbare. There's not a burn or a mark of candle grease on them. *Ha!* he exclaims as he turns them over, finding a neat monogram in one corner: *A. T.* Below it is the crest of Glasgow University.

So, lad, I doonae think you be much of a scholar, eh? And he slaps two palms on the polished oak counter. *Eh?*

The boy casts around wildly like a dog in a trap, backs towards the door, and is off, with Mackay behind him – Mackay, who has nothing better to do on this slow morning. And when the boy has the great misfortune to crash into a barrow of smokies in London Street, Mackay is there to seize him by the arm and hold it aloft like a prize justly won.

Some days later Dr Allen Thomson, the university's Professor of Anatomy, will call at 43 Trongate to thank Mackay personally for the recovery of university property stolen from the drying line between Professors Court and New Vennel. And a column in the *Glasgow Examiner* noting that *the shopman, Mr A. Mackay, deserves great praise for his energetic conduct* will sit, framed in scrolled silver, above the counter of the Old Exchange Loan Company.

Her family

The library of the Genealogical Society was busier than most public libraries and staffed by volunteers. Willa noticed that nearly every head in the room was a shade of grey or silver, that she was among the youngest there. Genealogy seemed to be a passion that struck the slowing heart, and she wondered what was at the base of this. Was it something as pragmatic as the freeing up of time for a new and pleasant hobby, or some deeper, more spiritual compulsion in the human psyche to commune with one's own dead before meeting them in the hereafter? Ancestor worship for the twenty-first century?

All around her, eyes peered at microfiche screens as though they were reliquaries, their cache of names and dates holy, precious things. It was connection they sought, Willa mused, to touch history in this intimate way. To breathe the same air. She, too, was seeking connection, looking for Little Jock through genealogical channels, daring to believe that a person with a family was a person whose story might be discovered, however partially, through other stories, glimpsed in kindred bondings, fugitive glancings.

She sat at the microfiche reader with indexes for the Glasgow census of 1861, the year before Jock's final conviction, and a map of the city spread out on her right. Her journal, on the left, was open at a page drawn up into columns, the first listing surnames and variant spellings:

King
Rafferty
Lennie/Lenny
Lonie/Lonnie/Lonney
Loany
Looney/Loonie
Lunney

The second list was smaller:

John/Jock/Peter/Patrick
Mary
Bridget?

And the third comprised jottings:

native of Belfast?
native of County Tyrone?
age 24 in 1862?
23 High Street?

The indexes provided only the name, age and place of birth of those in the city's inventory of souls, and the search for Little Jock was like trying to piece together an old jigsaw puzzle whose tattered pieces – those that remained – had been torn or had worn away into shapes no longer resembling the original. Or perhaps they were imperfectly formed to begin with, and never fitted together, for what madness to expect a whole picture of something so mutable as a human life.

The map didn't help, for nothing on it gave a clue to which of the 1861 census districts might contain High Street. There was no choice but to check them all. It was laborious work, examining fiche after fiche. She continually had to adjust the focus on each screen of names, blinking away the blur in her eyes. But Willa felt a mounting anticipation as she wrote down likely combinations.

At the end of the morning, she perused her page of John Kings, Mary Raffertys and sundry Lennies and Loonies, discarding some who were clearly too young or too old, putting question marks against those born somewhere other than Ireland. There were individual names that could not be ruled out, but what took Willa's attention, what her pencil circled, was a group of three in the Central District that bore the same book, page and line references: a family living together.

Lennie, Bridget, 20, Ireland
Lennie, Mary, 63, Ireland
Lennie, Peter, 28, Ireland

The age of this Peter Lennie did not match the trial records or the Convict Register, but she had a feeling about this little threesome. She was convinced Mary did exist, that she had found her Little Jock.

∞

Only one person replied to the email she sent to the Lanarkshire listserv.

From: jdonaldson@galileo.net.uk

Date: 14 October 2004

To: willasamson@trident7.com.au

Subject: Re: [LANARK-L] request
_____

on 13/10/04 3:08 PM willasamson@trident7.
com.au wrote:

>Dear group members

>Could anyone please look up a census at

>the Mitchell Library, Glasgow, for me?

>I have page reference details from the

>index.

  >With thanks

  >Willa Samson

  >Perth, Western Australia

Dear Willa Samson

Please send me details & I will be happy to
look up your family.

  I have been trying to trace a relative
on my mother's side who emigrated to
Fremantle, Western Australia, 1887. Could
you look up possible marriage for Hamish
James LAIDLAW?

  Regards

  James Donaldson

She'd hesitated before sending off the request, typing it,
deleting it, typing it again. What she had always valued about
the net, especially in the half-year since losing Imogen, was its
cool, anonymous distance. This was different. After all those
months of avoiding communication, here she was, practically
inviting it. What's more, it felt presumptuous, seeking goodwill

from strangers. But the library volunteer who told her about the listservs operating through genealogy sites had been cheerfully encouraging. *We do it all the time. It'd cost you a fortune to pay for a researcher. People just help out when they can.*

They are, she'd thought when finally sending her Lennies into the ether, the most obliging bunch of people, these family historians. Even so, she was relieved that James Donaldson wanted something from her in return, which spared her the burden of indebtedness – and made the exchange of emails less daunting.

Two days later she emailed him again, hoping he would be pleased to know that his antecedent had done his bit to populate Australia. Hamish J. Laidlaw married Elizabeth Greay in Perth less than a year after his arrival, and Willa had painstakingly trawled through the index of births for subsequent years to find Alice, Jean, Alexander, Lily, James, Andrew and Nora Laidlaw.

All those children! She had never understood the attraction of large families, could not imagine how love could be split so many ways. She had told Matthew, who had five siblings and, she suspected, certain expectations: *No more than two!* But one, as it turned out, was more than the universe had intended them to have. She had felt hurt when Matthew's parents did not appear at the hospital in those frantic weeks after Imogen was born, thinking they didn't care, or not enough; it was much later that she found out that Matthew – confused, embarrassed, *ashamed* Matthew – had asked them not to come. At the time, she had told herself that the genial Harry and Dawn were old hands at this, and although they had said they were *as pleased as Punch* to hear of the impending arrival of their youngest son's first child, they already had sixteen grandchildren *and counting!* They were never going to be as invested as were her own parents, for whom Imogen was the all, the only.

But she wondered, now, looking at that long list of Laidlaws. Perhaps it was safer in the long run when you had to stretch yourself to cover many, when what love you had to give settled on the shoulders as lightly as a pashmina shawl, instead of smothering like a swaddling blanket.

Chas and Orla had hovered in hospital corridors after the birth, listened outside closed doors, lain in wait for news. It would have been impossible to have kept the truth from them. The diagnosis had silenced them briefly, and in those few seconds Willa had seen a look pass across their faces that would remain with her forever, though they wiped it clean in the hush of a breath and would have denied it had ever been there. They were relieved to know that something could be done to *fix the baby*, and threw their weight behind the wall of secrecy that was set up to protect Imogen and put a halt to gossip. *Children in the playground can be so cruel!* In the years to come, Willa would wonder whether an army of playground bullies could ever have hurt Imogen as much as all those good intentions had done.

∞

From: jdonaldson@galileo.net.uk

Date: 20 October 2004

To: willasamson@trident7.com.au

Subject: your family

Attachments: lennies1861census.doc, looneys1851census.doc

Dear Willa

So many Australian relatives we never knew about! Thank you for beginning another branch of the LAIDLAW family tree. My

brother, Alex, & I are now keen to trace
any living descendants but we won't impose
on you any further, at least for now. I'm
sure you are more interested in news of
Mary, Peter & Bridget LENNIE. The full
transcript from the 1861 census is in the
first file attached.

As you were so diligent in looking up
LAIDLAWS, I took the liberty of checking
the index for the previous census (1851),
also. Couldn't find any LENNIES, but noticed
there was a LOONEY family (see file) with
some matching first names, though the ages
don't add up (mind, they never do; in those
days, people just guessed how old they
were). Could be your family?

Unfortunately, I can't check the 1841 &
1871 censuses for you because there are no
name indexes for these.

Hope this helps.

Regards

James Donaldson

Generous man, Willa thought, touched by the detailed
reply and the effort he'd gone to. She opened the attachment,
and suddenly there it was on the screen. Her little cluster of
three plucked from the microfiche index had burgeoned into a
family:

Parish of Outer High or St Paul, 93 High Street:
Mary LENNIE, Head, Widow, 63, Housekeeper, Ireland

Peter LENNIE, Son, Single, 28, Shoemaker, Ireland

Michael LENNIE, Son, Married, 38, Collier, Ireland

John LENNIE, Son, Married, 40, Dealer, Ireland

Bridget LENNIE, Daur, Single, 20, Mill Girl, Ireland

Roseanne LENNIE, God Daur [in case you don't know, Willa, 'god daur' means daughter-in-law], Married, 22, [no occupation given], Ireland

Hannah LENNIE, God Daur, Married, 23, [no occupation given], Paisley

Bridget LENNIE, Grand Daur, Single, 18 mths, Glasgow

May LENNIE, Grand Daur, Single, 7 mths, Glasgow

The Looneys of the earlier census, living at 97 New Vennel, comprised Mary (45, collier), John (22, collier), Michael and Bridget (12 and 10, both heddle makers), and another son, Felix (18, Lucifer match maker). All were born in Armagh, Ireland.

Lucifer opened one lazy golden eye as Willa punched the air with an elated *Yes!*, grinning at the intensity of her response. Little Jock had left behind a whole family in Glasgow. And she was certain that the Looneys at 97 New Vennel were indeed *her family*, that the evolution from Looney to Lennie was not the ploy of a petty criminal; it was a name change adopted, for whatever reason, by all of them. She pencilled the skeletal beginnings of a family tree in her journal.

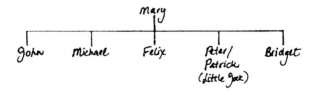

Where, though, was Jock – at that time known as Patrick – in 1851? She pulled the thick folder of papers down onto the desk and searched through the trial records sent from the National Archives. There it was:

> Patrick Loony, Central Police Court, 12 March 1851: 60 days...applies to the prisoner Peter Lennie...

Yes, the 1851 census was taken at the end of March, so he was probably away in prison.

Willa sat back in her chair, tapping her pencil on the desk. This Police Court trial in 1851 was the earliest record she could find for Little Jock, and the family name seemed to be corroborated by the census. *Patrick Looney*: was this, then, the name that most closely approximated the truth?

She typed a brief reply to thank James Donaldson, but her finger hesitated over the 'send' button. The tone of his email was so *jolly*. She didn't feel capable of chit-chat, but she couldn't reply like this. Her email was as cold as a note from the bank. Perhaps a postscript?

```
I am such a novice at this that I did not
even realise there were censuses for every
decade. It was kind of you to look further.
```

It wasn't much but it was the best she could do.

∞

In the far back corner of Orla's garden was a bed that had run to seed long ago. Chas's raised vegetable strip, once so abundant with beaded heads of broccoli, tomatoes – three kinds, always in season – pumpkins and trails of pale corn silk, was now a strangle of couch and parsley, and a cemetery for all of Lucifer's small offerings.

She had tried to save the lizard; she snatched it away, took it outside and laid it on the grass. But Lucifer, so proud when he deposited it on the computer keyboard, must have held it too firmly within the cage of his teeth. After wrapping the lizard in a clean, white tissue, she threw Lucifer in the laundry and slammed the door so she could dig out a square of couch and bury the poor crushed body.

He stalked away when she let him out, would not look at her.

The computer chimed as she reached the study. Another email from James Donaldson, who seemed to have taken her under his wing, with the address of a government web site called *Scotland's People*.

```
You can find records of births, deaths
& marriages from 1855, when compulsory
registration began. If you've the time &
money, that is. Moolly lot, they are, making
us pay for the records of our own! Don't
waste your money on the Old Parish Records,
because they're only for the Church of
Scotland. You won't find your (probably
Catholic) Irish family there.
```

Willa had been wondering what happened to Felix, the brother not listed on the 1861 census, and decided to try out this web site to look for a record of his death. She opened an account, warily entering her credit card details. Pounds sterling disappeared at an alarming rate as she clicked on screen after screen, trying out all the versions of 'Looney' that she could think of. But Felix must have died before registration came in, or left Glasgow, for there was no trace of him here. What she found, instead, were entries recording the fleeting existence of two infant Felix Lennies, Jock's nephews, the neatly scribed notations conferring on them a dignity in death that they almost certainly lacked in life. In the process, she happened upon yet another member of the Lennie family: Jock's brother Hugh, a soldier.

Genealogy is as addictive as it is frustrating, she decided, charging up her account again. More precious pounds. Small scraps of information on one record threw out tantalising hints, set you on the path of a whole new line of investigation, and so it went on, if you were lucky, growing the shoots and tendrils of family trees.

If you were not lucky, though, you found yourself puzzling over the gap between the theory of compulsory registration and the reality as it must have played out in the slums of Glasgow. She could find no death record for Mary, nor for any of Jock's siblings, though she noted sadly that baby May died a month after her life was recorded on the 1861 census. Was the absence of records for the rest of the family a sign of ambivalence towards authority, or did it mean that they, like Jock, died somewhere else? It seemed to Willa unlikely they would have gone far, given their tendency to cluster around the tenements in High Street. But it was not hard to imagine the dismal alternative: that they died unnoticed by doctor or priest, and informing the city of their passing had been no great priority for those left behind.

She found records for the birth of several other Lennie infants and for the marriage of Michael and Hannah, the latter yielding the unexpected gift of the name of Jock's father: *Felix Lennie, deceased*. Father, brother, two baby nephews: none of the Felixes in Jock's family survived.

After redrafting the family tree, adding names and relationships, Willa leaned back in her chair, mulling over all of this new information. Would any of it get her closer to the heart of Little Jock?

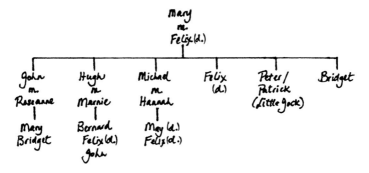

It was dark when she exited from the *Scotland's People* site and turned off the computer. Lucifer, roused from sleep by the familiar shutdown sequence, sprang from the top of the filing cabinet and complained for supper, and she swept him up in her arms. *All forgiven*, she declared, knowing that although it was true on her part, he had just forgotten he was a cat with a grievance.

The next morning Willa set it all out before her – the printouts of registered births, deaths and marriages, the census listings, the trial records – and as she read them again, it occurred to her that she had been focusing too much on the broad brushstrokes, when it was in small details that stories revealed themselves. High Street, New Vennel, Havannah – names she had seen in captions beneath the photographs of slums. A family always moving from one hovel to another. The theft of soap, of a shirt, of tobacco. Babies born and babies dying. This was the world that had confronted her from grim, gothic images in the pages of a book. In this world hundreds of people crowded into tenements shoddily thrown together to absorb the influx of people from the Highlands, from the north, from Ireland. Rooms housed extended families; beds slept many, and in shifts. People changed names but could not reinvent their circumstances. People disappeared. When injured or sick, they suffered untreated; when suffering exhausted them, they simply died. And what of difference in the hard slums of Glasgow? Would those who bore its mark have been demonised or exploited? Violated? Or in a world dominated by matters of survival, would difference be a thing of scant concern to all but those it directly touched?

I have to go there myself.

There: she had spoken it out loud, this worm of a thought, uncurling, flexing, niggling at other, more rational thoughts. How could she contemplate something like this when there was the chance, the remotest chance, that Imogen might…

Might what? Need you? Do you really believe that?

Money should concern her, she thought, and how shameful that it did not. Work should be her priority, but that would mean negotiating the idea of herself as Willa Samson, not Imogen's mother. She wasn't ready for that, wasn't ready to accept anything that smacked of *moving on* – which was just another term for *giving up*. And she hadn't given up: stasis was not surrender. But at the same time the idea of engaging with people, with ideas, overwhelmed her. How could she care about other people's words when her head was full of Imogen's? It was a goal that seemed too far ahead, the ground between here and there too riven, and she could not make the leap. And yet she – she who had barely stepped out of the house for months, had only just begun to manage rudimentary conversation with strangers – was thinking of flying to the other side of the world. The audacity took her breath. And for what? What could she hope to learn about Little Jock there that she could not find here, and what did any of it mean anyway when she was not a historian, not a genealogist, not a bona fide researcher, just a mother with motives open to dispute?

Still the thought would not be suppressed: I have to go.

December 1853

Glasgow

Duke Street is not on Bridget's way home from the Molendinar
Threadworks, but lately she has often taken this longer route past
the gaol. She stares at the imposing grey archway crested with a
cross, a lattice of iron bars behind it, the shadowy turrets rising
within grounds enclosed by a stone wall too high, too smooth, for
hands and feet to scale. It is a strangely silent place, and Bridget
thinks of the skipping game that girls play on the Green:

> *There is a happy land*
> *Doon in Duke Street Gaol*
> *Where a' the prisoners stand*
> *Hanging on a nail*
> *Ham and eggs they'll never see*
> *Bread and butter fur their tea*
> *Live their lives in misery*
> *God save the Queen*

She imagines Patrick hanging by his shirt on a nail until it
is time for him to be yanked down for the day's work, and then

being hung up again when night comes round. She knows this
does not happen, because Patrick has been away twice in Duke
Street already, and there *are* no nails – he told her so. But still
she imagines him, suspended in the moonlight, his feet flailing,
arms beating like the wings of a goose. He has been gone so
long this time, gone since summer, but Mam says it could be any
day soon that he will turn up, hungry as a beggar and looking
for his worsted coat.

Mary has not seen Patrick since she sat with the rabble of thieves
and harlots on the public benches in the Sheriff's Court and
listened to seven witnesses confirm that this lad of fifteen did
wickedly and feloniously steal and theftuously carry away a quantity
of brown soap, his offence aggravated by housebreaking in
this instance and by previous convictions. It had earned him
a promotion from Police Court to Sheriff's, an escalation
in sentence from sixty days to nine months, and the label
'delinquent' – but he had been whisked away to the cells before
she had been able to deliver her own damning verdict on his
abject foolishness: the risk of gaol again, compounded by the
blethering idiocy of stealing *soap*, do you mind! Soap, when they
had no bath for their bodies, no boin for their clothes! Only a
fool burns a lump of coal without warming himself. He might as
well have taken a horseshoe or the strings of a fiddle.

But there are no recriminations the day she arrives home
from Dixon's to find him thawing his fingers before the fire, and
she contents herself with a cuff with the heel of her hand before
enveloping him in a pungent embrace of wet wool, sweat and coal
dust. And then she busies herself with the dregs of yesterday's
broth, performing practised rituals of stretching one meal into a
thinner second, a pot for seven mouths into a pot for eight.

Marnie Malone, a regular at teatime since Hugh returned to the barracks (*for peace*, says John, and none would disagree), has never been shy about declaiming every meagre thought in her head. She complains bitterly of the watery brew. She scowls at John's wife, Roseanne, shedding glittering scales, *too spineless to tuck a herring in her sock* after a day's gutting at the market. She passes judgment on Bridget's unmannerly capering with Patrick on the stair before tea, Michael's unconcealed irritation at the infant crawling all over him. She demands to know what Patrick thinks he is about with his *oot* and *noo*, his *cannae* and *dinnae*, and *is it not good enough for him, the way his mammy made him?*

He stares at her. *Hugh himself says 'tis better not to shout 'Irish!'*, he ventures, but no answer is apparently required. She is declaring herself shamed to be supping with the likes of him, *a thief fresh from Duke Street.*

Bridget gapes like a fish when her mother flings a lump of coal across the room, hitting the woman on the shoulder and knocking her tin bowl to the floor.

The fire has dwindled to mere ash in the grate when Mary eases her tired body onto the only spare length of mattress on the floor. Patrick turns slightly and she can see his eyes are open, restless with the duelling emotions of repletion and loss.

Felix – when? he whispers.

In the autumn, may God rest his sweet soul. An explosion at the works. Three died alongside him. She pauses and then asks for confirmation of what only now seems clear. *The soap you took. It was for Felix? To sell?*

He is silent in the dark and she watches the rhythm of his breathing. There is something else she must know but she cannot find the words to ask, afraid of what he might answer.

You were not…hurt?

No.

They did not…?

He turns to face her. *They see what they think they see.*

Somewhere in the city a clock chimes thrice. Still his eyes are wide and sleepless; still thoughts scurry like rats. He creeps to the door to find his coat, discarded earlier in a pile of clothes and scarves and boots, and pulls it around his shivering body. A stirring on the mattress closest to the window chastens him: see, he has woken someone with his creeping and rummaging. But no, he can make out a rhythmic movement, limbs bare and indecently spilling from the square of blanket. John and Roseanne. He should look away, but his eyes are watchful, grow accustomed to the uneven darkness. He is no child to be goggle-eyed and breathless over adult things. There is nothing lascivious in his gaze, no impulse to gape. He has seen it before, this hunger of the body. The first time, Mary had yanked his head from sleep, clapped her hand over his mouth, made him look at Hugh and Marnie threshing naked while all else were snoring. *See what comes of sweet whispers?* she hissed.

He had looked at her, confused.

You are safe only while no one knows. Can you not see? If you let yourself be touched…

He remembered the man and his probing fingers, the blind eyes of the tiny children trapped beneath glass.

You cannot trust a soul, child. If lusts you have, keep them to yourself, for I fear for you if the truth be known…Remember: you cannot trust a soul.

He studies the bodies moving on the floor, contours beneath the thin blanket. An arc to rise over, cleave to; another to hollow out, be filled. *It must not be, it can never be*, but his body is a wakeful thing this night. The slight arching of his spine is all that betrays imagination, flexing first to mimic John; contracting in the curve of Roseanne.

Finally, imagination spent, he turns away in a huddle of coat, face to the wall, hand to his flesh.

At a market stall beneath the bridge at Briggait, he rubs his left arm as though shoring up comfort in advance of the pain. He has seen the Clydeside lads, sailors and wharfmen, with their anchors and wheels, sails and mermaids. In Duke Street there had been all manner of promises and threats stencilled onto skin in the form of dragons, crosses, hearts. Scrolled words, too; he could not read the proclamations but was told their meaning. *Forget Me Not. Ireland Forever. Cannot See God But God Can See Me.* He has come this far, far enough that he can smell the ink, smell his own ripe fear at the sight of the bloodied needle, and he will not back out now. There is something to be claimed, to stymie doubt, gainsay any whisper, in this simple act of self-inscription. A ritual of men. And there is something to be remembered. He will carry it with him always: the memory of the Bearded Lady glimpsed through painted canvas sheets of gold and scarlet. Were it not for Mary, that could be him, a fairground freak for sale.

He tells the man with the needle what he wants – simple shapes, meaningless on their own, meaningful in combination only to him. A crescent moon, a star and a flower.

December 1857

Glasgow

Crowds jostle along the route to the Justiciary Court, held back –
at times none too gently – by members of the constabulary under
the barking orders of captains Smart and Mackay. Wailing
rooks take to the sky, unable to compete with the skirl of pipes
from the 60th Rifles Band leading the procession from the
Queen's Hotel. A detachment from the same brigade marches
behind, forming an escort for the party of dignitaries lately
imbibing tea and rum at the Queen's, supposedly to keep the
cold at bay. The Lord Justice Clerk and Lord Cowan reign in
the lead carriage, swaddled in pomp and fur and boredom, with
lesser cabriolets drawing the sheriffs of Lanark, Renfrew and
Dumbarton, the Lord Provost, and a grave gaggle of magistrates
and civic officials. And trailing in their wake, through a slush of
snow and horse dung, comes a closed van, little more than a
parvenu barrow, bearing the prisoners to be tried at the Winter
Circuit Court.

Mary and Bridget are among the well-wishers lining the
steps to the side entrance of the courthouse in Jail Square,
craning their necks to get a better view. As the prisoners file out

of the van, clanking chains, there are optimistic shouts of *Keep yer 'eart up, Tom! You'll soon be oot, Hughie!* and the odd harangue: *Dan McDougall, you black-hearted scoondrel! And what's t' become of y'aun weans noo!* Patrick has been in the Tollbooth since October, awaiting the quarter sessions that will determine his fate, and Mary knows that this time, if convicted, it will not be fifteen months in Duke Street. This time it will be hard labour and he will be a convict; it will be years before they see him again.

Lacking air in her own lungs to squeeze through to the front, she pushes Bridget forward, but the girl emerges a few minutes later, distressed and dishevelled. *I could no see him above the shoulders of the guards. I could no see his face.*

They crowd in at the rear of the courthouse as the Reverend Doctor Craik offers an ode to justice and a prayer for the righteous.

The prosecutor outlines the case, before Lord Cowan, against Peter Lennie and Thomas Campbell, charged with the theft of a red Crimean shirt from a display outside the door of a drapery warehouse at 20 High Street. Peter Bryson, bookseller, who was having a smoke at the confectionery stand opposite the warehouse, noticed two men and a girl behaving suspiciously. He then witnessed Campbell take the woollen shirt while Lennie shielded his actions and the girl looked on. Bryson alerted the shopman, William Hope, to the theft, indicating which way the thieves had gone, and Hope ran around the corner into McPherson Street in pursuit of *two men walking very sharply*. One, he said, was trying to hide something beneath his coat. The two men ran, and when Hope caught up with them Lennie threw the shirt to the ground. Hope conducted him back to the shop and called for the police. Campbell got away but was later caught.

Mary listens, heart sinking, while Bryson and Hope are sworn in and give their evidence, corroborated then by a second shopman. *Lennie at the time was leaning on Campbell's left shoulder, as if to cover Campbell's actions. Lennie was looking at the shirt at the same time. Lennie had the shirt concealed all the time he was in my sight, till he threw it away as stated.* As Patrick's deposition is read, she prays for a miracle.

> My name is Peter Lennie. I am a native of Belfast, nineteen years of age, a collier, and I reside in High Street Glasgow. I was in High Street between twelve and one o'clock yesterday afternoon in company with a girl named Hannah McGregor. While she and I were standing together I saw the Prisoner Thomas Campbell snatch and carry off a Woollen Shirt from Millars the Drapers Shop door in High Street. He came running up to me and offered me the Shirt but I refused to take it, and seeing this he threw it from him and ran away. A Shopman came and got the Shirt where Campbell had thrown it and the Shopman put me into custody and had me taken to the Police Office on suspicion of being concerned in the theft but I had no hand in it. I had previously been in Campbell's company and walked with him from the Railway Station in Tradeston to High Street. And this I declare to be truth.

Mary knows that her prayer, as it so often does, has gone astray somewhere between her lips and the Lord's ear. His name is not Peter Lennie. He is not a native of Belfast. There is much else that is false in his declaration of truth – but then he knows for himself, and because of the pact between them, that truth is a servant, not a master. When Lord Cowan demands the account of previous convictions, it is clear that hope is lost.

A Criminal Officer in the Central District testifies that convictions against Patrick Looney in 1851 and 1852 apply to the prisoner Peter Lennie. *This is truth*, he declares. Two Sheriff Officers confirm that convictions against Patrick Looney in 1853 and Patrick Lonney in 1855 can be sheeted home to Peter Lennie. The Central Police turnkey concurs – *And this is truth.*

Lord Cowan glances down in disdain at Peter Lennie a.k.a. Patrick Looney or Lonney or Lunney, no doubt believing him feeble for thinking to escape his past with such transparent subterfuge. But there was more to it than that, Mary knows; anyone who had walked a mile in Irish brogues in Glasgow would know. 'Lennie' was a label less Irish than 'Lunney'.

He is standing before the presiding judge, this small nineteen-year-old thief, as the sentence of four years' penal servitude is read. He is not Peter Lennie. He is not Patrick Lunney. But she weeps because he is hers. And this is truth.

Seeing ghosts

The chill air was relentless, finding any exposed skin. You could don thermal socks and thick boots, swathe yourself in scarves over a cashmere-blend overcoat, cover your ears, your skull, with a hat pulled down low and your hands with leather gloves lined with lambswool, but unless you muffled yourself in tartan hijab – and some did – you could not protect your face.

Willa's face felt anaesthetised, and she dared not lick her lips for fear of a nascent film of ice forming on the surface of the skin. She plunged an awkward gloved hand into her pocket for a tissue, embarrassed that her nose, like everyone else's, might be dripping, but could not even feel the features on her face, let alone distinguish whether they needed to be dabbed.

At the foot of the road sloping down from Garnet Hill, the early-morning ice in the gutters and at the edges of the bitumen was so thick that careless bicyclists skated sideways into the kerb. Brakes squealed incessantly as cars skidded around the corner. She crossed carefully, her feet unsteady on the frozen road, and made her way up the concrete arc bridging the intersection of four major thoroughfares. At the apex of the overpass, she stopped, relieved to have left behind the throng of pedestrians far below. Before her was a commonplace view of people and traffic and city made fascinating because they were people and traffic and city of another hemisphere, in a climate she had never before experienced. *This is Glasgow*, she told herself, seventeen thousand kilometres from the southern summer. Seventeen thousand kilometres from the sanctuary of home, nervously entrusted for two weeks to deadbolts and luck; from Lucifer, whose plaintive howls she imagined she could hear from a four-star boarding cattery. Seventeen thousand kilometres from Imogen.

She watched people trudging to work, to school, to somewhere, and now she appreciated what *trudging* meant, that you could not properly *trudge* unless your body was cocooned in wool and your head was down, your shoulders hunched against biting winds and the pellets of ice being tossed at you from the sky by some cosmic schoolboy prankster. This was how she must have looked, dragging herself through the days, the weeks, the months after Imogen left, and she was sad to think that climate, too, could do this to people, could effect in appearance, if not in spirit, a defeat so close to dying.

Melting ice dripped from benches. Rooks circled the skeletons of trees.

When Willa told Matthew she was going to Glasgow, it was only a communication of courtesy. *Just in case*, she said.

She could hear it all the way from Sydney, flooding through the telephone line, the relief that she was *pulling herself together at last*. Matthew and Chas, for all the animosity that had existed between them in the end, always did have a lot in common.

Research, she had told him, deliberately vague, but he assumed, of course, that there was some purpose to it, something to do with work, study for a higher degree, perhaps, and she had no intention of disabusing him of the notion. He didn't need to know the extent of this seemingly pathological estrangement from work, the former anchor of her existence; that she was living guiltily, precariously, on the small income from investments inherited from her parents. And he would have cursed her to hell had he known that she was financing what he would see as another morbid obsession, a completely speculative, directionless little excursion into the past, through the sale of her father's Admiralty Blue 1969 Rover P5B. It had lain abandoned, unregistered, for four years in the old garage at the garden's rear boundary. It meant nothing to her, but Matthew had coveted it with a rare passion in those years when he was Chas's golden boy, joining her father in quarterly meets of the Rover Aficionados Club. If he'd known it was still there, he would have made an offer in a flash, no doubt after castigating her for allowing it to sit idle in that decrepit, white-ant infested shed abutting the lane, with no more security than the vice-like embrace of the trumpet vine holding the four disintegrating walls together. But Willa had sold the car to a stranger who didn't care why she needed the money.

In the background at Matthew's end she could hear the distant thump of a bass drum, the skirl of electric guitars tuning up. Matthew's son must be into metal.

Perversely, she was reluctant to hang up. *Does it make you crazy, wondering how she's managing?* she wanted to ask Matthew, the only person to whom her suffering could ever be voiced. *Do you think of her night and day, hear her voice, imagine what she would say if she were here? Do you worry how our daughter is getting by without us to love her?*

You'll email me if you hear anything? she said. *I'll check every day.*

Why would I hear anything? he snapped. *I'm the last person…* His voice trailed off, as sad as Christmas. *She's not coming back, Willa.*

She laughed silently into the mouthpiece of the phone. As if she needed *him* to tell her that.

It was warm inside the Mitchell Library, uncomfortably so. Willa discarded her bulky coat and jumper, the wool still stiff and cold from the walk, in a metal locker that smelled of mould and old sweat. It was her second day in the city, her second visit to the library. At first she'd felt exposed, nervous that someone would ask what it was she was doing, question her right to be doing it. But if the people rifling through shelves or engrossed in books had looked her way, it was just to smile and nod as they stretched their limbs or gave their eyes a rest. Today she felt a tremor of anticipation, taking her seat among the community of microfilm readers. The archaic machines were poorly lit and had to be manually shuttled – with the aid of a winder if you were lucky enough to find one – but she needed them to trace Little Jock's family.

Hugh Lennie, the newly found brother, was not in the 1861 census index, but she located him in 1851. He was living at the same address as the rest of the family but kept a separate household, with his wife Marnie and baby son, and two Irish lodgers.

The creaking old machine rolled forward a few pages, and there were the rest of the Looneys, just as James Donaldson had described them, and it was only through this act of winding on the reel, turning the handle again and again, that the statistics she had been reading about tenement housing took on meaning in flesh and blood. On and on she wound, pausing to check after every few pages of the census book, but yes, these lists of names were still for 97 New Vennel. She returned to the beginning and did a rough tally of lines and pages: 300 inhabitants crammed into this one building.

Dazed from the shuttling of life before her, she walked across to the windows, surprised to see, as she glanced up at the clock, that hours had passed. She tried to focus her eyes, but the streetscape three floors below seemed black and white, like the images of the nineteenth century that were still floating in her mind. It took a few minutes for her to understand what she was seeing, that while she had been concentrating on the small, cramped writing of census-takers, Glasgow had been dusted in snow.

That was it. Willa returned her reels to the shelves and donned her woollen armour. The Mitchell would still be here tomorrow, but right now it was snowing.

It fell silently as she got off the bus, studding her coat with pearls of white, gathering around her boots in drifts. *This is High Street*, she told herself. *I am walking in Little Jock's footsteps.* It was hard to reconcile the touch of bricks and stone with the weight of history. According to the book she had been reading, High Street was the oldest thoroughfare in Glasgow, dating back to the 1100s, the spine of the ancient city linking the river with the cathedral. The vast vacant block to her left, an eroding wilderness of weeds and refuse, was once the site of the university, built in 1540. Willa tried to imagine the imposing spires and towers rising above the squalor. By Little Jock's time, High Street had degenerated into a seething borough of crime and poverty, impossible to conjure in her mind as she kicked through the snow. Duke Street, Havannah, New and

Old vennels and College Open skirted the boundaries, pressing uncomfortably against the university's walls. She had read that whenever typhus visited the college grounds, those within would look darkly towards the high stone walls, no doubt in their minds as to its provenance.

In the 1870s the university was moved to the wholesome meadows of Gilmorehill, and by the end of the century those dreaded wynds and vennels around the abandoned site were swept away to make way for progress in the form of the Central Railway Goods Station. Today the station had disappeared, too, leaving this sad, derelict space. Willa wondered what its next reincarnation would be. She could find no plaque or stone to mark the site's history; the closest thing to that was across to the right at number 219, where a grimy whitewashed inn proclaimed itself the 'Old College Bar, established 1810'.

She walked on, feeling colder by the minute as the laden wind numbed her face. With eyes shielded, she tried to look up at the buildings either side, searching for numbers as she marked each block, but by the time she reached Glasgow Cross, the cold had her. Driven to seek shelter in the first warm doorway she found, its golden arches an unlikely sanctuary, she gulped down tea and picked at a serve of fries, palatable only because they were scaldingly hot. It took ten minutes of central heating for her face and fingers to begin a painful, prickling thaw. She moved closer to the window. Opposite, an alleyway off Trongate not much wider than a duffle-coated body gave some hint of the claustrophobic dimensions of Victorian Glasgow. But most of the streetscape was relatively new, coming in the wake of redevelopment after the old slums were demolished. Only a few landmarks remained: the Tron steeple, the grand Tontine buildings, and, to the side of the

Cross, the Tollbooth steeple. The steeple was all that was left of the Tollbooth itself, where witches had been burned in the 1600s – or so said one of the tourist bus guides. Little Jock had once been imprisoned there.

The snow subsided, and Willa, fortified against the cold with caffeine and cholesterol, set off down High Street again. She was looking for number 23 – that address Jock had always claimed as home – but there was nothing between the Celtic Shop at number 21 and the Indian takeaway at number 25. A brief tour of the Celtic Shop left her dismayed and vaguely lost, the green-and-white glare of football merchandise conspicuously at odds with her sepia-toned imagination. She walked up and down outside, trying to picture the tenements that once stood here in the shadow of the Tollbooth, but it seemed an elusive thing, this number 23, like the mailing address of an offshore company or some non-existent abode thought up by an unreliable witness. The family had also lived at numbers 75 and 93, but those, too, were long gone, and no hint of what came before could be gleaned from the shabby mercantile buildings that stood in their place. The whole of the High Street area seemed forlorn and neglected, its history not thought glorious enough to honour.

As Willa turned back and began retracing her steps towards the Cross, the sky darkened and the wind picked up, driving icy grit into her eyes. Her peripheral vision fragmented, and she sensed something hovering there. A figure – was it tailing her? She looked around, saw no one, but it was there again, the feeling that someone had just ducked into the shadows of a nineteenth-century close, scuttled up steps to a long-ago landing. Turning back into the wind, she cannoned into a disgruntled shopper, and as she backed away, apologising, she thought she caught a glimpse in the distance of a cap pulled sideways to hide a face – and then it was gone. Am I seeing things, she wondered, seeing ghosts? But Willa could live with ghosts. It was strangely calming, the idea that a spirit was keeping watch over what she was doing. He was suspicious of her motives, and rightly so, for what lengths he had gone to to cover his tracks.

Long fingers of light snapped in her field of vision, and she realised what was happening. Damn! She didn't have time for a migraine. Veering towards the line of shopfronts, she flung out an arm for something solid against which she could steady herself. The green and orange signpost for the vintage tour-bus company was just ahead, but as she turned away from the wind, in the direction the bus would come from, one of the clanking old double-deckers lumbered past on its meandering circuit around the city. It would be thirty minutes before another one arrived, and she could not wait that long. Stars were spiralling before her eyes as she hailed a taxi. By the time it pulled up outside the budget hotel on the crest of Garnet Hill, she could barely see.

Pain cuts its grooves into memory. As she struggled up the stairs, she at least knew what to expect.

The first time, she thinks she is going blind, or mad, unfamiliar with the surreal strobe flashing and haloing of the aura preceding the pain, the sudden skewing of faces before her eyes. One minute she is watching Imogen, whispering to her, stroking her face, and then she is confused, moving her head slowly, trying to focus, reeling backwards, reaching for Imogen's panicked grasp. She cannot black out when her child needs her – her child, a struggling butterfly pinned to a table, her thin little legs fastened into stirrups meant for women, not girls. They move towards her, the company of lab coats with their clipboards, latex gloves, the glint of stainless steel around their necks. Their concerned heads are bent like a row of commas, and she is gasping *No, I'm all right* to them, *Mummy's all right, baby-girl* to Imogen, and pushing their helping hands in the direction of her whimpering child who is illuminated under a great bowl of light, naked from the waist down, her body split open like an overripe fig, nerveless striations of scar tissue white against rosy flesh.

It is only the precursor.

What comes next can be tamed only by sleep, silence, a darkened room. And Willa learns this astonishing thing: that pain, like so much else, can be put on hold until a child is safe in bed and all that must be done for her is done.

It was not a bad one, as migraines go, but she did not wake until after eleven the next day. Her long, drug-induced sleep was fractured by the roar of a vacuum cleaner and the bantering voices of cleaners, almost incomprehensible in their thick Glaswegian burr, on the landing outside her room.

…I' weel ony go the wurrse if ye'll no tell 'im. Jus' do i', f' Goad's sa'.

D'y' think Ah doan know tha'? Gauny tell 'im, gauny tell 'im tonight…

She looked at the clock radio beside the bed, and groaned. She had lost the end of one day and the beginning of another. She sat up slowly. The jagged pain had turned molten, swilling dully around the bowl of her skull. Pulling a tracksuit top over her nightdress, she stood, testing her balance, and peered out of the door. *Good morning, ah, hello?*

One of the women was dragging the vacuum cleaner into the room across the hall; the other, resting on her hip a plastic tray of dusters and sponges and cleaning fluids, glanced around at Willa. Dressed in jeans, T-shirt and running shoes, she was much younger than her voice suggested, and Willa could see the spikes of a barbed-wire tattoo beneath the sleeve of one arm.

Don't worry about my room today, she said. *I'm running late.*

The gauny-tell-'im girl looked at her blankly. *Eh, sorry?*

I don't need the room cleaned today.

Ah c'n come back in a wee while, she said helpfully.

No, no, that's fine. Thank you.

The girl shrugged. *Suit yersel'.*

Willa was ravenous and nauseous at the same time, and it was no bad thing that she had missed the sensory assault of the Full Scottish Breakfast, with its smell of kippers and oatmeal and deep-fried haggis rising up the stairwell. Just bearable was this makeshift brunch of dry crackers and decaffeinated tea, helped along by aftermath painkillers.

The thick curtains were drawn to keep the room dark, but she could see from the small uncurtained pane of glass above the window that there was no sunlight to speak of, the sky the colour of asbestos. She tried the drapes gingerly, looking down on the road, but even this muted scene of snow-laden taxis and black umbrellas made her flinch. Turning her back to the light, she sat at the tiny desk, kneading her forehead, temples. Her notes from the previous day were in front of her, but where to start? She read through them again and then, allocating a fresh page in her journal to each member of Little Jock's family, she filled in what she had learned so far. It did not amount to much, but it gave her clues about where next to look.

The clock radio read 15:06 by the time she had finished – early enough for a few hours in the Mitchell – but her head was as thick as sludge and she knew her eyes would not stand the blur of the microfilm readers. She slumped back on the bed, staring at the yellow ceiling with its hairline crazing.

Where is Imogen? she wondered. What is she doing?

There were sixty computers in the Mitchell's Internet Centre, and she glanced curiously at screens as she headed to her allocated seat. Most people seemed to be accessing email accounts, although some screens flashed with bright animation. She turned her face away, still exquisitely sensitive to light and movement even after two days.

The connection was rapid and she sat with her finger on the 'delete' key, ready to dispatch the day's spam. She was not expecting anything from Matthew, was sure that her heart would stop if his name appeared in her in-box. But she was surprised to see a name she did recognise there among the list of strangers offering Vicodin, Viagra and vacations to Florida. James Donaldson.

```
Dear Willa
How are you going with your genealogical
meanderings (or is that maunderings)? You
mentioned being new to the genie game, so
I thought I would pass on some info about
Irish research - presumably your next leap
backwards into the LOONEY/LENNIE line -
that I gained the hard way while trying
to track down one of our miscreants. Not
good news, I'm afraid. Civil registration
records only from 1864. Before that only
parish records & the poorest classes often
didn't bother to register with the parish.
```

Too busy getting on with the tough business
of living, I suppose. If you'll permit me
to venture a guess, your LOONEYS/LENNIES
might have been in this category, given the
impoverished areas they settled in here.
(Maybe came over during the Famine?)

It gets worse. Few surviving census
records until 1901 & the Poor Relief records
are nothing as detailed as ours.

There're listservs for various counties
in Northern Ireland. Have you tried them
yet? Maybe someone can look up census
substitutes for you at PRONI (Public Records
Office of Northern Ireland – in Belfast).

Irish stuff isn't my forte, but ask if
you need some help & I'll put on my wee
thinking cap.

Regards

James

It struck her suddenly that her blinkered, fearful mode of
operating in the world was singularly lacking in grace. Would
it not have been a simple thing, a matter of courtesy, to tell
James Donaldson that she was visiting his city to follow up
the excellent leads he had found for her? Especially given his
seeming willingness to mentor a perfect stranger. She could
feel her face warming, the race of her heart, for she knew such
conventions of nicety were beyond her. What if he were to
suggest their meeting over coffee? How could she refuse without
causing offence? Still, as she signed off the log-in sheet and
made her way to the reading room of the Glasgow Collection,

she kept her head low – guilty, a little sad but also panicked at the notion that James Donaldson could be anywhere, maybe no more than a table away from where she slipped, unobtrusively, into her seat.

After a whole day of trawling through reels of the unindexed 1841 census, there was still no trace of Looneys, Lunneys, Lennies. But she suspected, anyway, as James Donaldson had done, that the family was still in Ireland then, oblivious to what the devastating Famine had in store for them. The next day, she tried the 1871 census – also without index – and by sheer chance located Jock's brother John and his family. Buoyed up by this discovery, she kept checking, screen by screen – the neighbouring houses, all along the street, up and down the closes that ran parallel and crossways – but nothing. The Lennies seemed to have gone their separate ways, no longer the family unit clustered around the widowed matriarch. It might take days, weeks, to find them, if they were there to be found. Was this the end of her search? It especially frustrated her that she could find no record of Jock's mother, Mary, whose fate she was desperate to know. Mary, who understood, who by 1871 had also lost her child.

In the late afternoon, already dark, she walked through slush to the railway station in Buchanan Street to buy a ticket for the ferry to Belfast, and that night, huddled close to the single strip of central heating, she went through her lists again, ticking things off and planning her last day in Glasgow.

She had passed the McLellan Galleries in Sauchiehall Street nearly every day on her walk from the Mitchell into the city food hall of Marks & Spencer. Today was her last chance, and it would have to be a lightning tour of the eclectic collection representing the treasures of Kelvingrove Museum, which was undergoing a three-year program of renovation. She walked through the 'Glasgow Style' gallery featuring the distinctive furniture and stained-glass designs of Charles Rennie Mackintosh, through room after room of rich oils, cracked varnish, old, dead masters. Rembrandt. Faed. Constable. In the 'Italian Renaissance' gallery, among the Botticellis and Bellinis, a small painting arrested her eye, oddly whimsical in a procession of conspicuous consequence. *A caprice landscape with ruins*, the display card read. *Oil on canvas. Giovanni Antonio Canaletto.* In the catalogue she had bought in the gift shop, there was a paragraph beneath the reproduction of this unremarkable vista of a place unknown to her:

> This type of painting is called a 'caprice', which means it is a mixture of real and imaginary details. The town is recognisably Padua but the ancient group of classical ruins in the foreground is invented.

The words remained with her as she walked down several flights of stairs and out again into the grey morning. The landscape of Little Jock's life she was trying to paint from archival remains and speculations was not unlike Canaletto's little caprice, although there was a frothiness associated with the word that made her frown. *A mixture of real and imaginary details.* It seemed to Willa that this was the essence of memory, perhaps even of history itself. And that there was nothing capricious about it.

∽

She took the tourist bus one more time, a round trip of Glasgow's sites of interest neatly parcelled, if you stayed on the bus, into an hour and twenty minutes. Willa loved the feeling of familiarity that came from seeing the city this way. Having taken the trip several times, she knew the standard patter by heart, but looked forward to any special flourishes individual guides might throw in. *Big Bertha*, announced the tartan-clad young woman who was doing her best with a dodgy microphone. The huge crane rose above the docks like a steel-girdered crucifix, lament for a city's dying industry. Beyond, the tall ship *Glenlee* came into view. Willa had stopped here one morning and toured the ship, sliding on the sleety decks and trying to imagine the deafening slapping of ropes and sails at sea, the blackness of the dingy hold at night.

The bus wound around the hill, passing the Cathedral, the Necropolis and St Mungo Museum of Religious Life, and then the stretch of Duke Street where there were remnants of the old university walls. Along High Street – *her* High Street – which the guide optimistically called the 'mercantile quarter', Willa watched passers-by, seeking out elusive shadows, but the streetscape today was distinguished only by its shabbiness, an aura of decay decidedly of the twenty-first century. As the bus lumbered around the corner at the Tollbooth steeple, towards the 'Barras' weekend market and People's Palace Museum, the guide struggled again with the microphone, which clicked intermittently, cutting out words: *Glasgow Green...where women washed and dried their...home for many years to Mumford's Penny Geggie...known for his moralising sermons...while soundly drunk himself, which he claimed...to warn his audience about the demons of liquor...*

Willa smiled, thinking of the 1852 editorial in the *Glasgow Free Press* she had copied into her journal:

> In Dickens' Household Words of the day we observe
> the following: – 'It has been stated, as we fear with too

good truth, that in Glasgow alone twenty thousand people go to bed drunk every Saturday night.' This, we presume, is exclusive of those who are so drunk as not to be able to go to bed at all. Truly, our good town has a nice reputation!

The hypnotic rumble of the engine briefly lulled Willa's thoughts, and she woke to the sight of the university's gothic spires: *home*, the guide was saying, *to the world-famous Hunterian Museum*. At last the bus approached the Mitchell. Willa rang the bell and stepped off for the last time.

∞

While checking her emails, she re-read the message from James Donaldson, to which she had not replied, and sat there stewing, feeling guilty anew. And a line caught her attention:

```
Few  surviving  census  records  until  1901
&  the  Poor  Relief  records  are  nothing  as
detailed  as  ours.
```

How could she have missed it? She logged off and hurried back to the desk of the Glasgow Collection, accosting the librarian to ask about Poor Relief.

In situations of extreme poverty, people could apply to the city for relief, of a kind – welfare before there was welfare, if you like, he told her. *An inspector would be sent out to investigate whether the applicant was genuinely destitute, and deserving, before the meagre help on offer could be given. That's what the records are: copies of the inspectors' reports.*

An appalling greed enveloped her at the possibility that Little Jock might have been driven to hold his life before the gaze of a welfare inspector. That she might glimpse him, glimpse Mary, through these contemporary eyes.

Are they kept here? Can anybody access them?

They're held in Special Collections, just on the other side there, but as you can see…

Willa looked up to where he was pointing, a sign advising users of temporary closure to facilitate the replacement of microfilm readers and redevelopment of the area. *The archivist apologises for any inconvenience.*

How long? Willa held her breath.

Ah. The contractors said two weeks but there's every chance they'll naw be done in three.

She collapsed onto a sofa outside the reading room, dumbfounded that it had come to this: foiled by the flaws in her own preparation. And then she took out pencil, journal, pocket calendar, wallet, travellers' cheques, ferry ticket and the printouts confirming flights and accommodation, and sat there fiddling with dates and figures, reading fine-print conditions on the reverse of documents, weighing up consequences. Trying to make something work that clearly would not.

February 1861

Portsmouth Convict Establishment, England

Snow catches in the prisoners' hair, in the turned-up cuffs of their trousers, and though it deadens the screech of winch and pulley in the dockyards, wardens have keen ears for anarchy. Stealthy *What-are-ya-in-for?* whispers are punished, when detected, as the one thousand inmates of Her Majesty's Convict Establishment at Portsmouth lumber in gangs on public works. And it is forty-eight hours in the black hole for physical contact of any kind beyond that made unavoidable by the proximity of men in crowded mess halls and queues for the closets, and working together on the same backbreaking tasks. At dusk they are stacked like goods in storage, one prisoner to each windowless, corrugated-iron cell. The order rings out to remind them – *Silence!* – and again it will sound whenever a whistle is heard, a bout of coughing, a grunt from a habitual masturbator. But not all noises can be policed. Just outside the prison the sea surges in the narrow channel between Portsmouth and the Isle of Wight. Gulls shriek. Glacial winds roar through the prison yards, scouring the Anchor Gate and unsettling the chapel bell into a musical quiver. Men groan and mutter in their sleep, unaware of their audacity, and some throw back their heads and howl like beasts, knowing the consequences but nonetheless compelled to assert this perverse humanity.

The only permitted speech is in the chapel, where one hundred prisoners at a time crowd into the makeshift schoolroom for their weekly half-day of instruction in reading and writing, rudimentary geography, multiplication tables, and the aliquot parts of weights and measures, pounds, shillings and pence. Though little enough, it is more education than most have had as free men, and nearly all will leave, if ever they leave, with at least some cause to be thankful for the reforming zeal of the penal commissioners of the mid-nineteenth century.

Portsmouth inmate number 5407 could sign the name 'Peter Lennie' at the time of his last conviction, and after eight months in Wakefield and more than two years here, he has absorbed words and numbers through the sheer weight of repetition, aided by the gift of a quick mind. He is not yet ready to admit to literacy – and indeed there is little incentive for it that he can see, for none of them at home can read. Even if he were to manage to put enough words on a page to make something resembling a letter, where would he send it? The family is always moving – escaping landlords under cover of night – and has probably changed address half a dozen times since his detention at Her Majesty's pleasure.

If he could write, he would not wish to tell them of life here; he would describe, instead, the journeys between prisons, the five hundred miles travelled through the spine of Scotland and England. Sleet and snow had cloaked the first, from Glasgow to Wakefield. But on the second, to Portsmouth, the feeble sun of summer had not yet died away. He had shared a closed-in box of a railway van with forty other sweating convicts, hands chained behind them, and it had taken much manoeuvring to angle his eye against the corner join of the wooden van. From here he had caught occasional glimpses of autumn-coloured fields stitched together like a quilt, the spectral outline of an abbey rising from the crest of a hill, distant towns and villages, silver-lit rivers, a blur of green someone whispered was the haunt of a thief of old who gave what he stole to the poor.

And then there is the sea. Michael and John would want to hear of it, this restless expanse of blue stretching out before him as he breaks stone on the Anchor Gate Road, the Isle of Wight in one direction and the channel in the other. Some months before, he had watched the *Palmerston* sail away with forty-seven Portsmouth inmates bound for the new world, to serve out their time at a place called Swan River. Would it be a blessing or a curse, he had wondered; God's own or the devil's? Today the harbour teems with masts and sails of merchant ships and naval vessels. In the distance, sinking into mud in the Spithead shallows, are the broken ribs of the *Stirling Castle*, the last of the prison hulks to be taken from service when the Convict Establishment was built. The others had been towed away years ago, but these rotting timbers remain, oozing a slick of slime. They remind him of what he has heard whispered of the hulks, of just how much worse it could be – for one such as him, for anyone.

In his cell at night, pressed like a herring between other cells, he thinks of what Mary would want to know, things he could not write in a letter. She is always afraid of disclosure, of what harm would come to him, imagining how, in an instant, he could become something more than he seemed to be, something other, and a thousand times more vulnerable. He could never bring himself to say, in a letter or to her face, that he is vulnerable even if they do not know. He has seen enough to understand that so far he has been lucky. The risk is not, as she supposes, from the cursory medical examinations carried out at each new prison, and each quarter after that: prisons are interested only in infection and contagion – consumption, typhus, the pox. Beyond that, they look for those gross deformities that would prevent a man from hard work, relegate him to his cell to pick oakum fibres from the core of tarred old rope – six pounds a day from ten scabby fingers, rising up like a mountain of virgin silk. But this is a world of the desperate, and for all that the prison governors seek to isolate and contain, in truth no one is safe.

He shivers in his thin smock, setting the hammock rocking as he curls his knees into his chest and wraps his arms around them. A scuffling somewhere near the heavy wooden door – inside or out, he cannot tell – warns him that rats are out tonight.

He is summoned next day to the governor's chamber, shuffling in chains that will later couple him to the gang marching to the dockyard, a spectacle to be despised by all free men. A parchment from Whitehall is read, informing him that, three years and two months after his removal from Glasgow, *Her Majesty is graciously pleased to grant to Peter Lennie Her Royal Licence to be at large in the United Kingdom during the remaining portion of his term of penal servitude unless it shall please Her Majesty sooner to revoke or alter such licence.*

Governor Henry Babington Rose sets the parchment down and intones a few words on *good behaviour* and *reforming the soul* but inmate number 5407 is no longer listening. Perhaps he is permitting himself to form the word *home* in his mind, to laboriously spell it out as something that might be his again. And perhaps he is wondering about this person called Peter Lennie, whether his luck will hold.

April 1861

Glasgow

The census-taker looks up at the decrepit tenement building at 93 High Street, known as Pipehouse Close for its connections to the pipe kilns and cellars of the last century. He sighs. All those windows! There must be fifty houses in the building, sixty even. If he is brisk, and if there are not too many *furriners*, still it will take him, as like as not, all day and into the night.

By midday his back is playing up and the piles are biting and he is cold and tired. All those stairs! He suspects most of the residents whose thresholds he has crossed thus far are liars but it is not his job to judge. He dutifully scribes their responses to the standard set of questions: name of each member of the household; relationship to the head of household; marital status; age and sex; occupation, trade or profession; place of birth. He waits patiently while they concoct the plausible and palatable, confer over the contentious. One question seems to give the greatest cause for bickering. Only the youngsters born after 1855 are on the books and official; the rest, when it comes to how many years they have drawn breath, are at the mercy of memory or expediency. He doubts there is one in Pipehouse

Close whose age declared today is exactly ten years more than that recorded on the last census.

He blots the page carefully from his crouching position in the doorway, balancing the large ledger on one knee and praying that he will happen on an abode on this floor – surely there is *one* – that boasts the amenity of a chair.

Nine, then, Mrs Lennie. That's the lot? No lodgers?

Nine. The widowed matriarch, strangely fearsome for all her rheumy-eyed frailty, looks momentarily doubtful.

Nine, yes, nine, he repeats impatiently, and counts off the list he has copied down. *Mary, Peter, Michael, John, Bridget, Roseanne, Hannah, Bridget – ah, that's another Bridget, the bairn – and May. Is that right?*

And whyever would it not be right? the old woman demands.

Why indeed, he mutters to himself, showing her the entry, though it is mere formality. One of the younger women, with a grizzling toddler fused to her skirt, peers over his shoulder at the smudged and uneven letters and exclaims tartly at the *dorty page.* He bites down his scorn as he snatches back the ledger, thinking it unlikely that the old widow or the pert young quean or any one of them in this wretched hellhole could read so much as their family name, let alone form it with pen and ink. He could record them for posterity falsely, compound their lies with carelessness or those of his own making, and none would be the wiser.

∞

So, we're all of us Lennies now?

No harm to keep them guessing, eh, Patrick-Peter-Polly-or-Paul? John's smile stretches over a mouthful of sour teeth.

The young man known as Peter Lennie shrugs, ventures a grin in return, though in truth cheer eludes him. He has been back a week, but it is still fresh, the shock of seeing what three and a half years has done to his family. As he watches the play of light from coalfire and lit tallow on haggard faces huddling around a pot of soup, he feels the stamp of luck on him again, undeserved, confounding. Lord knows his own lot has not been one of ease, but they seem to have fared worse, for all that freedom gave them. The blood has darkened beneath Mary's skin, knotted with veins. Her eyes are cloudy, a veil between her and a world she has no longer the heart to see. When he arrived at their door, she had grasped his face, weeping shaking her bony shoulders, and he felt the weightlessness of age in her, as though it was only the anchor of his face in her hands that kept her from floating away. He handed her what he had – a shilling from some worthy society, patron saints of prisoners – but had been anxious to find work, to give more than he took from Mary. It seems, though, that the basic skills he learned at Wakefield – in forming leather, squaring heels – are thought too basic to be worth a thing. Or perhaps employers cannot clear their minds of that other stamp that is upon him: the all-over bristle of scalp and cheeks, the ill-fitting tunic and trousers, as clear and as loud as Her Majesty's broad arrows.

They have not been lucky with the little ones, he thinks. Two little Felixes he has never met have been buried as paupers in Dalbeth: Michael and Hannah's lost to gastroenteritis, Hugh and Marnie's to scarlet fever. He feels a rush of sorrow, even for the Malone woman, but has no cause to regret that Marnie, all the great doorful of her, had moved with her brood to her own house to take in lodgers when Hugh joined up again. *She do be having army pay again*, Mary says, *and good luck to her*.

He hands a piece of bread to his new sister-in-law, Hannah, who nervously watches her husband. He glances too at Michael, but looks quickly away from a face that seems to have grown newly brutish. Hannah cradles baby May, never lets her go, as though loving arms will compensate for all. Hushed and ashamed, Mary had told him of Michael's desertion. John had to hunt him down – easy quarry that he was, nursing a dram of kill-the-carter in a wee shebeen in Gallowgate – and *shame* him into coming back. But it is clear to see that, if truce it is between Hannah and Michael, it is a truce of air. There is a darkness in Michael that has nothing to do with the hue of coal ingrained in his skin.

John is happy, he says, happy to be a scaffie. Night scavenging for the Cleansing Department is cleaner toil than being down the pits. Although he earns just threepence a ton for the middens he shovels, there is sometimes scrap iron to be had if a man is of a mind to be watchful, and more than once the little beam on his cap has lit upon something saleable in the city's waste. *Look*, he says, taking a rag from his pocket and carefully unwrapping a coil of wire thick with the muck of tenement leavings. Little Bridget reaches out a sticky hand, and Roseanne slaps it away.

Bridget, *his* Bridget, looks like a wraith; he can almost see right through her. She had cried to see him home, cried and held him tight, but he knew there was something...

She is weak, Mary whispered to him later as Bridget stared at the fire, *but she will heal*.

Bridget rises from her place beside him, stumbles, and as he steadies her he glimpses the little girl he remembers struggling within this broken young woman, a mismatched reflection in a warped mirror. She smiles at him uncertainly, muttering. *Patrick?*

∞

When the rest are asleep Mary looks at the small, nuggety body crouching beside her, close to the fire. Who would believe? She shakes her head.

He glances up at once, wary of any movement.

Grasping a fold of skirt, she wipes the filmy grit from her eyes, the better to search his face. Are there traces here among these whiskered planes, these quick, furtive eyes – traces of a little Irish child? She sniffs, satisfied with what she sees. And sad.

Will ever she be coming back?

Mary blinks, sucks in a panicked breath, but no, he is speaking of Bridget. Of course, Bridget. She looks away.

You said you would tell me. Well?

She blinks again, clears the thickness in her throat.

They had moved a few doors down the road, she and Bridget. The girl wanted to be free, just once, from crying babes and Marnie's sharp tongue and brothers wanting this done, and that, in the free hours she had between the factory and sleep. But Mary's pretty girl, her foolish, pretty girl, flew at freedom like a giddy goose with no mind to what her mother had to say about *young men in closes*. And soon it was past the time for warnings. Bridget was faint, dropping like a stone on the stair, on the floor, at her place by the loom – *'Tis a wonder she broke no more than a shoe* – and heaving every mouthful she tasted. She took to her bed, sure she was dying, but Mary knew the signs and that it would not kill her, though it was every bit as terminal.

Who? What lad was it?

Wheesht, Mary says, closing her hand over his fist. *She would not say, not even to her mam.*

Bridget missed her shifts and lost her wages, fretted what to do about the lodgings.

We should have gone to John. But no, she do be a stubborn girl, independent. She had heard them talking at the mill of applying to the parish. I told her, I knew what would happen…but she did it anyway, all by herself. Mary rocks, remembering.

The parish inspector had tut-tutted into his voluminous book as he poked around their room, lifting the mattress with the tip of his cane, peering into their saucepan, prying, prying. And for naught. He offered but a temporary dwelling, and, thinking he knew a malingerer when he saw one, told Bridget she must return to the mill at once. Bridget, shamed, complied. She returned to the mill at once, and she came home with a broken bobbin-skewer, proving she had been attentive to years of women's talk in factories.

It looked for all the world like a slaughterhouse, Mary says. *You could scrub for days, for the rest of your life, and not ever be free of the sight of that child's blood.*

Widow O'Neil came – she knew what to do and, unlike the doctor, did not ask for five shillings. And when Bridget was heavily dosed, and poulticed with comfrey, Mary sent for John to bring them home.

She will heal. Again Mary avers it, hugging her chest, daring him to say otherwise. A fierce little refrain that neither of them believes.

It is midnight in Glasgow. Beggars without tuppence for a shared bed of straw wheedle and whine. Women of the *poor, unfortunate class* hiss from close-mouths, *Sir, eh, sir! What's your wish?* Gangs of boys who should be abed circle the unwary, feeling for silver: they have jostling perfected to an art. Policemen trundle barrows to Central, carting the dead, the incapable.

He knows this midnight city like the tattoos on his arm.

In the rear stairwell behind Pipehouse Close, his pockets rattle with stolen baubles, bribes to coax back his lost Bridget, to buy from her a smile. Lizzie McFadden, brazen as the bright new pin on her coat, thrusts a small, pink tongue into his mouth and little shocks run through his veins as her hands creep down, down, and he is hot and alive and maddened enough to think that maybe he can do this, push himself against her body, up against the cleft of her, and maybe the worst that will happen is that she will raise her brow and think him still a weanling... But her plump hands are on his fly buttons now and he thrusts them away, for the sudden thought is like a douche of ice: that of all the girls there are in Glasgow, Lizzie McFadden must surely be one who will know, with a mere touch of her hand, that all is not as it might be.

You cannot trust a soul.

Mary's whisper comes unbidden as he flees into High Street. And perhaps he will run back to the close-mouths of Gallowgate where he can be careless with secrets. Where the women have no soul.

Crossing

The bus ride from Glasgow to Stranraer took most of the morning. She sat at the front of the bus where she could watch the thinning out of the city into suburbs and then into a bleak winter landscape that matched her mood. On through farming land and marshes and quaint towns with narrow streets, and eventually the bus cut through to the South Ayrshire coast. With the dark ocean tracking along at her side, she opened her journal at the set of pages reserved for Jock's family. How little was recorded there. She despaired to think how much more there might have been had the Poor Relief records been available, if she could have extended her stay. What had she gained from her six days in Glasgow?

What did you expect? The voice in her head was Imogen's and she could not answer.

What did you think dates and names written in old ink were going to tell you? What did you think they would conjure up simply through being found?

*I thought there might be signs that I could read, clues to how he managed…*She faltered. It sounded an unconvincing reason for travelling clean across the world.

The Imogen-voice was scornful: *As if people would be so careless with secrets. You, of all people, know better than that.*

She was nervous about the crossing, and the great solid bulk of the ferry rising from the grey waters of Loch Ryan did nothing to calm her. Cars rolled from the wharf onto decks at one level, passengers boarded on others, and the sight of those bow doors, gaping wide like mouths, made her shiver.

They were so clear in her memory: images of a ferry just like this. She had seen them years ago on a TV screen in the corner of a waiting room.

Imogen is fretful and twisting in her arms, and Willa is weary of the baby's droning wail, almost cannot hear it any more, so surely has it become embedded in the aural texture of the day. The receptionist joins another patient standing in front of the television and turns up the volume, no doubt to drown out Imogen. Willa is called into the surgery by the specialist himself, who seems annoyed that his intercom is unattended.

She wants answers, *they* want answers – she speaks, too, for Matthew, *especially* for Matthew, away on another training course in Sydney. They are tired of reassurances, patently untrue, that the surgery was successful, that *these things take time to settle*. Matthew becomes tense to the point of rudeness on those rare times when anyone – even his well-meaning mother (poor Dawn) – knocks on the door and enters their domain. It is so consuming, his fear that someone will put it together, break the code of all they do not say, that Willa has learned the same response, feels the presence of people as an intolerable burden. So the only one who is there to see is her mother, and Orla is blunt, says what Willa cannot bear to: *She doesn't look normal, not anything like it, and wasn't that the whole point of the surgery?* Willa tells the specialist her concerns about recurring fistulae, the constant need for antibiotics – surely that can't be good for the baby – and her observations, diligently recorded in a notebook, that disposable nappies cause Imogen pain, as does the gentlest glycerine soap, and even the passage of a breeze across her naked body. All the while he is probing, palpating, and she wonders if she will ever get used to seeing her baby touched this way. And the thought occurs to her, sucks the breath from her lungs, that these raw, inflamed tissues might carry in their cells, long into the future, a memory of violation.

As he writes another prescription, Willa dresses Imogen tenderly, shushing her cries with little kisses and promises she knows are as empty in effect as they are sincere in intent. His words repeat in her head: *Anxious mothers end up with anxious babies!*

The receptionist is back at her station, but her eyes are still fixed on the television. *Dreadful, isn't it*, the woman says, nodding towards the screen. *Like watching the* Titanic *go down. They're saying most of them would've died of hypothermia.*

Willa turns around, jogging Imogen on her hip. Words are crawling across the bottom of the screen, BELGIAN FERRY DISASTER, while the news broadcast flashes footage of carnage in a grey, icy sea: boxes, luggage, cars, buses, trucks, bodies. LOSS OF THE 'HERALD OF FREE ENTERPRISE', HUNDREDS FEARED DEAD. And they are playing an animated simulation, again and again, as if unable to comprehend that it takes only ninety seconds for eight thousand tons of steel to lurch, list and capsize into the shallows of Zeebrugge harbour.

Engines vibrated beneath the soles of her shoes.

As the ferry began to pull away from Stranraer, she hoped, prayed, they had closed the bow doors.

∞

It was low season and only some of the ferry's bars, restaurants and fast-food kiosks were open. Willa held her breath as she hurried past them, nauseated by the shudder of the engines, by the smell of deep-fried cod. In the little gift shop bursting with leprechauns and Guinness-shaped keyrings and Irish blessings stamped onto linen tea towels, she bought maps of Northern Ireland and Belfast and took them to a table close to the panoramic windows at the front of the ferry. Here she could watch their progress through the channel that was Loch Ryan, the rocky peninsula of the Rhinns of Galloway on one side and the bulge of the Dumfries coast on the other. The sheltered waters of the loch were slate-grey, with an occasional irritation of foam as they got closer to the open sea. When the white streak of the Corsewall lighthouse appeared up ahead, she could see, from the detail of the tip of Scotland shown on her Irish map, that they were approaching the curve of Milleur Point and would soon leave land behind them.

She took out a book, a late purchase, from its W. H. Smith paper bag, and began to read about the Irish exodus to Glasgow during the Great Famine of 1845–51. They came in waves, thousands of them every month, from Londonderry, Sligo and Belfast, and as they came, slumlords threw up those shoddy tenements to house them. The impoverished 'Paddies' or 'Barneys', always at risk of deportation if their abject poverty be known, earned the Glesga natives' enduring hostility by their willingness to work at bargain wages, their readiness to step in as strike-breakers in the mines and factories. And they brought with them a welter of beliefs and superstitions along with the Roman religion and all of Ireland's sectarian baggage. There was no welcome for those dazed newcomers staggering down the gangplanks at Broomielaw, the lucky ones who survived the journey.

Willa looked out at the seamless blending of wave and cloud before her, and felt blessed to be crossing in weather so unseasonally mild. The ferry had picked up speed now. There was an effortlessness to its movement through the swell of the sea that she supposed must come from size and engineering, as well as good weather. She thought of Little Jock and his family, wondered what manner of vessel carried them over the Irish Sea, how they felt about leaving behind the country she looked for now in the featureless distance.

In her book there were no photographs of the little paddle steamers that ferried Famine immigrants from Belfast to Glasgow, but they were said to be about the size of a modern tugboat. Willa tried to marry the image of such a vessel with the information that they carried up to fifteen hundred people, most of them weak, many sick, on a journey of between nine and twelve hours; that there was no seating, only decks and cargo holds. It was imaginable only by dredging up twentieth-century referents of horror: Jews crammed into railway wagons en route to death camps like Belsen. The Irish holocaust, the Famine has been called. Willa thought, too, of times she had seen trucks bound for the port of Fremantle, loaded with sheep for live export – the crazed eyes, the stench of excrement, the snort and bleat of fear.

She closed the book and looked around at the passengers eating chips, doing crossword puzzles, talking. From the table beside her came a bicker of voices, and it was the tone rather than the words that caught her attention, a strained pointlessness in the way each sought to hush the other.

Don't – do NOT *– tell me…*

All I'm saying is…

You've no right to interfere, do you hear? As far as I'm concerned you've given up your…

And whose fault is...

Fault? Don't make me laugh...

Her surreptitious glance was caught by a small, pale-skinned girl sitting outside the huddle of mother and father, pouring salt and pepper into a speckled pool on the tabletop.

Willa looked away.

It had been easy for Chas and Orla to cast Matthew as villain. Heartless Matthew, who abandoned his three-year-old daughter, a daughter he could not bond with, found hard to love. Matthew, who abandoned a wife struggling with a sick child. They turned on him immediately, repudiating overnight the son-in-law on whom they had hitherto bestowed their unquestioning allegiance, their hard, shining, alabaster love.

It was easy for Willa, too – constructive, even. There were times when the flare of energy generated by hating Matthew – *bastard, coward* – had been the only thing that dragged her from her bed in the hard, lonely hours before dawn.

It was easier to hate than admit the truth: that Matthew left because Willa and Imogen had become Willa-and-Imogen, a self-contained unit, impenetrable, off limits. Matthew left because his bond with Willa had sundered, because Willa was the one who was hard to love.

There were no explosive arguments, no undercurrents of acrimony, but over the course of those first few years, while they waited for *things to settle* with Imogen, Willa and Matthew closed off parts of themselves that once they had shared. Each made small, irreversible incisions in the weave of their lives together, so that when it became clear that things were not in fact going to settle, their marriage was a tattered thing, all loose threads and fraying.

She knew Matthew was going to leave long before he did, so his exit was not the stuff of drama. When he left, it was like the completion of a sigh, and life went on.

He told her he would always be there for them, would always support them, but he could not stay, *not even for the baby*. She smiled faintly at the patent nonsense of Matthew *being there*, but not being there at all. It was curious, pitiful, the way his eyes flicked towards her and away, again and again, as though desperate for reassurance but unwilling to look too closely for fear it wouldn't be there.

Stare at anything long enough, she thought, and you can see the atoms, cells, pixels, threads – whatever it is that makes it whole; you can almost believe in the absurd claim of physics that matter is not solid at all. In the panorama of grey on the other side of the glass, shapes began to form, and she thought she could make out the curve of a hull, the peaks of masts, the hump of a paddlebox. And bodies, a crush of faces and limbs and coats and hats – but now they, too, were dissolving before her eyes, dematerialising, re-forming into something else, some other grey on grey, stretching out on either side of the glass.

Her view was obscured by people gathering by the bow windows, and the level of noise was raised a notch. The woman at the next table, who had been silent for some time, led the little girl to the glass and knelt beside her. Willa heard her exclamation:

Look, Caitlin! Can you see? That's Ireland. We're home!

September 1862

Glasgow

Home, ah dear God, let me go home.

He snatches a glance at the fellow beside him, whose plea, in thick Irish brogue, seems directed at no one and nothing in particular, just a moan from the soul of a man not long from across the channel.

As the sun makes a rare break from the clouds, the idea of *home* glitters like glass before his eyes. It has been a lifetime since it has meant for him the place longed for by this plaintive Irishman, the green and shining land of childhood turned to waste by famine. Home lies between the prison gate and the Tollbooth tower, a mere distance of a few city blocks. For the seven months he has been in Duke Street awaiting trial, he has glimpsed the tower at the end of High Street, knowing that between it and him are those he calls family, part of the same world yet beyond his touch. It has been a slow weaning, perhaps a kindness, a gentle scoring of the surface before it is cut. But he can sense the blades are sharp and ready for him now.

Waiting with the others for the van that will take them the short way to Jail Square, he gives a single moment's consideration to the possibility of fleeing, taking advantage of the temporary absence of chains and the inattention of the guards – dull and heavy-bodied fellows, all of them – and disappearing into the maze of close-mouths and wynds and folk who are blind to absconders. But the cuffs are about his wrists before the thought is fully formed, and he knows there is no chance of flight while shackled to seven other miscreants. As Mary would say: God is good but you don't dance in a narrow boat.

Roll call, and though it has been all these months there is still a pause after the demand for *John King* to answer. A name is just a name. When apprehended, he had looked up at the blue enamel sign hanging over the shop near Pipehouse Close: a barrel encircled with brassy hoops. It belonged to John King the cooper, a jovial man as full and round as his own stout merchandise. As good as any.

John King! The guard is frowning now.

Aye, he responds hastily. He had better get used to it. This new name, with so little thought behind it, is now the barrel that will have to carry all the things he is and will be.

Dry leaves churn and crush into autumn dust as eight pairs of prison slippers shuffle towards the van. The Irishman beside him sighs, a slow, sad expulsion of hope.

It is an uncommonly fine day but few are in the streets around the square, or opposite on the Green, to enjoy it. The Autumn Circuit Justiciary Court is the centre of gravity today, full to bursting with bodies, pulsing with an obscene hunger for the gruesome and sensational. It is a congregation in waiting, reluctant to absent themselves to seek out pie or ale for fear of losing their place: the next prisoner led to the dock may be the comely one they have all come to see. Many of them spent the whole of yesterday seated so, only to leave disgusted at the day's adjournment. But today – it could be today.

There is a collective moan of disappointment as the next case is called before Lord Ardmillan in the New Court chamber. It is clear that the city officials, the court scribes, the learned advocates awaiting their turn to step up, the impatiently murmuring spectators – probably even the jury – desire a speedy dispatch of the case against John King and Robert Hutchison, trivial housebreakers and thieves.

He stares at his feet as the sonorous voice of the prosecutor reads the witness statement of seventeen-year-old mill girl Marion Dunn:

> I know Thomas Hamilton's shop in Havannah Street. At half past ten o'clock pm of Monday 7th April current, while I and the witness Robert Gilmour were amusing ourselves with other young people about Hamilton's shop door, the accused John King (or Pat Looney as I know him by) came down the street smoking a pipe, and as he passed us he looked at us and I thus got a good view of him…

From his position in the defendant's chair, John King glances around the public gallery, which, judging by the titters, is finding the words *amusing ourselves with other young people* preposterous from the mouth of the portly Mr Adam Gifford. He scans the rowdy rows for a familiar face, without expectation. The last time he had seen Mary, she had been dangerously close to infirmity and too desperate for what he had brought home – food and blankets, shillings for coal and lodgings – to question where they had come from. No quantity of blankets or thick-knitted shawls could ease the cold in her bones, and he fancied he could see the shadow of Barnhill upon her.

Mr Gifford's recital drones on:

> …the first thing that attracted me was Pat Looney in the act of going into Hamilton's shop. He was just stepping in. I stood for a few moments at the close-mouth and listened. The street is very narrow and the least noise in the shop can be heard on the opposite side. After Looney went in I heard the noise of a drawer being pulled out and also the rattle of money…

He remembers it, the clink and clatter of coins in the till, the rush in his veins as a few spilled out and rolled along the wooden floor. Once he had stolen for need alone, but none could deny there were satisfactions to be had in thievery. The stealthy observation of likely target, the joint planning (he always worked in company, a loitering pair being less suspicious than a loner), the exhilaration of a good skin – it had become a sport as well as a way to triple, on any given night, the weekly wage he brought home from his job on the wharf. Brother John called him a fool, but John had eaten the bread, warmed himself by the fire. Ah'm a fool a' right, he thinks, but only tae 've trusted Hutchison's girl. She was supposed to divert the attention of Marion Dunn and Gilmour and occupy them in Close 44 long enough for him and Hutchison to get away clean. He should never have weakened, never have let himself be persuaded. Two's company; for him, three's always been a curse.

Gifford has moved on to the deposition of some nosy old harpy who claims to have gone to her door and seen the said John King and Robert Hutchison running as fast as they could down the Havannah: *I did not see them carrying anything but there was a jingling of money all the time they were running...*

His counsel, Mr J. Fisher McLaren, leans back a little in his chair, flexing his limbs with the ease of a dog certain of where its next meal is coming from. He has never spoken to the learned Mr McLaren, serving as *agent for the poor*, but it is clear, from the way the man offered the plea of Not Guilty with an air of apology to the court, that he sees *poor* and *guilty* as much the same thing.

He rolls his eyes when Robert Jeffrey takes the stand, all spit-and-polished and proud to own the title of Criminal Officer in the Western District of the Glasgow Police:

> I will prove that these convictions apply to the accused John King, whom I have seen in custody and identified, the first under the name Patrick Loany, the second under the name Patrick Looney, and the third under the name Peter Lennie...

Lennie, Lonnie, Looney, Lunney – he barely remembers what came before that. A name is just a name. But he will not take Mary's with him this time. *John King*, he knows, will be convicted today: let *John King* take his chances.

Gifford is back on his feet, listing the items stolen: ten shillings in silver, ten shillings sterling in copper, fifteen shillings in copper, two and a quarter pounds of tobacco, and a wooden till.

Not a bad skin, he thinks, for all that he had to share it with Hutchison and his wretched girl. Only a halfpenny and a farthing and four ounces of tobacco were on them when they were caught at Hutchison's lodgings; the rest had been delivered to where it was needed and where it would never be found.

You the said John King, Gifford is intoning, *ought to be punished with the pains of law, to deter others from committing the like crimes in all time coming.*

A boy in the front row yawns lavishly and he feels the pull of his own jaw, cannot stop the intake of communal fatigue.

As he is led from the dock, his eyes make one last sweep of the room. Relief overpowers regret. He knows that seven years' penal servitude means transportation, and it is good she is not here to witness this last act of severance.

In the prisoners' cells in the basement of the courthouse, he passes by a cell holding the alleged murderess Jessie McLachlan, drawcard of these Autumn Circuit Sessions, accused of killing the housekeeper of her former employer and stealing an assorted cache of silver tablespoons, a velvet cloak and silk dresses. She glances up at him, serene and composed in her lemon pinafore dress and ruffled cap, no vicious cast to her face that he can see, and perhaps he will wonder at the absence of some sign to mark out a person who would strike another with a cleaver, again and again, on the face and forehead, severing the neck and fracturing the skull.

The twenty-four-year-old who answers to the name John King thinks hard before declaring to the scribe in Glasgow Prison his next of kin: *Mother, Mary Lennie, 23 High Street, Glasgow.* He has no wish to sully her name, but if he makes no claim of belonging, she might never hear what becomes of him. She saved his life and it grieves him to know that he can do no more than this to honour her generous heart.

Irish blood

The heating in the canteen was turned up so high that the frilled linen cloths seemed to wilt on the tables and every face was pink. Stainless-steel cauldrons of stew and dumplings and some meaty-smelling broth sent curls of steam into an atmosphere already humid with the breathing and coughing of construction workers, archivists, clerks and visitors, and Willa knew that if it were not for the icy blast scouring the room every time the door opened, she would probably have passed out from the heady fug. The prefab box, more like a caravan, at the edge of the parking area was a temporary arrangement during renovations to the Public Records Office of Northern Ireland, but she was glad of it, relieved she didn't have to brave the high winds along Balmoral Avenue just for a cup of tea.

James Donaldson's warning about Irish research was well justified, she thought, turning the pages of her journal. The results of a morning in the archives were scanty, largely irrelevant. She had worked through indexes and familiarised herself with what the archives held, but already her energy was stalling. There were too many variables in the story she was gathering, too many unknowns. Names, dates, places – especially places. According to the court papers and the census records she'd found in Glasgow, Little Jock might have come from Belfast (County Antrim) or County Armagh or County Tyrone – or all of these might have been lies. And as for which parish – where would she start? In the indexes there were Lunneys, Looneys and Loneys aplenty, but none of the individuals listed related to her family in ways that were clear to her.

Her family. Once again it assailed her, that furtive feeling of trespass. Back in Glasgow, a woman who had shared with her the library's one decently lit microfilm reader had tried to draw her into an ancestral contest. *Ah can trace ma line back tae the Battle of Langside on one branch and the tobacco lairds on another*, she boomed, brandishing a set of complicated charts like weapons against mortality, and she had clucked pityingly when Willa admitted to researching a family not her own. Willa wondered whether blood could bind her more closely to the family emerging, however obscurely, from her fragments of research, and was chastened to realise that she did not even know the full name of the great-grandmother who had bequeathed to Orla her avowedly Irish soul.

As she stood, gathering journal and scarf and coat, her handbag clipped a bottle of tomato sauce on the table behind her and it fell, exploding on the metal floor, shooting sauce and glass in a spectacular plume clear across the room. She dropped everything and sank to her knees, scrabbling frantically with a thin serviette and canvassing the mess. Everywhere people were rubbing at trouser legs and picking fragments from the laces of their shoes and the buckles of their boots and no one was looking at her or saying a word. Even the aproned man who bustled from behind the urn with a dirty mop and a wet rag motioned her out of the way, concentrated on the task in hand, said nothing in response to her gasps of apology. Realising, finally, she was just in the way, she grabbed her things and fled, leaving behind a flight of *sorries* like clay pigeons in the muggy air.

In the rest room of the main building, she plunged paper towels into cold water and sponged the sticky boots and the hems of her jeans. A glance in the mirror. What a sight. And a memory flooded through her, warm and sweet like mulled wine.

Do you remember when you dropped the cake, Mummy? Imogen's eyes widen. *Do you remember that?* And she begins to giggle.

Orla's hands are on her hips. *You couldn't possibly remember that, Imogen! How old was she, Willa – two or three?*

I do! I do! and she jumps, hanging on Willa's arm. *The cream went splat! and you said shit-shit-shit!*

Willa claps a hand over Imogen's mouth in mock protest and they both shake uncontrollably while Orla looks flustered and says *Surely not* and *Your mother wouldn't say that.*

She did! She did! Shit-shit-shit!

How Imogen – *that* Imogen – would giggle now at her anxious frown and the spicy odour permeating her clothes and the mound of soggy paper growing round her ankles. They would both collapse laughing when she described herself down on her knees, trying to soak up a river with a square of tissue paper, the dour faces of people fussing at their trousers – and in the telling she would make the sauce redder, the spill bigger, turn the people into ogres with horns and tails. She could hear that little voice, see her face, could almost touch the skin of memory. Suddenly she knew: moments like this were the difference between loneliness and being alone. She was used to aloneness, even comfortable with it, but loneliness existed in the seams of ordinary days and you didn't know it was there until you looked in the mirror and there was no one to tell, no one to take the edge off a stupid accident, to laugh at your terribly serious face.

It was visceral, a punch to the gut: *I miss her.*

A gale of a wind spawned from the Arctic gusted her back along Balmoral Avenue to the bus stop at the Lisburn Road corner. She let the first bus go, knowing it would take minutes to pull bloodless fingers from gloves and fumble for the right combination of coins, but another soon drew up. When she asked, *Do you go past Malone Avenue?*, the driver grinned, imitated her accent in a tortured twist of vowels.

Too right, ma-aa-ate!

The bus was bursting with people and briefcases and umbrellas and bags of shopping, and she squeezed in near the front, struggling to look through the window for landmarks. As supermarkets and video stores and pizzerias flashed past, the thought struck her: How everyday it all seems. And yet in the taxi from the wharf yesterday, not far from the quiet, elegant neighbourhood of her bed-and-breakfast, she had been confronted with the menacing image of a giant mural. A masked figure, rifle raised, and a crudely painted warning, explicit, non-negotiable:

You

Are Now

Entering

Loyalist Sandy Row

Heartland of South Belfast

Ulster Freedom Fighters

Painted in red, bracketing the words ARE NOW, was a pair of clenched fists. The taxi driver had been engaged in a non-stop monologue about the building of the glorious *Titanic* in the Belfast dockyard, but on hearing her intake of breath he segued into his commentary on the Troubles, pointing out the succession of faces and slogans, the red, white and blue, looming from every corner. She accepted his offer of a quick detour down Falls Road – *'Tis only right you see t'other side* – and they crossed the motorway into the green, white and gold of Sinn Fein territory.

These don't have the long history of the ones down the Shankill and Sandy Row, he explained as they drove past murals drawing on global solidarity: 'George Bush – America's Greatest Failure,' 'Palestine – Largest Concentration Camp in the World.'

They began painting 'em in the eighties to honour the hunger strikers. He looked in the rear-vision mirror for some sign of understanding from her. *Those Republican bhoys in gaol, you know? Political prisoners they were, said they – refused to be called terrorists.* He gestured at an enormous portrait, the face of an angel. *Bobby Sands, he was the first of 'em to die.*

After circling back at a roundabout, he had pulled over and idled the engine for a few minutes. *Look at that, then. Beautiful, is it not?* And she could see, without his having to explain it, that the scene depicted on the blind brick wall was of a 'coffin ship', one of the sailing vessels – larger than the steamers for the Glasgow run – that made the long, often fatal emigrant voyages to America during the Famine. The artist had painted the ship in the top third of the frame; the larger focus was the descent of its human cargo to the sea floor below, the ship passing over the bones of the Irish poor.

∞

Now, as the bus rattled along, she remembered the poignancy of the coffin ship set among images of machine guns and balaclava-ed men and barbed wire. She was learning that Belfast was a place of paradoxes like this.

She pressed the bell when a familiar church steeple appeared on the right, trusting this was her stop. The driver, unaccountably cheerful despite the harassment of rush hour, confirmed it with a mock salute as she alighted, and his loud *Hoo-roo, cobber!* put a smile on her face as she stepped onto the pavement.

Night fell quickly. She had been admiring the gracious streetscape from the window of her small attic room, the tree-lined pavements and Victorian sandstone terraces glowing in muted light. But in the time it took to pour boiling water into a cup and hang her hand-washed underwear on the central heating bar, the soft colours had hardened into illumination and shadow, cold in the glare of streetlights and headlights. A community of terraces had closed their eyes, shuttered themselves from the world.

She sat, warming her hands around the cup, reading the disappointing notes that were the sum total of a day's work. Nearly all nineteenth-century census records had been destroyed by fire. The archivist had told her that genealogists used property valuation records as 'census substitutes', but these were of little value to her. Even if she had known which area to look in, she thought it unlikely that her family would have been farming tenants. She had leafed through extant records for Armagh and Tyrone but the dates did not marry up with her Lennies. And the surviving Poor Relief records were just minute books recording dry administrative decisions and listing columns of figures.

She stood, looking out over the street again. She had never expected to find Little Jock here in these affluent Victorian suburbs. Nor had there been any sense of him when she stepped off the ferry and saw the world's largest cranes rusting in the sky, walked onto a ghost of a wharf that had once teemed with shipbuilders and dockworkers and sailors. Nothing in Falls Road: Catholic he might have been, but the Troubles were not part of his history, for all the efforts of nationalist mural painters to weave the Great Famine into their story. She had not even found him, not one trace of his existence, in the Public Records Office of Northern Ireland.

It was as though Jock's birth had never happened. She would be leaving Belfast empty-handed, her research, once more, having reached the finality of a full stop.

What next? she said aloud, but the breath of her words obscured the glass. She drew the curtains on the dormer window and curled up in front of *The Bill*.

Today, beneath the long black coat that had been on her back or under her arm since she stepped off the plane nine days ago, she was wearing something new: a sweatshirt bought on impulse from a shop near the Europa Bus Station. It was undeniably kitsch – green with white shamrocks stencilled on each long sleeve – but seemed a fitting gesture for an Irish pilgrimage. *Not* that she had succumbed to the ancestral roots Orla always said would one day claim her; in truth, the whisper in her ear that her mother might be watching from afar and smiling her satisfied smile was almost enough to quash the idea entirely. It was a matter, she reasoned, of pragmatism and proximity. Omagh, the town Orla called her *ancestral home*, was only sixty miles away – by Australian reckoning, just down the road. It seemed churlish not to go.

Rain fell continuously during the two-hour bus trip from Belfast around Lough Neagh and west across County Tyrone, through Dungannon and Ballygawley to Omagh. She looked out at the wet, green land and marvelled that country so lush and productive could have forsaken its people in the Famine years. She wondered, too, about Jock and Mary, Bridget and John, Michael, Felix and Hugh. The census of 1861 had recorded their birthplace as Armagh, but Jock had claimed, among other things, County Tyrone. Perhaps a Glaswegian census-taker listening to Irish brogue mistakenly noted the county 'Armagh' instead of 'Omagh', the county town of Tyrone. Could it be that this was their country, too, as well as her great-grandmother's? And would either of these connections be enough to make it hers?

Omagh is a pretty town built either side of a riparian curve where the Camowen and Drumragh rivers converge to become the Strule. It took Willa no more than an hour to complete the historic walk trail of churches and civic monuments, following a map produced by the 'tourist office', a desk in the corner of a newsagency. After returning to collect more brochures and a district map, she shook out her sodden umbrella on the pavement and set off in the rain again, heading for the library.

It had been three days now since she'd checked her email, so there was a daunting and irritating collection of spam. Nothing from Matthew. No surprise. She clicked on James Donaldson's last message, the one she had received in Glasgow, and it sat there on the screen like a dare. She would have liked to thank him for his advice, share with him the fruitlessness of her search in Belfast, but that would have required explanations and excuses that would at best bewilder and at worst offend.

She scrolled back through his previous messages, the kernel of an idea swelling in her mind. There it was: 'My brother, Alex, & I are now keen to trace any living descendants but we won't impose on you any further, at least for now.' Was she only imagining the hint of invitation in these words? What, anyway, had she to lose?

She began to type:

Dear James
Thank you for the information about the
Irish records. You are right about them
being frustrating. I managed to arrange
some searches at PRONI in Belfast, but there
is just not enough to go on.

I was wondering whether you would consider
a further exchange of research. You mentioned
that you and your brother hoped to trace your
Western Australian family further. Perhaps
I could help with that, and in return you
could look up some Poor Relief records for
me in the Glasgow City Archives?
Please let me know if you're interested.
Kind regards
Willa

Guilty about the half-truths but pleased with her idea, she hit 'send'.

∞

Window-wipers slapped across the wide front windscreen, as steady as a metronome. She looked at her map as the small tour bus pulled out of Omagh station en route to the Ulster American Folk Park.

Her fingers traced the environs of the town shown on the map, straying over musical names like Dooish, Seskinore, Owenreagh, Curraghchosally. A swathe of blue shown curled around the folk park – a stream with the deliciously intriguing name of Fairy Water – reminded her that this was a country steeped in myth. Wee folk of the Otherworld, solstice worship, Celtic goddesses, venerated spirits, sacred wells, portents, changelings.

When the bus turned off the A5, into the parking area of the folk park, it was still raining steadily.

The open-air, interactive museum celebrates the cross-Atlantic emigration of the Irish during the eighteenth and nineteenth centuries. Laid out in the form of a journey, it re-creates the 'Old World' of Ulster, the sea voyage from Derry, and the 'New World' of rural Pennsylvania. Willa saw all of this mapped out on the guide, but she lingered in the 'Old World', coming back again and again to a single-room cottier's cabin made of roughly cemented limewashed stone. She looked up at the pitched roof of sword-grass thatch, collected from the bogs, pinned in place with scallops of hazel; down at the dirt floor, black and damp, the peat fire smoking in the grate doing little to dispel the pervading gloom.

In the days before the Famine, a whole family might live in one of these. A costumed docent stood at the door, a smiling, elderly woman in long skirt and tunic of coarse, humble fabric and a fringed woollen shawl.

And after?

The woman shook her head. *There was no after. They disappeared from this land, wiped out, a whole class of our people.*

As Willa neared the door, she noticed the docent's smooth, pale face, unblemished by the sun. The woman's back was straight, her hands graceful. Why had she thought her elderly?

Murmuring thanks, Willa emerged into the curious half-light of a weak sun struggling through rain-laden clouds. She followed the path down through the 'Old World', running her hand along layers of stone that formed a barrier between the footway and boggy paddocks planted in furrows with some leggy-looking crop. Everywhere was the sheen of moss, wet and luminescent.

She leaned against a slatted gate, closing her eyes, seeing the woman's face in her mind and imagining it to be Mary's. She did not know in what manner of place Little Jock had been born – landless cabin, urban servants' quarters, tenanted cottage? But she did not need to imagine the cast of his mother's face when first she gazed on the infant's body, nor the stealthy guilt that would have crept into her heart. Physicians in the nineteenth century believed in 'maternal impressions', that if the eyes of a pregnant woman chanced to fall across some physical deformity, the foetus she carried would take on the same grotesque mark. Was Mary Lennie one of those pitiful, guilt-wracked souls, believing herself cursed for looking where she should not?

She tossed the thought from her mind. As if Mary would have had time for self-recrimination, occupied as she would surely have been with keeping her family alive. And if Willa knew one thing about Little Jock's mother, it was that no blame could be laid at her door. No stray ominous gaze caused her child's condition. Mary Lennie had nothing to be guilty about.

Willa envied her that.

When Imogen was born, Matthew's whisper had been the clearest thing she'd heard from the blur of all that was said: *My God, what have we done!*

Ha! she thought, walking back to the bus, the hint of a smile bitter, self-mocking. Poor pitiful, guilt-wracked soul!

The little tour bus returned to Omagh in the late afternoon, taking a circuitous route through the wild, barren moors of the Sperrin Mountains, the valleys of bog and slopes crisscrossed by streams, the herringbone paddocks, the woodlands dark as fairytales. It was beautiful in the way of beauty seen through glass, as removed as a documentary on TV, but as the bus reached the flatter terrain around Omagh Willa began to feel the land in her pulse. The endless rolling green of pastures broken only by hedgerows and grazing flocks – there was something about this open landscape that sparked an unlikely recognition, the shock of the familiar in a foreign world, and she wondered whether this was it, finally, the singing of her Irish blood. Or was it just that this country had the look of the South West about it, the corner of rural Western Australia she had experienced on childhood holidays?

An irritable wind buffeted the bus, and Willa grinned, hugging the green sweatshirt. She knew what Orla would say to that.

To ease the stiffness in her limbs, cramped from sitting in the bus, she walked to Tesco's to buy some fruit, and then browsed all along High, George and Castle streets, eavesdropping shamelessly on conversations, in love with musical voices and the charming occasional inversions and solecisms of Old Ulster English.

Yer wan seems for to be knowin' a bit too much for a girleen…

I asked do she be wanting to look like her poor oul' Mam…

Willa smiled to herself: was it only editors who were seduced by syntax?

In the window of an antiquarian bookshop was an old map of the British Isles, stuck to the glass with yellow tape that frilled and curled at the edges. She traced her journey on the glass from Glasgow to Belfast, Belfast to Omagh, and drew a wide arc down to the south of England. *We've been going in opposite directions, Little Jock.* But tomorrow she would leave Ireland, pick up the trajectory of his journey again.

It was evening by the time she reached the pub. As she was about to climb the double staircase to her room, a voice called out.

Ms Samson?

A ponytailed man stood in the open door to the bar, a comically beseeching look on his face.

There's not a soul in tonight, so I expect a kind lady like yourself would be wantin' to take pity on me and have a wee Guinness.

How do you know my name?

Ah well, you see, I'm the licensee of this humble establishment and you're the only guest.

She didn't recognise him. A young woman had written the receipt for her two nights' accommodation, held out the visitors' book for her to sign.

Y'd have met my niece when you checked in. He extended a hand. *Joey Duggan.*

She stood on the bottom stair, uncertain.

Ah, come on now, 'tis a free drink on offer and whatever have you to lose?

March 1863

Millbank Prison, London

The morning tramp of feet in the pentagon's airing ground yields an energy felt at no other time of the day, as the impact of boots on stone reassures men that they are still alive. John King marches in silence clockwise for thirty minutes and then turns on the order *Change!* for thirty minutes more in the other direction, all the time carefully watched for word or gesture, for *the evils of association*. He knows that to take your eyes from the heels of the man in front, to flex your chilblained fingers in suspicious ways, to smile, is to risk a week on bread and water or, at the very least, a kick to send you sprawling. And he knows, first hand, about the evils of association.

When the hour is up they are shepherded back to the cells through a honeycomb of passages, admonished to keep eyes to the front and bullied along by cries of *Make haste! Make haste!* Warders dispense mugs of oily cocoa and molasses to each cell, along with the day's work: coils of old rope for oakum picking, filling the air with the smell of creosote; lengths of flannel and paper patterns for the tailoring of soldiers' undergarments; squares of canvas to be sewn into hammocks, coal sacks, biscuit bags. Labouring alone in silence, each prisoner has a daily quota to meet, and each is instructed to reflect and repent as the long hours pass, to ignore the hum of London just over the Vauxhall Bridge.

He has heard it said, and knows it to be true: men go mad in Millbank.

The door to his cell in Pentagon 6 has an inspection hole the size of an eye, and someone long ago had daubed a pasty substance – dried skilly? – around the hole to fashion eyelids, lashes and an arched brow. Wherever he seats himself, wherever he angles his gaze, it follows, this Eye. There is nothing to stop him from rubbing it away with the sleeve of his smock, but five months' solitary makes a person reluctant to erase even the remotest vestige of human contact, even when human contact is a thing to be feared. He will put up with this crude representation, its incessant surveillance, in lieu of flesh and blood.

Squaring his back to the door to conceal his actions from the Eye or any passing warder, he uncorks a phial of Indian ink. He had asked the chaplain for this, along with a goose quill and a sheet of brown paper, and they had been granted in magnanimous recognition of good behaviour and the right tone of repentance. But his intention is not to write a letter. He has contraband in the gathered hem of his knickerbocker leg: a needle left behind by a careless warder when collecting the pile of sewn coal sacks from his cell at the end of the day. And tonight, by the flare of gaslight, he plies needle and ink to the skin on the back of his left hand, a shaky business, inexpertly done compared with the delicate tattoos on his arm. It has taken him many hours, point by point, but it is nearly complete, the rendering of this symbol that seems to follow him, making claims on mind and soul. He sees it in the chapel, a giant crucifix of smooth, gleaming wood, remote and untouchable and impervious to strains of 'Nearer My God to Thee'. It is chalked on his slate, drummed into him as the sign of summing numbers together. The Roman Catholic chaplain who visits twice weekly waits to see it dutifully marked on the breast. But it is not out of reverence for God or numbers that he tattoos his skin with a cross. He wishes to make solid, in the form of the revered, a mere slip of memory: an old woman in a mud cabin crying, *Away, child, you must, and may God protect you. And if you be spared, child, remember. Cross your heart, remember.*

What it was he should remember perhaps he cannot now say. But he has carried it with him, this exhortation to remember, and possesses no token but his body.

Picking up the blunt needle, he presses harder to break the skin. He will pierce four times, a dot within each right-angle of the cross, four compass points to mark out the course of his life to this time. Four claims on his heart. The old woman who cried. Another who smiled and opened her family for him to crawl into. A boy who died. And a child.

The edge of the known world

She slept on the bus from Omagh to Belfast, in the taxi from the Europa Bus Station to the city airport, in the departure lounge, on the flight to Gatwick. At Gatwick she had to follow signs from the terminal to the station and find the right platform, but once on the train she slept again, slept until someone gently prodded her arm and said, *Excuse me; this is Portsmouth Harbour; this is the end of the line.*

It was another room over another pub, but when she pulled back the drapes and forced the window open, a hint of ocean sailed in with the cry of seagulls on the cold, damp breeze. She leaned on the warped timber sill and looked out. Already it was growing dark, and even after two weeks this was something she could not get used to, the way days dissolved into nights so early. She could barely remember this particular day, other than for the trivial routines of travelling: wheeling her suitcase, lifting it up, down, handing over tickets, tumbling coins into dispensing machines for bottles of water. Many bottles of water. She could still feel the effects of the Guinness, the blood thick in her veins.

She had woken in Omagh alone that morning but the air had been heavy with presence. Sweat and tobacco, whisky, and an unmistakable smell she had thought belonged only to the past. Two cloudy shot glasses (had she been drinking whisky, too?) on the bedside table, a stiff ball of tissues, the wrapper of a condom on the dull, floral carpet. In the stillness were echoes of cries and murmurings; on her skin, a sheen she did not recognise. Someone had left prints on the intimate surfaces of her body.

Over the years she had become resigned to celibacy. Imogen came first, work second; she had neither hours nor energy for anything else. There had been times when the craving to be touched – someone, anyone, outside the small, tight fist of family – threatened to unbalance her, cast her adrift. Never, though, had she expected to succumb, because that would mean forgetting, loosening her grip. There had been one time, just one, she had let go, and it was inevitable that it would be Matthew. Matthew, who could be charming, to whom nothing needed to be explained, whose yearly visits to Perth to see Imogen were the only points of weakness on the boundaries of a circumscribed life. The humiliation afterwards had hurtled her back to earth, shored up all resolve. And gradually she had stitched desire neatly into the folds of her hairshirt. Imogen's Sacrificing Mother.

The voice was scalpel-sharp: *I never asked you to stop living.*

All day she had slept, hoping to keep at bay the bursts of light before her eyes. For surely they would come, given the accumulation of triggers: alcohol, the weight of her suitcase pulling at the tendons in her neck, the hours in motion, the flushed, incredulous surprise at what a mind could forget and a body remember. But here she was, cold and naked in the dark, breathing in the chill currents of a harbour city, and her head was clear.

Portsmouth is not like a mouth at all, she thought, studying the map on a signboard outside the Tourist Information kiosk. More the shape of a larynx descending into the throat of the sea. But it spoke of the ocean in the points of interest marked in red: Gunwharf Quays; the Fish Market in Old Portsmouth; Her Majesty's Naval Base, occupying a huge wedge of high-security land rendered blank on the map; the Dockyard tourist precinct where visitors could see the hull of Henry VIII's *Mary Rose*, discovered in the slime of the Solent twenty years before. Even the nameplates of public houses nearby, swinging and creaking in the salty breeze, exuded a nautical identity: Fleet and Firkin, Ship and Castle, Shipwright Arms, Sally Port. Perhaps it was no more than might be expected when the sea was in a city's name.

The city seemed less inclined to lay claim to its penal past. The first librarian Willa spoke to at the City Records Office looked puzzled at her enquiry about the Convict Establishment. *Do you mean the old Borough Gaol in Penny Street? Long gone, I'm afraid.* But the prison she was looking for was older still, a contemporary of national public works establishments of the mid-nineteenth century at Chatham, Portland, Dartmoor.

Another librarian thumbed through handwritten index cards and found an entry in the city corporation's records. *It will take a while to locate the volume*, she told Willa, and directed her in the meantime to a book on Victorian prisons. *You might find something of interest in there.*

After reading about the different stages of incarceration for convicts, Willa realised that Jock had experienced them all.

On his first entry into the system he had spent seven months in Wakefield before moving on to Portsmouth, but Wakefield, she saw, was something of a hybrid establishment – communal work in strict silence by day and solitary confinement by night. For his last sentence of penal servitude, he had been sent to Millbank, on the marshy banks of the Thames, now the site of the Tate Britain. At Millbank, which she learned was a penitentiary based loosely, and unsuccessfully, on Bentham's revolutionary panopticon, prisoners were exiled from human contact for twenty-three hours a day, and immersed in prayer and work. A prison reformer of the time, Sydney Smith, had laid down a simple prescription:

> In prisons, which are really meant to keep the multitudes in order and to be a terror to evil doers, there must be a great deal of solitude; coarse fare, a dress of shame; hard, incessant irksome eternal labour; a planned and regulated exclusion of happiness and comfort. A return to prison should be contemplated with horror.

From Millbank Jock had been dispatched to Portsmouth, to which he was no stranger. In Portsmouth men discovered the meaning of hard labour. Willa could imagine the small figure of Little Jock among the gangs chained and manacled on the dockyard or gunwharf. And in silence, and heavily guarded, for the fear of promiscuity was ever-present in the minds of Victorian prison governors. She wondered how he survived routine searches, medical inspections, exposure of his body when dressing and bathing. It would have…But she stopped suddenly, cautioning herself. Was she projecting here, inflating the extent of his difference among men when it might have taken the sharpest eye to discern any difference at all? Little Jock was not Imogen.

The librarian struggled out with a voluminous set of papers bound in worn black leather and set it down at a table for Willa.

According to the city's records, in 1851 the good citizens of Portsmouth protested vigorously against a proposal to build a convict prison in their borough – bad enough, surely, that for decades they had suffered the ignominy of hulks moored in their harbour, those infamous decommissioned warships converted to floating gaols, teeming with vice and pestilence. The hulks were to be scrapped, and a thousand blessings for that, but a convict establishment in their midst would be 'highly injudicious as well as injurious to the best interests of the borough.' Built it was, though, with the labour of those it would imprison, and when completed in 1852 it comprised

> an extensive range of fire-proof buildings enclosing a large yard, with a row of good houses fronting Anchor Gate Road for the Governor, Chaplain and principal officers. It had cells for more than a thousand convicts and accommodation for 100 warders. There was also an Infirmary with 40 beds. A chapel, which had room for all the prisoners and officers, was also used as a school, where 100 of the prisoners at a time were taught reading, writing and geography, etc., each convict having a day's schooling weekly.

Willa took the bulky volume to the desk. *Can you show me on a map where Anchor Gate Road is?*

But it no longer existed, and they could only venture a guess. *Probably somewhere in the old Dockyard, taken over by the military in the early 1900s.* The area on the map out of bounds, deliberately left blank.

∽

Wind lashed the harbour, and she felt the roots of her hair tugging at her scalp, her skin dry as driftwood. Soon she would leave this small island. She would board the train to Victoria Station, take the tube to Paddington and then the express to Heathrow, and by tomorrow's dawn she would have begun the long journey home. At the end of the ferry jetty, gazing out on the harbour stretching before her, and the ocean beyond it that she would fly across, she thought of Little Jock. The journey he made from this place was much longer than hers, and was forced upon him: an unceremonious shove off the edge of the known world.

And what of Mary? Did she torture herself with imaginings of what prison might hold for a child such as hers? Did she think of him toiling somewhere in England, working out his seven years? Did she become anxious as the years wore on, despair when he did not return? Or perhaps the authorities eased the misery of mothers, told them of the fates of errant sons banished from their own land. What was worse: to grieve the loss of a dead child, or to know your child was alive but gone from you, never to return? Willa could taste salt on her lips, felt it worrying at the corners of her eyes. Her heart broke for Mary.

She had suspected that the prison at Portsmouth no longer existed, that no trace would remain here, but now she understood her compulsion to make this one last journey. This was where it broke, the thread binding Little Jock to home.

Portsmouth Harbour, the end of the line.

January 1864

Portsmouth Convict Establishment

Sick parade can be a long affair, the work of a day for a prison MO, much of it spent weeding out the cunning – those seeking relief from toil or the ministration of a bit of boiled mutton – from the genuinely poorly. And there are plenty of the latter at Portsmouth. It is the same, he supposes, in any vice-ridden population. There is an unending monotony of coughs and catarrh, not to mention a freewheeling rotation of diarrhoea and constipation, the incidence of these last complaints dependent on the decrepitude of horseflesh flung into the day's soup, the proportion of middlings in a batch of skilly. These, of course, are infinitely preferable to the outbreaks of cholera and influenza that frequently ravage the prison, proving to him once more the inadequacy of his arsenal of remedies. As mundane as they are, his decoctions for the regulation of men's bowels can at least be ladled out with confidence.

Dr Crawford's dinghy is ashore, sir.

The MO sighs. It has been a long morning. But ninety-eight felons are due to board the *Clara* tomorrow, and he is required to assist the ship's surgeon to record their bodily marks and declare them fit for transportation. Crawford will be keen to ensure there are no fever cases, nothing to spread contagion on board, but both of them understand the administrative imperative to ship these men away. Blood-spitters, rheumatics and those with unnatural rhythms of the heart will be among any contingent 'fit for transportation.'

Right, lad, he tells the spotty youth in warden's greys. *Round up the lucky emigrants.*

There are two lines outside the infirmary, and as number 8092 gets closer he hears the order to strip. A flash of memory – *two queues, the girls, the boys* – and for a moment tough layers of brother-skin, felon-skin, are sloughed away and he is a child fighting down a futile impulse to run. He had quaked on admission to Wakefield, Portsmouth, Millbank, Portsmouth again, but these searches – all but one, and that back in Glasgow – had amounted to no more than a hasty rub-down and *off to the cells with you*. Medical inspections, too, had turned out to be matters for little care, for all his apprehension: a cold press of metal to the chest, a few idle questions (*Are you well, mmm? Are you insane?*) without pause for answer. And never, no matter how weak, how bilious, has he stepped forward to join the sick parade; never has he exposed himself to the dangers of being *physicked*.

A shove to the kidneys from behind, and he is tough again, shoving back. But as he takes another step the dread rises like bile.

Next but one to the head of the line, he begins the unavoidable process of unclothing – jacket, vest, knickerbockers, red and blue striped stockings, too-large slippers stuffed with toe-rags – and shivers in under-flannels at the infirmary door.

∽

The MO checks names against the indent papers dispatched from the Directors of Convict Prisons in London. He barks out questions. He measures. He grasps faces by the chin and peers into eyes. He stands back as though examining a painting, considering shape, assessing colour. He claps his hands behind heads, checking for deafness, waves like a man drowning to root out the blind. He quickly scans bodies for the obvious: scars, tattoos, pockmarks, moles, warts, cupping marks, birthmarks, crooked spines, missing fingers or toes or limbs or teeth, harelips, eyebrows that meet in the middle.

Down flannels! he orders, and is mildly curious to observe hesitation, laboured movement, resignation: compliance with this innocuous order seems to cost prisoner number 8092. But a knowingness replaces curiosity, and he suppresses an unworthy smirk as he takes in this man's insufficiency. He would not wish to disrobe, either, had he so little to show for himself. Consulting the papers, he sees the man was convicted in Glasgow. Ah, he thinks, poor wee mannikin.

Turn about, Little Jock, turn about.

A smatter of laughter from the queue.

He enunciates details to be scribed onto the indent papers in faithful black ink, and copied in triplicate, by the governor's sallow clerk.

Height	5 ft 1¼ ins
Hair	Dark brown
Eyes	Light blue
Visage	Oval
Complexion	Fair
Appearance	Stout

Distinguishing marks   Cut on forehead
                         Star, crescent and flower left arm
                         Left hand…

He looks up sharply, especially attentive to tattoos on hands. A row of five blue dots stretching between thumb and finger signifies membership of the 'Forty Thieves', and good riddance to those who carry them; who knows what new gang this crude design might represent? He calls to the ship's surgeon, busy with the other line of men, but William Crawford shrugs, his interest in ink daubings on the persons of convicts extending only to their proper recording on the set of papers he is entrusted to deliver to Swan River Colony.

Copy this exactly, the MO tells the clerk, thrusting the back of the prisoner's hand under his nose. The entry for transportee John King, Portsmouth number 8092, concludes with a pictorial representation: a cross dividing four dots.

A foul fog, thick as burgoo, steals in from behind the Isle of Wight as the longboat is pushed from land and the prisoners begin rowing. It blankets the Spithead, obscuring vessels that could be seen clearly only that morning: the troopship *Megara*, the paddle sloop *Hecate*, the store ship *Industry* and smaller merchant and fishing craft. Phantom fragments of human voices, disembodied in the pall, seem alarmingly close, and Jock looks up from his place at the oar, expecting some presence other than the convict in front and the convict behind. But the sounds disappear, thin into nothing, and he can feel no change in the weight of the air to suggest they ever belonged to flesh.

Ahoy!

This cry is different – he is not the only one to sense it. There is a pause in the slap of oars through the choppy swell and all the prisoners turn, crane to look. The warder on their boat returns the call: *Ahoy! Hull-oa there, Clara!*

Something begins to emerge from the fog ahead, a denseness, looming large, suddenly taking on the outline of a ship: three tall masts, bowsprit, a web of rigging, a limp riffle of sails. Haze dissolves at the waterline, revealing three other boats tied to the side of the ship, a cluster of men in new prison stripes climbing up a rope ladder, each with a bundle strapped to his back, busy seamen winching barrels and casks and baskets up to the deck. He spells out five bright letters painted in snaking script: c-l-a-r-a.

There is a clattering in the longboat as oar after oar falls slack in the rowlocks and men jostle for a better view of this, their prison, their whole universe, for the next three months.

He snatches a last look at the harbour receding in the longboat's wake. Farewell Portsmouth, wretched, miserable Portsmouth – nothing to commend it but its physical connection, through hundreds of miles of roadways and railway tracks, to a family huddled around a fire in a High Street tenement.

All he can see is fog.

His place

Lucifer slunk low to the ground, close by Willa's ankles, his head swivelling left, right, up, down, as though expecting demons behind terracotta pots and the shrivelled weeping fig by the laundry door, the same demons that had spirited him away in a wire cage, far from home, from Willa.

She stroked his loose-skinned flanks, but he would not be comforted yet, not until he had circuited his territory with her, the rooms of the house, the verandahs, the terrain of the gardens front and back, and then returned alone to scent each marker with a rub of his glossy black chin. She unpacked her suitcase, walked to the post office to collect her mail, bought bread and milk and walked home, and still he was engrossed in the business of reclaiming his place.

Tired from travelling but too unsettled to sleep, Willa flicked on the computer, cheered by the welcoming sound of its start-up routine, and then did her own circuit of the house. She had lived here as child, adolescent, university student; it had been from here she made the leap from daughter to wife, and then came back with Imogen and Lucifer nearly five years ago when Chas and Orla died. Home, she thought, pushing up the sash window in the study. There should be comfort in such a word. The air on her face was warm, with the humidity that midsummer often brings, and she opened the front door, too. The large room on the other side of the hall, mirror to the study, was unused other than for storing boxes of her parents' belongings, and the panelled door was always closed. Behind these rooms were two others, smaller but still with dimensions that soared compared with those of modern houses: her bedroom on the right, and the French-shuttered dining room on the left. Beyond that, another bedroom, the one that had been the lair of her childhood and still, if you knew where to look, bore the traces of her younger self: initials drawn in red felt pen, and enclosed in a heart, on the inside wall of the built-in robe; a loose floorboard under the desk by the window in which she had once stashed a strand of shells filched from the Freo markets that she was forever after too guilty to wear. She had hoped this room would be Imogen's when they moved from the flat, but her daughter, by then sullen and withdrawn, chose instead a small cave of a room at the rear of the house, beyond the kitchen, the bathroom, the laundry, that Orla had used for storing drygoods and Chas's homebrew and thought she might one day convert into a dark room or a computer room or a quiet little nook for reading the classics. Willa glanced at the bare face of the door. It had always seemed a one-way thing, a membrane through which Imogen's silent resentment poured in an unrelenting stream. It was still shut, but, unlike her parents' room, this one was always waiting.

Where is she…? Anxiety began to rear up but she fended it off, held it down: the only way she could keep her promise not to search for Imogen was to quash the terror of not knowing what a mother needed to know.

Raising the blinds in the open-plan living area – an extension that had been built while she was in her teens – she looked out on Orla's garden. It had managed to survive the two weeks without her. Lucifer, spent, was resting, eyes closed and chin tilted towards the sky to catch a river of light streaming through the trees. Willa smiled to think he was marking the sun as his territory, too. And though she was glad to be back in familiar surroundings, to have him home with her again, she wished she could bond as unreservedly as Lucifer with this place and its push and pull of memories.

An email from James Donaldson was in her in-box, enthusiastically accepting her offer of reciprocal research.

> Anything you can find out about that long line of Laidlaws would be welcome.
>
> Now, to your Lennies. Alex went into the Mitchell last night but the Special Collections area is being tarted up, & not before time, either. There won't be any access to Poor Relief records for another week or two. But we'll get on to it as soon as we can.
>
> Do you have anything to add to the list of family members on the 1851 and 1861 censuses? I'll check the index for all of them.
>
> This is going to be fun!
>
> James

Willa picked up her journal, turned to her sketch of the family tree, and began to type a reply, telling James about Mary's deceased husband, Felix, their soldier-son Hugh and his wife Marnie, and the several other grandchildren she had found. She also wanted to shepherd him towards Little Jock.

> Peter Lennie a.k.a. Patrick Looney is the one I'm interested in, the link to Western Australia. He was transported in 1864 under the alias John King.

There. It did not seem much for the hours spent on the *Scotland's People* site, not to mention two weeks that James Donaldson knew nothing about, that had cost her a vintage Rover P5B in immaculate condition. She sent off her reply, hoping there was enough here for him to locate something in the Poor Relief records. Guilty about the brother's wasted trip to the Mitchell Library, she resolved to start on the Laidlaw research the next day.

Trawling through microfiche indexes of births, deaths and marriages was time-consuming and hard on the eyes, but otherwise not onerous. By mid-afternoon she had accumulated a list of dates and places for the evolution of James Donaldson's antipodean Laidlaws. It was a good start.

She glanced around the Battye Library, repository for archives, publications, photographs and ephemera relating to Western Australia's history, and it occurred to her that she might be able to learn something about Little Jock's journey to Western Australia. The help desk seemed besieged, so she called up the on-line catalogue and typed *convict ships western australia*. Among the dozens of titles that appeared on the screen was *Surgeon's daily journal, Clara 1864, transcript*. She located it on the shelves and settled down to read.

The *Clara*'s voyage took ninety-three days. It carried 301 convicts aged between seventeen and fifty-seven, drawn from Chatham, Portsmouth and Portland; eighty-seven pensioner guards with their families; and twenty-five others – warders, officials and crew. Twenty children were among those on board.

Willa flicked through to the index at the back, but frustratingly those misdemeanours of Little Jock's that had lengthened his sentence had not been of sufficient note for William Crawford, RN, to have named him in the journal. At the front were the ship's Rules and Regulations, covering matters of procedure, conduct, safety, hygiene and morality.

> The behaviour of the Prisoners must be decent and becoming at all times...
>
> Cursing and all foul language, quarrelling, fighting, selling, exchanging or giving away clothes are strictly prohibited...
>
> If at any time a Prisoner has reason to complain of provoking language or treatment from the Ship's Company or Guard, he is hereby strictly enjoined not to retaliate...
>
> Captains of Division are to check any impropriety they may witness...

With what stone-cold bravado would the surgeon-superintendent have instructed convicts that 'their future prosperity and happiness will depend upon their good conduct on board'?

She waded through the pages of daily life Crawford recorded for the authorities: the weather, the daily routine of washing and cleaning and fumigating, the number sick, the issuing of lime juice and medicinal wine, the conduct of divine service, and the punishment of both prisoners and their warders – along with a surprising number of pensioner guards' wives guilty of 'disgusting language'. Two children died at Portland, before the ship made ready for sea, and a child and the wife of a soldier were 'committed to the deep' en route, but this voyage of the *Clara* was remarkable for the fact that 301 convicts were embarked and 301 were landed. On two occasions the good doctor sought the captain's permission to order corporal punishment – twenty-four lashes for attempted murder, forty-eight for 'unnatural crime' – but otherwise it had been, for Crawford anyway, an uneventful passage. Little Jock, she thought, might have seen it rather differently.

Very insightful, Mother. How unlike you.

According to a footnote in a book on convict ships, the *Clara*'s chaplain was one of a few enlightened individuals who had encouraged the convicts in his care to produce a newspaper to while away the interminable hours. Miraculously, eight issues of *A Voice of Our Exiles: or the Clara Weekly Journal* were among those that had survived, and Willa ordered a photocopy on-line from the National Library of Australia. When it arrived a week later, she was enchanted by the sheaf of handwritten pages, ornately decorated with pen drawings and flourishes, edited by convict Francis S. Simpson, an erudite wine merchant who, according to the convict dictionary, cheated his twenty-year sentence for forgery by dying of typhoid in Fremantle five years after arriving.

What did it say about news media in the twenty-first century, she wondered, that her expectations of a convict newspaper fell so wide of the mark? She had hoped for a rag, prayed for ship's gossip, life on board the *Clara* through the eyes of someone like Little Jock – although this last was surely a fanciful wish, given that most of the convicts were semi-literate at best. She had not expected *this*.

The *Clara*'s voice was lofty, witty, classically educated and quintessentially Victorian in its glorification of the arts and sciences, its exhortation to readers to strive for redemption through learning, its passing of judgment on their collective predicament by debating Bentham's principles of reform and the vexatious question of 'What shall we do with our criminals?' There were 'West Australian Sketches' by the ship's chaplain, as fascinating to Willa as they must have been to a shipload of convicts en route to the unknown; the odd contribution that she guessed might have come from one of the ship's officers; and a poetic offering from the wife of a private, 'Mrs Daly's Ode to the Sea' – but the content otherwise appeared to have been solely from the convicts themselves. Essays ranging from the philosophical to the scientific were interleaved with letters to the editor and original verse, although Simpson had felt moved to caution would-be poets:

> There is a remarkable similarity of tone and sentiment, and a perpetual recurrence of the same eternal rhymes of 'prison cells' and 'bells', 'moonbeams bright' and 'starry night', etc. Would it not be better to write indifferent prose than execrable verse?

Not necessarily, she laughed to herself.

'The Phantom Horseman' and 'A Mysterious Manuscript', lavishly illustrated, probably would have grabbed the attention of more readers than 'The Screw Propeller' and 'Ancient and Modern Navigation' did, though the unnamed poet (probably Simpson) who offered 'An Opinion' seemed less than enthusiastic about fiction:

He who writes naught save fiction
Though thrice splendid be his diction
Is not entitled to, nor can he claim
With Truth's defender glory the same
For he who doth our minds entrance
With the images of vain romance
Whose story when we have it ended
And find not mind nor manners mended
We soon forget together with who penned it
But he who doth his time employ
In Truth's fair cause, gives mankind joy
And when thro' his lines we've run
We wish they were but then begun

Other than Simpson, convict contributors appeared to have been unwilling to identify themselves, preferring pseudonyms like 'Clutha', 'Veritas', 'Nemo' and 'Cato'. Who were these highly literate, often intellectual felons? Scanning her copy of the *Clara*'s convict manifest, Willa counted sixty-nine designated 'literate' – clerks, engravers, merchants – who could have been among the *Voice*'s scribblers and scribes. And which of them was responsible for the occasional foray into typographical inventiveness, like the *W* artfully tailored to reflect its singular context?

She tried to imagine the scene as the men took turns to read the newspaper aloud, the reception of their captive listeners to philosophical ruminations. How many convicts nodded sagely, how many sat dull or dumbstruck, as Simpson foretold the demise of literature, and, though he conceived it not in these terms, the coming of the internet?

> Men, in these days of steam and electricity, write too rapidly to write well. They cater to the public taste, instead of aspiring to future fame. The day will perhaps even come when books will cease to be written at all; when the thoughts of the learned will be interchanged, developed and modified, by action and reaction, with lightning speed; and newspapers and pamphlets will form our only literature.

She glanced at the tree of Laidlaws she had just finished drawing up for James Donaldson, that she would transmit to him *with lightning speed*. What would the brothers in Glasgow think of this gathering of strangers on the other side of the world, to which they were connected by blood? Their intrepid ancestor, Hamish, had journeyed from Glasgow half a century later than Little Jock, by a less circuitous – and no doubt more comfortable – route, and, judging by this filigree of names joining names and flowering into families over the course of generations, Hamish had found his place. Could the same be said of Jock?

On the open page of her journal was a question mark in violet ink, its open curves an unfinished lemniscate, symbol of infinity. The surgeon's journal and the *Clara* newspapers had widened her perceptions of the world Little Jock inhabited, but for all she had learned – or perhaps even because of it – she despaired of ever being able to understand how he had negotiated a place for himself in that world.

Mid-February 1864

Convict transport Clara, *latitude 15° 34' N, longitude 26° 34' W*

He sniffs the air, sunrise-cool and salty, violently fresh compared with the 'tween-decks prison and its steamy ferment of bodies that have not seen soap for more than a month. The shark's tail impaled on the tip of the bowsprit for luck – seamen being a superstitious breed – has desiccated to mere leather and no longer sends a wave of rank decay wafting across the decks. And the calmer weather, more moderate seas, have for days now relieved the decks of their swill of vomit. But nausea overtakes him as he approaches the big tub of stagnant seawater, noxious enough to a nose more at home with the peculiar stenches of tenements, cities, prisons. He hunkers down, naked, for his daily humiliation, a dousing with a bucket of water from the tub, accompanied by shouts – mostly jocular, some more sinister: *Ho there, Little Jock!* Scarcely bothering with the drying rags, he dashes down the hatchway ladder to reclaim his clothes. The flannels, coarse duck trousers and fustian shirt feel like a suit of armour, reinstating him as an unexceptional number in the ship's penal population.

In the cramped prison, newly fumigated with chloride of lime, he shakes out the horsehair blanket and rolls it inside his hammock for stowing up on deck. He is ravenous for his ration of skilly, the gruel known aboard the *Clara* as 'stirabout'. Fleming, convict-captain of his mess of six, ladles it from a cast-iron pot, all the while holding forth on what he calls *matters various, young Jock, matters pressing to men in circumstances such as ours.* Words, words, words. All very well, he thinks, wooden bowl in hand, but you can't eat words.

By ten o'clock the prison is sweltering, pungent with the smell of sewage from overflowing closets, but there is no respite for those messes held back for morning school. Jock wishes he was up on deck with the other group who, after holystoning the barracks and scraping the slimy bottom boards removed from the prison, will while away the morning as idle men, although they will stir themselves into some movement that passes as exercise whenever a warder heads their way. There is not one among them, up on deck or down in the prison school, who would not sell his soul for a plug of tobacco.

He tries to shut out the unbearable, unfamiliar humidity, the longing he feels for home, the distracting, lewdly configured bodies chalked on an abandoned slate, and concentrate on what Mr Irwin is saying. The chaplain and schoolmaster is a gentle being, though he can work himself up when he sees the need. And he sees the need, and takes it very seriously, for every prisoner aboard to acquire skills in reading and writing, or advance those he already has. Jock watches Irwin turn irritable, tsking under his breath, when the notes of a melancholy ballad slip through gaps in the ship's timbers from the narrow cell beneath the fo'c's'le. It's Kennedy, beginning his second of three days on bread and water in the black box for attempting – for reasons best known to himself – to destroy his mess's water cask. Irwin waves in the direction of Jock's mess, the point of his chalk focusing on the trustworthy Fleming. *Go and tell Kennedy to hush that maudlin nonsense, or apply himself more fruitfully to the hymns of Our Lord. Better yet, take the* Voice *and read him some improving literature.*

Jock follows Fleming up the ladder, brash as you please, hoping for Irwin's leniency: having expressed a strategic interest in leaving his old religion behind him, he is temporarily in the chaplain's good Anglican graces. Even so, he half expects Irwin to yank him back down, but the fellow simply calls the sentry on the prison door for a guard to escort them to the fo'c's'le steps. *Let them up.* Up and out. Oh, those few moments of breathable air!

Irwin supplies the paper, quills and ink, but it is Francis Simpson, convict editor, whose grand ideals animate *A Voice of Our Exiles: or the Clara Weekly Journal.* He is ably assisted by other educated convicts, Fleming among their number – men, says Irwin, *fallen into the lonely byways of disrepute and sorely eager for redemption.* Their efforts in the first two issues had been read aloud in the prison after supper, and although Jock did not understand all of what he heard, nor why the writers signed off with fancy monikers rather than their real names, he was secretly all the more impressed for that. There's something suspicious, he thinks, about the idea of allowing prisoners to express their minds – although much of what they have to say seems to toe the line of every sermon he has ever heard since entering the penal system. Is that, he wonders, why they encourage the paper in the first place? *Cunning.*

Fleming's voice is booming:

Torn from all which true Englishmen most cling to and revere – the poor prisoner mourns the position now sacrificed – which he has, certainly, in former days too little valued, perhaps despised. He would not be led into a mistake in supposing that high walls and iron bars alone deprive him of liberty. Nothing can secure the Englishman of that boon but the close following of those principles which characterise the upright Englishman...

Jock watches Fleming with a measure of admiration. Ever since the Portland contingent of convicts was received on board, he has wondered whether Fleming recognised him from the holding cells beneath the Glasgow Justiciary Court. Three of them now on the *Clara* had been tried at the Autumn sessions of 1862, but James Coates Fleming – merchant and shipbroker, convicted of nineteen counts of falsehood and forgery – knew a different Glasgow from the one Jock called home. The rat-eyes of the other prisoner, James Reilly, itinerant Irish thief, had followed him from Glasgow Prison to Millbank, from Millbank to Portsmouth, but Fleming he had not seen again until the man boarded the ship from Portland. He suspects Fleming might have had a softer time of it – not that you would think so to look at him now, just one among the *Clara*'s convict cargo. Jock has not asked: Fleming disdains to discuss his own fall from grace, speaks of *the convict condition* as though it is nothing more to him than to any man interested in the affairs of the day – a difficult feat to pull off when he is costumed from neck to toe in convict garb like the rest of them. Jock warms to his jovial condescension, though the man does go on, and his speechifying around the decks can be alarming.

The dramatic reading continues:

> He whose conduct compels him to crawl in shadows
> and live in mental bondage amongst his fellow men is
> but one step removed from the despised and confined
> prisoner – no self-respect – no national pride – no
> English heart beats in him...

Sensing he is losing his audience, Fleming flicks through the stiff foolscap pages, looking for something to cheer up the man sweating in the black box, so confined, so narrow that he can neither lie down to sleep nor find a comfortable stance for his body. He pauses with a snort. *Listen to Simpson, dizzy on his high horse!*

> We have received some verses, purporting to be original,
> entitled 'Confession and Resolution', and 'The Bible's
> Perfections'. As they have evidently been transcribed
> from the poems of a monkish rhymer of the fourteenth
> century, we decline to insert them in this journal. They
> first appeared contemporaneously with the 'Vision of
> Piers Ploughman' at a time when our English metre was
> still in an unsettled state, and are noticed by Wharton
> in his 'History of English Poetry'. The Plagiarist has
> not even copied them correctly.

Fleming winks. *Let that be a lesson to us all, young Jock.*

Jock cannot fathom what the joke might be but grins nevertheless. Fleming, though surely but a few years older than Jock, has a knack, with his superior air and his *young Jocks*, of making him feel as young as a pup, and every bit as eager to please.

Kennedy seems monumentally unimpressed with their improving literature. Turning his back on the two of them, he pours his heart into another lament.

∞

The midday dose of lime juice and sugar attacks the ulcers in Jock's mouth and he cannot manage any biscuit, the hardtack as rough as holystone on bloody gums. Reilly skulks along the deck, his once-pasty face damp and ruddy, and crouches by Jock in the boiling shade.

Would you not be wanting that, then, Little Jock? The sing-song whine lingers on the *Little*.

Jock is quick to hand over the biscuit and then hauls himself to his feet, preferring the sizzle of sweat on his skin to the dread he feels in Reilly's presence. He glances down on hearing a word muttered through a mouthful of hardtack, but perhaps it is the wind playing tricks on his ears, for Reilly seems fully absorbed, as though his life's work it is to chew thoroughly and chew well.

From the prison deck the men can hear the families of the pensioner guards, former soldiers who have surrendered their military pensions in exchange for a better life in the new world. Children's play, laughter, scolding and the slap of a hand, nursery songs, wailing babies, women conversing or quarrelling or cursing – if the prisoners close their eyes, these sounds are capable of taking them somewhere else, a place growing ever further away with each nautical mile the *Clara* sails. It is torture for men with families they will almost certainly never see again to catch these reminders on the Atlantic breeze, blown from the deck above them – men like Fleming, though Fleming vows his wife and baby boy will join him in Swan River Colony ere two years have gone by. Jock turns away when he hears this, tells himself he is lucky to be unburdened by such pulls on the heart. He glances down at the tattoo on his hand. He can do nothing for his own any more.

Dr Crawford crosses the deck with a grim face, and the murmur goes around that his patient, fearfully ill this last week, is unlikely to survive the hour.

…And the sea gave up the dead which were in it; and death and hell delivered up the dead which were in them: and they were judged every man according to their works…

The words of the chaplain drift down the hatchways into the prison. Poor lady, Jock thinks, glad she cannot hear this mournful drone, need not hearken to its *death* and *hell*. He, last to descend the ladder at day's end, had seen her carried up from the hospital to the quarterdeck, trussed in oatmeal bags sewn together and tied with sennit. The body of Mrs Trueman, wife of Corporal Trueman, departed from this life at four bells, was body-shaped still, smooth and featureless, as no doubt befits a corpse. Peaceful, too, he would like to think, as he imagines her sliding into the deep with more grace than Mr Irwin can muster for the occasion. He remains close to the hatch, listening.

…Amen.

After a few moments of silence, there is an unseemly splash.

He cannot get it out of his mind, the body of Mrs Trueman, a woman-shaped hull, lost without masts or sails, no wheel to guide her. Later he asks Fleming where she will drift, finally come to land.

She will not be washing ashore, young Jock, he says. *They will have weighted the corpse with ballast. She will sink with the fishes, may the Lord rest her soul.*

Oh, he says, unwilling to let his mind go to this terrible place. *But if they dinnae, what then?*

Fleming takes down one of his books, a library loan courtesy of the chaplain, and opens it to a map of the world, a mosaic of strange shapes with incomplete borders, vast stippled expanses that Fleming tells him are ocean.

We are about here, he says, pointing, *between Africa and Brazil, but closer to Africa.*

In his hammock that night, Jock dreams of the oatmeal-bag cerements drying in the tropic sun, bleaching white, perishing, on the African shore, and the body of Mrs Trueman spilling out into a new world to be judged according to her works.

Late March 1864

Convict transport Clara, *latitude 40° 44′ S, longitude 44° 59′ E*

The noise is worse at night, when only the requisite number of crewmen are awake and on deck, and those few subdued in the solemn, vast darkness. Without human activity to mask it, the restless character of the frigate-built ship is magnified: the ceaseless creaking expansion and contraction of timbers; the knots straining in the rigging, vibrating like the strings of a parlour quartet; the symphony of sails with their thrumming, whistling, skirling in the wind. And when the great gales of the Indian Ocean rage by and seas thunder against the hull, the stout masts of the *Clara* quake.

Jock is wide-eyed, still warm from the regulation half-gill of watered wine. Earlier Fleming had shown him the ship's location on the map, adrift in the limitless ocean, and when he saw how far they were from the solid shapes of continents, even from the tiny specks that are islands, he could not think how they could ever survive, find their way to land again. He shudders, overawed by visions of giant jaws and cavernous ribs, conjured from Mr Irwin's preaching. He is disinclined to believe that a man could live inside a whale for three days and three nights but Mr Irwin is a religious man and is not supposed to lie. And is that so different, after all, to being trapped in the belly of a ship, deep below the water line, the weight of the ocean heaving against the curved timber ribs and planking? He shudders again, remembering the story going round the messes: that the ship's hull, the only thing between soul and sea, is sheathed in soft, white pine as an offering for marauding worms, and that if the *Clara* should be prevented from reaching port in good time, Neptune's minions would eat through the outer layer and begin on the oaken hull. *Nonsense!* Fleming declared. *The* Clara *is not constructed that way: she is a modern vessel, well protected with plates of muntz metal. Nothing will be eating through that!* Jock knows it is Fleming's word he should trust, the word of a clever, educated man, but Fleming had not scoffed at Mr Irwin's story about a man living inside a whale – so who can be certain? This night, with the ship shrieking and the timbers groaning, so far from where they have come and where they have yet to journey, he fancies he can hear the slimy, sucking sounds of a thousand sea worms devouring the *Clara*'s sacrificial skin.

It is a mystery to him how the rest can sleep. He looks around at the occupied hammocks strung up like so many puddings in calico bags. There are always one or two empty, one or two figures prowling through the hold. He listens, trying to isolate those sounds – footfall, an unmuffled cough – amid the grunts and snores of the sleeping. A faint scuffling near the closet, not far from his mess. His first thought is of raisins. It is generally known that a quantity has been filched from the galley, though no one is admitting to the as-yet undiscovered deed, nor divulging where the treasure is stowed. Provisions are dwindling after fifty-eight days at sea, and the resulting monotony of salt horse and suet, salt horse and barley, salt horse and pickles, is wearing down spirits and needling tempers. He would like to locate those raisins for himself, but only a fool would steal from a thief in a shipload of felons.

Glad of the distraction, he tumbles noiselessly from the hammock and creeps towards the place where he thinks the sound came from, dodging the swaying puddings. Spying movement behind a stack of buckets, he grins, thinking to catch the raisin-thief and thus to be paid in kind for silence. But there are two bodies in the dark recess between the buckets and the closet, two bodies and not a raisin in sight.

He draws back, crouching, still. Here is intimacy of the kind repugnant to prison authorities, the kind they seek to nip in the bud by stripping out sleeping berths on convict transports and replacing them with hammocks. *The evils of association.*

He remembers.

The rat-eyes of James Reilly always remind him.

He had shared a cell with Reilly in Glasgow Prison. They were there only a month, between conviction in the Justiciary Court and transfer to Millbank, but what manna for the warden who conducted the hated dry-bath after admission, probing orifices for tobacco and homemade weaponry. *Strip – legs apart – arms up – mouth open – touch toes!* A man who loved his work.

Jock flinched, cried out, as the warden's pudgy fingers fumbled and thrust into him, unexpectedly breaching a fold of skin. He heard a sharp gasp.

Away and what ha' we here, then!

He spun Jock round, stared and stared, and when it seemed that his eyes could bulge no more he flicked a hand towards the nubby member sprouting from its wiry nest. *Weel, ye dinnae look like no lassie the Lord made. But ye'll do, aye, ye'll do, lad.*

The warden returned after dark with an iron bar and a tub of muttonfat. Six times in four weeks he returned.

The bar at his throat, the grit floor at his back, Jock became a child once more, a child on a journey from Omagh to Belfast, shrinking into nothing to escape – squeezing out of his skin, suspending the soft pith of himself just beyond reach, blind and deaf and senseless. Of the rape he recalls nothing, naught but an image after: his cell-mate Reilly, half terrified, half incredulous, witness to all Jock would will himself to forget. Reilly, silenced by the flame of the warden's candle held to his face, singeing his brows, and the mocking warning: *An' ye'll no' be saying nothing, neither. Willya, eh! Willya!*

It is different, what is before him now between the buckets and the closet of the prison hold. Lust, yes, and rough enough, but no violence – no more, no less, than the nighttime couplings of John and Roseanne, Hugh and Marnie. A thread of moonlight reveals the intimate lattice of their fingers, and he is humbled to witness such trust, surely a thing of wonder in a place like this.

Dropping his eyes, he creeps away, bumping into hammocks, stepping on the foot of another prowler.

The evening is calm, unnaturally still after the savagery of the previous night's gale. Surgeon-Superintendent Crawford blots the page of his journal, having noted the ship's position, the ambient temperature, the number of prisoners in sick bay, and ponders the events of the morning, which bode not to his liking. Taking up his quill, he records how he began the day by taking stock of prisoner Moore's bruising, he having been *rather knocked about in the black box during the night*. In view of the man's obvious repentance – *he had promised to be a well-conducted prisoner during the passage* – Crawford had opted for leniency. But he could not show the same in the case of the two who had been dealt with on the prison deck before noon.

Dipping the quill again, he writes his official account in the Surgeon's Journal:

> J. S. of 13 Mess, J. G. 13 Mess, were reported by several Prisoners and seen in the act of committing an unnatural crime by J. P. of the same Mess. Both these men have been punished with 48 lashes on the Buttocks in the presence of others who are suspected of the same offence. They confessed their guilt during Punishment and promised never to do the like again.

Jock shivers in his hammock, staring up at the timber planking forming the prison deck, its boards caulked tight with pitch and fibres of oakum. Red, it looks to him, and how could it not be so, soaked as it was with blood when the cat bit at their flesh, again and again until their arms, pinioned to the apex of the triangular frame, dragged with the weight of their slumped bodies. He has seen men flogged before, for plotting escape, for wounding, for violence. But what he witnessed this day – was hauled out especially to witness, it having been noticed that he, too, had been out of his hammock at night – has purged the heat from him. Fear breathes on his neck, curdles in his gut. *Unnatural*, they called it. Unnatural, and a crime. Even Fleming had looked pained, quoted fancy words from the Bible. Imagine what damnation the Bible might hold for one as unnatural as Jock.

He fingers the crescent, star and flower on his left forearm, feeling the stamp of them though the skin is smooth, and shivers anew at all the ways the world has thought up to punish what is not the same.

Nothing penetrates the seal of pitch and oakum, proof against the rush of ocean over deck in the strongest gale. But he lies awake expectantly, watching for the drip of blood.

Mid-April 1864

Convict transport Clara, *off the town of Fremantle, Swan River Colony*

Long before the low sandy shore of the Western board of Australia is visible, a peculiar and almost indescribable odour pervading the atmosphere intimates to the sensitive olfactories of the wearied voyager his near approach to land...

Life, thinks Jock, remembering Mr Irwin's lecture. It is the smell of life, the living come to wake the dead. And indeed, until that first intimation that land was ahead, life seemed to have left those on board the *Clara*, in spirit if not in the pump of the heart. There had been no sign of the world ashore for thirty days since, when a flock of Cape pigeons had followed the ship for some hours, the whites of their underwings and bellies dazzling in the sun. But they had grown tired of the *Clara*, as though knowing what was ahead and unwilling to join company with the ship's misery. All on board were sorry to see them wheel away from the bow. In the last sluggish weeks, the prisoners had dragged themselves through days in a torpor of despondency as though dosed with some potent soporific. Gone was the incessant babble of the prison hold as each man shut down, sealed off, wasted it seemed from the effort it took to imagine the voyage could end. Even the crew, perpetually in motion, had become listless during the ship's passage across the Indian Ocean.

Proving Mr Irwin's words true, this strange, sharp smell of life is soon followed by a cry from the watch: *Land!* Those below in the morning school abandon their slates and risk being ironed to swarm up the hatchways. By the time Jock finds some small space to squirm into, both sides of the ship are lined with men, a corrugation of heads like an ornamental railing, all scanning the low coastline on the horizon.

The nearer they get, the more each one feels a blanket of awe descending, a terrible, forbidding awe at the magnitude of their situation, brought fifteen thousand miles to a settlement that can scarcely be called such if this barren approach, this unpeopled waste, is its welcome to the world. *Mother of God*, the man beside Jock whispers. *They have sent us to purgatory.*

The first aspect of the place is anything but pleasing: for the only salient points from the ship's deck are the Prison, at one end, and Arthur's Head with its small light-house at the other, near the mouth of the Swan.

School is abandoned for the day, and all remain on deck for as long as Crawford tolerates their presence, which licence ceases at the approach of the government pilot boat come to guide them to anchor.

Down in the hold Jock feels the hush of uncertainty all around as men shuffle their feet, anxious to stand firm on land again but knowing themselves to be exchanging one prison for another. He glances at Fleming, composed as always, reading the *Voice* with the demeanour of a man with a cigar in his hand and a day of idle ease stretching before him.

Come now, young Jock, he says. *From a sink of mud might come a pearl. Hear what our good Mr Irwin has to say in his last missive:*

> We assert, without fear of contradiction, that the climate is healthful, and becomes agreeable when use has blunted the sting of the mosquito, and tempered the eye of the northern denizen to the glorious effulgence of a southern sun; that, without holding out the slightest prospect of the speedy acquirement of wealth, the colony offers a fair prospect of employment to all who mean 'work' – to those who do not – hopeless and unrequited toil – and that the right hand of friendship is never withheld from the honest and industrious convict-settler…

What say you, Jock? Do you see yourself in the guise of honest and industrious convict-settler?

While Jock is puzzling to himself on the virtue of honesty, word buzzes through the prison that the pilot has come aboard, and with him a consignment of fresh beef and vegetables.

By the time night falls, the ship rocking gently at anchor, he is not the only one to be feeling more kindly disposed to this new colony as a bountiful supper of stew is slopped into his wooden bowl. Slightly gritty it might be, but the plenteous serving and the glorious absence of strings of salt meat are blessings to more than compensate. He remembers that Irwin had warned them about Fremantle, all glare and limestone, how it had looked to him *like a town where all the inhabitants were bakers, everybody and everything visible powdered with a white sandy dust resembling flour.*

He does not think there would be one among them this day who would not willingly exchange salt for sand.

William Crawford, RN, writes his entry in the Surgeon's Journal for 14 April 1864. Only two more entries remain for this, the second voyage of the ship *Clara* to Swan River Colony, and then he will submit the journal in duplicate, his service over. He is proud to record that when the ship was inspected by the Superintendent at Fremantle, Mr Lefroy, and Colonel Bruce of the Volunteer Forces, *the former officer stated he had never seen men in such order.* No convict had perished under his care and supervision. One hundred had already been landed, chained and ironed, and marched from the jetty through town to the limestone prison situated on a ridge behind it; the rest will leave tomorrow, along with hammocks and blankets and undispensed medical comforts. This motley assortment of men from all over Her Majesty's realm will be someone else's problem.

He picks up the bound sheaf of foolscap he had found in the sick bay – an issue of *A Voice of Our Exiles* – and idly glances through it, pausing to read.

> Time, the great Physician, may heal the rankling sore, may mellow the chastened sorrow, but can never eradicate the deep, deep sense of soul-agony which a man can pass through in two short years. There are moments that seem months: there are events that require no note-book to record, no effort of memory to recall. They are scarred on the brain for ever. Such will occur to every thinking man during that blot in his existence – a term of penal servitude.

He considers appending it to the copy of his journal to be handed in to the Convict Establishment, as further proof – should any be needed – of his ability not only to command order but to engender proper feeling in the convict population under his care. In truth, though, he knows that in doing so he would be taking over-much credit and eliding the influence of his colleague Mr Irwin.

On second thoughts, he files the convict journal away among his own papers – a trophy of sorts, a curio to be exclaimed over by the eager folk back home.

Mother-in-waiting

Lucifer, in the midst of his fastidious ablutions, froze at the unfamiliar peal of the doorbell.

Willa scratched the space between his flattened ears. *It's OK, old boy*, she said, lifting him off the computer desk. *Let's go and see.*

She recognised the figure on the other side of the leadlights, though it had been a while since his last delivery. The courier was in the process of tucking an airbag under the coir mat when she opened the door, startling him.

Oh, you ARE here. He picked up the bag by one corner, gave it a none-too-gentle flick to shake off the sand, and thrust it at her.

She took the package, feeling the obvious shape of a book inside the thick plastic. *Do I need to sign?* But he was already skipping his way down the verandah stairs.

Willa gently deposited the squirming Lucifer on the floorboards, catching her reflection in the bevelled mirror of the hallstand as she stood up. Funny, she thought, how she could be oblivious to an image seen twice a day in the bathroom mirror.

But an unexpected glimpse like this, distorted in the ripple of old glass, took her unawares, snagged her attention.

It was nearly a year since she had shorn off her hair, scraped the surfaces of herself back to bone. Her hair grazed her shoulders now. She was not as thin, as ragged. Sunlight haloed the dull black of her jeans and T-shirt, seeking out the blue-green of her eyes and in the moonstone ring Matthew had given her – *from the baby* – when they found out that she was pregnant at last. Most of the stones were scratched, the result of too much attention from small, stubby fingers and milk teeth, but still they glowed as her hand moved to trace the lines on her face. *Adularescence*, it was called, this blooming of moonstone, and the thought occurred to Willa: This is what grief is like. Always waxing and waning as you move, but never dying away.

She had rushed to order the book after chancing on an internet review. How could she resist *a biography of a nineteenth-century surgeon well known in colonial military circles who was, on death, exposed as a hermaphrodite*? She curled up in Chas's high-backed recliner with the story of Dr James Barry. The book's back cover outlined the facts of Barry's life: his 'mysterious childhood', his obsession with anatomy, obstetrics and midwifery, the brilliant theses he wrote on the subjects of inguinal hernia and the comparative structure of the male and female pelvic anatomy, his successful career as an army surgeon, with postings at Cape Town, Malta and Corfu. But, as the blurb revealed, on the death of this distinguished medico in 1865, sensational claims were put forward that he was, variously, a woman or an 'imperfectly developed man'.

Willa had known, from the review, that Barry's was a fascinating story, that he was a complex individual full of contradictions – a 'noted dandy' belligerent in the face of authority, a passionate humanitarian who championed patients' rights and equitable medical treatment for the poor. But after reading long past dusk, stopping only when Lucifer howled at the outrageous absence of fish in his bowl, she found herself returning again and again to the biographical fact that had caught her interest above all others: that it was this same Dr James Barry who had performed the first successful caesarean section known to Western medicine.

Restless, she wandered around the house, switching on lamps and pulling down blinds as if such trivial routines could quell the rise of a memory that was buried deeper than the others, because it was a beginning.

Everyone is masked and white-coated, infused with urgency and purpose. But she can do nothing – she who should be the one labouring, she who has been disempowered, robbed of this right by the capricious mispositioning of a wayward placenta. And so she lies, conscious but dazed, sensation blocked from the waist down, a mother-in-waiting relegated to the wings of her own debut.

A dragging sensation as the bloodied body is pulled from her own, cradled in sterile arms, whisked away.

The evaporation of a clammy warmth when Matthew abruptly releases her hand from his.

The huddle of white coats under white light.

A pointless threshing, a helpless wrestling with the tube taped to the back of her hand, as they ease her onto a gurney – *No, no!* – and still she has not seen…has not touched…they said she could hold…where…

Silence when she wakes.

She longs for the comfort of cliché; the claim of all new mothers to superlatives, blithe assumptions, an inheritance of recycled images from every happy-ever-after movie ever made. She wants a nurse to place an angel in her arms and smile beatifically at her and Matthew and say, *Congratulations! You have a daughter!* But when they arrive, in their white coats, their stainless steel, with her baby in a plastic bassinette on wheels, no one coos and smiles. No one says *adorable* or *the sweetest thing*. No one says *perfect*.

It is not the way a love is supposed to begin.

She had seen it on the ultrasound, the way the unreliable placenta had lodged over the cervix. Somewhere on the periphery of awareness she had heard a nurse cluck: *Imagine trying to push a baby out with that in the way!*

Imagine.

Women died before Dr Barry proved they did not have to.

Tender from the afterbirth of memory, she jumped at the computer's sharp, tinny ring. Lucifer was stretched out in front of the humming screen, and she moved his tail from the keyboard to check her email. There, in the in-box, was James Donaldson's name, with a parade of exclamation marks marching across the subject line: poor relief records at last!!!!!!!!!!!!!!

    Dear Willa
    Success! I found Poor Relief applications
    for John & Roseanne, Hannah, Hugh & Marnie:
    full transcriptions in the file attached.
    Also some index references to check,
    possibly Bridget & Mary, but I ran out

of time (I forgot the Special Collections section closes at five – very public service of them). Nothing, I'm afraid, for your Peter/Patrick, either as a Lennie or as John King (a surprising choice of alias for an Irishman!).

I've always been amazed at how detailed the inspectors' reports are. Makes for fascinating reading.

Now, you'll see some references to Barnhill, a.k.a. Towns Hospital – this was the City Poorhouse. Barnhill was a dreaded fate, and it left its mark on Glasgow's memory. I can remember people of my parents' generation saying, 'Don't do such-and-such or you'll be ending up in Barnhill!' – & this was long after the place had been torn down.

As suspected, your Lennies did not have an easy life.

I wish you could see the microfilms for yourself. They take on a life of their own on the handwritten pages. You can almost see the expression on the inspector's face! Maybe one day you will come to Glasgow & I can give you the complete 'genie tour'!

Kind regards

James

A faint smile as Willa, just for one moment, imagined herself doing the things ordinary people did. It was hard not to like this James Donaldson. But she had been to Glasgow, she reminded herself. The smile faded.

She opened and printed the attachment and began to read. Scanning the pages quickly, she was struck by a common detail. What did it mean that the Lennies were unanimous, here, in claiming to be from County Tyrone? When welfare was at stake, were people more truthful, or more careful in presenting a consistent story? Or had she been right in guessing that the reference to County Armagh had been an error of transcription, a misrepresentation of the town Omagh?

Omagh. Tyrone. She felt a rush of connectedness, the likes of which Orla's St Patrick's Day parties could never have inspired.

She returned to the first page, reading carefully. James had begun with the earliest application, dated 1851: Jock's brother Hugh complaining of ill health and being admitted to Towns Hospital. Next was Marnie, Hugh's wife, who applied in 1860 when Hugh joined the army. She applied three more times in the same year, citing the illness of her children, but the inspector seemed suspicious, at one point noting that two of the children were 'not at school and not seen.' In the following year she was 'said to be dying' but clearly made a miraculous recovery: she was still around in 1884, by then a widow, complaining of 'debility and swollen feet.' She died in the Poorhouse in 1885.

Hannah's application, dated 1860, sketched a harrowing picture in few details. Residing in a Night Asylum with an infant born in the City Poorhouse, she had been deserted by her husband, Michael.

Willa felt a spasm in her throat when she read John's first application. Here he was, in January 1865, being described as 'Son of Felix Lonie a labourer and Mary Rafferty *both dead*.' Later, in 1874, he was admitted to the Poorhouse. The inspector who visited Roseanne and her four children remarked: 'Applicant's house and the manner it is kept makes it perfect hotbed for all description of disease.' In 1888 Roseanne, 'wholly disabled' with bronchitis, declared that John had died of consumption.

Willa laid aside the transcriptions. James was right: none of them had had an easy life. But it was learning of Mary's death, less than a year after Jock was transported, that affected her most, felt like a loss of her own. What might James find of Mary when next he was able to access the records?

The circle of moonstones glowed under lamplight, as green, as blue, as the ocean. She grieved for this Irish mother who had fled to Glasgow for survival, and for Jock, thousands of miles away in the new world, believing himself remembered. Would he ever have known of Mary's death?

Late May 1864

Albany Road work party

It has been raining all night – long, drenching showers that have filled buckets and boots and barrows. Huddling awake inside the hut, listening to the downpour drumming the earth around him, he half expected the land to saturate, send floodwaters swirling into the makeshift structure of brushwood and paperbark to carry him and his two companions off on a muddy stream. But the deluge has drained away, soaked into subterranean seas, and this morning there is no sign of scouring, just damp, damp earth.

No one else is yet awake, but a warm pink backlighting the rapidly receding clouds tells him it will not be long before the rest are up and grumbling for damper and treacle. Jock rummages in his bundle and pulls out a twist of newspaper, an old piece discarded by McGregor and still smelling of his tobacco. It is easy on the eyes, this strip torn from the front page, for the notices of *goods just arrived* and *healthful comforts* are in larger letters than the colony's news. *H-O-L-L-O-W-A-Y-S*, he spells out, practising.

DISEASES ATTENDED ON CHILDHOOD

Diseases incident to the early life fall more under the management of the mother than the medical man. Holloway's Ointment should therefore be regarded by her as a 'Household Treasure', as it never fails in bringing out the rash in measles and scarlatina; and for the removal of all skin diseases its effect is miraculous…

Many of the words are a puzzle but the idea of the whole comes through. He thinks of the baby Felixes who died, of Roseanne's little Bridget, and vows to send home a pot of this Holloway's Ointment when he is a man of means, and free.

Reading is easier than writing, he thinks, staring down at the blank square of paper, no longer pristine, that he was issued at Fremantle Prison a month before. He smoothes it flat with his jacket sleeve.

What to say? How to explain the riddle of this prison with no bars, no walls, no chains? A man could, if the fancy took him, turn tail and flee into the bush and just keep running, run all day and all night, run until his lungs panted dry, and never see another soul to call him to halt. But what gain? There are no vennels and wynds and tenements here, no mass of population into which a stranger could disappear, to emerge with a new name. The bars of this prison are the ocean and the desert; the walls are the certainty of capture by black trackers; its chains, the promise of early release, a species of freedom called ticket of leave.

Will they want to know this?

He looks over towards McGregor's tent, wondering whether he is yet awake and of a mood to be approached for ink or pencil. Already the camp is stirring and he can hear the fruity curses of the man whose job it is, on this sodden morning, to cajole a fire into life. The thought of billy tea, hot and aromatic, takes hold and he stuffs the paper back in his bundle and rummages for his pannikin.

Though his muscles gripe at the end of the day, the work is nothing to a Portsmouth veteran. The party of forty, led by McGregor, is forming the foundations of a section of road to replace a bush track so wheel-rutted and narrow he can scarcely believe it supports all traffic between Perth, the colony's capital, and Albany, its mail port on the edge of the Southern Ocean. There is something in his allotted task of carting gravel in barrows from the dump to the head of the works that brings to mind a lad trundling a whirley of coal in the dark heart of Govan. But it is only the merest glimmer of memory, for what could be more foreign to the Glasgow pits than this startling blue sky, this endless space, this glossing of every surface under a naked autumn sun?

McGregor is a man of the land, could live off its bounty, he says, *for good an' all if 't weren't for the love of me 'bacca*. He supplements the party's rations of flour, tea, sugar and potatoes with fresh kill. Kangaroo, rabbit, opossum and cockatoo have found favour with the convict workers, but bandicoot is another matter. Some of the men view with suspicion this scurrying little creature, muttering among themselves that they have *never yet sunk so low as to eat rats and willna be starting now*.

Jock has never eaten so much meat in his life. Listening to the evening's testimonials to McGregor's wallaby stew – *Sweet as chicken, dark as best partridge. No better to be had at the Frog and Whistle* – he thinks of home. For all that he has always valued bulk of any kind to line his stomach, he had come to loathe the tasteless mush called pease brose that appeared day after day in Glasgow. He would chide Bridget as she ground the dried peas under a pestle of stone and mixed it into a paste to be thinned and thinned again. *Muck it looks and muck it tastes!*

Ha! she would sniff. *So however did you get to be so stout on naught but muck, then?*

He wishes she was here, his Bridget. How she would heal and fatten – how all of them would thrive – on a goodly dose, and regular, of McGregor's meaty stew.

Darkness falls early in the new world, and the light is already failing as he digs out the square of paper again. McGregor's fire crackles to the accompaniment of a cranky applause as forty men slap at mosquitoes.

He stares at the page. Would they want to hear about the ragged screech of parrots at dawn, the dying cry of the raven dissolving into night? What it feels like to stand on this land, puny and powerless and at the mercy of its whims?

He claps palm over wrist, and blood spatters from a plump mosquito onto the otherwise blank page.

Away and be damn!

He shoves it back into his bundle. His letter has waited this long; it can wait till tomorrow.

Each Sunday, after their weekly shear-and-shave, McGregor unrolls the schedule with its rows of minute handwritten numbers. One by one they come up to inspect their accumulation of marks towards ticket of leave. Reading along the column for number 7756, Jock sees that McGregor is allocating him three or four marks a day: three for 'very good behaviour'; four, 'exemplary'. He had been dismayed to learn that minor wrongs aboard the *Clara* – failing to wash his spoon, being reported out of his hammock after dark – had added time to his sentence. But he understands it now, the simple equation of behaviour to reward, and is taking on in earnest the goal of getting his ticket a year from September.

Well satisfied, he retrieves the paper from his hut again and asks McGregor for the loan of pen and ink.

McGregor eyes him, surprised, and gestures at the page. *How do you come to have that? You know the rules, Little Jock. Only one letter every three months. You'll not be due yet.*

He looks down. *It's m'arrival allowance. Ah havenae used it.*

McGregor shakes his head and hands over a pencil. *The cart is due tomorrow, so best be quick about it. You'll be fretting, as it is, when the others get their replies afore you.*

Jock settles himself beneath a peppermint tree and picks up the page again, the paper grubby and dog-eared, a corner smeared with blood. Early-morning sun flashes through long fingers of leaves.

What, out of all there is to say, shall he tell them? What can he say with one square of paper and the words he knows how to form?

A shiny jewel, brilliant gold and green and splashed with rows of rubies, drops from the sky and lands on the page. Entranced, he waits for the creature to fly away, but when it does not he takes it as a sign. Johnson has a pink cockatoo that walks along his arm; Williams, a tiny possum called Glossop, says he, *after me uncle, because 'e's got a tail on 'im what makes me think of the old bastard's whiskers.* Jock aspires to such companionship but baulks at the idea of keeping as a pet something McGregor is as like to cook for supper.

Felix, now, there's a good name, a name he'd like to have an excuse for saying out loud again.

Balancing the paper carefully on his hand, he carries it to the wagon where McGregor leans in a reverie of tobacco smoke.

What've you got there? the man says.

Jock removes his cupped hand as though unveiling a prize.

Ah, it's just an Albany jewel beetle, man. You can find 'em by the hundreds when certain trees're in flower. Bloody nuisance. He peers closer, gives it a nudge with his yellow thumb. *Nearly dead, I'd say. They don't live long, a couple or three weeks. Just long enough to mate. What a life, eh?*

Jock returns to the peppermint and picks up McGregor's pencil again. He stares glumly at the page, blank but for the tremble of wings, the furious quiver of tiny antennae, and he is suddenly taken with the thought that he might, instead of labouring in the puzzle of words, fold his page in half and press the body of this creature between it, certain it could say as much, and delight more, than his struggling efforts with letters could do.

But he gently deposits it on a flower-cluster blown from a gum tree.

Dere Mery, he writes, *I yam arivd in Swon Rivvr I yam qite well…*

∞

When the supply cart arrives back at the Albany Depot, it carries an unsealed letter addressed in McGregor's black ink to *Mrs Mary Lennie, 23 High Street, Glasgow.* The Superintendent quickly scans the page and then, after stamping the missive with the Convict Establishment's waxen seal, records a deduction of sixpence postage from the account of number 7756.

Perhaps, after five months by sailing ship, rail and carriage, the cheap parchment square will be passed from door to door around the hovels of 23 High Street. And perhaps, eventually, it will be discarded underfoot, kicked and scuffed into the snow, pulped under horses' hooves and the wheels of barrows.

October 1865

Perth

The news that he would be transferred to the colony's capital to begin his ticket of leave had kindled Jock's homesickness for the teeming life of a busy city. It has taken him a month to become accustomed to the reality that is Perth.

His arms ache from carrying the basket high, stiff-armed and awkward, along the sandy track. It will be back to the depot if the goods are soiled before he delivers them, and he is anxious to hold on to his embryonic freedom. He has already had to detour to avoid the morning storm of dust and grit kicked up by the movement of the town herd down Wellington Street to the Commonage, a cloud that hangs thick in the air long after the cows have ambled by.

Relieved to reach the partially macadamised stretch of Cemetery Road, he pauses under a tree to rest his arms and takes a peek under the cloth protecting the large basket. *Beautiful.* He longs to, but dares not, stroke the fine muslin petticoats, with Kat's tiny stitches, invisible to eyes that have not seen her labour over them, and Bridie's loops and coils and petals in pastel silks. Surely the skirts will float when unfolded and flounced out, held against the frame of some rich colonist's wife or daughter. Imagine – he cannot – the feeling of such fabric, light as breeze, against the skin. Too bad it will soon be dragging in the sand.

Tucking the cloth firmly down, he sets off towards the large white house of Mr Phillips in Adelaide Terrace.

∽

The cathedral chimes ten as he heads back down Cemetery Road with an empty basket and a leisurely gait, having delivered to three fashionable Terrace residences. Mr Buchan's clientele is strictly 'city', as they are wont to call this village of sand and fleas and flies: there are none in the new town east of the swamp who can afford his wares, other than *certain ladies* in Stirling Street when particularly flush after race days.

At the cemetery gate he can see the trees beyond, and decides to take a shortcut, conscious as he does of the small pleasures of freedom. A pipe and two shillings in his pocket. Two pound-notes in the heel of his workman's boot. Unshaven whiskers lengthening on lip and chin. Which way he goes a matter for his own fancy. Who would exchange places with Kat and Bridie, plying their needles all hours of the day in a small, cramped workroom of corrugated iron?

On either side of the oystershell path through the burial ground are monuments of white marble with low friezework fences, angels on plinths of polished granite, tall crosses, weighty ledgers. Ivy and roses struggle in the sun. Dry grass grows among forests of wooden crosses plainly carved with names and dates. And across the road, separated from decent folk, is an allotment for the bodies of felons and suicides, unmarked and overgrown. The stench of the government slaughterhouse in nearby Claise Brook wafts across the cemetery and right through the new town whenever the wind gets choppy. But if the living can get used to it, he supposes, so indeed can the dead.

He reaches the stand of mulberries off Trafalgar Road and climbs up into a forked branch to fill his basket with leaves for Mr Buchan's silkworms. From here he can see across to the river flats, deserted this morning. But once when he had come near dusk, there had been a small group of natives, cloaks of kangaroo over their skinny frames, fishing in the shallows with long spears. He had seen natives in the bush near the Albany Road, was alarmed at first at their approach, until McGregor greeted them briskly and set about an exchange of a bit of flour for bush honey. But in Perth he has seen only those fishermen. According to Mrs Buchan, so Kat tells him, the town blacks are *beggars one and all, a shiftless bunch, infested with disease*. But Mrs Buchan has scarcely a soft word to say of anyone. Ticket-of-leavers such as he are representatives of the *moral contamination wrought upon us all by the convict plague. Vermin*, she pronounces the shiploads of Irish girls like Kat and Bridie, brought out, the colonists hoped, to be brides for expirees. *And you should hear that woman bray about public houses*, Kat says, *and 'the intemperate who are dragging the colony into ruin.'* He remembers the wary fishermen in their kangaroo cloaks, keeping to themselves any views they might have on the likes of Mrs Buchan. As do Kat and Bridie. As does he.

Kat, loud and luminous, had tried to tease him with a kiss before he had been at Buchan's a day. She laughed when he pulled away, the wet kiss sliding from his face like water from glass.

How ould are you, then? she demanded.

Twenty-six, twenty-seven, thereaboots.

Ach, the ouldest virgin in Swan River, to be sure. Or you've been too long with men in prison, is it?

Drawn to the lilt of her voice, the memory of belonging it stirred in him, he began to watch Kat – so often that she noticed, and mocked him. *Poor Little Jock has missed his chance and must look to his own self for a good time now!* He watched her at her work, silk trailing through her fingers, skeins looping around her hands. He watched her slip out with Aled, the wheelwright's boy, to the laneway behind the stable, and heard the rush of his own blood, *missed-his-chance, missed-his-chance*, plumping up those places in him no one must see. When he flung himself face down on the palliasse beside the copper, he was watching her still, *no-chance, no-chance*, body chafing against the horsehair blanket. Late one night he watched unseen as she rose naked from the tub before the kitchen fire, hair pale as tallow dripping down her back. And he knew then that the one thing he wanted more than Kat was to be her, to step inside the guise of that cool, white skin.

He felt himself warming to the other girl, the sullen, plain Bridie, who also clearly wanted to be Kat and for whom it too could never be.

It is mid-afternoon and he is only a block from Buchan's iron cottage in Beaufort Street, the basket full of mulberry leaves on his arm. A commotion of scrapping fowls draws his attention to a side lane, and there in an open-air workshop he notices a man on a low stool, intent on shaping the sole of a shoe, tapping it with a cobbler's hammer. The shoemaker looks up from his work to speak to his master, and Jock sees again the rat-eyes of James Reilly.

In Glasgow Prison, he had been terrified Reilly would tell, knowing that the only thing to hold at bay Mary's fears of disclosure was the silence of this sly Irishman. When the first shock quieted, Reilly had stared at him, recoiled in disgust, spat in a whiny voice turned shrill: *What is it you are? What manner of freak?*

And Jock had said nothing, nothing.

That night he had dreamed of Mary, come, he thought, to comfort, but she slapped him fiercely, hissed and railed: *You cannot trust a soul!*

And so when Reilly woke, Jock was standing over him, leaning close with threat in his face.

Say a word o' me tae anyone, one word, and Ah swear it will go the wurrse fur you. And how will you like that, Ah wonder, tae be known as the freak's lover?

Reilly had held his tongue in Glasgow, in Millbank, in Portsmouth, on the *Clara*, but Jock will not take chances when they need not be taken. He hurries away down Mangles Street, suddenly aware of how partial is this freedom he has gained for himself. The walls of Perth Gaol are visible beyond the row of cottages up ahead, on the other side of Beaufort Street. His precious ticket is in his tunic pocket, at the ready should the demand be made – *Bond or free?* – though none could be in doubt, thanks to the black uniform with stripes as bright as the yolk of an egg. Every night at ten o'clock the prison bell clangs, signalling the curfew for ticket men. It is the lot of all who have been granted provisional licence to be at large in the community to seek work and begin the long, slow journey to *a more respectable life than they deserve.* But some things he can never be free of: there will always be someone to prod his fears with a stick.

He stumbles on the track and curses this town, this mockery of a capital with its endless sand and sun, its corrugated-iron shambles, its stinking cesspools, its smug cruelties.

∞

Buchan stands watching, arms akimbo, as Jock unloads trunks from the spring cart and trundles them, one by one, around to the store-room, balanced on a barrow. They are so heavy that Jock is surprised to see the contents when Buchan prises off a lid.

Look at that, then, Mrs Buchan, he gloats, pulling back newsprint sheeting and layers of straw packing. *Finest weave from Manchester, that.*

Unrolling a length from a bolt of cloth, he caresses the delicate fabric. *Perfect for the Hamersley order, wouldn't you say, m'dear?*

But Mrs Buchan has pounced on the discarded papers on the store-room floor and is already engrossed in old news of a far-off world.

Late that night, after Jock has chopped wood, emptied the hogshead washing tub into the laneway and raked out the stables, he settles to a supper of bread and dripping by the stove. Mrs Buchan's voice can still be heard on the other side of the kitchen lean-to. He half listens as she reads aloud from mismatched pages of the *Manchester Guardian*:

Listen to this, George...

Oh, where's the other bit...

For her efforts, she gets but a grunt from Buchan, habitually engrossed in his columns of figures.

Kat and Bridie twitter like a pair of birds and it seems to him a thing of wonder that they still have words to say after a day together in the workroom.

You're a quiet one tonight, Little Jock, Kat declares with a pinch of his arm. *C'mon now, or Buchan'll be calling for the dead cart to come and take you away.*

It's leaving that's on his mind, heading for the bush in the south, where there is space to feel free even when you are not, and all you need is a wire snare to eat meat three times a day. He tells Kat and Bridie about the tiny pub-and-police-station hamlets dotted sparsely along the road to Albany, the farms hiring ticket men at double his present wage. He has made up his mind to apply to the depot for transfer to Plantagenet and try his luck as farmhand or shepherd. Dairymaids are wanted, too, he has heard.

Bridie shudders.

Kat arches a brow. *It's daft you are if you think I've come to the end of the world to milk cows.*

Mrs Buchan's voice floats into the pause as the two girls contemplate his plans.

> An incident is just now being discussed in military circles so extraordinary that, were not the truth capable of being vouched for by official authority, the narration would certainly be deemed incredible.

George…GEORGE! Are you listening?

> Our officers quartered at the Cape between fifteen and twenty years ago may remember a certain Dr Barry attached to the medical staff there, and enjoying a reputation for considerable skill. The gentleman had entered the army in 1813, had passed, of course, through the grades of assistant surgeon and surgeon in various regiments, and had served as such in various quarters of the globe. His professional acquirements had procured for him promotion to the staff at the Cape. About 1840 he became promoted to be medical inspector, and was transferred to Malta. He proceeded from Malta to

Corfu, where he was quartered for many years. He died a month ago, and upon his death was discovered to be a woman!

A woman, George! Did you ever!

Very probably this discovery was elicited during the natural preparations for interment, but there seems to be an idea prevalent that either verbally, during the last illness, or by some writing perused immediately after death, he had begged to be buried without any post-mortem examination of any sort. This, most likely, only aroused the curiosity of the two nurses who attended him, for it was to them, it appears, that the disclosure of this mystery is owing.

Mrs Buchan's reading breaks for a breath. Jock glances up: Kat and Bridie look thrilled with their own disgust.

The motives that occasioned, and the time when commenced this singular deception are both shrouded in mystery. But thus it stands as an indubitable fact, that a woman was for forty years an officer in the British service, and fought one duel and had sought many more, had pursued a legitimate medical education, and received a regular diploma, and had acquired almost a celebrity for skill as a surgical operator!

The conclusion of the story occasions a small eruption from Mr Buchan: *Stuff and nonsense! Don't believe a word of it!*

Kat tosses her hair and pronounces scornfully: *Plain as wheat flour, to be sure, a woman who could fool the likes of soldiers, dorty animals that they be.*

Caught between them as Bridie titters and Kat preens, Jock is as flustered as if he himself had been stripped by a pair of curious nurses, and was likely at any minute to be hauled away and put on display like the Bearded Lady. And yet there is a naked awe, too, in the flush of his cheeks, admiration for this Dr Barry who was no one's pet freak and had fooled the world. Imagine the clever things he had managed to do with his life!

Crawling closer towards the stove so the girls can't see his face, he nurses to himself a shiver of shame. The most he could ever say of his own life is the fact he has so far survived it.

There y' go, Albert, he whispers, offering a sliver of bread on the flat of his shaking hand, but Mrs Buchan's ginger tom sniffs and walks away.

Lost girls

Lucifer huddled in the wire cage beside Willa in the back seat of a taxi, whose driver had wound the window down and kept looking in the rear-vision mirror.

Isn't going to puke again, is it?

Willa said nothing. She leaned close to the bars, anxious and watchful, both hands holding the cage steady.

The taxi pulled up outside the veterinary clinic, and Willa threw a twenty-dollar note onto the front seat. She and Lucifer were gone before the driver had time to fish about in his bag for change.

Lifting Lucifer from the cage and on to the stainless-steel table, it occurred to her that a sick cat is as light as air, as though its tenure on life is more about attitude than anything else. She answered the vet's questions, watching distressed as his fingers probed around Lucifer's chest and abdomen. The rectal thermometer disappeared and Lucifer's low growl of generalised complaint turned guttural.

Temperature's only slightly above normal, the vet said, and Lucifer promptly retched again, though there was nothing left in his stomach to expel.

But I think we'll keep him in for observation.

And when Willa looked like crumpling, he added, *Just as a precaution. I don't think it's anything serious. He's in pretty good condition for a cat of thirteen.*

The walk home took forty minutes and all the while Willa was remembering the day Matthew had turned up at the door of their flat just before he left for Sydney with his new wife and infant son. He had always brought presents for Imogen – Barbie dolls and sweet lacy teddy bears and miniature furniture, quaint, exquisite pieces, for the old-fashioned doll's house he had ordered from England when she was a baby.

Judas gifts, Orla would always say, scarcely able to hide her gloating sniff at the fact that Imogen clearly didn't cherish Daddy's precious doll's house, though she always looked at it politely enough when Matthew was around.

But that day was different. Matthew brought with him a cardboard box that squeaked and scuffled and changed their lives.

∾

Imogen falls in love the moment Matthew lifts out the mewling little thing, all frizzled up like a black bottlebrush, and says, *Here you are, sugar, this is Lucifer.* He turns and shrugs at Willa. *Don't look at me: the Cat Haven named him.*

Imogen kisses the squirming kitten again and again and rocks it in her arms. *Lucie*, she croons, *Lucie-Lucie-Lucie.*

Lucifer, not Lucie, Matthew laughs. *It's a boy kitty, sugar.*

For now, anyway, he mutters with an exaggerated grimace at Willa.

She can call him Lucie if she wants, she protests mildly, but Imogen giggles.

Lucie-Lucie-Lucie-fur.

Willa is thrilled at Imogen's smile, rare since another hospitalisation earlier in the year. She glances sideways, and it takes her by surprise: the tenderness in Matthew as he watches their daughter. For one pure moment, a flood of warmth courses through her.

The kitten stops squealing and before long it yawns and nestles down into the crook of Imogen's arm like a soft, silky muff.

Listen, Matthew whispers to her. *He's purring. I think he likes you.*

Still rocking, exquisitely gentle, Imogen buries her face in the rumbling fur. And then she looks up at Matthew. *Why is he a boy kitty?*

Well. Because he's...because he's got...

He casts about helplessly but Willa is unprepared, too.

Well, look at his face, Matthew blusters. *He looks like a tough little chap, doesn't he.*

As Imogen peers uncertainly at the sleeping kitten, Matthew busies himself with keys, sunglasses, and parts tearily, promising Imogen he will be back to visit in the new year.

Willa takes the kitten while Imogen is in the bath and it crawls up her body, stares into her eyes, pats her face all over with the soft pads of its paws as though committing the features to memory. Her heart is lost, too, she knows it. But Matthew has left a ticking bomb. *Everything's in here, you don't need to buy a thing*, he had told her before he went, struggling in from the car with a wicker basket, a huge pack of litter and a bag containing a blanket, a ball, a fluffy mouse, two plastic bowls, a dozen little tins of food, a tray, a page of instructions. She reads the leaflet from the Cat Haven. Feeding, worming, injections, sterilisation. *Neutered cats are happier cats. Neutered tomcats are calmer, more content to stay at home, and generally do not spray.* There is an appointment card stapled to the page, a time and date printed on it.

The day of the surgery was burned into her mind like scenes from a tragedy:

Imogen gripping the basket, refusing to stay with Orla as planned, crying all the way to the Cat Haven's clinic.

Willa telling her, *It won't hurt*, wishing immediately she could haul back her words.

It will. It will so hurt.

It's just a little operation, all cats have them, and then he won't want to run away.

He won't run away, he promises. He will be good.

Hearing herself botch the whole thing. *But cats sometimes wander off and get themselves lost, and we don't want that, do we?*

Lucifer howling as they leave; Imogen rivalling the noise with her wild sobbing. *He's frightened, Mummy. Please, Mummy, please go back. They'll hurt him and he's frightened.*

Lucifer listless when they bring him home, uninterested when Imogen fills his water bowl with milk, not purring when she scratches between his ears. His tail down, tucked under his body.

Telling her, *Be careful, he might be a tiny bit sore.*

Where? Where is he sore?

Imogen silent when Willa cradles him carefully, exposing the flush of furless skin, pink and vulnerable, the empty scrotal sac grooved with two small wounds.

Finding Imogen lying beside the basket, still, quiet – child and cat two foetal curls. So still, so quiet, her eyes blank and tearless, all the words sucked out of her…

There were so many *should haves* whenever she replayed that day. *She was five years old; I should have been prepared. I should have recognised it as an opportunity. I should have talked to her. I should have drawn it out of her, what she was feeling. I should never have let it happen, never...*

A word cut through, in that cold, cold voice.

Coward.

∞

The house was quiet without Lucifer. It had been less than an hour, but she called the surgery anyway.

Resting comfortably, the vet's nurse told her, adding firmly that she could phone again at five o'clock.

Willa paced up and down the hallway, put a load of washing into the machine, massacred the roses, made a cup of tea, walked to the end of the road to buy a newspaper, read it from front to back without taking in a word, made another cup of tea, remembered she hadn't checked her email.

James Donaldson's name was there again, with another exclamatory missive: `mary & bridget applications!!!`

Willa drummed her fingers on the desk, excited yet apprehensive. This was what she'd hoped for, wasn't it? But... But it meant that Little Jock's mother and young sister had had to throw themselves on the mercy of the parish. Willa felt torn between wanting and not wanting to eavesdrop on the sorriest lows in their lives.

Glancing at her watch – 4.45 – she decided to wait until after she had called the vet, and paced the garden paving stones with the last of the day's sun at her back.

At five minutes to five she could be patient no longer, and picked up the phone.

Yes, you can come and get Lucifer, the vet told her cheerfully. *He hasn't vomited again, and his temperature's down. Whatever it was – maybe something he ate? – there's not much wrong with the old boy now.*

∞

Lucifer was starving, and she was alarmed at the way he gulped down his food, but soon he was trotting down the hall after her, as he always did. He jumped effortlessly onto the computer desk and reclined between the screen and the keyboard, regarding her regally, the traumas of the day already forgotten. How she envied him this, the pragmatic memory of cats.

She opened James's attachment and printed the file, waiting for two pages to fall into the tray. And then she settled into the chair and began to read.

> No. 6552, 12.45 pm, 20 November 1862
> Mary Rafferty Lennie
> Residence: 23 High Street, front 4 up left stair
> Born Ireland
> Widow, age 62, dealer

Willa paused at this, looked at her journal to check. Mary *couldn't* be sixty-two. Even allowing for the uncertainties of the time, she must have been only in her mid-fifties in 1862. But perhaps the inspector's sympathies could be counted on to increase with a hapless applicant's years.

> Disabled. Age+
> No dependants
> Children living at residence, not dependants: Bridget
>   age 16, earning 3/6

That wasn't right, either; Bridget was surely older than sixteen.

First application
Particulars of settlement: House by indoor inspector.
Did not go in.

Did not go in, Willa murmured. *Why, Mary? Why didn't you take the settlement offered?* There seemed such defeat in these few words. She flicked back through the pages of her journal. No, there was nothing specific, no concrete piece of evidence to explain it, but she felt a growing conviction that the bond between Little Jock and Mary was unique, unlike Mary's relationship with the other children. Perhaps it was not just coincidence that only two months after Jock's final trial, when Mary probably knew that she would never see him again, she resorted to parish relief for the first and apparently the only time. Had a habit of protecting this most vulnerable child transmuted into the habit of being protected by him?

There were two applications for Bridget. The first, in 1860, well before Jock left, described Bridget Lonie living with her mother at 23 High Street – 'back outside stair 1 up and right door.' 'Cannot say what is wrong – vomiting,' the inspector noted, and sagely concluded his remarks: 'I suspect this girl is pregnant.'

The date on the second application was startling: December 1902. Bridget was fifty-seven – no grand age now, though it might have been a different story at the turn of the century. But Bridget had entered Willa's consciousness as a girl, only a girl, and it was not easy to imagine her as old and haggard, as the application conjured her.

No. 7360, 11.15, 25 December 1902
Born County Tyrone, Ireland
Age 57, single, mill worker, Roman Catholic
Wholly disabled, dyspepsia
Earnings, means of earning: none
Wholly destitute
Parentage: Felix Lunney, weaver, and Mary Rafferty,
    both dead
Cohabited with James Thorburn, labourer, for about
    30 years
Previous means of support: self
Pauper has been unsettled for the last 30 years in
    lodgings and sublet houses about Calton and which
    she cannot detail
Disposed of: 25 December 1902, Barnhill Poorhouse.

25 December 1902. It was Christmas Day when Bridget was
admitted to the hated Barnhill – Bridget who at nineteen might
have been pregnant but was never to have a family, Bridget who
seemed to have been lost, unsettled for thirty years.

Willa put her head in her hands and wept for lost girls.

It was late when she typed an email to James Donaldson, thanking
him for following up the Poor Relief records. She was grateful,
so grateful, to know the fate of Little Jock's family, though she
could not explain even to herself why it should have mattered
so much, for there was nothing here to enlighten her about the
riddles of Little Jock's life, other than the undeniable fact that
his had been a hand-to-mouth existence. But looking back over
her journal, she stopped at the census record of 1861. It seemed
that this archival portrait of the Irish matriarch surrounded by

her children and infant grandchildren was the last time that the family was together. Jock had just been reunited with them after his release on licence from Portsmouth. A year later he would leave again, this time for good, and the family would scatter...

A great hollow sadness was beginning to balloon in her. They were real, these Lennies; they had become more than just census statistics. They were the people Little Jock had loved. But she realised the time had come to leave them behind. There was nothing more that Mary could tell her.

Lucifer stood, stretched, looked at her with a quizzical expression that could only mean he was still hungry. She held him tight as she carried him to the kitchen. She could not have borne it if anything had happened to him. When Imogen left, she had taken her cello, her books, her computer, her worn and tattered Babar. The only thing she loved that she did not take was Lucifer, and Willa clung to the sliver of hope to be found in that.

September 1866

Kojonup

He walks to the spring at dusk to purge the smell of dung from his nostrils. All day he has been carting cow pats to the modest little market gardens planted to supply the government gangs between Kojonup and Albany. A boodie rat darts across his path as he passes the Barracks, now used only sporadically for military purposes. Children's counting and rhyming songs can be heard here on most mornings, while on the Sabbath hymns from a small congregation float out over the ten-acre pensioner grants and struggling farmlets, reminding one and all that this is an outpost of God and Empire. He has never been asked, nor would he expect, to join the worthy citizenry of Kojonup in their self-guided praise. It is not a requirement of his provisional release to attend divine service, as it had been when he was in prison or on the road gangs; once a man is a ticket-of-leaver, it seems the Convict Establishment takes no further interest in his soul.

The Roman Catholic pensioner guards and their families, like the Noonans, the Shinners and his employers, McDonnell and Sweeney, do not attend the humble Anglican service. He had assumed that some, like he, had never been enthusiastic communicants in the old country anyway and now considered Catholicism a relic of the past. However, the arrival of a visiting priest had proved him wrong, bringing forward a gathering of respectable size on Mrs Noonan's verandah. Even so, he has noticed that, whatever the religion, however pious these free settlers think themselves to be, they are as like as not to make welcome the unlicensed gallon men who ply gin along the track to Albany. In fact, Kojonup has gained something of a reputation for drunkenness, though you would be hard-pressed to believe it if you heard those ragged Sunday voices. *Lucky sods*, he thinks. Escape in the guise of a thick green glass seems a fine thing to aspire to, and the one thing, the only thing, that keeps him a rotgut-virgin is the prospect of losing what freedom he has and putting at risk what more will be his due. If found in possession of grog, his ticket would be twitched away in the blink of a blind man's eye.

The spring attracts kangaroos and tammars at this time of day, and screeching parrots of the type that an enraged McDonnell brings down in showers of buckshot and emerald feathers when they descend on his small grove of figs and almonds. But for all the racket of the birds, and those blood-chilling cries from unknown creatures deep in the bush, he feels more at ease here than in McDonnell's barn, and will delay his return until he hears Sweeney striding towards the Barracks to sound the curfew bell. Most nights he and the two other ticket-of-leavers employed at McDonnell's press their fingers over their ears to muffle the shouting, the scuffling, the crash of tin plates and cutlery against stone walls. The first time it happened, he had been appalled to see Mrs McDonnell's face, swollen and purpling in the clear light of morning, but soon realised from the state of old William himself that Maryann was no meek lamb and could match her man blow for blow. A good twenty years younger than her husband, and handsome for all her slovenly ways, she takes pains to let the workers know it will be her fury they will deal with if the work is not done, or done other than to her liking.

It is here, by the spring, his feet propped up against a granite slab, that Jock stares for hours at the night sky. In Glasgow people don't look up. Stars are dull things glimpsed behind roiling fog and the smoke from chimneys; the moon, blurred and blowzy. When Fleming had told him, in the dark fug of the *Clara*'s hold, that sailors set their courses by the stars, he could not imagine this could be so. But here in the new world he sees the true lie of the universe, the thin ink of night poured across the sky, nothing between him and stars so glassy bright and glittering that he can believe they bring men safely home. Nothing between him and the moon. He knows from Fleming that the sky is ever the sky, but it does not seem possible that the same heaven above him gazes down on Mary and Bridget.

The vastness spread before him tempts thoughts of what lies beyond the twelve-month left of his ticket, when he will taste the next level of freedom in this prison colony. He could do worse than to settle here in Kojonup, where there will always be need for hard workers and men content enough to live with their own company as shepherds on the outlying runs. There is talk of a public house, even a store, and they say the Barracks will be closed for good by year's end. To walk free of the shadow of the Convict Establishment would be sweet as a peach.

He drifts, dreaming of fields of green that roll away as far as the sky, as smooth and clean as church glass…

Suddenly he is on his feet and running, roughly jerked back to the present by the clang of the Barracks bell.

October 1867

Albany

The assistant warder looks up from his dried pork as Dr Baesjou rushes past with his gladstone bag and a distracted air, muttering something that could have been *Good morning* or equally could have been the continuation of a monologue requiring no response. To be safe he says, *G'afternoon, Doctor, sir,* but Baesjou is already slamming the dispensary door behind him.

He is about to resume his lunch when a small figure appears in the archway of the depot barracks, doubled over in a fit of wet, gluey coughing. Eyeing the man with some disgust, the warder puts his pork aside and calls out, *You there, you! What's your business here?*

The man shuffles over and grips the rough slab of sheoak that serves as a desk, to steady himself.

Ah'm here aboot ma conditional release, he says in a hoarse whisper.

Mmm, registration number? Name?

The man coughs and splutters. *King. 7756. Ah'm due it soon.*

There is nothing in the correspondence book and nothing in the orders.

Ah know Ah'm due it soon, the man repeats anxiously.

The warder runs a finger across the schedule of the district's ticket-of-leavers. *Look, you've another two weeks at Duffy's, according to this. We know where you are. The Superintendent will have you report when the paperwork comes.*

Ah'll come back next week, the man croaks. *To see.*

Suit yourself.

Dr Baesjou strides out of the dispensary, frowning, at the same time that King 7756 is overcome by a fresh bout of hacking. The warder watches as the doctor stops abruptly and orders the fellow to open his mouth, and the little man does it with that unthinking obedience that comes from long periods in institutional servitude.

A spot of linctus will fix that, Baesjou announces. *Come, man, and let's check you over.*

But alarm flares on the man's face and he backs away, mumbling, *Th's no need, no need for tha'.* He slips out the door, not bothering to wait for any linctus.

The doctor slumps into his coat and his habitual frown deepens. He turns to the man at the desk as though about to ask a question, but then sighs and heads back to the dispensary, his original errand apparently forgotten.

The assistant warder stares after him, wondering what it is about this town and its medicos. Dr Finer had been shipped back to Perth and admitted to the asylum where, so they say, he'd done himself in. And now Baesjou, so well thought of, as good a man for a bad tooth as for when a leg needs coming off, but such a melancholy air. The Superintendent has been overheard to say you never knew where you were with Baesjou these days.

He turns his attention once more to the pork, as tough as saddle leather, wishing he had an ale to wash it down.

༂

The main intersection of Albany town – the corner of York Street and Stirling Terrace – can be a dangerous place after heavy rains, when runoff from Mount Clarence and Mount Melville pours down the slope of the semi-cleared street and floods across the terrace before gushing into Princess Royal Harbour. And to be on that corner after staggering out of the Freemasons Hotel at closing time carries dangers of its own. Jock might, at another time, give the proper observance to these twin perils, but, as it is, he is too drunk to grasp more than three alarming facts: he is wet to the knees, he is having trouble keeping his footing, and PC Gilchrist is bearing down on him with obvious intent.

The police station being momentarily flooded, he finds himself at the town gaol, grit-eyed and garrulous. *You cannae do tha'. Ah got ma condishnal 'lease today. Today! Ah'm m'own master noo.*

Settle down, PC Gilchrist tells him, averting his face from the potent fumes. *You're not being arrested for curfew. You're drunk, man, you're flootered!*

Jock belches lavishly as he empties his pockets of a folded parchment, two ounces of Negrohead, a pipe and a sixpence. *John King*, Gilchrist reads on the printed form, and Jock is at pains to correct him: *Jock. L'il Jock noo.* It seems funny and he chuckles.

Along the corridor to the cells, the constable's lantern throws ghostly shafts of light onto rough whitewashed walls obscenely bulging like rolls of flesh in a tight flannel shirt. Bodies, he thinks. Bodies in the wall. He giggles again and belches.

Gilchrist guides him into a narrow box equipped with palliasse and bucket, and throws him a blanket. *Sleep it off, Little Jock. A fine place you've chosen for your first night of freedom!*

A woman moans in the next cell. *Where's that doctor? I'm sick, I tell you. I need the doctor.* She thuds on the cell door.

Hush, Harriet, Gilchrist says mildly. *You don't need the doctor; you likely just need a drink.*

Hope flowers in the briefest pause. *So get me a drink, then?*

The constable laughs. *Your fourteen days're up tomorrow and you can get it yourself.*

Bastard! She kicks the door savagely and howls again. *Fetch the doctor!*

Shut up, woman, Gilchrist hisses over his shoulder. *There's no doctor to fetch any more. No wonder Baesjou cut his own throat, having to deal with the likes o' you.*

The cells are doused in darkness. Jock slides down the wall, humming, grinning at oblivion.

The next morning he stands before the Resident Magistrate, unsteady on his feet and sour with vomit, and listens open-mouthed as he is fined a pound, plus two shillings in costs.

Can you pay the said amount? asks Magistrate Cockburn-Campbell, looking doubtfully at the property book.

He looks down and mutters, *Ah'm owed ma wages from Duffy. He said he would settle up wi' me today.*

Very well, then. PC Gilchrist will escort you to collect them.

By midday he is standing at the top of the York Street hill, head thrumming, a substantial dent in his wages. But he is a man with a conditional release, his own master, and free to say what the next move will be.

Turning his back on the blue forever of the ocean, he sets off on the Albany Road, north towards Kojonup.

A hardy little symbol

Willa's phone hardly ever rang, so she was not prepared, still less for the long-distance pips and a familiar voice with an offer of work.

I wouldn't be pressing but Gabrielle asked especially. She enjoyed working with you last time, and I think she's a bit nervous – second-book syndrome – wants someone she knows.

Consternation gripped Willa and she could not speak.

I warned her that I didn't think you were taking anything on at the moment, but I'm hoping you'll tell me otherwise.

Um, no, I really…I can't.

Oh.

Willa hated this. Celia had always been a good client, good to her.

OK, well, I'll just have to give Gabby the bad news. But look, keep in touch, OK? Her voice changed. *How are things, Willa? How are you?*

Willa didn't know how to respond. What did Celia Long imagine *things* were? It was nearly a year since Willa had phoned to tell her, *Don't send that manuscript we discussed; I'm taking*

248

a year's leave, since she had forestalled all questions with her standard reply: *I have lost my daughter…*

She would always break off deliberately, insert the ellipsis at the end of her words, knowing it could do the work of a whole story. Such a hardy little symbol, reliable in spite of its seeming hesitation, its suggestion of doubt. It could force the air from an exchange as surely as a seal of wax – but kindly, for the other person was unaware of the impress, the weight of it. In closing down and sealing off, it left a space for someone else to fill with assumptions. Any one of the world's sad stories would do:

Runaway on Street Corner.

Tepid Bath Hastens Exsanguination.

Broken Body in Twisted Wreck.

Malignant – Inoperable – Terminal – Sorry.

She had never had to say any more, and the ambiguity of *lost* could keep its wings, hover unencumbered by explanations. Soon, surely, she would have to breach the gap with words. But not yet, she thought in a mumble of *sorry* and *thanks* and *I have to go*.

She had been languid for days, unsure of what to do now, where next to look. With sources in Scotland and Ireland exhausted, she was no closer to finding Little Jock, to detecting clues to the monumental sleight of hand that was his life. No closer to the truth. She caught herself, smiled at the notion. Truth, whatever *that* was.

When the phone rang again, she looked at it wonderingly. It was not like Celia to push. She steeled herself for another uncomfortable conversation, but it was the library. The books she had requested were in.

∞

Over the years, she had edited several local histories; many rural communities chose to celebrate centenary milestones during the 1980s and 1990s by publishing a worthy book. Willa had always found them interesting, up to a point – usually the point at which the historian seemed finally to succumb to the pressure of the commission and got down to the business of cataloguing the minutiae of local government evolution. She had wondered, then, about the market for books like these, but since had discovered they were collectors' items and much sought after by library patrons.

She had not before seen the two she pored over now, which dated back to the 1970s, and turned the pages with a fascination she would once have found hard to credit. In the histories of Kojonup and Albany were glimpses of the world Little Jock inhabited, even photographs of places he would have been, and though, of course, he was not listed in the indexes among the names of venerable settlers, she paused at some of the references, sources she had not thought of. She would have to go back to the state archives. The humble could not be found in books.

It was not as if she was expecting answers any more, she told herself, but still she could not let go of Little Jock.

She found him in the day-to-day transactions of small towns. There he was on a 'Nominal List of Probation Prisoners Transferred from the Establishment of Perth and Fremantle to Albany Road Parties':

> Reg. 7756 John King joined 16 May 1864 rationed from 4 June 1864, party attached to A. W. McGregor. To Fremantle 16 September 1865 for discharge on Ticket of Leave.

She found him, too, in the diary of a Kojonup settler, Thomas Norrish, as an occasional visitor to the 'Ettakup' property and on its lists of seasonal shearers.

He was also on the Kojonup police station's licence register, buying the right to cut sandalwood in 1880 and, in the 1870s, applying for dog licences. Kangaroo dogs were obviously considered the superior breed, but Little Jock could afford only sheepdogs – half the licence fee. Willa flinched at the word for female dogs: *sluts*.

The surviving Police Occurrence Books for Kojonup and Albany occupied her for days, for they provided social snapshots of 1860s and 1870s life, a history less lofty than that celebrated in centenary tomes. There was an intimate sense of community in their pages that reminded her, ironically, of George Sullivan's article in *Past Lives* – his description of how the local people had sought to assist police in finding evidence about Jock's murder. The good citizens of Albany had taken on this ghoulish task with alacrity, said Sullivan:

> Horace Egerton-Warburton visited the Sinkings on 5 November and found a piece of skin with hair adhering to it, a piece of cloth, a fly net, two fingernails, six pieces of tweed, some sand cemented with blood, and a portion of a flannel shirt sleeve. How the police managed to search the site and miss these items can only be imagined. *The West Australian* applauded Egerton-Warburton 'for his exertions'; the reaction of a crime scene investigator today would no doubt be less congratulatory!
>
> The public holiday of 9 November brought forth a veritable army of amateur evidence-hunters to the Sinkings, and storeman Thomas Palmer was rewarded

with the discovery of a bloodstained axe. But the grand prize came on 11 November, when Constable Spencer Hayman made the grisly discovery of legs, wearing boots stuffed with toe-rags, socks and a portion of trousers, buried in the vicinity, and William Finlay, erstwhile policeman and currently customs clerk and tidewaiter, dug up a head some 100 yards away.

Sullivan's matter-of-fact rendering of the shocking facts was, Willa realised now, not unlike the tone of the large, hardcover Police Occurrence Books. Laboriously handwritten by officers of varying literacy skills, they revealed the community's darker side, its foibles and its transgressions. There were serious criminal offences – 'violent' assault, rape, murder, infanticide, spearing, arson, fraud – but these were outnumbered by incidents of domestic violence, desertion of families, neglect of child support. One recording officer was careful to note that it was a *spinster* who was charged with failing to register her child within the time required by law. When another *spinster* accused a man with 'being the father of the child she is now pregnant with,' he was ordered to pay birth expenses and maintenance.

Page after page, Willa read of offences concerning alcohol: drunk and disorderly, drunk in charge of a team, drunk and incapable, selling grog without a licence, supplying convicts with spirits, supplying rum to 'natives'. Serial offenders were placed on the 'prohibited' list for thirty days, banned from licensed premises for the duration. And it seemed that those who weren't drunkards were thieves. Mentally noting the various acts of theft, Willa began to wonder whether anything had been held sacred. People stole clothes from washing lines, robbed shepherds' huts, illegally detained property in boarding houses, and broke into homes and stores and fowlyards. Children took grapes from vineyards, oranges from backyard gardens, and a thirteen-year-old girl who stole from a shop a bottle of scent worth two shillings and threepence earned herself a month's hard labour in Albany Gaol. It would have been no small undertaking, Willa thought, for a ticket-of-leaver to stay out of trouble in a society so strictly policed and seemingly so criminally inclined.

Upright citizens were no strangers to the police courts, either. A storekeeper, she noted, was charged with 'having in his possession one weight which was not according to the standard,' a publican with 'not having his name painted on his cart,' and the keepers of lodging houses were always in trouble for permitting 'reputed drunk and disorderly persons' to remain on their premises. Settlers failed to brand cattle, licensed boatmen conveyed contraband goods ashore, and employers of all kinds refused to pay wages owing, while shepherds absented themselves from their flocks and servants and seamen absconded from their duties.

Willa read with amusement that it was an offence to 'ride furiously in the street,' to drive scabby sheep on a public road or to permit one's privy or cesspool to be emptied between the hours of 6.00 am and 10.00 pm. Children were cautioned for 'damaging a municipal water tank by bathing in it,' while Albany's doctor seemed forever being charged with allowing his horse to stray or tethering a cow in a public street. Parents were fined for not sending their children to school, and outraged citizens accused each other of profane or obscene or abusive language. There were people who loitered, people who exposed themselves, and, gravest of all, people who 'lay in the open with no visible means of subsistence.' And there were prostitutes, though Willa was intrigued to see that until the mid-1870s the magistrates seemed coy about using that particular word for the women who offended.

While on conditional release, Jock was convicted of selling a bottle of gin belonging to his master, William McDonnell, and was speedily despatched to gaol. But Willa was delighted to see that he was no meek milksop to be pushed around: litigious as the rest of them, he took the same master to court for refusing to pay wages. The complaint was dismissed and he was fined more than eight pounds. How, she wondered, could a servant ever have hoped to manage that?

A much later Police Court entry in April 1882 caught her eye:

> Sergeant McLarty charges Lewis Davis expiree and James Stevens free with that they did on or about the 31st ultimo feloniously steal, take and carry away from the person of one John King one silver watch and Albert chain, over the value of £5. Committed for trial.

She had come across several John Kings in the records: could her Jock have been the owner of a silver watch?

Finally, after reading them all, all the books that the years had spared, she looked at her page of notes detailing Little Jock's trivial misdemeanours. There had been no mention in the Scottish court papers of his being the worse for liquor, but here it was a different story: 'drunk and making use of obscene language,' 'drunk and refusing to go to his place of abode,' 'drunk and disorderly.' Willa's skin crawled at Jock's carelessness, the power of alcohol to make him vulnerable. *Take care, you must.* Was it Mary's urgent whisper she thought she heard, or the echo of her own useless pleading when Imogen screamed that she would drink if she liked and no one would stop her, and slammed the front door so hard that one of its leadlight panels cracked?

The voice was as hard as granite, bitter as memory:

What were you frightened of, Mother? I'd already been raped, remember? Vaginal Dilation by Loving Parent.

Imogen's preschool teacher is on the phone, her voice taut with a familiar mixture of urgency and bewilderment. *You'd better come and get Imogen, Ms Samson. She's…she's distressed. We're not sure what to do.*

Willa reaches the playroom, finds it bedecked with crepe streamers twisted into double-helix garlands. There are mounds of large paper flowers and sheets of coloured cardboard with animal shapes to be cut out. The floor is alive with bunches of bright balloons muttering and jostling as they wait to be strung up on ceiling fans and suspended over the door frame. And in the corner, on a low plastic chair, is Imogen, doubled over, her arms clamped tightly under her knees.

The teacher is gabbling. *The children were helping to decorate the room for the Sully triplets' birthday party after kindy. Imogen…I couldn't interest her in making flowers or cutting out; she just sat there, watching me with the balloons. And when it was time for recess…well, she doesn't seem to hear me.*

Willa registers two things simultaneously: she knows nothing about any birthday party, and Imogen's gaze is fixed on the balloon pump on the floor. The nozzle of the pump is a familiar colour and shape.

She places herself between it and Imogen, grasping her shoulders, and watches the eyes unglaze, refocus, lock on to hers. Imogen opens her mouth and finally it is out, a long scream that tears through the membranes of twelve dozen balloons and makes the Sully triplets cry and sears Willa so soundly that she will forever feel the shiny ridges of scar tissue on her heart.

It had been a daily ordeal for both of them, the insertion of the dilator to keep open, keep *patent*, what the surgeon had had to re-create – and he had warned Willa that if she faltered in this, his work would be undone again; there would be no choice but to operate a third time.

Imogen was so brave, Willa had always thought, so heart-breakingly stoic. It devastated her to see the savage pain beneath all that bravery, pain that could be triggered by the sight of a mould of white plastic plunged into the neck of a balloon.

But rape? *Rape?* She had never imagined, until she began to read those stories on the internet, that this might be how Imogen would remember it.

How could I never have imagined that?

Imogen's voice, for once, was silent.

There were black spaces on the page in front of her, explosions at the periphery of sight. She returned the last Police Occurrence Book to the desk and hurried to the train station, anxious to escape to a darkened room. But in some perverse way she welcomed these signs of the coming migraine. Like blood from self-cutting, they proved she was alive. And they distracted her from another pain, one she could not bear.

May 1868

Kojonup

The two small rooms of McDonnell's cottage are hot and smoky, partly from the twin fires of banksia and mallee root that burn in back-to-back fireplaces. A dozen or so people, mostly men, all with clay pipes or thickly rolled cigarettes, fill the cottage and spill out into the lean-to kitchen – arguing around the rough-cut table, playing cards on the plank-lined floor, leaning against walls to scratch that space between shoulder blades that fingernails cannot reach. Not one is without a drink in hand, a bitter, gut-stripping gin that would likely find a place in an apothecary's inventory among diuretics and other purgatives. But let not anyone mistake McDonnell's as aught but a private residence where friends gather on any given night to share the events of the day. And if William and Maryann McDonnell choose to offer their friends a drop, well, whose business is that other than their own?

George Baggs has had enough friendship for the night, but thinks it will be wise to take a bottle away with him, for emergencies. After a quiet conversation with Mrs McDonnell, he begins to make his way to the barn but finds himself stumbling over mounds in the earth. He falls forward, a knee plunging into something that bursts, wet and sticky-sweet. Melons! McDonnell has abandoned his market gardens for a more lucrative enterprise, and a section of his acreage has been left to rot and self-seed and flourish where it will. Baggs staggers to his feet, cursing softly, and picks his way through the wayward melons.

In the barn he finds McDonnell's servant, explains his quest, and perches on a bale of canary-grass while the man disappears somewhere behind the barn. It occurs to him he should follow, spy out where McDonnell's store-room is, but the servant is back with his bottle of gin by the time he has found his feet. *Ta, Little Jock*, he says, handing over six shillings, and then, with the bottle safely under his coat, he threads back to the track of sand and gravel called Soldiers Road.

It's morning, and Jock stands, fuming, in the frame of the milking shed.

You can take it up with my wife, if you've the stomach for it, McDonnell tells him, his face scarlet and stubborn. *I've told you before: if an agreement was made – IF, I say – it was with her. I know not a thing about it.*

Jock stalks across to the cottage, where Maryann McDonnell is up to her elbows in flour, pounding a damper on the grimy table in the lean-to. Knowing that McDonnell has already warned her of his claim, and that the pair will stand together on this if on nothing else, he wastes no time in preamble.

Two poonds a month, tha' was our agreement. By ma reckoning, tha' makes eight poonds one and six you owe me, after sundries. And he offers her a page from a notebook with pencilled sums and subtractions. *See?*

She slams down the dough and glares at him. *Never mind that. Show me this agreement.*

Ah cannae show what wa' spoken.

Well, then. And she turns her back on him.

Look, he says, *Ah'll walk away noo wi' five and call it done. Save me the bother of going into town.*

She swings around. *Odd jobs for board. That's what I recollect of this 'agreement'. And that's what I'll tell the magistrate. Who will they believe, d'you think?* She shakes back the hanks of hair falling around her face, narrows her eyes. *Think, Little Jock. You've been coming to us for work since you was a ticket-man, on and off. A shame to leave angry. And with nothing. Two pounds a month, you say? Well, maybe that's a fair bond for a workman-servant, and maybe I'll agree to it – if you stay on.*

He snorts in contempt and snatches an apple off her table. *Ah'm off this night, then, and before the week is oot you'll have ma complaint tae answer.* After pausing to bite the apple, he adds, *And mebbe more, aye, mebbe you'll have more tae answer.*

Don't you be threatening me! she yells as he walks away.

The thin note of anxiety in her voice gives him wondrous satisfaction. He spits an apple seed into the dirt.

Jock stumps off down Soldiers Road with his small cloth bag of possessions, planning to camp at the 160-Mile overnight and set out for Albany in the morning. McDonnell's dog prances beside him, attracted by the smell of dried meat wrapped in his spare flannel vest.

Ah've a mind tae take you wi' me, he says, tousling the mutt's head, *but they'd call me a thief an' have me afore the magistrate b' Friday.*

He looks back at the cottage, home these last five months, where he has cut hay, fetched and carried, tended the horses, helped build a barn, repaired shoes, and driven his employers – all la-di-da – about in their trap. He owes no thanks, nor fine feeling, to William and Maryann McDonnell, but through them he has met good people, all manner of people hereabouts to whom he can offer his labour, and for that, he supposes, he would have remembered them kindly had they paid him his due.

Lyin' bastards!

He tramps away, ripe with that plump and pious grievance of the thief turned honest.

June 1868

Albany

The Resident Magistrate's Court dispenses justice to a procession of petty offenders, the nature of the punishment wholly at the discretion – some say the whim – of the despotic Alexander Cockburn-Campbell.

William Smith, Expiree, lying in an outhouse at 2.30 am with no visible means of subsistence, and not giving a satisfactory account of himself. One month's hard labour.

Harriet Church, drunk in the London Hotel. Fifteen shillings plus eleven shillings costs.

John McKenzie, summonsed by Louisa Nicholls for assault. Case dismissed.

John Carrotts, CR, possession of an unlicensed dog. One pound plus three shillings and sixpence costs.

Native Mirott, robbing a hut belonging to Harry Hale, TL, shepherd. Twenty-one days plus eighteen lashes.

Margaret Beard, summonsed by Louisa Nicholls for insulting language. Twopence costs, each to pay half.

Isabella McKenzie, selling or supplying spiritous liquor to Johnny Wongineal, Aboriginal. Five pounds plus four shillings costs.

John F. T. Hassell, riding furiously in Earl Street. Cautioned.

Ann Gregory and John Hayes, using profane and abusive language towards each other. Five shillings each.

Margaret Beard, drunk in the closet of the Freemasons Hotel. Fourteen days' hard labour.

Cockburn-Campbell is heartily sick of the community it is his lot to judge: *If they are not quarrelling, they are falling down drunk*, he tells his wife, Sophia, daily over oatmeal and bacon. But to his great vexation, his applications for transfer elsewhere, anywhere, have consistently been ignored.

Surely we are done for the day! he snaps waspishly at the constable on duty. But there is one more case to hear.

PC Moan reads the complaint of John King, CR, of Kojonup, against his former employer for refusing to pay him the balance of wages due.

Cockburn-Campbell eyes the two men standing behind the constable, hats in their hands. One is old and stooped, uncomfortable in an imperfectly preserved suit reeking of mould and camphor; the other, a short, rotund fellow in workman's kit. An unprepossessing pair, the magistrate thinks. *Which of you is the complainant?*

The younger man steps forward.

John King, CR – how long have you had your conditional release? Since September last. Sir.

Cockburn-Campbell looks at him with distaste, thinking it a good thing, a very good thing indeed, that the colony's days of taking Mother England's dregs are done.

Very well, then, he says, *let us hear your story.*

It is a convoluted recitation of dates and wages and work performed, and as the little man stumbles his way through it all, Cockburn-Campbell takes stock of him, irritated by the long, dark hair falling in his eyes, the way he scratches at ginger whiskers when straining to recollect some trivial detail. But it takes little to irritate Cockburn-Campbell on this long, dreary day of minor crime and petty nonsense.

The complainant finished, thank the Lord, Cockburn-Campbell looks at the other man. *And you, McDonnell, how do you answer these claims?*

With an injured air, McDonnell whines, *I never made any agreement with King, sir, nor did I hear my wife make any. She has never told me that she did make any agreement with him, sir. He came to work out one pound, which my wife lent him. He did not pay for his board. He did for that little jobs about my place. I cannot say much more. Sir.*

There are no witnesses? the magistrate asks hopefully.

But PC Moan is smoothing out two sheets of paper and clearing his throat. *Witness statements, Your Honour,* he says. *Obtained by PC Hogan at Kojonup.*

Cockburn-Campbell sighs and waves a weary hand. *Proceed.*

Maryann McDonnell, wife of the defendant, says: 'King has been living in my house five months. He would make no regular agreement. He wanted to work on his own account. He was to do odd jobs for McDonnell in his leisure time for his food. When he left he said he could go where he liked – he was his own master.' It is signed Maryann McDonnell her mark.

And there is the statement of William Brown, ticket-of-leave labourer at the McDonnells': 'I was present when King asked McDonnell to settle up with him. King gave him a bill for ten pounds and McDonnell tore it up and he said I'll give you neer a one now. Mrs McDonnell said that he did not come there to work for her but for himself.' Also signed and sworn.

Cockburn-Campbell turns to the complainant, fixes him with a sceptical stare.

Any more statements? he asks PC Moan.

No, sir, Your Honour.

Very well, then. I am dismissing this case against William McDonnell and ordering the complainant, John King, to pay the costs of this court, and mileage, which amount to…

He pauses to peer at the sheet of ruled paper PC Moan hands over.

Mmm, yes. John King to pay eight pounds fifteen shillings and eightpence, or serve one month's hard labour in default. Can you pay? No? Then take him into custody, Constable.

Three days later, John King again appears before the Resident Magistrate, charged with having in the month of May sold, bartered or otherwise disposed of one bottle of spirits – to wit, gin – his master's property, to George Baggs at Kojonup. Cockburn-Campbell, his choleric temper frayed to ribbons by these upstart fellows who abuse the licence extended them, dismisses King's claim that what he did was in the McDonnells' service, and sentences him to three years.

Perhaps Cockburn-Campbell will have a moment of disquiet when, five months later, the McDonnells' house is searched, the pair suspected of *having a quantity of spiritous and fermented liquors in unlicensed premises and illegally selling to another.* More likely he will not even remember the conviction of John King that resulted in his being sucked back into the prison system, all licences cancelled.

The stuff of story

Dear Willa

Well, thanks to your sterling efforts, we have our letters typed & stamped & all ready to go. But last night Alex had a few qualms: 'What if they think it's some sort of con?' I admit it had been niggling me, too, that this type of unsolicited contact, a letter out of the blue announcing long-distant kinship, might be unwelcome. Some people (most people?) find genealogy peculiar, even a bit morbid. My daughters, Janet & Catherine, roll their eyes & say the whole thing's pointless (though I have high hopes of Katie: they say things like this can skip a generation!) Heaven forbid we should come across as stalkers or somesuch!

Alex said 'Ask Willa.' (We don't have any Australians among our acquaintances so you have been elevated to Oracle.) Of course,

this sort of thing is personal, not cultural,
but even so we'd like your opinion.

So. What do you think? How would you
react if you got a letter from across
the world saying 'Guess what? Your great-
grandfather was my great-grandmother's
brother.' Interested? Suspicious? Annoyed
at having someone snooping through your
family's past? Or would you just say 'So
what'?

Kind regards

James

PS What say your children (if you have
children - do you?) to your digging around
in family history?

Willa thought about James's email – mentally erasing the
postscript – as she went out to the letterbox, along the brick-
paved path thick with summer-brown moss. *How would you
react?* She imagined such a letter arriving from County Tyrone,
some long-lost descendant of Orla's Irish line. How pleased she
would be, now that she had some other reason for cherishing
the connection. A year ago, though, she would probably have
stuffed the letter in a drawer, something she felt compelled to
keep because of the tangible link with her mother but not a
thing to respond to, act on.

Walking back to the house, she unfolded the Genealogical
Society newsletter and tore open the plastic wrapper.

How would she react? It was all relative, and even though
he might enjoy the pun she couldn't tell James Donaldson that.

Lucifer sprang on to the kitchen benchtop, where he was absolutely forbidden to go, and she lifted him down absently while reading the newsletter. She perched on the edge of the table, turning the page, and he jumped again. This time she looked up, noticing his expectant crouch, the great yellow moons of his eyes and the ears flat to his head.

Bad boy, Lucifer! Down!

He leapt off, satisfied that the world was as it should be.

As she reached down to scratch his back, an announcement at the top of the page caught her attention.

ADVANCE NOTICE

CONVICT ANNIVERSARY

To mark the 140th anniversary of the end of transportation to Western Australia, the Genealogical Society will publish 'Convict Lives' in 2008, a volume celebrating our convict forebears and the lives they made in a new home that was not of their choosing. Short articles (1500 words max.) are invited from descendants and historians. Stories of all convicts are welcome: the famous, the not-so-famous and the infamous!

Below it was an article by the newsletter editor, clearly meant to inspire contributions.

Most people, when asked about Western Australia's convicts, think of the bushranger Moondyne Joe (*Pyrenees* 1852) and the Fenian John Boyle O'Reilly (*Hougoumont* 1868). But in the coming issues we will introduce some names you might not be so familiar with. Here are a few to whet your appetite:

Thomas Palmer (*Sea Park* 1854): Schoolmaster, active in the public affairs of Albany.

William Chopin (*Norwood* 1867): Chemist (unqualified), teacher. Operated 'Medical and Veterinary Dispensary' business in York. Eventually reconvicted, after repeated trials before the Supreme Court, of abortion. Known for his compassion in ministering to desperate women and frightened girls.

John Coates Fleming (*Clara* 1864): Journalist with the *Inquirer*, headmaster of William Street Academy for Boys, Colonial Superintendent of Telegraphs. Honoured by the London Society of Engineers for his pioneering work on the Perth to Albany and Albany to Eucla telegraph lines.

These brief notes are sourced from Rica Erickson's 1985 *The Brand on His Coat*. We hope that the forthcoming volume will include the results of research undertaken in the years since this ground-breaking work was published. Make sure *your* convict is in it!

Where did Little Jock – *her* convict, for no one else would claim him – fit into this proposed commemoration of *the famous, the not-so-famous and the infamous*? *All stories*, they said, but it was clear from the examples given in the article that what they really wanted were either splendid law-breakers like Moondyne Joe and O'Reilly or those industrious fellows who had made good. She had not known of Fleming's illustrious colonial career but remembered him from the *Clara*'s muster of names, among the educated number who may have contributed to the ship's newspaper. He was an obvious one to honour. Even the re-offender William Chopin seemed to have secured his place in posterity through professional achievement, rendering heroic his subsequent crimes as abortionist. Without a measure of the extraordinary, it seemed a life was just a life, not a story.

She frowned, thinking of Little Jock. In many ways, his life was probably more extraordinary than any other convict's, but she could not prove it; nor could she construct a narrative of 'making good' out of the fragments she had collected. If she were to lay them out, all the things of which she was *certain*, only one would qualify as the stuff of story: the brutality of his death. George Sullivan had already written that tale. And she could not bear to think that after all her research, the one indisputable marker she could bestow on Little Jock was *victim*.

Who are you trying to fool? His victim status is what drew you in.

Willa decided she would reassure James Donaldson and his brother Alex. She had tracked down more than a dozen living descendants of Hamish Laidlaw, using – bumbling amateur that she was – a probably unnecessarily complicated combination of registration data; birth, death and marriage notices in *The West Australian*; electoral rolls and telephone directories. A more experienced genealogist would no doubt have identified dozens more, but her list was the product of luck rather than skill. If anyone should feel like a stalker, she thought, it was unquestionably she, once again trampling over someone else's ancestry without the tie of blood as justification. She had no idea, none at all, how these people scattered around the suburbs of Perth would respond to James's invitation to be enfolded into the Donaldson–Laidlaw family tree, to the sudden flesh-and-bloodness of a Scots heritage they might be only vaguely aware of. But she sensed a real vulnerability lying beneath the lightness of James's email and had a feeling it would take only a few words to dissuade him and Alex. And if there were one person on that list of theirs who cared – well, what a loss that would be.

It was his postscript that unsettled her: *What say your children, if you have children – do you?* In other emails he had volunteered a few personal snippets. He had resigned from a high-pressure job at a boys' grammar school when his wife became ill, and was now teaching part-time. His daughter Janet worked in London, and the other, Catherine, lived near him with her husband and little Katie. But Willa had pretended not to notice the invitation implied in these offerings. This direct question was different, more difficult to ignore.

She typed the reply she hoped would put an end to it:

```
I  have  lost  my  daughter...
```

Look at that, said the voice in her head. *Evasion comes so easily.*

∞

Her eyes are fixed on Willa's face.

Even before Imogen could speak, Willa would catch her daughter watching, as though waiting, as she bathed and cleaned and hummed and reassured, *Everything is all right, baby, everything will be all right*. And for a long, long time after she could form questions in her soft, childish voice, still Imogen watched and waited. But at the age of ten, at the end of a day when she has been subjected to another *review*, a string of medical students gawping at her genitals as though they were abstract, a plaster cast of some monstrous stillbirth, she finally puts into words what she has been waiting for, letting them flow over the soft fur of Lucifer's back as she holds him tightly to her.

Mum, what's wrong with me?

Willa, pinioned, pierced through the heart, hates herself for the dishonest mangling of words that she knows will come out of her mouth, the practised way she will skate over the truth of her daughter's body. *Nothing's wrong. There was a little problem when you were born, but everything has been fixed. You're perfect.*

It's what they told her to say, all those years ago, to avoid frightening Imogen or giving her a reason to feel different.

Imogen looks at her gravely. *Then why...?*

She doesn't know whether Imogen's bravery fails her or whether she senses, and spares, Willa's discomposure, but the question is left hanging, incomplete, unanswered, suspended between them like a strand of razor-wire.

I have lost my daughter...

The cursor pulsed beside the ellipsis, like the beat of her heart.

She held down the 'delete' key and it swallowed the characters and spaces one by one. And then she started to type again.

October 1870

Albany

A perishing wind from the Southern Ocean rushes up York Street, undermining the warming effects of the sun. Jock puts down his spade and rubs blanched fingers against his thighs.

The roadworks are finished, as far as the official record is concerned – the project of levelling, widening and metalling that has occupied the town's small convict population for five years. But there remain some tasks of clean-up and beautification, as befits a thoroughfare now reputed to be the finest in all the colony. The gang is clearing away spoil dug out during the construction of gutters, and carting it to the P&O depot for sale as ship's ballast, causing one town wag to remark, *Yes, go on, take our sullage and why not leave it in Smelbourne in return for all the scarlatina and influenza they've given us!*

Jock turns his face to the wind, towards the terrace, where an approaching huddle of passengers from the *Salsette* en route to the eastern colonies is being blown up the hill in a flurry of mockery and complaint. As the visitors come level with the convict gang, he can hear scraps of conversation tossing in the wind.

Not a thing to commend it…
Whyever is there not some manner of conveyance for visitors?
Nature has done all possible for the place and man, very little…

Staring their disdain full in the face, he picks up his spade and plunges it into the rocky spoil with as much menace as he can muster, and is gratified to hear a squeal from a man in a silk hat. When they make a hurried left turn into Grey Street, his smile broadens. There is nothing down there but sand and decrepit allotments of rhubarb and arum lilies. Before long, they will be forced to stop and empty their unsuitable shoes.

He is inattentive today, daydreaming of freedom again, another chance at it soon to be his. Hooves clatter behind him and he swings around in time to see Hassell's fine grey mare out of control and bearing down fast, with Jeremiah Coghlan, one of the town's incorrigible drunks, half slipping from a saddle he has no right to be on. Diving sideways to escape the horse's gallop, Jock crashes face first into the lip of a barrow.

The narrow sash window of the prison infirmary throws a single shaft of light across the otherwise gloomy ward, and it is into this blast of brilliance that a face appears, hovering over the cot beneath a halo of pale, frizzled hair. Jock blinks rapidly and the image flickers – on–off, there–not – until gradually settling long enough for him to realise where he is.

With lucidity comes pain. His head aches, his face hurts, and there is a more insistent throb from his right temple that he tries to explore but meets the resistance of a wad of lint damp with blood and phenol.

His eyes dart back to the face, becoming clearer now, regarding him in a thoughtful, speculative manner.

Chopin.

He has a reputation for peculiarity, this sallow-faced man who, being conscripted into Rogers's service as an orderly, has blossomed there among the phials and unguents in the dispensary, tending the sick in the hospital ward, laying out the departed in the dead house. It is said that he has the confidence of the town's medical officer, Dr Cecil Rogers, who seems to look on him as some splendidly convenient unpaid apprentice. But whether this is because of the convict's skill or a matter of the doctor's own pressing social priorities, who can say?

Jock had once glimpsed Chopin through the dispensary door with Rogers's precious microscope, peering at wriggling things on bits of glass. Chopin is looking at him now with that same intensity, as though taking mental notes, practising observation.

He tries to sit up but falls back weakly, pain slicing at his temple.

Lie still, Chopin instructs in a low, soothing tone. *You have a concussion, and bruising, and a cut to the head.*

He feels himself sliding into night, and then jerking awake again. His fingers touch some soft weave of fabric, lighter than a blanket – *not* a blanket – nor the lining of the palliasse beneath him, either. He is wearing it, *wearing* it! No sign of the coarse duck trousers and vest that are the uniform of convict gangs.

Where're ma clothes? he demands, but his voice wanes to a whisper.

Soiled, Chopin says. *Only fit for the fire. Dr Rogers can't abide filth in his hospital. But don't fret, I kept these for you.* He fishes in his pocket and deposits on the cot a folded strip of newsprint and a small grubby handkerchief. *Found them in the lining of your shoe.*

Jock snatches them up in his fist and glares at Chopin until the man drops his curious eyes and leaves.

Motes of dust dance in the stream of light pouring from the window, minute particles of the world at large.

Do you bleed?

Jock looks at Chopin, nonplussed, and his hand goes instinctively to the wound on his head that the man is dressing, a deep gash from temple to forehead that meets up with an old scar carved by a coin in a fist.

No, no, I mean do you ever bleed...from your privates?

Jock's eyes widen in alarm and he shakes his head vigorously.

What about pain? Here or here? And he gestures either side of his gut.

Jock remains silent, wary as the orderly ties off the bandage, and the moment it is done he is on his feet.

Chopin looks at him intently, like a man with so many questions to ask that he cannot decide what the first should be. But when Jock backs towards the door he shrugs and calls for the warder. *Go, then, for now,* he tells Jock, *but the doctor will want to look at that wound when next he does his rounds.*

As the warder escorts him back to the cells, Jock reflects on the pleasing prospect of his impending release on ticket of leave, for the second time, with a ten-day pass to seek work. In all likelihood he will be able to avoid Chopin for the next four days. He isn't afraid of coming before the doctor: Rogers won't be doing rounds at the depot any time soon, not when the *Salsette* is in port.

But later, lying on the straw palliasse, he stares up at the mossy roof and thinks again of Chopin's question. He understood

275

the man's meaning. He remembers the bloody mess of Bridget's rags. Mary had told him to watch for blood, *For we cannot know that the curse will not yet take you.* But time went by, years, and there had been no sign of the dark clots that oftentimes he had seen in lavatory closets. *Thank the Lord*, Mary had whispered. *'Tis easier to believe a dog is not a duck when it don't be having wings.*

He pulls from the heel of his new slipper the two items retrieved by Chopin, and unfolds the paper, drawing a finger down the claims for Holloway's Pills:

> THE FEMALE'S BEST FRIEND
>
> For all debilitating disorders peculiar to the sex and in every contingency perilous to the life of women, youthful or aged, married or single, this mild but speedy remedy is recommended with friendly earnestness. It will correct all functional derangements to which they are subject.

Were it not for the memory of Bridget's monthly rags, he might not make the connection, for not all the words are within his grasp. But he fathoms that he has been spared some great pain. Why, then, this pull at his gut?

Confused, he shakes out the once-white handkerchief, still as soft as down, a cluster of lilies embroidered in one corner. If Kat missed it when he left, it was unlikely she would have attributed the loss to him, would never have pictured him holding it to his face and yearning for Lord-knows-what.

June 1871

Albany

The boarding house of Ann Gregory in Earl Street is a lively den, even at those times when a lodger might wish it otherwise. Mrs Gregory – the *Mrs* conferred as a title of form rather than fact – has only one test when it comes to accepting boarders: the wherewithal to hand over four shillings sixpence-ha'penny a night, in advance. As a result, her clientele is an eclectic mix of seamen, sandalwooders, labourers, travellers and all species of men from outlying areas come to town for a spree. But for all that these paying guests are capable of disturbing the peace, and do so regularly, the cause of many a police visit to the low iron cottage with the pea-green door is Mrs Gregory herself.

On the momentous day when he is to become a free citizen of Swan River Colony, Jock wakes to a welter of profanity barrelling through the flimsy walls of the shared lodgings room. Scindian Foote, the other occupant – *citizen of everywhere and nowhere*, he is wont to claim, on account of his having been born at sea on the first convict ship to the colony – opens the window shade a crack.

Margaret Beard, he reports, seeing Jock is awake. *Drunk. Accusin' Annie of all manner o' scandals. Better'n a play, I tell ya.*

Jock groans and begins pulling on trousers and shirt over his flannels. *Where's Andrews?* he asks.

Just watchin'. Havin' hisself a hoot.

The screaming continues even after PC Hogan steps in, and even when he leaves with a struggling Mrs Beard in cuffs. David Andrews, Mrs Gregory's violent sometimes-partner, back on shore for a few days, surveys the sorry scene from the front verandah, smug and virtuous for once, for it is usually he who a constable must drag away. Andrews will tell anyone who will listen that he left a wife and four children in Edinburgh when he was transported, and declares this enforced desertion to be the only favour Her Majesty has ever deigned to grant him. He nods amiably as Jock shoulders his canvas bag and heads off down Earl Street, and although Jock briskly returns the gesture he resolves to spend his four shillings sixpence-ha'penny elsewhere this night, knowing the heat of Andrews's rage and that it is not in the man's nature to be peaceful two nights running.

Princess Royal Harbour sparkles in the winter sun, as blue as cornflowers. From the Spencer Street hill he can see all the way across to Stuart's Head and Limeburner Point, an expanse of land and sea and sky that has the power, still, to make him gasp, a token of incredulity from a child of northern slums.

By the time he turns from Grey Street into York, the little town is awake and going about its business, and he passes people whose stories he has heard. Bobby Gardiner, the bird man, ambles by with a big white cockatoo in a chickenwire cage. The bird is famous for screeching outrageous rhymes as Bobby sells possum-skin rugs and lamp-stands made from emu legs on the wharf, and Jock has noticed that this is sometimes good for business and sometimes not, depending on the refinement of the steamer passengers. Louisa Nicholls, savagely beating a rug looped over a tree branch outside her *boarding house* – so they call it – glares in response to his nod. Bedevilled by unreliable men and illegitimate progeny, Mrs Nicholls finds solace in rum and litigation, neither pursuit endearing her to the Resident Magistrate. John Carrotts looks decidedly queasy as he clutches Jock's shoulder and says, *How do.* Carrotts is in town from Balgarup for a few days, and certain to be charged at least once by the constabulary for being drunk while in charge of a team, and probably by Mrs Nicholls also for insulting language. Schoolmaster Thomas Palmer, a splendid example, held up to all, of transportee made good *and it's a pity there's but one of him*, nods from the door of the Standard Bakery Tea Rooms. Jock skirts around Catherine Covert, who is trying in vain to keep her cows from straying on the road and from the attention of PC Fagan. Mr Finlay bids him a hearty *Good morning, Jock*, and stops a moment to enquire after the status of his freedom. Once a police inspector but now the town's tidewaiter, the man is always fit to burst with gossip and affairs of importance.

As Finlay bustles away, Jock wonders whether he will look different to the former policeman – to all these people – when next he passes this way; whether the certificate of freedom he is about to receive will change the cast of his face, his posture, his gait. Pausing outside the premises of William Munday, he takes stock of his glassy reflection in a window framed with boots tied together in pairs with string.

What does a maybe-man, a nearly-man, a soon-to-be-free-man, look like? He peers closer, curious. It is not often he glimpses more of his likeness than the portion that fits in a small piece of shaving glass. He has always thought of himself in terms of a shape, as formless as the figures he and Bridget used to draw in the dirt on the stairs. But here, staring back, is a face like other faces, with the details of skin and hair and bone that mark out one from another. An oval face lengthened by chin whiskers, broadened by a soft moustache curving to meet them; deep, grave eyes; a sweep of long hair, straight, parted on the right. A face of thirty-three years, youthful fleshliness gone, its planes scarred by acne and circumstance. When he looks only at the shape in the glass, he sees what all else see, but in this face is a story that none would believe.

Perhaps, after seven years, two months and six days in the Swan River Colony, John King, 7756, will walk away from the Albany Depot marvelling that freedom is conferred in such small tokens: a square of parchment, signed and stamped in wax, the label *Expiree* that he will carry always, and the phlegmatic benediction of two words: *Good luck.*

Imogen's face

The library copy of *The Brand on his Coat* was open at a photograph of William Chopin, the convict who had become a chemist and later an abortionist. The nineteenth-century equivalent of a 'mug shot' on the occasion of his 1893 reconviction, it showed a frail, elderly man with ethereal white hair and a long wispy beard. Two views – profile and portrait – were conjoined like Siamese twins, and while Chopin-in-profile gazed dutifully to the right, the hooded eyes of the portrait view looked piercingly at the camera. His hands were folded protectively across his chest, his prison number above them. Willa brooded over this image, wishing it had been the colony's practice to photograph all of the nearly ten thousand convicts who had arrived in the middle decades of the century. What she wouldn't give for a photograph of Little Jock.

She closed her eyes, trying again to summon up a picture of his face, but the image that played out was too far away – a furtive figure disappearing nimbly into a High Street close in a swathe of fog, with a cap drawn low across the brow – and she had to zoom in to capture him in close-up. *No*, she corrected herself. *That's not right. I'm conjuring a child, an adolescent.* But she could not find in her imagination the face of the convict who arrived at Swan River at the age of twenty-six, and was startled to realise that it was because she had been giving Little Jock Imogen's face.

When Imogen was nearly fourteen, her face changed forever.

In that hard year, a year in which Imogen began to shed some of her unconditional childish trust, to revisit questions, pick away at answers, Willa returned to the specialist. *Is it time?* she wanted to know. Was it time to admit that the hormones Imogen had been taking since she was eleven years old were not just to strengthen her bones? To explain to her why she did not have periods like other girls? To talk openly about her scarred genitals instead of vaguely referring to *things down there* needing *fixing up* when she was born (when had she started sounding like Orla)? In effect, to prove to Imogen once and for all that she could not rely on her mother to tell the truth about the least little thing?

Age-appropriate explanations only – only – if they absolutely cannot be avoided, the specialist had advised from the beginning. As the mother of a newborn, Willa could never imagine what could be appropriate in circumstances like these, and allowed herself to be persuaded of the inherent kindness of secrecy and silence, all wrapped up and sanctioned, as it was, by the medical profession. But as her daughter grew older, Willa had to suppress the needling suspicion that the only thing more toxic than the truth was her oh-so-responsible lies. She had asked the specialist, hopefully, about the possibility of counselling but there was none to be had – not in this highly specialised area – and later when she mentioned the conversation to Orla there was a small, controlled explosion and she was left in no doubt that her mother thought counselling was for the demonstrably broken-down; the merely damaged *bucked themselves up and got on with it.*

Bring her in for a review – long overdue – and afterwards we will just see what questions she might raise, the specialist said, and although the hint of joint culpability in that suggestion appealed to Willa, she knew what a *review* would entail for Imogen and kept pushing it from her mind. And so that hard year stuttered on, from question to question, until the accident eclipsed everything else.

The suddenness of Chas and Orla's death left Willa stunned. It was so incomprehensible that she felt benumbed, could scarcely keep her feet moving, her hands washing cups in the sink, her mouth forming words when the phone rang. Not until she went to the house, alone, to choose the clothes in which her parents would be buried, did the torpor break. There on the benchtop was a banana cake, left on a rack to cool. A minute more at the club, lingering over morning tea – a few seconds more of conversation – and Chas and Orla Samson, Club Pairs Champions, would have come home. Her mother would have iced the cake while Chas complained for the hundredth time that it was better just with walnuts on the top, while Orla declared, as she always did, *But Imogen likes lemon icing, so lemon icing it will be.* They would have been safe, living their ordinary lives, oblivious to the existence of a kid in a stolen Monaro who had run a stop sign, who had ploughed them into a limestone wall, who had walked away from a tragic palette of twisted green metal and bloodied bowling whites.

And so it was a stale banana cake that undid Willa, unleashed in her a feral cry for the senseless waste of love.

She began to worry for Imogen, listening to the turbulent vibrato of the cello mourning from her room. The loss of those two central, irreplaceable figures in her daughter's life found its language in Dvorak's elegiac 'Largo', Saint-Saëns's 'The Swan'. Grief swung from passionate weeping to subdued defeat at this brutal revelation that life could be snuffed out *like that!* Willa held her, rocked her to sleep. But in time the sickly perfume of Oriental lilies – from Matthew, from the bowling club, from cousins Willa hadn't seen in fourteen years – began to fade. Tentatively she broached the subject of moving into Chas and Orla's house, a house they both loved, and Imogen seemed to take some comfort in the idea of this enduring connection.

The task of dealing with her parents' effects was daunting, sorting what would remain, what would need to be boxed up for storage, what could be thrown away. In the kitchen, Willa rummaged through Orla's vast array of gadgets and appliances, glad enough to keep most of them, though she stared, perplexed, at a professional-looking preserving kit complete with four dozen jars in six sizes. She thought of the scrawny, stunted plum at the bottom of the garden that *had never delivered the goods*, as Chas always said; the apricot trees that had to be dug out when all three succumbed to leaf curl because Orla refused to let Chas spray anywhere near where Imogen played. A smile softened her sombre face. How like her mother, to be well prepared for a glut of fruit that never materialised.

Chas's study made her wonder whether his much-lauded retirement had actually left him with too much time on his hands. It looked impressive, with the glossy desk flanked by filing cabinets, the gold-plated pen-and-pencil set. But when she began rifling through the suspension files – and what an unforgivable intrusion it felt – she noticed the labelling on the files' plastic tabs. Alongside compartments for share certificates and bank statements were those marked 'Groceries', 'Newspapers', 'Homebrew Supplies', and it saddened her to imagine her father in his shirt and tie, his slippers, cataloguing every transaction of his day-to-day life.

The glass cabinet in the dining room caused her some disquiet, but eventually she sat down with sheets of butcher's paper and began wrapping figurines, plates, decanters, trinket cases, firmly ignoring Orla's protestations running through her head: *But it's Lalique…it's Lladro…it's Dresden!*

There's no right way of doing this, she thought, no way to avoid blundering through the history people leave behind, trampling over the things they valued. The only comfort is that they will never know.

Arriving home at the flat, exhausted, she was pleased to find that Imogen, for the first time in weeks, was not pink-faced and weepy. She had even made a start on packing up her own things after school.

Next morning, next room, and it was the little things that tore at Willa's heart: Chas's familiar felt hat, an old pair of midnight-blue suede gloves that reminded her of feeding ducks on blustery days and holding her mother's hand. Orla's oak armoire was an eclectic time-capsule filled with old passports and birth certificates, Willa's school reports, tissue-wrapped baby shawls, tiny knitted boots, trophy jewellery Orla had never worn. And there were photo albums, dozens of them. Willa started stacking them in a box: plastic folders of holiday snaps, a wedding album with silver-embossed covers, cardboard books containing small black-and-whites, each page interleaved with transparent paper, brightly coloured records of her own progression through childhood, volume after volume of Imogen's. She picked up one, expensive-looking, with padded covers of pale pink velvet. But as she scanned through it, her face became hotter at each turn of the page. She had not seen this before, but she could guess what it was.

Orla had placed side by side photos of Willa and Imogen at around the same age, paired portraits no doubt for her to rake over and compare, gauge the features on Imogen's face, the shape of her body. She could imagine her mother noting welcome similarities in the soft swell of lips, finely tapered fingers, the thick lashes fringing blue-green eyes. More worrying, those shoulders, arms; Imogen's square jaw, disturbingly Matthew's. But Orla wasn't looking for traces of her detested son-in-law; she was comparing daughter with mother, alert for telltale legacies of prenatal testosterone – *boyishness* – that would need to be disguised, when the time came, with cleverly applied makeup, tricks with the cut of a jacket, the styling of hair.

Damn you, Mother.

When she returned home in the late afternoon, the flat was quiet. Imogen was not in front of the TV, not in her room, though Willa could see she had been busy again, taping down boxes, marking them with a thick black pen.

Imogen, she called. *Imogen?*

There was a hush in the flat, a chapel silence, and a shrill note of panic entered her voice. *Imogen?*

A box half filled with clothes in the door to Willa's bedroom.

The wardrobe door ajar.

Books and papers and X-ray films scattered on the floor.

From a distance, the photographs in the journal open on Imogen's lap looked vaguely pornographic. But when Willa drew closer, she could see her daughter's fingers splayed like parentheses around the abstract Willa could recite by heart:

...diagnosis of chimerism, the result of one XX embryo
and one XY embryo undergoing complete fusion in
utero to produce a singleton with admixtures of
genetically male and genetically female cells (karyotype
46XX/46XY). True hermaphroditism in humans
is extremely rare. It was observed that the subfertile
mother had been undergoing fertility treatment at the
time of conception, to regulate oligomenorrhoea, but
the precise causality is unknown...

Imogen turned and looked up at Willa, stricken, words
arrested in the quavering pulse at her throat. Years of formless
suspicions confirmed in print and illustrated in colour for the
world to see.

William Chopin's prison photograph, with its twin faces, was
still on the desk in front of her. She looked at the frail, elderly
man gaoled for helping powerless women and girls. He was
doing what he believed was right, she thought. Rather his guilt
than hers.

The cause of Willa's infertility had been single, easily
correctable by a common fertility drug. *Sub*fertility, the
gynaecologist had called it, in fact, and if they were patient in
time *nature might take its own course*. But she and Matthew had
not been patient; they had wanted their family early, in love with
the idea of being young parents. The drug came with fine-print
warnings about (rare) side effects; the gynaecologist had rattled
off a list of (rare) *negative outcomes*. But it was like the waiver
you sign before surgery: you never think of (rare) potentialities
as having anything to do with you. She and Matthew had
discussed – dismissed, if she was honest – the risk of multiple

birth, reassuring each other that they could handle twins. As if that were the worst that could happen.

The precise causality is unknown but still she could not forgive herself; it had felt like a punishment for wanting what she was never intended to have. And in trying to set the world to rights so that Imogen should not suffer the weight of it, she had succeeded only in hurtling herself beyond forgiveness for all time. It wasn't a drug that had caused the change in Imogen's face.

No, you did that yourself. You and your lies.

The Brand on his Coat was due back and she walked to the library to return it. As she was opening the front door again, a sharp chime from the study heralded the arrival of new mail.

It had been more than a week with nothing from James Donaldson, no reply to an email she wished she had never sent. But here he was, apologising, pleading a bout of late-winter flu. It was her instinct to disbelieve him, to think instead that the unexpected story she'd added to her last email had frightened him away. But there was concern in his gentle words, concern and kindness, and a blind sort of faith that, for once, she did not resile from:

> My late wife, a canny woman, once told me that when it comes to family history, motivations are as important as consequences. And if you will permit the opinion of a man whose biases about families you already know: blood will find its way in the end.

Once again it assailed her, the capacity of the world to surprise.

December 1872

Kojonup

The Semblance of Old England, like most public houses in outlying parts, is a haven of democracy, enfolding all who pass through Kojonup into its levelling embrace. Governors and bishops, explorers and graziers, merchants and salesmen, labourers and erstwhile felons – all seek hospitality of some sort, at some time, under Mr Elverd's shingled roof, and all meet the curiosity of a small community avid for news of elsewhere. Over the previous months the townsfolk have been well served by contractors of the Electro-Magnetic Telegraph Company, who have been clearing the line between Perth and Albany, and cutting and erecting poles. And tonight they are expecting the society of the company's supervisor, here to connect the wire with his team of ticket-of-leavers (the latter *not* welcome at the Semblance).

On the wide verandah, William Weir is warming up for a hearty evening. His concertina accordion quavers, coughing out dust from the bush track into town, before gathering enough momentum to accompany him in a popular air:

Oh, where have you been, Billy Boy, Billy Boy
Oh, where have you been, Charming Billy
I have been to seek a wife, she's the joy of my life
She's a young thing and cannot leave her mother

Jock, sweating inside on his usual perch, nurses the dregs of an ale and watches Elverd run around like one of his wife's fowls. With a full house – and a rowdy one at that – the publican doesn't look like a man who would take kindly to the suggestion of a modest loan. But there is naught but a few pennies in the pocket of Jock's moleskins, and it would be a waste of good words to ask Garretty on his left or his mate Joe Hall on his right, both of them poor as bandicoots.

Jock winces as Weir tries to strangle a jig out of the melancholy 'Annie Laurie', to honour the arrival of the company supervisor who is, they say, a Scot. The next offering, 'Loch Lomond', though equally mournful in lyric, is far more amenable to Weir's jaunty rendition, and a thin applause comes from the crowd on the verandah.

Ach, don't encourage him, Jock groans to no one in particular.

Hall eases himself off the packing-case bench. *I'll see if he knows 'Rose of Tralee' or somesuch*, he says. *Put all you Scotchies outta yer misery.*

Mrs Elverd bustles in from the store-room with a gallon bottle under each arm. *Another, Jock?*

He shakes his head glumly.

Look, she says, *shall I fill your mug and you do something for me in return?*

He looks up hopefully, as does Garretty.

The Queen's on the list, and I don't have time to watch out for her. Keep your eyes peeled, eh, and come fetch me if you see her?

His mug and spirits brimming again, Jock leaves Garretty pleading with Mrs Elverd for the same arrangement, and ambles over to the open window to watch the shadows. He chuckles to himself at the notion of his being commissioned for such duty. He has been thrown out of the Semblance himself more than once, and from Mr Tunney's up the road, but in truth so has nearly everyone. The town's Resident Magistrate has found cause to relieve him of several shillings in fines but has never yet put him on the prohibited list – barred from even entering licensed premises. He cannot say the same of his old nemesis, Maryann McDonnell, better known these days as the Queen of Kojonup.

A voice whispers in his ear. *So this is the Semblance of Old England, young Jock. Not much of a semblance that I can see!*

He swings around and gapes at the supervisor of the Electro-Magnetic Telegraph Company, all dressed up like a shilling dinner. Fleming.

∞

Do they know you were a convict? He keeps his voice low and glances around.

Fleming dismisses Jock's question with a mercurial wave of the hand. *There's many who must, and good luck to them. But to those who don't I volunteer nothing. Appearances are what talk, young Jock. I have made my little forays into education, journalism, and now there's this ambitious enterprise of Horace Stirling's. That is how most know me. Appearances.*

Jock is awestruck by the magnitude of Fleming's bravura confidence, no more evident than in the readiness with which he is prepared to acknowledge, however quietly, his former *Clara* mess-mate.

There's value in keeping your own counsel, young Jock, he says gently. *There's much to be said for declining to tell all to all who may want to know.*

Approaching with a mug in each hand, and looking every bit as though he has business to discuss with the telegraph supervisor, is Mr Chipper. For all Fleming's nonchalance, Jock is unwilling to embarrass him with the taint of the past. He inclines his head in warning and half turns towards the window.

Fleming accepts the proffered drink from Chipper, allows himself to be led away to a table of the town's respectable men, but as he takes his seat he glances in the direction of the window and winks.

On the verandah, on the other side of the window, fists are being thumped on tables, epithets tossed around. The farmhands from Spencer's reckon it's a disgrace that Shanahan was put away. *Raping the Queen, d'ya mind, the Queen! When it's known to all she's a liar, and worse.*

Jock has heard it all before, heard it and felt unmoved other than for an uncomfortable twinge of satisfaction he would rather not own. Armstrong, his master, had been in Albany at the time of the trial and had reported to all and sundry the deposition of Maryann McDonnell. Shanahan, said she, had broken into her home, threatened her with an axe, dragged her out to the waterhole and thrown her in. Later, he came back and barged in again, slamming her down on the kitchen table. The new Resident Magistrate had dismissed the charge of rape, and if it were not for the evidence of Mrs Loton, attesting to the extent of her neighbour's injuries, he might not have entertained the charge of assault, either.

That magistrate knows a hen with three legs when he sees one. Still, eighteen months is eighteen months. Done for a woman like that!

Jock has no love for Maryann McDonnell. But the encounter with Fleming has done its work this night – nothing like a brush with the past to raise up demons. Ornery as a goat, that woman was, and a liar and no mistake. A mean woman, mean and hard. But as he broods darkly into his empty glass, unbidden images form in the thickness of noise and tobacco smoke. Her face as Shanahan tears at her clothes, pushes her down on the kitchen table, her hair in the flour, breaking her open, breaking through the mean, the hard, splitting her body, spilling blood bright as pomegranate...

And the face he is imagining becomes his own, the one broken is he, the splitting open, the blood spilling, his eyes on Reilly cowering in the corner, bright as pomegranate, those rat-eyes on him...

A burst of laughter jolts him back to the Semblance.

Jock slips outside, around the back of the pub, his guts turned to water. He has heard it all before, but now he heaves beside the water barrel. He has heard it before and felt unmoved, but now the fit of his body loosens inside his skin.

He heaves again and again.

Outside the store-room door, waiting for Mrs Elverd, Jock hears fragments of conversation around Chipper's table, Fleming's booming voice.

...young John took to Fremantle like a duck to water...

...Emma's involvement with the church...

So, true to his word, against the odds, Fleming had done it: he had brought his wife and child out to the colony. Jock looks down at the tattoo on his hand, the pale blue hieroglyph of family that soothes and wounds and reminds him of where he has come from. There had never been the slightest chance he could bring his family to the new world. Mary would have been too frail to come, anyway. He doubts Bridget could have been persuaded.

Would they even remember his face if they could see him now?

Ah'm ill, he tells Mrs Elverd as she struggles through the door with half a dozen mugs hooked onto her meaty fingers. *Ah cannae stay tae keep watch.*

With Garretty already pressed into service, she frets only for the loss of Jock's refill. *What sort of a man do you call yourself that can't handle two pints!*

A small gathering turns out two days later to farewell Mr Fleming, who has supervised the wiring and the installation of equipment, and trained the new telegraphist, Mr Chipper's daughter, in Morse code. Jock, in town to fetch supplies for Armstrong, watches from Elverd's vine-covered verandah as Fleming acknowledges Kojonup with a regal wave and rides off with his ticket men to connect the next section of the line.

Wounded storytellers

The wisteria was straggly, dropping its leaves, exposing a crosshatching of old, gnarled canes. Willa tried to ignore the flaking paint on the fretwork and the timber posts, the alarming sag of the bullnose verandah. If she needed any confirmation of the uselessness of contemplating repairs, there was a credit card statement in her hand that would do the job nicely.

The other envelope that she had pulled out of the letterbox was for Imogen, and Willa frowned at it as she closed the door behind her. Imogen's financial situation, though long beyond Willa's control, was an abiding worry. How many part-time hours could she manage while studying? Willa had transferred her own savings into her daughter's account when it had become clear that Imogen's leaving was only a matter of time and nothing could be done to stop it. But that silent help was all Imogen had accepted. Matthew had tried to make a deposit in her account, but he phoned Willa in consternation when the bank informed him that it had been closed and would give him no further information. *Do you know where she's living?* he demanded. *Do you have an address?* But Willa could not speak. It had been one more rejection, one more message to stay away, to keep the promise she had reluctantly made.

The quarterly statements for the small trust account set up by Chas and Orla, payable to Imogen at the age of twenty-five, were still posted to Willa's house, still addressed to Imogen Gates. She put the envelope with the others for safekeeping in a box on top of the filing cabinet, her fingers straying over the little stack of mail. If a life depended on it, she could probably track down the address where it should be forwarded, though she had resolved not to, certain that whatever might remain of her relationship with Imogen could be preserved only by staying away. She told herself she was respecting Imogen's choices, giving her the space she'd demanded, making reparation. But she knew that was only a partial truth. In spite of all she had said and all she professed to believe, she was waiting for her daughter to come back.

She stared at her desk, the blank computer screen, replaying the day that Imogen began to leave.

∞

Four troubled years after Imogen discovered the truth hidden in her mother's wardrobe, Willa finds a square of notepaper lying on top of a manuscript on her desk – put there deliberately, weighted down with a corner of the *Larousse Dictionary of Literary Characters*. She is puzzled when she picks it up and sees a web site address written in Imogen's large, rounded script. Opening her web browser, she types in the address: <www.thewoundedstoryteller.org>.

A home page springs on to the screen in deceptively soothing tones of aquamarine:

WELCOME TO
THE WOUNDED STORYTELLER

Kierkegaard wrote of the ethical person as editor of his life: to tell one's life is to assume responsibility for that life...In stories, the teller not only recovers her voice; she becomes a witness to the conditions that rob others of their voices.

Arthur W. Frank, *The Wounded Storyteller:*
Body, Illness, and Ethics

The Wounded Storyteller invites victims of intersex genital mutilation to bear witness to what society has done to them, to reclaim their voices and the truth of their own bodies.

We deplore the long-established system for treating infants of ambiguous gender. This system, which we call the Playing God Protocol (PGP), prescribes the surgical assignment of gender, based largely on consideration of genital 'acceptability' over and above reproductive, chromosomal and neurobiological considerations. Parents are instructed to reinforce what doctors have created through rigorous social conditioning of the child according to the assigned gender (*read:* reinforcing stereotypes), drawing a veil of secrecy over what came before.

We are not the first to note that PGP must be the most unethical form of treatment ever devised, requiring parents to raise children in an atmosphere of shame and denial, and doctors to perform irreversible, life-changing surgery without patient consent and therefore without being able to meet the fundamental responsibility of their oath: 'First, do no harm.'

If well-meaning parents and medical professionals are in any doubt of the legacy of PGP, we invite them to listen to, and with, the adult intersexuals who have chosen to tell their stories through this site in the hope of healing themselves and others.

As several of our contributors passionately point out, the existence of intersexuals throughout human history exposes as a lie the rigid categorisation of humans as male or female. We argue, instead, that gender is a continuum between male and female, linking rather than polarising. And we call for an end to the practice of mutilating the healthy bodies of intersexed infants in the name of cultural expectations.

Willa's hands are shaking but she can't feel them, can't feel anything, not even the pressure of her fingers on the keys as she clicks randomly on the names listed in the left margin – wounded storytellers, all of them.

Raph D.
When I finally got my medical records, there it was, written in my file: 'Successful surgical outcome.' So proud of their handiwork, the wankers. Successful to who? Not me, that's for sure. Sexual response: zero. Orgasm: what's that? No, successful in *their* terms: size, colour, cosmetic appearance. Their heterosexual terms. A hole for a pole...

Herculine
I asked my mother what I looked like when I was born, what deformity was so terrible that it had to be cut away. All she could do was cry. It was as if there were no words for what I was...

Jas
It isn't our bodies that need changing; it's the sickness of a society that can't accept difference. The same society that demonises the third world for circumcising baby girls...

Regan
I don't want to be touched, ever again. No one would want to touch me, anyway...

Mx S.

I had vaginoplasty at the age of four months. Couldn't they have waited till I was old enough to have an opinion? Can someone tell me why a four-month-old needs a vagina?

Sensing a presence behind her, Willa swings around to find Imogen at the door with Lucifer in her thin arms. With her hair cropped close to her skull (how Orla would weep: *Your beautiful curls!*), her face is all eyes, all pupils, as large, as still, as Lucifer's. She looks achingly vulnerable but suddenly grown up, as though she is done with screaming, with those helpless rages of adolescence, and is trying on for size this cold, brittle shell.

I wish I'd been born in another time, when you couldn't have done what you did to me.

Lucifer springs down, slinks behind the door.

You blame me, I understand that. But try, Imogen, please try to understand. We thought we were doing what was best for you.

Because I was a monster and you couldn't let me be.

No! No…

Imogen's voice breaks into shards. *So you edited me, made me into something you could love.*

Love? Imogen, I've always loved you, more than anything, anyone. But that's why I had to choose. To defer choice – that's what this web site is saying? – well, that isn't safe and it isn't an answer. I had to choose for you. And I suppose I always knew that you would damn me, whatever choice I made…

Why did it have to be about you choosing? You could have called me a girl if that's what you thought was right. You could have dressed me like a girl, brought me up as your daughter. You could have done all that without carving me up to make you feel better.

*Please…*Willa begs, but it seems Imogen has taken a long time to gather the words and she cannot stop now until all of them have been spoken.

Did it ever occur to you, she says softly, *that you could have been a grandmother?*

Willa tries to speak but her daughter bats the words away with the palms of her hands. *It didn't occur to anyone, did it? You sacrificed a possibly fertile boy to create an infertile girl. You neutered me. Like an animal.*

Long after Imogen leaves, Willa keeps the page pressed to her cheek, as though the touch of her daughter's hand can be drawn from ink on paper.

She sat at her desk, surrounded by the folders and files of Little Jock's life. *I wish I'd been born in another time.* That's what Imogen had told her before she left. Well, here it is, she thought, and it isn't pretty.

Little Jock was born into an extremity of poverty you could not imagine, Imogen, and lucky for him that he didn't have the saltwasting form of CAH or he would have died within a few days. And lucky for him he wasn't abandoned by his family and consigned to hell as a circus freak – that's what the Victorians thought of hermaphrodites, Imogen. But he survived, and just look at *what* he survived: the Great Famine, the Irish diaspora, the slums of Glasgow, years and years in prison, transportation to the end of the earth, work gangs, uneasy freedom in a distrustful society – and yes, a lot of what happened to him happened to thousands of others, but think of the risks posed by that *unedited* body, Imogen, the need to conceal from surveillance a maleness that might not have passed muster. The crippling danger of intimacy, the threat of exposure in the confines of so many all-male spaces. And then, after surviving all of that, after being so unremittingly *lucky*, he is butchered and dismembered and his remains left to be worried at by native dogs and kangaroo rats and the whole damned township of Albany out on a forensic picnic and the police and the courts and newspaper reporters and finally, finally, by fakes like me who call themselves researchers, and do you think, Imogen, do you really think that the brutal obliteration of Little Jock was a matter of a few pounds and a load of sandalwood, or can you bring yourself to believe it just might have had something to do with the fact that he was intersexed, like you, but that because of when he was born, his parents had no choice but to *let him be*.

So this is it. All your fears for the ambiguous body wrapped up into a neat bundle called Little Jock. And I suppose you expect me to thank you for saving me.

Head sunk into the cross of her folded arms, she felt spent, too leaden, too dull to move, until finally a benevolent, throaty purr asserted its presence. She raised her head onto one elbow. In front of her were the piles of research material – the facts and fragments answering none of her questions. A soft warmth grazed her cheek and she came eye to golden eye with Lucifer.

He blinked companionably.

I still want to know, she told him. It was time to go back to the trial records. To begin at the end.

June 1877

Near Kojonup

The grey of late afternoon is deepening as a small covered cart rattles along a bush track cut by much larger wheels. The driver nudges the old mare on through a narrow trail on one side of the track, though it is tough going and the horse shies, skittish as acacia branches whip at its flanks. When the trail opens out into a clearing that few, surely, could know existed, the driver dismounts. He tethers the mare to a sheoak, loads his haversack with several bottles from the cart and takes down a lantern, as it will be dark by the time he returns. He sets off into the thick undergrowth, towards Norrish's north paddocks.

Jordan knows the whereabouts of every shepherd's hut between Kojonup and the Gordon River and south to Balgarup. He knows, too, that if he times his visits just so, just as the winter sun is fading, he is likely to score a supper of cold mutton and hot tea, as well as a respectable sale. They are a lonely breed, these shepherds, mostly ticket men or the newly free, and the appearance of a visitor is such a rare happenstance that they will gladly share their rations to prolong the novelty of hearing another human voice.

The bush begins to thin and soon he is in a hilly paddock of native grass. He trudges across it with his heavy load, carefully avoiding sheep dung and tangles of hovea, climbing towards the stand of thick scrub and banksia near Solomon's Well. As he crests a rise, he sees Norrish's flock, well covered in winter wool, shuffling with that restlessness of animals impatient for dusk to be done. Two black and tan sheepdogs fly out of the thicket and rush towards him, yapping and growling, but Jordan is prepared for shepherd's mates. He feels about in his coat pocket for some strips of tough old hide, and tosses a couple at the dogs, one in each direction. As they scuffle with these offerings, he heads towards the brushwood hut he knows lies beyond the banksias.

The shepherd, alert to his approach, is standing by a fire blazing in a half-drum, peering in his direction. By the time Jordan reaches him the smell of cooking meat has reclaimed the dogs' attention and they race back, barking madly around him.

There, now, Watch. Guid lad, Monty.

The dogs quieten at the shepherd's voice and flop to the ground, panting.

That's a well-trained pair o' mutts y've got there, Jock, he calls.

The little man smiles, beckoning him welcome.

As Jordan reaches the encampment, with its modest rush-roofed hut, his stomach lurches in disappointment. It does not look promising, no, not at all. The blackened pan on the fire sizzles with a glistening pink carcase that is not mutton. If he did not know it already by the smell, it would be clear from the skins pegged out on the banksia trunks that Little Jock's staple diet was possum. Only two reasons a man eats possum when he could eat mutton, he thinks. Low rations or no rations.

His suspicions are confirmed when the shepherd offers him a tin mug filled with tea from the billy. Only it is not tea but burnt tommy, a brew made from boiling up a piece of damper crisped to black in the fire – a poverty brew, clear as day.

Looks like you're due a visit from the boss, he says, unshouldering the haversack with a clink of bottle glass. *How 'bout some grog to liven things up round here?*

But, to Jordan's surprise, the little man shakes his head and stumps over to poke at the fire with his crook. *Ah could be discharged, you know that. Forfeit what's owed me, be sent on ma way.*

The sly-grogger looks at him sceptically. *Never stopped you before, Jock.*

Aye, true enough, he concedes. *But Ah'm putting by noo, saving ma poonds and shillings. A spree in town at the end of a month – tha'll have tae do me.*

Jordan grunts, his mercantile heart sinking to the soles of his bluchers. *Nothin' wrong with puttin' by, as puttin' by goes*, he says. *But what can a man do with a hoard all the way out here?*

Planning to buy masel' a sandalwood rig in a year or two, Jock says, hooking the possum carcase with the curved end of the crook and rolling it over.

Ah, well. And Jordan takes up the heavy canvas haversack again. He is about to heave it onto his shoulder when another line of enterprise occurs to him. *How are ye for togs, Little Jock? Togs and rags? I keep a small stock on hand for fellows such as y'self. You couldn't buy cheaper.*

The merest hesitation on the man's face is all the encouragement Jordan needs to plunge his hand into the haversack and fish out a tight roll of multi-coloured cloth from the bottom. An eclectic assortment of items of clothing appears as he unrolls and unravels.

Jock picks up a pair of shapeless flannels tinged with that yellowing grey of the well worn and worn again. He snorts. *Y've been snow-gatherin' in Albany, Jordan, Ah see. Whose line did you thieve this mingin' lot from?*

Now, I didn't say they're new. Only that they're cheap. What is it y're wantin'?

Jock doesn't say, but carries on poking around through shirts and gaiters. He picks up another item, so scrunched up as to be scarcely recognisable as a woman's vest. He raises an eyebrow at Jordan.

As good a dishrag as they come, Jock. Or for blowin' yer bugle. Look. And he smoothes out the wrinkled garment. *Let's say fourpence.*

He cannot fathom Jock's expression.

Fourpence, man, and y'll still have yer pounds and shillings!

It is raining by the time Jordan reaches the little clearing off the Ettakup track where he left his horse and cart. His clothes are wet, his bluchers reek of dung and he is only fourpence the richer for a night's work.

Hah! he cries, spurring the old mare on, back towards the track. *Hah!* The charcoal taste of burnt tommy is still in his mouth and he spits in disgust.

Dusk, and the dogs start their yapping again, tear off into the bush towards the Ettakup homestead. Jock leaps up from his place by the fire, but waits, listening, before setting off to investigate: it is too early for wild dogs. *Rabbits, more like*, he mutters. *Guid lads.* Watch and Monty are as fed up as he is with possum supper. But the dogs are returning and, to his surprise, a horse and rider are with them. It could only be Norrish. Jock sighs. Mr Norrish will size up the situation in one glance, and though he will not baulk at supplying next month's rations in advance, he will want to know the reason why, and Jock will be loath to tell him.

∞

Thomas Norrish studies the little man, a most reliable shepherd in nearly all respects. Good with the lambs – that he is – and you don't need to tell him a thing more than once. But this business with the natives…

Old Paddy, then, was it? Or Scandalous Dan?

Jock says nothing.

Look, you must know who's been about and likely to have done it, and we can't keep turning a blind eye. Robbing huts is no small crime.

There is no getting round it. The man can be stubborn. Norrish pulls from his saddle-bag a suet tin of Christen's melon jam wrapped with newspaper and tied with string.

You're not encouraging them, are you, Jock? The natives'll never learn to respect property if we're not firm about what's ours. He looks at Jock sharply, suddenly wondering whether the man's silence is a mask for shame or a guilty conscience. *It can be lonely out here, none would doubt it, and Lord knows a man shouldn't judge what he's not called upon to suffer himself, but…Look, Jock, no lasting good can come of it if you encourage the women…*

The little man cocks his head but he doesn't seem chastened.

Norrish feels he must press. *Look what happened with Peters. Now, that was a nice, clean little girl he took up with, but when the baby died she turned wild again and off she went, back to the bush, and no one's seen her since.*

Thanks, Mr Norrish, Jock says, taking the package. *Tell Mrs Norrish Ah'm obliged.*

I'll send Weir out with your rations. But look, if it happens again, I'll have to be getting PC Hogan out here. And you can be sure he'll be wanting names!

Jock raises his lantern and waves as Norrish rides away.

∞

When the sounds of the horse can be heard no more, Jock settles by the fire again. It's nearly eight, according to his silver watch. He looks with satisfaction at it, this prize he bought from John Norrish last summer – handsome, and a bargain. Thomas, John at Warkelup, George at Oakfarm – the Norrish brothers have always been fair, and never mind how a man made his way to these shores.

He remembers when he arrived at Ettakup, months ago, in search of work. It was dark, and a farmhand had sent him up to the house to see the master.

He could hear voices coming from inside, voices and laughter and the cry-babble of young children. The pretty sprigged curtains were not yet drawn, and he peered through the window into the middle room, already lit by lanterns. Around the table were the Norrishes with their three toddlers and a babe in a wicker basket. A little cluster of family, a gladdening sight for a lonely soul.

Thomas Norrish was reading aloud over the general din, holding a folded newspaper close to the lantern, while his wife fussed with sticky faces and fingers.

Whatever do you have in your hand, Liza? she was saying, and exclaimed when the little girl's fist flew open to show her, showering a mush of broad beans.

Ow, the smallest boy wailed piteously, flailing at bits of green. *Ugh! Ow!*

Jock smiles. The strongest memories, the ones summoned up in colour, are those that claim a little piece of the heart. It was the solemn Liza, with her messy russet curls, who did it. She had the look of Bridget about her.

He feels a stab of loss. What has become of his Bridget? He prays there is light in her face, flesh on her bones, that she has a brood to heal her. Bridget's bairns – surely they would be striplings by now. What would that be like, to watch them laugh and cry and grow, to know they were your own to love, and would love you back?

Muttering a blessing, he moves closer to the fire and unfolds the stiff yellow pages of the *Inquirer and Commercial News* that were wrapped around the melon jam. In the bottom right corner is a familiar box of words peddling hope.

> PILES, FISTULAS, AND INTERNAL INFLAMMATION
>
> These complaints are most distressing to both body and mind, false delicacy concealing them from the knowledge of the most intimate friends. Persons suffer for years from Piles or similar complaints when they might use Holloway's Ointment with instant relief, and effect their own cure without the annoyance of explaining their ailment to anyone.

It has been years now since he wrapped the package with brown paper and string and handed over a shilling to the post-master at Albany. But he does not know what Mary thought of the ointment, how Bridget found the little pills. Although he was careful to print the return address in clear letters – J. KING, C/-ALBANY POST, SWAN RIVVR COLONEE – there has never been a reply.

The coals have died to nothing and still Jock cannot sleep. The air is so cold that his breath, exhaled in puffs of white, seems a brittle thing, like thinnest ice. A wail echoes through the night, sorrowful enough to seem human.

He never sees them, the natives who sometimes visit the hut while he is checking the paddocks beyond the lambing station. Only once the girl came. Shared his meal. Stayed. He would never forget the warmth of her skin, the smoke and ash on her hair as she sidled into the hollow of his throat – nor the shriek that cut up the night, scattering parrots and stripping the leaves off trees. She recoiled hysterically, shrank from his regret, her eyes, as she backed away, wild with fear, with loathing. But she told no one – could not have done – for still the others come and go like spirits, taking some but never all. Surely they would have speared him as a demon if she had told.

As he shivers under possum skins tacked together into a blanket, a dog at his side and one curled into the pit of his knee, his thoughts turn to High Street: the nights he would huddle close to Felix or Bridget for the heat of another body; Mary, old and stooped, skinning onions, soaking peas, cajoling a flame from snow-damp coal; thefts committed daily by people he worked with, by neighbours in the tenements – thefts that were acts of need, impossible to deter by the playing out of consequences. Food and warmth, warmth and love. How closely they are bound, he thinks, with all manner of trespass.

When he wakes, stiff-limbed, from a fitful sleep but a few hours later, his mind is blurred from the distortions of dreams. For the briefest moment, he mistakes the frost-covered possum skin for Mary's old tweed coat.

In the clear chill of morning, Watch and Monty keep the flock moving up the rise, responding in part to Jock's sharp whistles and in part to instincts all their own. Once the sheep are settled on the grassy slope, an area already scouted for poison pea, he climbs further up into the scrubby granite hilltop, a place called Little Hell for reasons that must be known to someone. Here he can see for miles, miles that he knows, has tramped through, skirted around with Norrish's flock. Large tracts of banksia bushland. Paddocks of native grass, and the neater ones planted with hay crops around the Ettakup homestead. Soon seasonal grasses will die and wheat and barley will struggle. Great expanses of yellow and brown will appear. But now the land is winter-greening, assailing his memory. There is something about this place, some sweet sense of belonging he can scarcely credit, so remote is its origin in time and place. *Endless green. Smooth and clean as church glass. A child who wanted to stay with the snow-sheep forever.* They catch him in the heart, too, these memories of a long-gone child. Beat there softly like fingers on the bodhrán.

Later, after satisfying himself that the flock is at ease, with Watch and Monty resting but alert, he retreats into the granite outcrop. The cave, discovered some months before, looks as he left it, no evidence of visitation, and he draws out a bushel sack stowed behind a boulder whose lichened surface had been grooved long ago by the rubbing of a stone axe. He takes the sack out into the sun.

In his pocket is Jordan's dishrag, a fourpenny garment of soft muslin. He smoothes out the wrinkled fabric, pulling it into the shape of a woman's vest, brushing with callused fingers the delicate embroidered posies of delphinium spears and full-blown roses wreathed in scrolls of ivy and jasmine, the exquisite silk stitches surely the work of some immigrant Irish girl.

He holds the cloth against his body, moulding its shape to his. And then he folds the vest and stows it gently in the sack with other small, improbable fancies.

September 1880

Near Kojonup

Listen to this.

Thomas Knapp reads aloud from a month-old copy of *The Age* that has found its circuitous way to the dirt floor of the shearing shed at Ettakup. His forefinger, black with ink, underscores each halting word.

'If my life teaches the public that men are made mad by bad treatment, and if the police are taught that they may not ex–ex…'

Dever looks over his shoulder. *Exasperate.*

'…and if the police are taught that they may not exasperate to madness men they per–per–secute and ill treat, my life will not be entirely thrown away.'

The twelve men of Norrish's shearing team are quiet for a moment, taking in the calm philosophising of the celebrated inmate of Beechworth Prison.

D'ya think he'll swing, then? Knapp asks at length.

Every one of them has an opinion.

Nah!

Sure to.

They don't hang heroes.

The police will see to it that this one do. He murdered one of theirs, remember.

Jock gets up and takes a lantern, his day's work not yet done now that he is a man of property. While he is here for the shearing season, earning ready cash to finance the next sandalwooding trip, Norrish allows him to hobble his team behind the dairy, where there is plenty of spare feed at this time of the year. He pauses at the door, listening to George Whitten invoking a tired old recipe for the ills of the world: evil, crime, punishment, deterrence, protection, and yea, the good shall triumph. He thinks to toss in a former felon's reply, but who would gainsay Whitten when he is boiling like a billy? And to what end? If Ned Kelly's words are as nothing, then Jock knows that his own stand not a chance.

Wait till there's no iron mask between his bloody neck and the bloody noose, Whitten snorts. *I daresay he'll not be prattling about 'teaching the public' then!*

Jock slips away to check on his horses.

The light is fading fast when he sees Christen Norrish, leaving the dairy with a cloth-covered dish, stop and peer down at some small movement by the door. She leans forward, trying to reach it, but the solid mass of her belly threatens to unbalance her.

He rushes to scoop up a tiny mewling kitten, its ginger fur standing stiffly on end as though starched.

Goodness! she cries, looking around for somewhere to put her dish. *You're far from home, little one. Thank you, Jock.*

Ah can carry the butter, he offers.

Good, she says, exchanging the dish for the squirming kitten. *John is up at the house and will be leaving in the morning. Why don't you come up with me and bid him goodbye.*

He walks slowly, in step with her laborious waddling gait. She is, he supposes, about the age of Mary as he first knew her, but with a motherliness of a gentler breed. Christen Norrish is a soft Englishwoman turned farmer's wife in a struggling colony, and none would say her life was free from care and toil, but she is blessed if she but knew it, blessed with luxuries of a kind that come when survival is a given.

You are well, Mrs Norrish? he asks, stealing a glance at her flushed cheeks.

Yes, yes, and soon to be better.

How soon? he wants to ask, his eyes straying downwards, marvelling. It is as if she has swallowed the moon, as if it is dwelling there beneath the drab plaid skirt, ready to shoot back to the sky at any moment. His palms itch. He longs to reach out and touch it, the moon-child growing there, to feel life moving in his hands, the writhe of it beneath his skin, to keep it safe for as long as it will consent to stay.

He says nothing, and keeps a firm grip on the butter dish.

When they reach the stables, Mrs Norrish beckons him over to a flour bag in the corner, where a large white cat with marmalade patches is nursing two kittens just like the runaway. She hands him the kitten. *Put her in with her neglectful mother, will you, Jock? For shame, Bessie, for shame.*

The Ettakup homestead is always a flurry of children and babies – seven it will be with the impending new arrival – and tonight two little cousins add their voices to the general din. John and Margaret Norrish, with their boys, are spending the night, passing through on their way to Albany to take up the lease of the Weld Arms.

Jock waits uncertainly at the door, folding and refolding his billycock hat in his hands, until rescued by the affable John.

Ah, Jock my boy, he says, bringing two mugs out to the verandah. *Thomas showed me your team. Fine wagon you have there, too. How did you find it at the Pallinup?*

Trees there are fur the grubbing, Mr Norrish. But the wurrk is sore, aye it is. He turns up palms that still, after weeks, smell faintly of sandalwood and bear a fretwork of scars and calluses. Other sorenesses can't be shown and trouble him more. He shakes his head. *Ah'll be needing tae wurrk faster if Ah'm tae pay off ma debt to Mr Hassell. Ah owe him still fur ma tools an' rig.*

What about taking on a partner? John suggests. *Plenty do. Someone to strip the branches and clean off the bark while you do the pulling.*

Ah've been thinking on it, Jock admits. *One of the young Garrettys might be willing. Joe Hall, mebbe.*

You'll be right, Jock my boy.

He is bemused that John Norrish, nigh on ten years younger to be sure, always calls him *Jock my boy*, but then he would probably forever be *young Jock* to the likes of Norrish and Fleming and *Little Jock* to the world at large. Such is the way, it seems, when he is less than middling men in stature, lower still in status.

Hard worker such as yourself, you'll be right, John repeats. *And when next you bring in your load to Albany, I'll be counting on you to drink your profits at the Weld!*

An enormous pepper tree shades the yard of the police station, where explorers' parties have rested on their way through town, small groups have gathered to await the magistrate's sessions, and Aboriginal prisoners and convicts have been chained. Jock guides his team of six under the tree, bringing them to a halt on ground flattened and compressed by years of hooves and wheels. He jumps down from the wagon, flinching on impact, the familiar ache dragging at his sides, across his back.

As he takes off his hat and enters, a plaintive verse of 'I'll Take You Home Again, Kathleen' can be heard from the far end of the station, where a door of oiled jarrah as thick as a man's arm separates police quarters from the cells. PC Hogan, pen in hand, looks up from the daily occurrence book. *Weir*, he says, nodding towards the corridor. *Caught in Chipper's fowl house with a bird squawking under 'is arm.* He shakes his head. *And what can we do for you, Little Jock? Haven't seen you in the cells for a good long while.*

Jus' ma sandalwood licence, he says, grinning, and counts out two shillings and sixpence onto the constable's desk.

No dogs?

He shakes his head regretfully. It had broken him to leave the lads with Norrish's new shepherd, but dogs were luxuries to a man in debt for a wagon and team.

Right you are, then, says Hogan, pulling the licence book from a drawer.

Jock watches as he enters the details in bright blue ink, making one Jock King a legal sandalwooder until the end of October.

Have a good trip, then, and we'll see you back next month.

Weir is building up to his finale, strangling every vestige of melody from the refrain:

> *And when the fields are fresh and gree–ee–een*
> *I'll take you to your ho–o–ome ahhh–gain*

Jock throws Hogan a sympathetic wince as he turns to leave.

Could be worse, says Hogan gloomily. *Could've brought 'is bloody accordion with 'im.*

Jock snaps the reins and the team pulls out onto the Albany Road. His five-ton wagon, empty but for dry stores, chains, tools and sundry utensils, rattles as the wide iron rims bounce over stones and lurch through potholes.

A few hours out, heading towards the Pallinup River, he passes the track to Ettakup and promises himself he will return in high summer for a break from grubbing. He will always have a place at Ettakup – Thomas Norrish has told him so.

He settles back to enjoy the mild spring day. He is a man of honest livelihood, with a team, a rig and a second-hand silver watch. A man with a place to go and a place to come back to. A happy man.

A dialogue between two

It was late, and Lucifer looked up, tetchy at the interruption, as Willa returned to the study with a mug of tea. *Grumpy old thing*, she told him, scratching the side of his face with her free hand, and he tilted his head dreamily, magnanimous.

She shuffled paper aside to make space on the desk for her mug, and looked at the records of the murder trial, the stacks of A4 all tagged and annotated, read and re-read so many times that she fancied she could hear the words as they would have been spoken: earnest voices giving their depositions, breathless reporters narrating events for readers of the colony's newspapers. *I'm listening*, she said. *Tell me what really happened.*

Instinct led her back to the evidence of the doctor, Rogers. Those two *inorganic substances* in either side of the pelvis whose presence he could not explain but which Willa speculated were ovaries. *I feel confident they are the result of disease*, Rogers had told the judge. She scanned through the depositions, taking notes.

Robert Walker: 'He remarked to me once in the bush he was not so stout as he used to be, and he had shortened his belt.'

James Donohue: 'I went to King's and helped him to load his team.'

William Jeffries: 'I understood that Collins had been helping Jock's team in bad places.'

John Norrish: 'The last time I saw King he said he meant to cart seven more loads of sandalwood – that would clear all his debts, and then he would sell the team, divide the money with his mate and go to my brother as shepherd.'

A picture began to form in her head of a teamster weakened, struggling to manage horses, rig and load, with the physically tough toil of sandalwooding – perhaps planning an easier life for himself. Little Jock wasn't old. Might he have been ailing? In the early stages of – what, cancer?

She shook her head. Even if that were true, how could it be relevant to his murder – unless, perhaps, it made him more vulnerable, an easier target?

Could his murderer, in the intimacy of a lonely camp, have discovered the truth about Jock? She considered the scenarios: bathing (wasn't there a well at the Sinkings?), donning cleaner clothes before riding into town after a long stint in the bush. Impossible to guess at what Jock's naked body looked like – but she had come to believe that his genitalia must have been sufficiently virilised to pass as male through all the superficial exposures that the prison system would have demanded. She had discounted the possibility of womanish breasts for the same reason, and a certain amount of breast tissue could be expected in the case of a fleshy male. Little Jock had always been described as 'stout'.

A sexual relationship, though – that was different. She sat back in her chair, pondering. There was nothing in the records, nothing at all, to hint at Little Jock's sexuality. He remained single after gaining his freedom, but that was the norm among expiree convicts, and of course was no indication of desire.

The biography of Dr James Barry suggested that the celebrated surgeon had had a sexual relationship with Lord Charles Somerset, Governor of Cape Town; there had been a libellous placard displayed, accusing Lord Somerset of 'buggering Barry'. But with Barry's exact medical condition remaining a mystery, his case made for an uneasy comparison with Little Jock's. Willa grabbed a file of medical articles and rifled through them until she found the account of those few nineteenth-century intersexuals who'd had contact with physicians. One doctor reported – somewhat approvingly, she thought – that Matthieu Perret had lived as a man and 'showed no inclination towards either sex.' Maria Duriée, encouraged to shed her spurious female identity and become Carl Durge, was described as having had 'some predilection for the female sex but no sexual desire.' Willa had underlined these passages and made a note to herself in the margin: *Asexuality? Are they suggesting that opposing levels of male and female hormones neutralise sexual drive?* But there was also the story of Catherine Hoffman, who 'fulfilled, though imperfectly, male and female sexual functions.' So no pattern there.

These three were so-called 'true hermaphrodites', like Imogen: they had both ovarian and testicular tissue as well as mixed genitalia. If Willa's lay diagnosis of congenital adrenal hyperplasia was correct, Little Jock was a 'pseudohermaphrodite':

masculinised genitalia with female reproductive organs. Did that make a difference? She searched the medical file again for the article on Guiseppe Marzo, the first person to be described (in 1865) with CAH. Although genetically female, he 'transacted all of his affairs of life, including sexual intercourse, as a man' – heterosexual intercourse, presumably. And according to an article she had downloaded from the net, lesbianism was common among women with CAH – a result, so doctors claimed, of prenatal androgenic hormones 'masculinising' the brain.

Willa's jaw tightened. Hormones? Was it as simple as that? As clichéd? She resented it, this idea of sexual desire as programmed, a formula, when surely, surely, it was enigmatic, mercurial, impossible to pin down with science or logic or reason.

Listen to her. She was hardly in a position to make pronouncements about desire. Or perhaps she was. Perhaps it was precisely the yawning waste of loneliness, of all those years, that conferred on her a special brand of authority.

As for Imogen, she didn't know.

You don't want to know, do you?

Her daughter was nearly nineteen, for God's sake, not a little girl, but still Willa was reluctant to place them side by side in the one thought: *Imogen* and *sexuality*. She wondered whether this was true of all mothers…

…or just those who have meddled with the precious formula.

Imogen had been started on high doses of oestrogen at the age of eleven. It was all part of the prescription, the final stage. Prepubertal hormones to help mould breasts, feminine curves; to prevent facial hair, a lowering of voice – legacies of that long-excised testicle. But at sixteen she had finally refused to continue hormone treatment. Willa pleaded with her: *At least see the specialists first, listen to what they have to say, weigh up the consequences.* But Imogen vowed never again to entrust her body to the *caring* profession.

I feel like a lump of dough that's been pounded and rolled and cut, she spat. *I want to know what shape I really am.*

Willa pulled the blind and looked out on the empty street, the canes of wisteria strangling the verandah posts. Little Jock had lived at a time when autopsy was the only surgery he would ever have been likely to face, when hormones had not even been named, and he had survived in the shape he was meant to be. But his death…

She dropped the blind suddenly. It didn't matter whether the murderer accidentally discovered the truth. For all she knew, Jock, faltering at the edge of mortality and desperate for a witness to his life, might have decided to tell someone – and chosen the wrong person. But murder was a transaction, a dialogue between two. She had to listen not just to Jock but also to the man tried, convicted and hung for killing him.

She had become convinced of John Collins's guilt. It was not because of the flimsy motive put forward by the police, that Collins had killed Jock for material gain. Even the prosecution had decided at trial to distance itself from the idea that Collins had committed such a brutal and complex crime for what in the end amounted to a sum of forty pounds. In his opening address, the Crown prosecutor, the wily S. H. Parker, had told jurors, 'Motives were usually adduced to strengthen a case, but it was not necessarily incumbent upon the prosecution to assign a motive.' He suggested they 'might discard the question of motive from their minds altogether.'

No, it was the evidence of Thomas Masters that persuaded Willa that the jury had got it right.

Several people had passed by the Sinkings on the night of 1 October 1882. Horace Egerton-Warburton was the last of them to see Little Jock alive, and had left him and Collins together at their campfire at midnight. Four hours later, when Thomas Masters rode by on his way out from Albany, he found two teams but only Collins at the murder site. According to *The West Australian*:

> He arrived at the Sinkings about 4 o'clock, and, as he approached the camp, he heard a noise, as of a man groaning. Going up to the camp he went into a tarpaulin tent, near the fire, from whence the noise appeared to emanate, and found the prisoner there alone, groaning in his sleep. Witness woke him up and asked for a drink of water...Witness asked him if he had seen the comet that morning, and he replied that he had not. The comet was visible at the time, but the prisoner did not move...'When I woke him up he merely lifted his head up. He did not appear startled, but seemed somewhat distant or reserved...I mean that, judging by his manner, he did not wish me to remain on the camp.'

Was it in small details that stories revealed themselves? Stories, yes, but not necessarily the truth. There was no more reason for her version to be true than for any other, but Willa imagined a man of calm, wary surfaces, a man lying prone in his tent, anxious for Masters to leave, unwilling to move lest the blanket slip and reveal his bloodstained clothes; a man with demons concealed beneath those calm, wary surfaces, rising up only in the unconscious groans of a bloodstained nightmare.

As she had suspected from the start, it was the portrait of a madman she was beginning to paint.

And so Willa opened another page in her journal and began re-reading her transcription of the Supreme Court file, searching for anything that could help her to understand the mind of this murderer, Collins.

It seemed strange that there was so little in the depositions. The Albany sandalwood merchant John Hassell described him as 'honest and straightforward in his dealings.' Sheep farmer Arthur Treasure claimed Collins 'once threatened to put a scythe around my neck' but had been quick to concede that he, Treasure, was 'in a temper at the time' and had given Collins plenty of provocation.

The newspaper reports were more forthcoming, and more colourful. Collins was reported to have responded to the trial judge's sentence of death 'jauntily', claiming, 'I have never shed blood in my life,' 'My mind is easy enough,' 'I can die with a good conscience' – and left the court 'apparently quite unconcerned.' He 'burst out into loud laughter,' and told a friend outside the court that he would 'go up like a game cock.' He had conducted himself 'with utmost callousness and bravado to the very end,' said one newspaper; 'in a most defiant manner,' said another. Willa was unsure of how much faith could be placed in interpretations like these, given that the *Albany Mail*'s correspondent had reported erroneously that Collins, a common thief, 'was formerly transported on a capital charge.' But there was a sense, here, of instability, of recklessness. Perhaps that was all she could hope to find.

∞

The next day she returned to the State Records Office in search of the Convict Register for John Collins, number 6540. When it shuttled into view on the screen, her first thought was how bare it was, how few details were recorded on the grid. There was no trace of family. Collins had been convicted in Manchester of larceny and had previous (unspecified) convictions. He was transported from Chatham Prison and arrived in the colony on the *York* in 1862, two years before Little Jock.

Now familiar with the process, she travelled upstairs to look at the Prison Commission index, but Collins was not listed. Finding an annual return for Chatham Prison in the Home Office records, she laced up the microfilm reel. Criminal lives spun by until there he was on the screen – but once again it was disappointing. The entry gave minimal information, and no new offerings.

Under the heading 'Character' was the notation 'Very good.' As she looked at the handwritten words, a rare wave of certainty flowed through her and she startled the man at the neighbouring machine by exclaiming out loud.

I don't believe it.

After a fruitless hour at home, searching the net for sources, she still didn't know how to tackle the enigma of John Collins when there was so little to go on. Court records might be a starting point, but if they existed where would they be? London? Manchester? The woman she phoned at the Genealogical Society wasn't sure. *Try both*, she suggested. *And write, don't email. For some reason, they seem more inclined to respond to letters.*

Willa felt frustrated at the prospect of waiting, but suddenly it occurred to her that she knew someone who might hurry things along.

Lucifer didn't stir when she moved aside his sleek black leg draped across the keyboard and began to type.

```
Dear James
Do you happen to know anything about
English county court records? I am trying
to find an account of an 1861 trial (Quarter
Sessions) at Manchester...
```

∞

James Donaldson was quick to reply, enthusiastic about her new interest in Manchester.

```
I'll check with Alex & let you know. We've
a Mancunian on one of our branches & Alex's
daughter married one, so he does a bit of
dabbling in the archives when he visits
Susan. Send me the details & I'll pick his
wee brains for you.
```

But he was curious, too.

```
Is this another convict in your tree? How
does he fit in with the LENNIE ancestors?
```

The irony hit Willa as she read the email. She had told this stranger about Imogen, something she had not told another soul, and yet he still knew nothing about Little Jock. *Stop hedging*, she ordered herself, and hit 'reply'.

```
Dear James
Thank you for offering to help. I don't know
```

```
where to start. What little information I
have is as follows:

   John   Collins,   born   ?1840.   Convicted
of  theft  24  June  1861,  age  twenty-one,
Manchester   Quarter   Sessions.   Previous
felony convictions.

   You asked about his connection to me and
to the Lennies...
```

She stared at the screen for a long time, trying to construct an answer, wondering whether her ineptitude with words was because she was reluctant to confess to a 'real' genealogist that Jock was not technically *hers*, or that in sharing the story with someone else, part of her was letting it go.

March 1882

Near Albany

In the coruscating heat of early afternoon, five sandalwood carters, travelling in company, drive their teams into the campsite below the King River bridge. They have spent all morning loading up with stores in Albany, and although the camp is only seven miles from town, a mere fraction of their long journey back to the Pallinup, it is a good place, they find, to ease into the transition back to the land, from goosefeather bed to blanket roll. Tomorrow they will leave, refreshed, at sun-up on the first day of the three-day ride.

By two-thirty a pan of fish sizzles in dripping, and the thrum of cicadas is thick in the air, its rhythm getting into the blood, slow and sluggish. Jock pours warm water from the river in an arc around the fire, to prevent sparks from catching the bleached grass, but it runs off in rivulets. A second bucketful also snakes away, but the third pools, and then slowly, slowly, drains into the resistant earth, the dry grass snapping and popping.

Offer dips his mug into the billy and swirls the brew around. *Give us a bit o' treacle, willya, Jock?*

Ha! the little man snorts. *It's more'n ma life's wurrth! Joe Hall'll be looking fur his treacle afore he bothers tae ask how much we got fur the load.*

He scratches the head of Dixon's dog and reaches into his sack for a bit of dried pork. *Guid lad!* he laughs as the dog leaps to catch it.

The men look up from their tea when the dog throws back its mangy yellow head and howls. Another team is clattering over the wooden bridge. Within minutes a large rig of eight horses thunders into the camp, kicking up grit and swirls of dust.

The driver is a stranger to Jock, who looks at Sounness, raising a brow.

Collins, Sounness tells him. *Works out towards the Salt River, beyond Chesters. Not bad country, that. Might give it a go meself next season.*

Collins jumps down from the wagon, raising an arm in salutation, but remains in the clearing, busying himself with the team.

From beneath the shade of a peppermint tree the men watch him, ruminating on idle thoughts and sweet fried fish, passing round a bottle of mother's ruin.

Moody bastard, Ryan says quietly, inclining his chin towards the florid-faced newcomer.

Offer spits out a mouthful of fish bones. *Don't drink, neither,* he sniffs. *Never know where y'are with a man of unnat'ral inclinations.*

Didn't pay 'is fare out, Dixon says darkly, and then looks sideways. *Beg pardon, Jock.*

Jock shrugs and puts down his tin plate, wiping his hands on his trousers. *Ah'll have ma watch back noo,* he says to Offer.

The man grins. *Yeah, reckon yer safe for another spell.* He extracts from his coat pocket a package wrapped in frayed linen that looks like waistcoat lining. *How many times have yer sold it back ter Norrish and bought it from 'im again?* he asks, handing Jock a hefty silver pocket watch with an ornate Albert chain.

Jock shrugs again and drapes the links of rolled silver over his fingers admiringly, holding them up like a jeweller's web. *Guid as money in the bank.*

And it wouldn't be John Norrish if he didn't make a pound on the deal each time, I'd venture. Just like the bank, all right.

Pocketing his talisman, Jock is quick to defend the publican of the Weld Arms. *Ah'll not hear naught against Mr Norrish. Always been guid tae me, he has.*

Yeah, so long as 'is account's paid. Reg'lar prince is Norrish.

Collins stretches out in the shade of his wagon, back to the wheel, and pulls down the brim of his hat so that he can, without appearing to, keep one eye on the men up on the rise.

Look at them, with their empty bottle, their open mouths, snoring in grunts and whistles. Why they bother with hard slog at all is not a thing he cares to guess at, for what they don't piss away on the hard brown earth they are as like to pay in fines for brawling. Not one of them has the measure of his own rig, paid for in full, free and clear.

The new world, he has found, can be much to the liking of a man who understands the usefulness of invisibility. It had taken little effort to get by – in prison, on ticket, on release – for it was more a matter of what one did not do than of what one did. The essence of the 'good behaviour' so prized by the Convict Establishment was simply the good sense not to exhibit bad. The sought-after 'hard worker' was the man who stayed out of trouble rather than the one who expended energy. And a man could gain a reputation for being honest (yes, *honest*) just by refraining from the reckless stupidity he saw around him every day.

And so John Collins had progressed in the colony formerly his prison, quietly and with stealth, and what he has to show now, as an expiree, for his twenty years in Swan River is this fine sandalwood rig, this team of eight, this wary eye on the world.

The yellow mutt, which has been lying near the other men, absorbed in the business of crunching fish bones, shambles to its feet and takes a few cautious steps in his direction. Collins gauges its skinny neck. He could snap it like a sapling with one quick twist. His fingers feel around in the sand, close over a flint of granite. *Just one more step*, he whispers, ready to take aim. *C'mon, c'mon, y' daft mongrel, just one step closer.*

But the dog retreats, belly low to the ground.

By four o'clock the sun has not lost any of its glare, its glistering heat, and sensible men will have none of it. But Jock is drunk.

In the clearing by Dixon's wagon, he is pink and frazzled, dancing unsteadily on burning feet, bare arms and shoulders flaming beneath a grey flannel vest.

His travelling companions still snore beneath the peppermint tree, but James Stevens, newly arrived, watches open-mouthed as the little man throws impotent punches.

Although he is not much taller and far less stocky, the other man, Collins, at first stands firm, almost amused, dodging the flailing of small balled hands with the slightest of movements. But then Jock takes him by surprise, lowers his head and barrels into his body and they are down, scuffling in the dirt like a pair of mongrels. It is a short scrap only, for Collins, no longer amused and no longer surprised, brings it to an end with a series of savage thumps to the gut that leave Jock winded, all the bluster sucked from his body.

It is then, while Jock is gasping up at the sun, eyes turned to slits and onion-streaming, that Stevens spies a gleam of silver in the dust.

Collins washes his face at the riverbank and stalks back to his wagon, mean-eyed and muttering and in no mood for conversation, but curiosity finally gets the better of the laconic Stevens.

Upset 'im, did ya?

Collins takes a long breath that restores the calm mask to his face. *Weren't my plan*, he says mildly. *Heard he was called 'Little Jock'. Crossed my mind to ask him why.*

Stevens waits, but nothing else is offered. *And?*

And nowt. Bugger went mad. Well mithered. Collins smirks. *Little Jock! Little Dick, I'll wager.*

May 1882

Albany

Jock is beset by the sensation he is shrinking into some smaller stamp of himself as he stands before the Resident Magistrate, Mr Loftie – even though this time, this one time, he is on the side of the law in these chambers.

The magistrate urges him to continue.

Ah was under the influence of liquor. Ah swear this watch is mine. Ah've had it fur a long time. Ah can identify it by some portion of the lid spring being gone, and Ah know the chain.

James Stevens jumps to his feet, begging leave to cross-examine on his own account. *Can you say on your oath it was me what took it?*

Jock looks apologetic.

Ah won't swear you picked it up, no. Ah lost it at the King.

Rowley Crozier Loftie leans forward. *But you are sure, absolutely certain, that this is your watch, yes?*

Aye, Ah've no doubt in ma mind.

At the end of the day's hearing, it is clear that the fine silver watch with its rolled Albert chain is going to cost Stevens twelve months' hard labour. And Jock, in spite of everything, is sorry for it. What pie-eyed luck, he thinks, for Stevens to have sold his spoils to Lewis Davis, because Davis, through some devilish flick of fate, took it into his head to try to sell the watch to the one man who knows it as well as Jock himself does: the publican of the Weld Arms.

At the police station, Sergeant McLarty counts out fifteen shillings for two days' lodgings and one pound fifteen shillings for five days of travelling. And then he takes out a soft cloth bag from his desk drawer. *You can have it back now*, he says, tipping the contents into Jock's hand: a slither of chain, a solid casing of silver. *Sign here. And here.*

Jock writes his name in the evidence book and again on the loose sheet marked 'Witness Expenses'.

How's Hall's leg? McLarty enquires. *He was pretty poorly when they brought him in last week.*

Aye, it's a bad break, very bad. Dr Rogers says he'll be laid up fur a guid while tae come.

So it's back to Chesters for you, then?

Aye, Ah'm off in the morning.

Well, take care of that watch. And Jock?

He looks back from the door.

Stay away from the grog!

A strong wind gusts through Stirling Terrace, whipping at skirts and trouser legs, wrenching bonnets and caps from heads. Jock clamps one hand on his billycock hat and strides directly into the blast, salt from the Southern Ocean burning his lips and the skin on his face. He is glad to have the weight of the watch in his waistcoat pocket, the tick of time against his heart.

Ducking into the laneway abutting the Albion Hotel, he skirts around the back and is confronted by a woman adjusting her skirts by the hotel outhouse. Slightly the worse for gin is Charlotte Parsonage, but he can see she remembers him – oh yes, without a doubt. When intimacy is a commercial exchange, you don't forget a client who leaves before he's had his money's worth.

Eh, she says, approaching unsteadily, *eh you, c'm 'ere*.

But Jock is already bolting towards York Street, leaving behind him a wail of petulant curses.

Merchants are beginning to pack away displays under the wide verandahs; keys rattle as shop doors are locked. He breaks into a run to cover the half-block to Munday's, hoping to arrive in time to purchase new gaiters and have his measurements taken, for the hole in his leather is widening and can be patched no more. If there is one thing he knows, it's that the bit of shoemaking learned in Wakefield ill fits him for the fashioning of brand-new watertight boots. But he reaches the little shop just as William Munday is winding a scarf around his throat and preparing to leave.

Steady on, there, Jock. We're still open. My man will see you right.
Thanks, Mr Munday. Sir. And guid night tae you.

He pushes open the door, to find the teamster who had trounced him on the day he lost his watch.

Travel-stained and obviously just in from another haul, John Collins leans against Munday's counter, inspecting a pair of slippers. *Ah, Little Jock!* he says mockingly.

Jock nods. Grunts.

Heard ya was in town. Reilly was just tellin' me how Stevens and Davis got done t'day all in t' glory of y' silver.
Reilly?

Munday's man. He's just out back, gone to fetch his measure.

Boots are knocked to the floor as Jock hurries from the shop, back out into the greying afternoon.

Dusk settles over bungalows and vacant allotments in Earl Street, muting the brightly painted doors and beds of poppies but not the spirits of seamen on shore leave, prowling for company. There's a commotion on the verandah of Mrs Gregory's cottage, and a partially clothed Lascar is bundled down the steps, followed by socks and shoes and trousers.

And don't you be bringing your pox to this door again!

The muttering sailor struggles into his clothes, glaring as he pushes past a small figure catching his breath by the gate.

Jock rubs his aching back, staring in awe at the dishevelled woman on the verandah. Who would have thought Annie Gregory had it in her still? The woman must be, what, sixty if she's a day?

The Earl Street hill has done him in, that and the twist in his heart after hearing the name *Reilly*. The last time he had seen the man in the flesh was years ago, in Perth, when he'd been tapping shoes in an alley a few blocks behind Buchan's, but that face, those eyes, can be summoned from hell whenever he is afraid. What Reilly knows is a blind boil, a poison beneath the skin that could break any time. And now he is here. Speaking of him. To Collins.

Brooding, he slams the pea-green door of Mrs Gregory's boarding house behind him.

On a mattress of lumpy down, Jock threshes and groans, dreaming of naked sailors and the pitted buttocks of Ann Gregory tattooed with flowers and stars and crescent moons.

Kat rises from the tub in a rush of waves crashing over the bow and she cries, this ragged child, weeping into the knees of strangers. *Patrick! Patrick!* And wax drips onto her thigh as the man holds the candle closer, thrusts a finger deep into secret skin, and Reilly is watching and hissing *Freak!* through a mouthful of biscuit, while Sergeant McLarty and Mr Loftie laugh and point and pull at the beard to see if it's real, tug at the long silver ringlets piled on his head. *You cannot trust a soul!* And he is running, trouserless, panting down the Earl Street hill and he is absolutely certain that this is his watch, the one with the Albert chain and the tiny silk lilies embroidered in the corner. Gold and scarlet petticoats flounce in the dust as a child gathers them into a bouquet to press against her body, and from the crazed window of a tenement someone is shouting, *Porridge! Porridge!*

He sits up, breathless, disoriented at the sound of rapping on the door.

Porridge! calls Mrs Gregory. *Come on, now, up with you. It's getting cold!*

He looks around the empty room. *Forty-four, Ah am,* he tells it. *And no one knows ma name.*

The wind is still howling down Stirling Terrace the next morning when he collects his supplies from Hassell's. From his position high on the wagon, he can see the choppy harbour lapping at the feet of the town and threatening to consume it. He reaches into his coat pocket for the bottle of Holloway's Pills and swallows two in one dry gulp. Time, he thinks, time Ah am away.

Darcy

The streetlight across the road was glowing, illuminating the bare wood of the wisteria. She left the blind up, the light off, and turned on the computer. The pain was still a weight dragging at the base of her skull, but she swallowed two tablets and willed herself to ignore it. Twelve months ago today Imogen had left. Willa believed in anniversaries, that even the sad ones should be hived off from other days so their meaning did not become part of the flotsam of time passing. Every year she laid roses on the graves of her parents; every year on the date of her wedding she toasted herself wryly with chocolate cake. She had not intended to spend the anniversary of Imogen's leaving in bed with the curtains drawn, and now it was nearly over.

A scuffling caught her attention, followed by a thud, and she padded back to the bedroom. The sliding door was open again – those damned runners – and she pulled aside the hangers, flinching at the scrape of metal on metal. Lucifer was trying to keep his balance on the loose top of the tea chest, and as she lifted him down, the lid came with him, its soft fibres caught in his scrabbling claws.

The chest was such a flimsy-looking receptacle for dangerous goods. After moving into the house, she had manoeuvred it in here, into the deep recess of the wardrobe, among a buffer of coats and jeans and jumpers. Imogen had never asked to see the contents again, and Willa had felt an uneasy sense of vindication in this; if Imogen preferred denial, maybe the doctors had been right all along. She had tried to talk about it, had tentatively raised the subject of counselling, but Imogen wanted none of it. Her daughter shrugged off questions and slid away from the soft, whimpering guilt of mothers. All she would not say she bowed furiously into the strings of the cello, and Willa felt it physically, the notes like blows, the long chords winding round her throat, her head. Late into the night, light would pool under the door of the cramped little room at the back of the house, and Willa, hearing the clack-clack of the keyboard, hoped Imogen was studying.

Months passed. A year. Two. And a wall grew between them, made of all that needed to be said.

At sixteen Imogen shaved her head. Left the house at all hours. At eighteen she disowned her name. Left forever.

As Willa pulled the chest forward, intending to seal it again, she spied her mother's photo album lying there, lethal in its pink velvet covers. She picked it up, turned the pages reluctantly. All those side-by-side pairings of her face and Imogen's, held in balance like clauses either side of a colon. Babies in finery of white crocheted wool threaded with satin ribbon. Hesitant toddlers in pink jodhpurs, smocked floral prints, broderie anglaise. A whole series in the Irish dress – how Orla loved those puffed sleeves, the frills of lace across the bodice. Willa's high-school ponytails beside Imogen's unmanageable curls. And that was where the pairings ended, the last one of Imogen – her before-face – taken not long before Orla died.

Something was wrong.

Puzzled, she went back to the first page and started again. Her vision was still migraine-hazy, but this was not, surely, just illusion. She had hated this album when she first found it, a repository for all her mother's fears, but after scanning the pages from cover to cover for the third time, she could find scant trace of whatever it was she had hated. Where before she had seen a cynical surveillance, she now saw the tracking of two beloved faces. Could the creation of this album have been, all along, an act of love?

Not for the first time, it occurred to Willa that her mother deserved more credit than she had ever given her. *You hypocrite, Willa*, she told herself. *You hypocrite, Caoimhe.*

A sharp ring from the front room, announcing new mail, jolted her back to the present and she returned to the computer screen.

There had been no immediate reply from James Donaldson, no reaction to the story of Little Jock, so she was relieved to see his name in her in-box again.

```
Dear Willa
Sorry I haven't emailed but I knew I would
soon have news - & here it is! Alex went on
one of his jaunts to Manchester last week.
He had been planning to go at the end of
the month but was so excited after reading
about Jock & that Collins fellow that off
he went, a week early. I don't mean he
was excited about the poor wee man being
```

murdered (very sad, & such a puzzle) – you know what I mean!

Well, good news & bad. He found the court records in the Manchester Archives: three cases (see below). But they don't give us any clues about the man's personal history. Alex was hoping to find an address, something to link to the censuses, family background, but there's nothing – & without that, we're stuck. The census indexes are incomplete & Collins is a fairly common name. Alex, bless him, spent a few hours looking through the partial films & there were hundreds of Collinses!

No local prison records, either. So that just leaves the court summaries. Here they are, starting with the earliest:

Manchester Quarter Sessions, 20 February 1855: John Collins & Patrick Colcannon, labourers, theft of one hundredweight & one half of a hundredweight of lead fixed to a building of Robert Anglezark Pilling on 29 December. (The documents say these lads 'did feloniously rip, cut, break, steal, take and carry away' the lead 'against the Peace of our said Lady the Queen, her Crown and Dignity'!) Tried & found guilty. Collins: nine calendar months' hard labour. Colcannon: four years' penal servitude. (No prize for guessing who was the ringleader!)

> Manchester Quarter Sessions, 23 November 1857: John Collins, labourer, theft of twenty-eight pounds weight of lead fixed to a building of William Arnold McGill on 20 November. Plead guilty. Four years in penal servitude.
>
> Manchester Quarter Sessions, 24 June 1861: John Collins, theft of twenty pounds weight of lead fixed to a building of Richard Gatenby on 24 May. Tried & found guilty. Seven years in penal servitude (which of course meant a free pass to the colonies).

Lead, you know, was as good as shillings in those days. Sheet metal cladding, slotted roof shingles – that sort of thing. Apparently there was a Fagin-like character in Manchester called One-Armed Dick who had a gang of young lads thieving lead for him. Orphans mostly. Maybe our Collins was one? If so, he must've been quick on his feet, because he wasn't nicked until the grand old age of fifteen!

Alex hopes all of this helps & sends his best regards, as do I.

James

PS Keep up the good work. You are doing Wee Jock proud.

Willa's mind was racing, trying to process James's information. Lead. Hundredweights, pounds, of lead. As good as shillings.

A gang of children assembled for gain, schooled in the value of metal, scaling the roofs of buildings, creeping along walls in pairs, small hands ripping, cutting, breaking, stealing, taking and carrying away. Small hands on lead. Years and years of it...

The codeine was beginning to take effect, radiating its little opiate shivers. She should lie down for a while, let it do its work, but an idea was beginning to gestate.

It took only thirty minutes of searching the net, leaping from site to site, to convince her. The printer had spat out a dozen pages, and she began marking words and phrases with her highlighting pen, pupils contracting at the bright smears of iridescent yellow:

> dramatic escalation of lead use around the time of the Industrial Revolution
>
> among the most significant predictors of adult criminality
>
> erosion of mental processes
>
> cruel, impulsive behaviour
>
> loss of self-control
>
> aggression
>
> violence

Hitting 'reply', she began to type quickly.

```
Dear James (and Alex)
Thank you, and especially thanks to Alex,
for finding the Manchester records. You are
both so generous, and I appreciate your
interest in Little Jock.
```

You know, those records got me thinking: perhaps there's a clue here to the bizarre savagery of Collins's attack. I've just been reading about the links between childhood lead exposure and adult violence and psychological deviancy. Lead exposure would have been common in the decades following the Industrial Revolution – fumes from smelting processes, dust from pipes and building materials – although obviously not everyone was affected in extreme ways. But hand-to-mouth ingestion after handling lead was especially dangerous, and children were most at risk. The absorption was even greater in undernourished bodies. Lead accumulates in the bones, has a half-life of at least twenty-five years, and childhood exposure has been positively linked to criminality and psychosis in later life.

So, it's only a theory, but what do you and Alex think? Something set Collins off that night – I don't know what – but then he struck Jock with an axe, hacked his forehead and torso, severed his head, dismembered his body; calmly rode into town and sold his goods; laughed his way through the trial. Just another madman, or a man with the tick of lead in his bones?

Willa hit 'send' and sank back in her chair, marvelling at the little icon transmitting her speculations through copper wire and satellite and optical fibre in processes she couldn't fathom. She had forgotten the pain in her skull, now numbed to an ache, so buoyed up was she by the results of her research and the wash of goodwill and generosity from the other side of the world. For a moment she almost forgot what she had resolved to do on this anniversary day.

She glanced at the time displayed in the corner of the screen: 2.08 am. The day had slipped by. But she would do it anyway.

There was a time, in the weeks after Imogen left, when typing the familiar URL into her browser had been a form of addiction, a ritual of self-harm no less potent than the cutting of skin with the blade of a knife. She had not gone there for a long time, promised herself she would not. Was this a test, she wondered, waiting for the link to be made, a test to prove she was strong enough? Or was it a relapse, one more flick of the whip?

The screen filled with those drowning aquamarine waves. WELCOME TO THE WOUNDED STORYTELLER…

The words had not changed but they felt less like weapons aimed solely at her. Consciously slowing her breathing, she scanned through new links to research, reviews, articles in the press. An intersexed person in Perth had achieved a world first in having the space indicating 'sex' on a passport marked 'X' rather than 'M' or 'F'. More physicians were adopting the patient-centred model of care advocated by groups like the Intersex Society of North America, rather than the old 'concealment' approach that had 'unintentionally harmed many individuals and families.' *Breathe, breathe.* She glanced at the list of names on the left sidebar of the screen, each one representing a self-conscious declaration of testimony. There were many, many more than there had been six months ago.

Suddenly the breath turned ragged in her throat. It was there, the name she had refused to acknowledge, had resisted saying, even to herself. She whispered it soundlessly, bereft of voice, and the click of the mouse was like the clanging of hammer on anvil.

Darcy

I was born 46XX/46XY, a chimera, twins in the same shell. I am a boy and a girl, both and neither, and all the treatment meted out for my own good cannot change that. My body was cut up, remade into the shape of a girl, and I was dressed in pink, given dolls, plastic pots and pans, toy vacuum cleaners, taught to walk with a book on my head, keep my knees together. I didn't hate all of these things. But there were other things I wanted to do and to be and to have.

I didn't heal properly for a long time. I think of it as akin to an organ transplant: my tissues rejected the gift. I was always a sick child, always being watched and examined by people in white coats. Even if it was my throat that hurt, still they'd gather at the foot of the bed and I would be exposed, opened up for view. No one told me why. I was ashamed, knew it must be the most grotesque, unspeakable secret.

When I found out, the truth swallowed me alive. And then came the rage, so consuming I thought I would die of it – of all things, to die of *this*. My mother, my distant father, doctors: I turned on them, hated them. Not because of what they did, not just that, but because they lied, colluded in falsifying the record so thoroughly, so desperately, that I thought I must be a beast like the Chimera of myth, that no one was like me. And then I found out that that wasn't true, either. Others like me took me in, accepted me. They saved my life.

I am not the girl they tried to make. She is someone else, has another name. I think of her as my mother's daughter. I am a student, a cellist, a poet, a half-hearted, not-very-good, only-do-it-because-I-think-I-should political activist.

I am a beer drinker, a Dockers supporter, the doting owner of a speckled grey cat called Mabel. I'm told I am a good friend. I am 46XX/46XY, an androgyne, not a boy, not a girl. Not a myth.

Flooded with moonlight, Willa was transparent, silver-veined. Sparks flew from cranial nerves, short-circuited thought, threatened blackout.

All she could grasp was that she had been granted a gift beyond anything she deserved: the knowledge that this wounded storyteller, this precious human being, could transcend her own history. *She has made a life for herself. She is happy.*

Late August 1882

Near Kojonup

Perhaps Christen Norrish will tell her husband over supper that for the briefest moment she thought it was a woman driving Little Jock's wagon up to the homestead.

The face of the driver was turned slightly from her and she had seen a long fall of hair from a hatless head. But mostly what misled her was the shape – a softening, a whittling away, of that familiar stoutness, that fleshy gourd of a body always cinched in the middle by a thick leather belt. *Mark my words*, she will tell Thomas, *that man has lost some weight.*

We weren't expecting you this year, Jock. I'm not sure the team can use an extra. But let's go and see, shall we?

Thomas Norrish claps a hand on his shoulder and Jock is cheered by the warmth of the gesture.

Ah cannae do the shearing season, Mr Norrish, tha's no why Ah'm here, but Ah'd like tae come back shepherding soon. He looks intently at Norrish's face, hoping his meaning is clear. *Tae stay. If there's a place.*

Well! And what about your team? You've worked hard for it.

347

Aye, he says, *aye. Ah'm not afraid o' wurrk.*

Norrish waits expectantly, but Jock says no more.

Well, come back and we'll be glad of it. There never was a better shepherd at Ettakup.

Jock looks away and speaks to the post of the verandah. *Ah cannae come till the new year. Ah've a wee sum yet tae pay Mr Hassell, and Joe Hall's still laid up in Albany. Ma partner*, he explains, turning back. *Fell under the wheel May last and busted his leg.*

Yes, I heard about that. Little wonder you look tired, man, working by yourself. Take your supper in the shed, and why not rest a while, if you've time before you go.

Jock heads off to the shearing shed, but Norrish hails him.

If you've a mind to have a yarn with some of your teamster mates here for the season, they're camped up near the north paddock clearing, just off the road.

Jock gives his thanks and waves goodbye to Christen Norrish as he walks away.

It is late when he leaves Ettakup with a full stomach, the horses fed and watered. A good distance from the clearing on the track, he stops. After yoking the horses loosely to a banksia stand, he cloaks his lantern with an old kerchief. He has no wish to have a yarn with the men at their camp – prays, in fact, that they do not spy the dim light as he scouts around the far perimeter of their noisy gathering and picks his careful way through the bush and across the north paddock.

When he sees the thicket of trees fringing Solomon's Well, the temptation to stop by the old hut is great, but a distant smell of wood smoke and mutton coming from that direction warns him off, carrying as it does the threat of dogs and discovery. His feet hurt, blistering from the stiff new watertights. Munday's new man – a welcome sight for wary eyes on the lookout for the departed Reilly – had stuffed the toes with rags to fit, but still the leather rubs. His back aches cruelly as he tramps up the rise, the ever-present heaviness dragging at his gut. He is relieved when the granite peaks of Little Hell appear up ahead, their quartz crystals catching the glow of the moon.

Jock's trek to Little Hell has not gone unnoticed. John Collins, always on the margin of any camp, sees the moving shadow with its lantern and watches it disappear into the paddocks, to emerge as a fitful light, faint as a firefly, jerking up the hill.

He slips away, follows at a distance, his boots noiseless on the wet grass.

Jock holds the lantern high, illuminating the deeply riven walls of the cave, the small falls of rubble, the grains beneath him that are the ashes and dust of earlier stories lived on this same land. He gasps, and immediately lowers the light so as not to disturb any further the dense shadow above him, alive with the murmur of bat wings. Setting the lantern down, he runs his hand over the scarified surface of a boulder, feeling where the edge of an axe has been sharpened against it, eaten into it, one stone drawing potency from the yielding of another. He has never stroked the tattoos on his hand and arm without feeling ridges and grooves like these, though he knows – of course he knows – they are only imagined.

The bushel sack is where he left it, and for a moment he kneels on the cold sediments, shivering. And then he draws out an embroidered muslin vest, a long linen skirt, a cap edged with scalloped lace, a shawl, and lays them down before him like the shell of a girl.

The truth of this place

Lucifer gave her a baleful look as she slipped out into the darkness. *Mind the house, boy, I'll be back tonight,* she whispered. He turned his back, flicked the plume of his tail.

She closed the door quietly behind her, shivering as she turned the key, and pulled her coat over the green Belfast sweatshirt. The forecast promised a warm, autumn day but it would be hours before the sun delivered. The last time she had felt this cold was in Ireland.

Willa didn't like driving. It had been no great hardship when her noisy, smoke-wheezing eighteen-year-old Corolla was given a yellow sticker and she couldn't afford to have it overhauled; by then she hardly left the house anyway. But her hands and feet seemed to respond without conscious thought to the business of stop–go–turn. Not that there was much of that to do once she left the semi-rural suburbs of the Darling Ranges, just before dawn, and turned south-east towards the Great Southern. Over the course of several hours there were only a couple of tiny hamlets, then Williams, and then a long, unpopulated stretch to Kojonup.

When a sign warned that she was approaching the town, she looked down at her watch. She had a long way to go in the space of a day. There was no time for deviations. Even if she could have stretched to a second day's car hire, a night's accommodation, she had Lucifer to think of: she couldn't bear to send him off to the cattery again. But only last night she had read on the net about an 1850s cottage in Kojonup, now a museum, that had been built by a certain William McDonnell, one of the pensioner guards stationed there when the embryonic town was little more than a military barracks. Intrigued by the notion that this McDonnell might be the William McDonnell, market gardener of Kojonup, whom Jock had challenged for unpaid wages, she could not just drive past.

She pulled in beside a cafe, just opening up, to ask for directions and then stood by the car in the sun, sipping scalding tea from a polystyrene mug. The woman from the cafe bustled out.

Sorry, love. Bill reckons the house is closed mid-week. But apparently you can phone one of the Historical Society people and they'll come out and give you a tour. She pushed into Willa's hand a scrap of paper with a number written on it.

Willa thanked her but knew she couldn't wait for a tour. After pouring the dregs of the tea into the gutter, she headed back along the highway to Spring Street and turned left, and then right into Soldiers Road. If nothing else, at least she could see what remained of this place where Jock might have lived, the ground he might have worked.

It was a little stone cottage, painted white, with a lavender hedge and a low fence of chickenwire strung between weathered posts. To one side, an enormous pine tree cast a partial shadow, rendering the dwelling strangely ominous for all its quaint prettiness. Willa stepped out of the car and walked around the perimeter, feeling joins in the rough outer skin where rooms had been added. She peered into windows but the interiors were too dark to make out much more than the shape of stone fireplaces, back to back, in the two main rooms. At the rear of the house was a wild, tangled garden of fruit trees and ground-trailing vegetables, cottage flowers and weeds, and a prickly native bush all around the boundary. The props for an old clothesline were still standing. She ran her hand along the weathered timber of a rickety race, the remains of a milking shed, and gazed at the rural vista beyond the garden: tree-lined paddocks in all directions, fallen timber, huddles of sheep here and there. What would Little Jock have seen when he stood here? Was this once McDonnell's market garden?

Regretfully, but telling herself she must not linger, she returned to the car. As she looked back one more time from the driver's seat, the mottled shadows cast by the pine revealed a small figure, there behind the apple tree, face obscured beneath the bowl of a billycock hat – so real to her that she had to get out of the car and run back down the driveway. The earth around the apple tree was undisturbed but for the rippled prints of her own runners.

So you're staying here, Little Jock. You're not coming with me, she mused, picking up a pinecone in the driveway and rolling the rough scales between the palms of her hands.

As she turned on to the highway, sun streamed through the windshield and she turned the visor down. Her eye caught sight of the white envelope on the dashboard, awaiting action, awaiting courage. She had addressed it care of Student Services – as she had suspected, the university would not give her an address – and printed in large letters at the top: PLEASE FORWARD.

When the Australia Post sign appeared up ahead, she made one more stop, and felt the blood flood her face as she dropped the envelope into the box with a prayer to the sky.

Albany Highway was an easy drive, wide and smooth-surfaced in its current incarnation. The original cart track, a crude, meandering thoroughfare of sand, had first been transformed into something resembling a road by the labour of convicts, gangs of them, who cut trees, cleared scrub, carted rubble and limestone and gravel. She remembered finding Little Jock's name on a list of prisoners working on what was in 1864 called the Albany Road. There had been no indication on the list of where his work party had been stationed along the four-hundred-kilometre route, of where his handprint might be found on the road she was travelling.

On either side of the highway were undulating paddocks already showing signs of rebirth after another summer bleaching. The last time she drove this way it must have been winter, although she could not remember exactly which month. Some details of that long-ago trip were hazy and others sprang to life as though they were spooling out before her eyes. She had stopped at every service station along the road from Perth to Albany – it seemed there were more of them then, though that can hardly be true – for toilet breaks, to buy those raspberry ice-creams Imogen liked ('Push-ups' – is that what they were called?), cans of lemonade, more toilet breaks, anything to release the irritable string of drivers backed up behind the car as she drove carefully with her precious cargo, ten kilometres under the speed limit. Imogen sat with Babar in her safety chair in the back seat, singing to herself. She pointed at horses and cows and tractors and trucks – *Look! Look!* – and at the distant patches of white spotting the rolling green paddocks. When Willa explained that these were sheep, she looked doubtful and when she began to sing again her voice rose to a query: *Baa-baa-black-sheep?*

Lush and green – that's how Willa remembered the South West; that's why the landscape of Tyrone had nudged her memory.

She wouldn't have time to drive through Albany town to its coastal beach, but she did not need to remind herself of that beautiful place where Imogen had seemed to unfold, unpack her tight little body limb by limb, drinking in salty air that replenished every cell and fibre. That was Willa's abiding image of Albany: her daughter running through milk-white sand with her shoes off, her skirt tucked into her pants, her arms reaching up to the winter sun, backlit by the brilliant blue of the Southern Ocean, and looking for all the world like a normal child.

The photograph she had snapped in that one perfect moment was spoiled by the glare of the sun: a blur.

She slowed, approaching a major roundabout just before the town, where two highways and a road intersected, spiralling out like the arms of a star on the map she had studied before leaving. She veered left onto Chester Pass Road, which took her north again but further inland, and after a few minutes she pulled over to take bearings, gather thoughts.

The morning had become warmer and she eased out of the sweatshirt, felt the black cotton T-shirt absorb the sun. She looked for her map among a sheaf of papers on the passenger seat, grabbed hurriedly from her desk, and found among them the printout of yesterday's alarming email from James Donaldson, inviting her to attend, on behalf of him and Alex, a reunion of the Western Australian descendants of Hamish Laidlaw by the riverside at Crawley. *Please consider going, Willa*, he had written. *You would be the family's special guest, an 'honorary Laidlaw', for if it wasn't for your help their reunion wouldn't be happening. Alice will send you a proper invitation if you will give me your snail mail address.*

She folded the page into a small, fat cube, and then unfolded it and smoothed it out, read it again. It was an honour, this invitation from a man to whom the ties of family were no small thing. An honour and a kindness. But the thought of a crowd of strangers, of questions, evasions…James had no idea what he was asking of her.

She left the printout where she could see it – a reminder to think about it some more, conjure up some plausible excuse – and concentrated on the map. It was a photocopy of one dated 1883 that the staff at the State Records Office had located for her. There, on King River Road, on the side opposite a tract of land designated as belonging to H. E. Warburton, was an annotation: 'Well – The Sinkings.' Elated at the find, she had placed the photocopy beside a glossy colour map showing tourist attractions, accommodation and the small blue and red utilities symbols recognised by travellers all over the world. The scales were different, but she had worked out the ratios and marked the corresponding spot on the tourist map on the route now called Chester Pass Road. Five miles from Albany – just as it said in the newspaper articles of 1882. And right on that spot was a square of blue etched with the symbol of a barrel. The Sinkings seemed to be located on the site of a winery.

She turned on the ignition again and set off to find the place where Little Jock was murdered.

∽

It was clearly not a good time. Willa, directed to a little office at the back of the cellar, waited by the door as a grey-haired woman in denims spoke briskly on the phone. She nodded, mouthed *Won't be a minute*, but Willa felt uncomfortable when she heard the tone of the conversation change and the woman turned abruptly to grab a file off the desk. She backed away from a barrage of sharp words – *wrong colours…labels by Friday… no, THIS Friday* – and stood on the gravel driveway, surveying the trellised slopes between the cellar and Chester Pass Road. It was a good ten minutes before the woman emerged from the office.

Sorry about that. Now, what can I do for you?

She listened to the cautious speech Willa had rehearsed in the car on the drive down.

The Sinkings? Never heard of that name. And I've lived around here all my life. But a well…

Willa followed her as she strode down the drive towards the roadway winding up to the cellar.

There are two old timber posts in a swampy patch of ground along the boundary of the far paddock over there. See? Beyond that line of trees?

Willa squinted in the direction she was pointing, across cleared paddocks on the side of the drive opposite the rows of vines. She wasn't sure what she was supposed to see.

Now, they're what's left of an old well, really old, collapsed now. Only know it's there because the owner's son used to burn through on his trail bike when he was a nipper. Clipped one of the posts and took a spill.

Willa held her breath. *Is it about a hundred yards from the road, would you say?*

She considered, then nodded. *About that, I think, although…*

Could I see it? She blurted it out, this thing she so desperately wanted, and her words sounded harsh, demanding.

The woman raised a brow.

Look, I'm sorry. It's just that, it's…Somebody died at that well.

Died? the woman barked. *You might have your bearings mixed up, after all. This place has been in the owner's family a long time. Everyone knows everything that happens around here. And nobody's died here, I can assure you.*

This was in 1882.

She laughed, looked relieved. *Oh, well! That's different. So what's your interest in all of this?*

Willa paused only a second. *Family history.*

This seemed to be a satisfactory answer, and Willa wondered again at the tolerance of strangers towards the crazy things people did in the name of their family tree. She felt guilty about the lie, but it was only technical. She hadn't said the family was hers.

The woman called over a young man moving cases of cleanskins on a trolley. *Dave, this is Mrs – I'm sorry, I don't think I asked your name?*

Samson. Willa Samson.

Mrs Samson here wants to have a look at those old well posts in the bracken. You know, out between the south paddocks? Take her over, will you? Just watch out for snakes.

The phone began to shrill in the distance, and the woman grimaced wryly as she shook Willa's hand. *Duty calls. But good luck, and come back, will you, and tell me what you find?*

∞

The uncleared strip running between Chester Pass Road and a dam at the rear of the property was fenced. It loomed up ahead: tall eucalypts, the odd conifer, straggly banksia, swamp tea-tree.

And a low coppice of bracken and bulrush – a patch of brown among the foliage. A seed of panic germinated in Willa as she tramped over the paddock, following Dave, who was thumping at the ground every so often with a stout branch. Was she just unnerved by the likely presence of snakes, or was there actually a residue of threat radiating from the marshy-looking anomaly visible up ahead? When they reached it, Dave stopped, looked at her doubtfully.

Sure you want to go in?

She nodded.

Shrugging, he executed a clumsy hurdle over the wire fence, boots first into the bracken, and waited for her to climb over.

The fleshy bracken thrust up to their elbows, some over their heads – long, brown spears bearing fronds curled in tight fists. Dave ploughed a path for her to follow, and she flinched as fronds whipped back and forth. The grab of rushes and old, dry bracken about her legs and hips made her shudder. After only a few steps, Dave's head disappeared.

Here! he called.

Willa crouched down beside him.

Don't know what you were expecting but there isn't much to see.

The two wooden stumps were ravaged by age, as dry and weathered as railway sleepers. It was hard to make out the surface of the ground, but there seemed to be no obvious presence of water. The vegetation, though, the ferns and the rushes, told her that the water-table must be high around here. She grazed the blanched, splinterless wood with the heel of her hand and then stood up, bolder.

Is it OK if I stay here awhile? By myself?

The young man snorted. *Just you and the dugites?*

I'll be OK. And I won't stay long.

Right, then. He grinned and handed her the branch. *You'd better take this.*

It was perfectly still, no breeze to rustle leaves, flurry the undergrowth. If there were snakes, they were hibernating, or lulled to oblivion by the hypnotic call of unseen insects. *Tick-tick. Tick-tock.* Caught in the firm grasp of bracken spears, Willa looked around her, trying to see this, too, through Little Jock's eyes: cleared pastureland on either side; Albany Highway beyond the trees with its drone of engines; the homestead and winery in the distance, up over the rise; a stretch of trellised vines just visible through a line of trees. But it was useless. He would not recognise this place. The Sinkings in 1882 had been a well in a clearing, a campsite in the heart of virgin bushland reached by a track pounded hard by the wheels of sandalwood carts, the hooves of their teams.

What had really happened here?

She closed her eyes, intent on summoning forth the truth of this place, trying to assemble it from all the little pieces she had found and imagined:

A campfire, a midnight sky, rich with stars, the aura of a comet like some fiery sign from heaven. A man with lead in his bones, volatile, unpredictable. The blade of an axe. Blood spilt on the hard earth…

No, the picture was eluding her. She tried again.

A campfire, a midnight sky…

But she could not fit them together, could not reach that darkness. The sun permeated the lids of her streaming eyes, insisted on anchoring her to the here and now, the cloudless void of the sky.

30 September – 2 October 1882

The Sinkings, near Albany

The sky is as pink as a new-picked peach beyond the trees fringing the Kalgan camp. James Donohue smothers the coals of the fire with a bucket of sand, stamps his feet with a shiver.

Ready? The little man atop the wagon seems impatient to be away.

Donohue freezes, a hand poised in the air. *Listen! What's that?*

Through the din of parrot screech and restless twitter comes a clopping of hooves, the pace slowing the closer they get, until a large rig appears on the track. Its driver waves and shouts, *Ya heading for the King?*

Donohue glances up at the man in the wagon, surprised that he hesitates a moment before acknowledging the greeting with a wave of his billycock hat.

Are you right there, Little Jock? Donohue asks.

Aye, says the man, *aye*, but he looks like a chap who's bitten a lemon.

Donohue hauls himself onto the wagon heavily loaded with sweet-smelling sandalwood trunks and they creak slowly up to the track, drawing in behind John Collins.

∞

Jock regrets the departure of Donohue in the late afternoon. He had not found the man's company a chore, was glad in fact to give him a ride as far as Geake's land, where Donohue had left a pony hobbled on the outward trip. He was glad, too, of the help, as Donohue was strong and willing. Now he has Collins as sole companion and there is not a thing to be done about it. Rough bush etiquette, although you would be hard-pressed to find a teamster to admit such existed, will not countenance a man refusing to fall in with another if both are bound for the same destination.

Part of him – the part that is unaccountably, irritably tired, struggling at times to control his team – welcomes the presence of another teamster, for the same unspoken rule that demands he travel in company with Collins compels the fellow to render assistance when such is needed. But he cannot deny the unease he feels in exposing need before a man like Collins.

He swears when the wagon sways badly on a curve in the track and one of the longer logs nicks a tree.

Need a bigger wagon, Collins pants after they manoeuvre it back onto the tray. He slaps his hands on his trousers, half grunting, half laughing, and Jock squirms under the man's sly grin. His look seems as loaded as his wagon, and though there is naught in his words to give just cause for alarm, Jock is afraid. What does Collins know?

When finally they set up camp, Jock for once does not rue that the chores involved in feeding and watering the horses are so many; that the branches he gathers for kindling are damp enough to make the task of getting a fire roaring no small feat; that these and other acts of survival occupy nearly all the hours and minutes between their arrival and the moment he will take to his tent, with little pause or need for conversation. Each of them eats a makeshift supper while busy with sundry tasks, and it is only when they are at last helping themselves to tea over the fire that the silence is briefly broken.

Collins, chewing furiously on a piece of dried beef, spits out the tough fibres in disgust. *I've a mind for some real food tomorrow. What d' ya say to possum stew, Napoleon Bonaparte?*

Jock's taste for possum has waned to nothing, but by the way the other man laughs it was clearly no real question.

Collins throws down his mug, takes a large wire snare from his wagon and, without further word, disappears into the bush.

Swaddled in a thin blanket inside his tent, Jock wakes suddenly, and listens. Familiar camp noises: distant bush rustling, the spit and crackle of a fire, snorting horses. And then he hears something else, some small throaty whimper of a sound. He wriggles towards the tent flap and looks out.

The camp is ablaze in the cold, clear night: the fire, the moon, a universe of stars and that strange, brilliant spectacle that has adorned the sky for two weeks now – the fiery streak of a comet like some arrow from the gods pointing the way to heaven. But Jock's eyes are drawn to the fire, where Collins is squatting, blank-faced, where he is holding a big, black-handled butcher's knife against the throat of a tammar wallaby, where he is pressing the blade just enough to draw blood and then releasing it, again and again, where the earth beneath him is blooming crimson.

Not until Collins is asleep does Jock creep to the wagon. All night he crouches alert by the wheel, the handle of an axe gripped in his hand.

In the morning, the two wagons continue along the soft, boggy track towards Albany, slowed by the weight on board. Jock is edgy, jumping at every raven's cry. And he is exhausted. More than once he must shout for help with his fractious team, hesitant at the approach of another hill, and Collins complies but with less and less grace as the day wears on.

As dusk begins to fall, they approach the track to the Five Mile camp. Collins is in a foul temper, and pulls his team roughly to a halt.

Jock hesitates. It's only five miles to Albany town, to the boarding house with the pea-green door, but five miles in the dark with a fractious team and a full load might just as well be fifty. Reluctantly he follows Collins into the Five Mile, a clearing a hundred yards off the road, better known as the Sinkings.

The well, a shallow soak just beyond the sheoaks, is loosely covered with bush timber, and you can tell when a team last stopped here to drink by the state of the ground around it. Jock steps across fine circlets of newly shooting grass and begins to prise away the logs, but the tender green blades are obliterated by the time the horses have finished.

After watering his team, he tethers the blind grey mare and the skittish colt to the wagon; the others he allows to wander, alert to their whereabouts by the gentle clink and jangle of bells and chains. Close to the wagon the heady scent of sandalwood, this scent that he breathes every day, almost brings him to his knees; it is the heartwood, that potent nub near the base of the trunk, the richest in oil, the darkest in colour, the point of greatest resistance when the tree is pulled, and the most precious for all these reasons. Jock is no whittler, has no artistry in his fingers or vision dancing in his mind, but he has often thought he would like to take the heartwood of a sandalwood he has grubbed from the earth and carve some trinket for remembrance, for these hard days on the road are drawing to a close. The new year, he told Thomas Norrish, and he has done his sums, worked it out. Just seven more loads and he will sell the team, give Hall his share and pay off his debt to Hassell. He can return to Ettakup, free of care and obligation. Get himself a pair of dogs. For all his unease over Collins, there is a smile on his face when a horse and rider clatter into the clearing.

Fagan, one of Horace Egerton-Warburton's farmhands at Millbrook, does not seem to mind whiling away an hour by the fireside at the Sinkings, although Jock would venture to guess it's the meaty stew simmering on the fire, and not the sandalwooders' company, that is the kernel of his contentment.

What news in Albany? Jock asks.

The same, the same, just more of it, says Fagan, screwing up his weathered face to think. *Still talk of the railway. Folk as usual reckon there's those in Perth delaying things on purpose as usual.* He licks the gravy off his fingers and thinks some more. *Was going to be a concert at the Court'ouse t'night. Some bugger with a blow 'orn and fancy girls, so they say. Oh, and the Nicholls woman got 'er smalls lifted off the line again,* says she. *Though oo'd want a bag o' underflannels belonging t' Louisa Nicholls, the Lord don't know and nor do I.*

Make any damper? he adds hopefully.

Run out o' flour, says Jock.

Fagan seems to study him for a moment, then jumps up to fetch a bottle from his saddle-bag. *How about some grog, then?*

Ta.

After taking a good long swig, Jock waves the square-cut bottle in Collins's direction.

Keep it, snorts Collins.

Fagan raises his eyebrows at Jock.

The bottle sails to and fro a few times before Fagan bids them goodnight.

As the fellow rides off in the direction of Millbrook, Jock finds himself wishing he had stayed a while longer, for the comfortable combination of his presence and the warm gin seemed to snuff out all manner of tensions. He can sense that Collins is looking at him again, that there are things he has been storing up to say and he is about to say them. That day in Munday's boot shop, Reilly's startled cry of recognition as Jock fled – *had* there been a cry or had he imagined that? Collins had been there; Collins had heard; Collins had remained. Collins and Reilly.

What did Reilly tell him? What great lumping stick might he have given this watchful man by the fire?

When Collins speaks, his words take Jock by surprise.

The lovely Louisa's underflannels, eh? We'll 'ave t' be on t' lookout for those, won't we, now, Little Jock.

Riding up to the Sinkings, John Garretty has the raging thirst of a man who was well and truly liquored at noon. He flops down by the fire, drains his kidskin waterbag dry and downs the proffered pan of tea in one long draught.

Ahhh, ta, Jock.

His bleary gaze surveys the tents, the wagons, the fire, the two men, the night sky with its fearsome arc of gold, the wet leaves in the bottom of the pan, finally coming to rest on the anchor clasp on Jock's belt.

You've 'ad that belt f'r a good while now.

Jock looks down, runs a thumb over the dull metal clasp. *Aye, tha's true. But Ah've had tae cut masel' a new notch. Not so stout as once Ah was.*

Garretty's eyes travel, stop. *Good stout boots. Need a new pair myself. Get 'em offa Munday, did ya?*

Jock nods.

Garretty stretches out his lanky legs to gauge his own scuffed boots against Jock's. *Smallest feet I ever did see.*

Any grog going? he adds.

It's tea or nowt, Collins grunts.

Ah, well.

Garretty falls silent, his breathing becoming thick and heavy. And then a voice jolts him alert.

Where're y' headed, then? Collins says.

Millbrook. Camping there a while, doing some odd jobs. Will take the team back out in a coupla weeks.

Stay till morning if y've a mind tae, says Jock.

But Garretty has sobered up just enough to be aware of the need to be at Millbrook at dawn for the job he's being paid to do. It's now or never, he thinks, so best it be now.

When later he is asked if he saw anything amiss at the Sinkings that night, he will declare, honestly, that he did not.

Since Garretty galloped off, all loose in the saddle, Jock has managed to engage Collins in talk of tonnages and trees per day, provisions and prices, and is grateful for the safety to be found in sandalwood. It is late when they hear the approach of another horse.

Who's there? calls a big bluster of a voice, and the rotund figure of Horace Egerton-Warburton appears, balanced on a slim chestnut mare. He dismounts nimbly – a sight to behold for a man of his size – and answers his own question. *Ah, Little Jock. Just the man I wanted to see. And Collins, is it?*

Collins gestures towards the billy, but Warburton demurs and pulls out a flask from his coat pocket. He offers it to Jock.

Heard you've a horse to sell.

Jock is surprised. *Who tol' you tha'?*

Can't rightly recollect, but what's it to be? I'll pay decent money for a good carthorse.

Weel, no, Jock considers. *Ah'm in no mind to break up the team jus' noo.*

Someone's misspoke then. Let me know if you change your mind before you head out again.

Jock hands the flask back. *Sit awhile, if you like. How did you find Albany?*

Saw a fine show at the Courthouse, he tells them. *Voices like angels, them women, as fine as ever I've heard. Could have done without the chappie on the bugle whatnot, though. What a screech to rattle the bones of the dead.* He grimaces, making the thatch of hair on his lip jump and bristle like the tail of a startled cat.

Heard Joe Hall's on his feet again, he adds, passing the flask again.

Ah should hope tha's the truth, declares Jock, *seeing as how Ah'm going in tae collect 'im. Ah've a pile o' wood waiting fur him tae clean up past Chesters.*

Well, then, if you're sure about that horse?

Jock nods, glum to be relinquishing the man's hospitality.

Collins stares after Warburton as he rides off. *Every man and his bleedin' 'orse come callin' t'night,* he mutters.

The night air is cool. Jock staggers to his feet to scout around for more wood for the fire and to check the wagon for warmth of a different kind – hopeful, as only the oiled can be, that a bottle might suddenly have sprung from nowhere. He thrusts about in his canvas sack but there is no friendly clink of glass.

And wot might Little Jock be hiding in 'is dilly bag?

Jock swings around unsteadily, chilled. He is no great size, this Collins, but he has inches over Jock, and muscle to his flesh.

C'mon, Little Jock, Collins wheedles, *c'mon now, show Johnny wot's in ya bag.*

Jock rubs a hand across his eyes. The belligerent face is rippling like water. He upturns the sack and the contents tumble at their feet: a piece of soap, a blunt knife, a twist of pork.

He stares at the boils around the man's neck, which look like they are ready to pop, at the face red-blown and churning.

Did ya think no one knew owt or nowt of wot y' get up to up past Solomon's? You and ya manky little faggot clothes?

Even blearied with gin, he can see it. There's no mistaking loathing when it looks you in the eye. Jock blinks, stumbles, flings out a hand to steady himself, and Collins bursts before him.

Keep y' hands offa me! he bellows, slapping like a madman. *I know wot y' are, y' faggot freak!*

Fear makes Jock sober and nimble. He turns. Flees.

But he doesn't know that you cannot outrun the insane.

There he lies, by the well at the Sinkings, gasping into its dark waters. Time feels as though it is suspended, held taut as a string, and he will die when the string is severed, as it surely will be. There is a sheen on the surface of the water, lit by the heavens, so he cannot tell whether the thing is above him, reflected, or floating in the heart of the well. It does not matter – what can it matter? – for he is going to die. He closes his eyes, shuts them tight, as his head is pushed into the water. But a voice whispers in thick, shushing waves, insistent, urging: *Open your eyes, mind what you see.* He forces his eyes wide, and it is there again. A face. He remembers, has seen it before – not this face, but another, shimmering in the dark waters of a well. *Mind what*

you see, but the child could never understand why Ga'ma could not see it, too, the face of a man with long, dark hair swept to one side, whiskers on his chin and lip and a scar in the centre of his forehead, and the child was afraid, not of the face, but because Ga'ma could not see it, and so the child would not tell. And now there is this small, fluid face, rippling in the darkness, with strands of hair fanning out, swaying like reeds, a face never before seen but known all the same. The face of a child.

He reaches out his hand.

The fist holding him under tightens its grip on his hair and he is wrenched away, hauled out, flung on his back. Left to lie, puffing, like a reeled-in fish. It could be minutes, it could be hours, that he lies there, until Collins comes back with an axe in his grip.

The comet blazing above him, he waits for the taut string to break.

All kinds of memorials

The old East Perth Cemetery is an anachronism, a fragile pocket of the past wedged nervously between markers of the modern world. Willa looked around at the townhouses of the East Perth redevelopment rising on one side; the ugly floodlights of the cricket ground towering, hunched like vultures, on the other; the casino in the distance, across the river. A band of National Trust volunteers maintained what heritage was left of the colony's original graveyard, disused since 1900, but more had been lost than preserved. In the early decades of the new century, tracts of the cemetery grounds had been resumed, human remains bulldozed and dumped, monuments destroyed for scrap metal. Vandals desecrated vaults, pillaged marble and slate. Jarrah crosses, those that had survived natural weathering and decay, were wrenched from the ground and burnt for warmth by destitute men and women in the Depression. Less than twenty per cent of known gravesites remain, the bones of the rest unmarked, unremembered.

This section of the cemetery had once been crammed with Anglican monuments: plain wooden crosses, long gone, outnumbering more lasting memorials. Willa paused to read the few surviving headstones, walked around the rusty lacework of cast-iron enclosures, examined headless cherubs, tombstones lurching at precarious angles. But most of this section was denuded of all but weeds, with only occasional earth mounds to hint at what lay beneath. She walked with her head down, kicking at spongy clumps of clover, dandelion. Here and there the dun earth was studded with white that from a distance looked like bone but was, on inspection, far less sinister: bleached snail shells, toadstool caps, the milky undersides of oystershells washed down the slope from the original path, gleaming fragments of polished marble. A smattering of wild convolvulus, small petals of pink and white, to serve as funerary flower.

She had been moved to read a small coda in the *Albany Mail*'s account of the trial and execution of John Collins.

> W. Finlay raised a subscription among the witnesses in Collins's case, for the purpose of giving the unfortunate victim, J. King, a christian burial. The remains were placed in a coffin and conveyed in a hearse to the Church of England cemetery, where they were interred.

Those beleaguered remains, examined and exhibited and re-examined, brought to Perth for the trial to be exhibited again, had been buried with respect by people who remembered Little Jock kindly – and as a member of their community, not as a felon, certainly not as a freak. There was dignity in that, a transcendence over the manner of his death that reminded Willa that Little Jock had made a life for himself, a life that had resisted all her efforts to make a symbol of suffering of him.

No stone for our boy, Mary, she whispered sadly. His name was on the cemetery register but no one could tell her where plot 1233 was. His disarticulated bones could be beneath her feet right now. Had William Finlay's collection stretched to a memorial? Perhaps there had once been an inscription – no room for an epitaph – on a wooden cross long since perished.

John King, d. Albany 1882

John King was not his name, but perhaps, she thought, the name that matters is not the one we are born to but the one we choose for ourselves. And walking back across the field of bones, she smiled to think that the good people of Albany had buried an Irish Roman Catholic woman as a Scot they knew as Jock in the Church of England cemetery.

There are all kinds of memorials, she told Lucifer, and his eyes, drawn to slits in the sun's glare, opened slightly, favouring her with two crescent slivers of gold. She poured blood-and-bone into the hole and a bucket of water onto that and mixed it up with the blade of the shovel, just like she had seen Chas do. The plastic pot came away easily, the soil moist and friable, and she hoped it was a good sign that the roots had not twisted themselves into knots, trying to escape the confines of the container. After she had compacted the earth around the new rose with the soles of her runners and trained the hose onto it, she stood back, satisfied. In spring there would be the usual profusion of pinks, lemons and ivories in Orla's bed of old-fashioneds, but in the centre would be the rose Willa had planted, her first contribution to Orla's garden. A hybrid tea, Blue Moon, not really blue at all but a beautiful, indeterminate blending. And without knowing where it came from, she had this conviction that her mother would not mind at all.

A dragonfly skimmed along her arm in a buzz of papery wings and she thought again of the idea she'd had the Sunday before, brooding in the bus on the way home from the cemetery. All week it had worried at her, insistent, immune to demurrals. She looked at the journal lying on the garden bench. It was a serious thing to attempt to portray a life. All it could ever be was a caprice: a mixture of the real and the imaginary, coloured by all the obsessions of the one who imagined it. The sum of all she knew from the things the world called history was a mere fraction of what was unrecorded, lost, deliberately concealed, simply unknowable. Could she re-member Little Jock, put the fragments of his story together in a way that made sense, when she didn't even know how the story began?

Brushing the earth from her hands, she sat on the bench and picked up the journal, the pencil tucked inside it. *Perhaps*, she wrote. Her hand moved across the page.

> Perhaps it begins with a lone carrion crow flying over a cabin. An ill omen.

If she closed her eyes, she could see that wet, green land, the dark cabin in Omagh with its mean little fire, the face of the docent watching her from the door. But she will not let that face be Mary's.

> The Handywoman shivers, pauses. It is only the familiar rhythm of the keening coming from inside that keeps her from turning back to the village. She had promised

the widow she would do for her girl, and who would break faith with a widow?

She wrote quickly, gathering flints of memory, recollections of old tales of portents and changelings. Myths to explain what could not be explained, the unthinkable, the impossible. To efface responsibility, absolve guilt.

…Let God take the blame, and let this woman choose.

Something left her body as she exhaled. It was a start, though an uneasy one, for she remembered the proud claim of her own child: *Not a girl, not a boy. Not a myth.* But Little Jock was not Imogen. *And you'll have to allow me a few myths*, she murmured, tucking the pencil back inside the journal. *Call it the Irish in me.*

Lucifer, reclining on the warm paving stones, gazed up quizzically. *You've got the right idea, boy*, she said, scratching his side. All four limbs flexed, each paw splayed like a starfish.

Suddenly he sprang up, ears alert, pupils eclipsing the gold of his eyes. As he slunk away, she pitied the poor slip of a gecko he must have spied.

She glanced at her watch draped over the arm of the bench. Sighed. She would rather stay here, the autumn sun on her face, enjoying the sweet smell of mint bruised from contact with Lucifer's paws, than go inside to shower and dress – and dress in what, she had no idea. Her usual black garb would not do today, not for a picnic. A picnic! But since she had committed herself, however reluctantly, to going to the Laidlaw descendants' reunion, she owed it to James and Alex to make an effort.

She got to her feet unwillingly, but the sight of the rose brought a rush of pleasure and she lingered over the lone late bud just beginning to unfurl its soft-hued petals. She turned towards the house, and gasped.

There was a figure on the top step of the back verandah, infused with light, brilliant in the shimmering sun of late morning. Hesitant, the apparition advanced, one step, out of the pure, white glare, and Willa saw Lucifer cradled in the space between arms and face. That beloved face.

She tried to speak but her throat constricted, saved her, for in that moment she was given a second chance, to substitute one name for another. She tried again.

Darcy.

ACKNOWLEDGMENTS

The Sinkings is a work of fiction. Although many of the events and people in Little Jock's story come from the historical record, and archival material is used, there is much imaginative embroidery around and between the stitches of historical thread. I have invented the motivations and personalities of actual people, and have freely interpreted events.

Gillian O'Mara first brought to my attention the existence of Little Jock and some early research done by Brian Purdue. I thank them both.

For research assistance I am grateful to Jane Kelly (Edinburgh); Lyn Todd, Bevan Carter and the WA Genealogical Society's Convict Group; Agnes Paini, Barbara Hobbs and Jack Cox (Kojonup); Rob Wignall, Julia Mitchell and Noel Inglis (Albany); Professor Tony Payne and Dr John Shaw-Dunn (University of Glasgow); Jim Rouse (*Scottish Mining* web site); Dr Stephen Pawley (Walter Road Veterinary Clinic); and staff at State Records Office of Western Australia (SROWA), Edith Cowan University library's Document Delivery section, WA Genealogical Society library, Mitchell Library (Glasgow), National Archives of Scotland, Public Records Office of Northern Ireland, National Archives (Kew), Manchester Central Library and Portsmouth Central Library.

Thank you to the team at UWA Press for their enthusiasm, care and good humour, to typesetter Keith Feltham and proofreader Sara Foster, and to Terri-ann White for selecting *The Sinkings* for her fiction list.

And finally, I thank Susan Midalia for her sensitive, insightful editorial perspective and for much encouragement; Annabel Smith, who gave generous feedback over a long period; and readers Francine Nababan, Wendy Bulgin, Karen Williams and Simone Lazaroo. Three people were, in different ways, this book's guiding lights: my supervisor, Richard Rossiter, fellow writer Robyn Mundy, and my husband, Ric.

Pen drawings (p. 189) and extracts (pp. 187–9, 194–5, 205–8) from the *Clara* newsletters are reproduced by permission of the National Library of Australia (MS 6037).

It is acknowledged that Babar, Barbie, Guinness, Lalique, Lladro and Rover are registered trademarks.

SOURCES

George Sullivan and his article 'A strange case of murder and mutilation' are fictitious, but the content of the article is based on archival and newspaper records. Also fictitious are the South West Historical Society, the journal *Past Lives*, the generic 'Genealogical Society' and its proposed publication 'Convict Lives'.

The invented web site *The Wounded Storyteller* was inspired by the excellent web sites of the Intersex Society of North America, the International Foundation for Androgynous Studies (no longer operational) and the AIS Support Group Australia (but does not necessarily represent the views of these groups), and I am indebted to the many people who have chosen to tell their moving stories on these sites. The web site draws its name from A. W. Frank's *The wounded storyteller: Body, illness and ethics* (Chicago: University of Chicago Press, 1995); Alice Domurat Dreger (*Hermaphrodites and the medical invention of sex*, Cambridge, Mass.: Harvard University Press, 1998) first made the connection between Frank's book and the treatment of people with intersex conditions (more recently known as DSD – disorders of sex development).

The research of many writers helped me to imagine lives for Willa and Imogen and all that cannot be known about Little Jock; not all can be named here, but the following were especially important: M. Bignell, *First the spring: A history of the Shire of Kojonup, Western Australia* (Nedlands: UWA Press, 1971); J. Burrowes, *Irish: The remarkable saga of a nation and a city* (Edinburgh: Mainstream, 2004); J. Colapinto, *As nature made him: The boy who was raised as a girl* (New York: Perennial, 2001); Dreger, *Hermaphrodites and the medical invention of sex*, and (ed.), *Intersex in the age of ethics* (Hagerstown: University Publishing Group, 1999); R. Erickson, *The brand on his coat: Biographies of some Western Australian convicts* (Nedlands: UWA Press, 1983); D. Garden, *Albany: A panorama of the sound from 1827* (Melbourne: Nelson, 1977); F. Haynes & T. McKenna (eds), *Unseen genders: Beyond the binaries* (New York: Peter Lang, 2001); and S. J. Kessler, *Lessons from the intersexed* (New Brunswick: Rutgers University Press, 1998).

Sources for quoted passages are as follows: trial records pp. 12, 19, 23–4, 317–18, 321–3: Supreme Court of Western Australia, Criminal Indictment Cases, CONS 3273, WAS 122, item 16, case 1031, SROWA, *The West Australian*, 19 January 1883, *Albany Mail*, 24 January 1883; quotes in 'George Sullivan' article pp. 21–2:

CSO records, Acc. 527, Reel 55, item 1448/119, SROWA, B. Purdue, 'Was one
a woman?', typescript of a talk given to the Friends of the Battye Library, n.d.,
PR 14617, Battye Library; quotes from trial documents, pp. 71–2, 110–12, 150–3:
AD/14/62/53, AD/14/57/92, National Archives of Scotland, Edinburgh; 'It was said
that those with money went to America, those with only a little went to Liverpool,
and those with nothing at all went to Glasgow' p. 75 adapted from J. House, *The
heart of Glasgow* (Glasgow: Richard Drew Publishing, 1987); quotes p. 76: Sir H. C.
Cameron, 'Notes on a case of hermaphroditism', *British Gynaecological Journal*, 29,
1904, p. 349, L. Tait, *Diseases of women* (New York: William Wood & Company,
1879), p. 23, H. Barbin, *Herculine Barbin: Being the recently discovered memoirs of a
nineteenth-century French hermaphrodite*, introd. M. Foucault (New York: Pantheon
Books, 1838/1978), p. 103; quote p. 89: *Glasgow Examiner*, 15 March 1851; extract
pp. 96–7: 1861 Census, Glasgow, vol. 644-1, book 30, Central; verse p. 104: People's
Palace, Glasgow, museum display text; 'Keep yer 'eart up, Tom! You'll soon be
oot, Hughie!' p. 110 adapted from A. Brown, *Glasgow 1858: Shadow's midnight scenes
and social photographs* (Glasgow: University of Glasgow Press, 1858/1976), p. 64;
catalogue text p. 126: McLellan Galleries, *Italy: Renaissance and beyond, Italian art
1350–1750*, 2004; tour guide commentary p. 127 adapted from House, *The Heart
of Glasgow*; quote pp. 127–8: *Glasgow Free Press*, 18 December 1852; quote p. 133:
Licences, Male, 1861, PCom3 reel 86, National Archives (Kew); Smith quote
p. 173: Old Town Gaol, Stirling, Scotland, museum display text; quotes p. 174:
W. G. Gates (ed.), *Records of the corporation 1835–1927* (Portsmouth: Charpentier Ltd,
1928), pp. 62, 66; quotes pp. 185–6, 202–3: W. Crawford, *Surgeon's daily journal, Clara,
1864*, transcript J. Kelly (Subiaco: A. J. Kelly, 1864/1996), Battye Library; dialogue
p. 197: Revelations 81:65; 'Strip – legs apart – arms up – mouth open – touch toes!'
p. 201 adapted from P. Priestley, *Victorian prison lives: English prison biography
1830–1914* (London: Methuen, 1985), p. 202; quotes pp. 211–12, 319: R. Holmes,
Scanty particulars: The life of Dr James Barry (London: Viking, 2003); quotes
pp. 215–16, 237–9: Poor Relief records, Glasgow City Archives; quotes pp. 229–30:
C. Savona-Ventura, 'Dr James Barry: An enigmatic army medical doctor', <http://
www.geocities.com/hotsprings/2615/medhist/barry.html>; quote p. 250: Albany
Police, Convict List, AN5, Acc. 364/88, SROWA; quotes pp. 252–4, 261–2, 264:
adapted from Albany Police Occurrence Books, AN5, Acc. 364/1–9, SROWA;
trial testimony p. 263 adapted from Albany Plaints 1868, WAS 1686, CONS 438,
item 65, SROWA; 'Nature has done all possible for the place and man, very little'
p. 273: *Albany Advertiser*, quoted in Garden, *Albany: A panorama of the sound from
1827*, p. 148; p. 290: 'Billy Boy', traditional; quotes p. 311: *The Age*, 9 August 1880;
p. 315: T. P. Westendorf (1875), 'I'll Take You Home Again, Kathleen'; quotes by
doctors pp. 319–20: G. F. Blacker & T. W. P. Lawrence, 'A case of true unilateral
hermaphroditism with ovotestis occurring in man', *Transactions of the Obstetrical*

Society of London, 38, 1896, pp. 286, 290, 306, A. M. Bongiovanni & A. W. Root, 'The androgenital syndrome', *New England Journal of Medicine*, 268 (23), 1963, p. 1283; quotes p. 323: *The West Australian*, 19 January 1883, *Albany Mail*, 24 January 1883, 7 February 1883; testimony p. 332 adapted from Albany Plaints 1882, WAS 1686, CONS 3468, item 112, SROWA; court summaries pp. 340–1: Quarter Sessions Rolls, Manchester Archives; quote p. 345: *Tips for parents*, Intersex Society of North America, <http://www.isna.org>; quote p. 371: *Albany Mail*, 24 January 1883.

Amanda Curtin is a writer and editor who has a fascination with history. Her short fiction has been published in *Island*, *Indigo*, *Southerly* and *Westerly*, and she has won the University of Canberra National Short Story Award, the Katharine Susannah Prichard Short Fiction Award and the Patricia Hackett Prize for best contribution to *Westerly*. She occasionally teaches writing and editing at tertiary level, and has a PhD in Writing. She and her husband share their home with an opinionated Siamese cat.

Lightning Source UK Ltd.
Milton Keynes UK
UKOW03f1915090517
300858UK00001B/16/P